WHITE POWDER

A NOVEL OF THE CIA AND THE SECRET WAR IN LAOS

LARRY B. LAMBERT

Niederhauser Andwendungen (Asia) Ltd.   ✳   Hong Kong

NIEDERHAUSER ANWENDUNGEN (ASIA) LTD.

Publishing Office
Suites 4301-5, Tower 1, Times Square
1 Matheson Street, Causeway Bay,
Hong Kong

FIRST EDITION

Library of Congress Catalog-in-Publication Data

White Powder: A Novel of the CIA and the Secret War in Laos / Larry B. Lambert – 1st Ed

ISBN 1449975852

EAN-13 9781449975852

Printed in the United States of America

FOR GRIFFIN AND ALYSSA

"Really, my dear chap, you seem to be reading too many romantic thrillers. This is no romance dear friend, this is reality."

–John Forsythe, *The Day of the Jackal*

AUTHOR'S NOTE

The secret war described in this book was real, but this is a novel, a work of fiction. Specific events and characters are imaginary with the exception of historical persons who appear from time to time in the story in order to frame it properly in the context of time and period.

I owe special thanks to people who influenced this work: to my buddy, the late Don J. Bennett of the Clandestine Service of the United States of America whose life was cut short during the War on Terror; to my editor, the late Marji James, who passed before this work was complete. Her unflagging support buoyed me and made this book possible; to buddies in 'the business', who cajoled, prodded and kept me working; and to my family (also known as) the Dragon, Mouse, Wishbear, Angel and Elmo, who endured periods of emotional absence while I wrote.

Tall trees in the Laotian highlands swallowed four silent, grim men under a full moon. They sat near each other, slowly going over their gear, field stripping their weapons in the darkness, all by rote and touch. Moon-cast shadows provided camouflage that left the world black and white with a broad range of gray. It was their first night out, always the most difficult.

They began the transition from civilized man to soldier-savage once more in a land where some residents believed themselves descended from reptiles. The valley dwellers lived in an uneasy alliance with dragon-like beasts that were merciless judges, jealous of human fortune. Men tattooed themselves to resemble reptiles, hoping by this artifice to escape being dragged into the water. Their magic allowed them to consult with spirits on all of life's enigmas. They took their dead to mountaintops where their corpses dissolved. The remaining spirits were thought to inhabit the rocks, trees and streams from where they instructed the hill clans. It didn't play that way back home, but Craig Burton was in Laos and the rules were different.

Burton learned early that survival on long duration, deep penetration missions through the ancient hills of Laos depended on a successful metamorphosis.

The army provided each of them an explanation of their place in the world. The army philosophy agreed with their own predilections and culture, allowing them through subjective belief to consider the rules back home the reliable author of objective reality. That way of thinking got men killed when they were alone and cut off from friendly forces. Burton's men were alive specifically because they were able to shed that skin. It always began on the first night out. There was no clean way for

1

them to operate on long duration patrols. Trying to reconcile what they did with the way things were done back home or within the Army proved to be as impossible as trying to pick up a turd from the clean end.

This is the story of Craig Burton, an army officer who became something else. To a lesser extent it's also the story of three of the men who went out into the hills with him. Burton's metamorphosis can't be explained except within the context of others who had their parts to play in the outcome.

It's also the story of spies from various nations with both personal and national agendas who congregated in Laos. They were willing to do more or less anything to meet objectives. The end inevitably justified the means. Chinese, American and French intelligence agents all gathered seeds of what might someday become intelligence and as they did so they succumbed to the bane of all professions. Largely unsuccessful, they became hectors, whose days were occasionally brightened by the currency of Indochina, White Powder.

Lastly, it's also a story of Charlotte Sabon, who met Craig Burton and in the end got both what she wanted and what she deserved.

LARRY B. LAMBERT

ONE

Tuesday, 4 July 1961 – 0800 HRS
Military Region One – Ban Kheun, Laos
About twenty-five miles from the border
of the People's Republic of China

The distinctive popping of Soviet ammunition fired from SKS or AK-47 rifles caused the American reconnaissance team to go to ground in dense jungle foliage.

Strange volleys discharged more or less away from the recon element and caused concern mixed with curiosity until they were able to determine it was range day for the People's Army of Viet Nam and their Pathet Lao allies.

The four heavily camouflaged Americans had been carefully stalking, crawling, and scrupulously avoiding both peasants and soldiers for the proceeding two days in order to approach the enemy military compound on the outskirts of Ban Kheun, a crossroads city in the Laotian Highlands sitting astride Highway 1. According to intelligence reports, the 8th Pathet Lao Artillery Regiment received a shipment of Russian artillery in violation of the Geneva Accords. The Green Machine wanted to know if the rumors were true and the only way to know for sure was to put eyes on the target. The 1st Battalion, North Vietnamese Infantry also called Ban Kheun home, making the sneak and peek mission more complicated.

The Tartar Team, now in a position to count and photograph Russian artillery tubes, operated in areas of total enemy control. Their infiltration into the enemy's camp had thus far focused on killing feral dogs and anything else that would be inclined to raise the alarm along the way. They managed the business with a silenced pistol, aptly named *hushpuppy*.

Jimmy Paint, a small, squarely built, Mescalero Apache, climbed a tree quietly and confirmed what the other three men on the ground were only guessing at. He whispered down, "Some round-eyes are teaching the zips how to shoot. Looks like maybe Russians."

WHITE POWDER

"Now that's interesting," Captain Craig Burton said to the two other men standing next to him, also looking up at Paint. "They've got to be Russians, Sparky." Burton said in the direction of Sam Willoughby, the tall, thin Army Security Agency man who handled both the radio and a rifle. "You speak Russian."

"I only know fuck words—enough to get laid in Russian." Willoughby replied, not wanting to be ordered to wiggle through the underbrush to get a closer look.

Paint crawled down the tree carefully and very deliberately, but he was obviously in a hurry. To Burton, "One of the Russians is coming this way in a big hurry."

"Prisoner?" Willoughby mouthed the word.

Burton drew his finger across his throat. They couldn't afford to alert anyone to their presence, and were too far from anywhere to interrogate the prisoner without allowing for the opportunity for discovery. Burton turned to Paul Gorman, lifting the Russian made AK-47 that he carried. Gorman understood. If they were discovered he'd shoot the Russian.

Gorman smiled. With all of the rifle fire, one more report from an AK-47 wouldn't be noticed. Because they resupplied themselves from enemy stores on their long duration missions, they carried the weapons of their enemies. Practical logistics aside, it also made a rifle's report something that didn't immediately raise the specter of an attack to the enemy. Many Pathet Lao troops had very poor weapons fire discipline in rear areas and it was common for them to shoot at one thing or another when they were in garrison.

The Russian was young, wearing an olive drab uniform with black shoulder boards. He came within twenty feet from Willoughby before they discovered that he was looking for a place to relieve himself. As soon as he squatted, another volley of fire erupted from beyond a line of trees fifty feet in front of the Americans.

Burton thought that the food must not agree with him. The kid was as far away from home as they were.

Then another thought crossed his mind. Proof of Russian troops would be useful, but taking the Russian here in his camp would be very risky. So risky that the Russians would be inclined to believe he had been killed by his allies.

Gorman looked at the Russian, then at Burton.

4

Burton made a hand sign.

Gorman put a single round between his eyes. The Russian's face bulged and then flattened as the round carried some the unlucky Russian's brain matter out the back of his skull and spread it over several meters of plant life.

Willoughby, understanding what was needed, sprinted from his hiding place and expertly went through the Russian's pockets, emptying them, while Paint, Burton and Gorman offered cover if needed. As an afterthought, Willoughby pulled his K-Bar utility knife and removed the soldier's thumb at the second joint, and slipped the watch from his wrist.

Paint, an expert tracker, cleared the back trail and made sure their path was obscured as the team pulled back and up a hillside, waiting to see if they had been discovered or followed.

Target practice continued.

They moved across and up the heavily wooded hillside carefully until they arrived at a spot just below the ridgeline where Burton called a halt.

Willoughby laid out a pay book, cheap wristwatch, and identity folder, counted out 230 Rubles, one Soviet Army issue prophylactic and the unfortunate soldier's left thumb. Squinting, he translated Cyrillic. "His name *is*, er— *was* at this point; Popov, Dmitry Borisovich, artillery. A junior sergeant, assigned to the 83rd Airborne Brigade. Hey, we did this guy a favor." Willoughby pulled a smudged photo of a plump young girl from the pay book. "She's ugly as a mud fence." He passed the photo around. They all agreed.

Burton knew the army would be thrilled with photographic proof that the Russians not only had been peddling artillery to the People's Army of Viet Nam but that said artillery was now in Laos in violation of the Geneva Accords. The presence of Russian advisors, as evidenced by what Willoughby collected would be additional proof of violation. But was one soldier's identification and property enough? Burton pondered the matter as they ate rice with fish sauce on the ridge. Taking out one lone Russian artilleryman while he took a dump was hardly heroic, but what if they could take them all out and drop a pile of Russian ID's and thumbs on Major Piper's desk?

5

TWO

Sunday, 30 July 1961 – 2000 HRS
Villa Aljaccio,
Ban Dua, Thailand

There were two types of CIA case officers in Laos. The dedicated career professionals and the dedicated thieves who manipulated the world and the secret war to their own end. Walter Kennedy knew he fit nicely within the second category.

In his capacity as manipulator and self-serving thief, Kennedy looked out from the veranda overlooking the Mekong River, smoking a Dunhill with one hand and holding a Baccarat crystal tumbler filled with thirty year-old Scotch in the other. The ice in the whiskey was transparent and he wondered to himself how Bruno Jospin was able to have clear ice made in this place.

Jospin, wearing a saffron yellow silk Chinese dressing gown, walked across polished teak decking to his guest. At the same time, Kennedy pointed to birds dipping in the water and in the marshes on the estate that overlooked the river from the Thailand side. The Land of the White Parasol and a Million Elephants, also known as The Kingdom of Laos, was on the other.

"See the speckled one with the sharp beak and the spikey feathers behind his head? That's a crested kingfisher," Kennedy said, pointing with the cigarette suspended between his first and second fingers. He delicately put the cigarette in his mouth, "and that one with the black head, white cheeks and grey feathers, the one in the mud with the spindly legs, is a River Lapwing."

Bruno Jospin glanced at the CIA man. Kennedy wore a nice suit, white shirt, silk tie and an expensive gold watch. A thick gold bracelet dangled from his other arm. The expression on his thin, somewhat angular face wordlessly conveyed sincerity, but the cold blue eyes held no emotion.

"Did you come here to banter about ornithology, Walter?"

Kennedy took a long drag on the cigarette and flicked it, arcing over

6

the water in the afternoon light to land in the muddy river and be swept a hundred miles to the sea. "All the Americans really care about keeping one up on the communists. They don't care about you. Not one bit." Jospin looked something like the paintings of Napoleon Bonaparte, also a Corsican, except that Bruno's hair was white and his black eyes were sunken back into his skull, forbidding and dangerous.

"We don't like Communists any more than they do." Bruno added, walking closer to Kennedy, resting his husky frame in a wide chair, motioning with a hand like a short flipper for Kennedy to sit beside him. "They know we are businessmen."

"Yeah, of course, but opium is not popular in certain circles back in the States. Don't get me wrong, the heroin market is alive and well, but drugs don't sit well with some people." Kennedy sat.

"Do you foresee any danger of infiltration from your people?"

"Infiltrating the Corsican Mafia is like trying to ram an apple up a rat's ass. I don't think you have anything to worry about." Kennedy assured Jospin.

"You're betting your life on your guess, so guess well, Walter." Jospin opened a clasp knife and drove it into a mango in a fruit bowl beside him. Lifting the mango from the bowl on the steel blade, he rotated the knife, severing it into two parts. The Corsican threw them over the edge of the veranda into the river. The gesture wasn't lost on Kennedy. "The intelligence agencies are plotting against us. The Red Chinese Guoanbu, the Nationalist *Kuomintang*, and the Thais want to take the bread from our mouths. You need to find out what they are planning, Mr. Kennedy. That's why we're paying you a lot of money. The French are keeping their noses in the business as well, trying to figure an angle, trying to keep their profit. I don't mind them dipping their beaks occasionally because they provide a measure of protection for the business at home."

"I'm meeting with Wu Ming, the Communist Chinese Rezident spook this next week." Kennedy said with a confidence he didn't feel. Even though Kennedy couldn't stand Wu Ming, they both lived their lives to serve their countries and stole as much as they could in the process. Common cause and overwhelming greed made strange bedfellows.

THREE

Wednesday, 2 August 1961 – 1300 HRS
Café Du Paris, near the Tonle Sap River,
Phnom Phen, Cambodia

Mutual friends arranged the meeting because each had something to say to the other and this is how such discussions began. It was a dance, almost a ritual, and it remained to be seen who would make the first move.

The restaurant where they met perched in the penthouse of a white-washed French Colonial style hotel within what once had been an expansive sitting room when the hotel was not a hotel, but the residence of the French Ambassador in the early days of the century.

At five-foot-seven, Kennedy stood the same height as Wu. Both were slender, each had been the recipient of a classical Western education and they both lived for the game that occupied their waking hours. Kennedy's hair was sandy brown and his eyes were bright blue. His hair was Ivy League short. Wu was classic Han Chinese but wore his hair longer than the fashion of the time dictated. Kennedy dressed for dinner, Saville Row: white jacket and black tie. Wu wore a coarse weave blue Mao jacket and trousers with sandals. To each his own.

Their dinner table had a broad view of the greenbelt, sidewalks and the Tonle Sap River beyond. They ate, passing polite pleasantries. Walter Kennedy preached gently, trying to make murder sound respectable. Wu Ming complained ritualistically about the pain his wife was inflicting on him through her extravagant spending habits.

"How is your boss's health?" Wu solicited.

"The new boss with the exotic haircut or the old boss?"

Wu clarified. "I know the one in Manila, the fat one who looks like two swine are coupling in his trousers when he walks. Jack Beckman."

Kennedy didn't like either of the bosses but he bore grudging respect for Beckman. He was morbidly obese but wasn't anybody's fool. The Station Chief in Vientiane, Montgomery Keene, was cast in a different mold. An ego with a pompadour on top, he bore the unfortunate nickname, 'Monkey King'.

8

Even though Kennedy was assigned to Manila, Pete Desmond, Chief of Far East Operations personally cleared him to pursue his case into Indochina. It meant that he didn't have to kiss ass to appease the frequently temperamental Monkey King.

Dessert arrived. Cake, authentic French, with layers of custard and cream, frosted and topped with dark chocolate flakes and crushed almonds. Kennedy's fork cut a generous piece from the wedge on the china plate. Wu picked at his cake with chopsticks and found his mouth without dropping it, a testament more to the rich, moist cake than to his skill.

Neither of them drank more than a glass of wine with dinner. To a dinner guest at an adjacent table it would mean nothing. On the other hand, the fact would have been significant to an outside observer who knew them, because both were borderline alcoholics. This meeting was serious. Their mutual issues were weighty and they didn't want to loose control with each other, the likely and probable result of drinking too much.

Sobriety slowed down the process. Wu's impassive face and diffident, self-effacing manner didn't betray his motives or provide a clue to what he wanted, no matter how Kennedy tried to divine his intentions. Kennedy's off-handed remarks and high-handed American homilies were equally effective in masking his purpose. By so doing, they'd been beating around the bush for hours. Now the desert tray stood empty before them. It was time for one of them to bring up their real business.

Walter Kennedy broached his subject first with maximum magnanimity. "We're working on a reliable way to tap into the Corsican mafia's backbone. The key word is *reliable*. Unione Corse has been collaborating with us since World War II but we're not close to getting all we want out of them." He flashed a crooked smile.

Wu nodded as Kennedy lamented the CIA's position. Faux compassion flitted across his features. His smile was a token of understanding, underscored by receding gums and yellow teeth.

Kennedy understood Chinese. They considered themselves to be Celestials, well above the rest of mankind in every respect. As a Celestial, Wu was reluctant to be frank. They'd beat around the bush for hours more if he didn't get down to business. Kennedy took the blunt approach because he believed it to be an American strength, not a weakness. "They're in play around the world with their drug distribution network.

They pay everybody off from here in Phnom Penh to Moscow and New York. We'd just like to know who, how much and whether not we could hitch a ride from time to time. That doesn't seem to be too much to ask but they're reluctant to hand it over."

"Did you tell them what you wanted?" Wu asked with a disdain for the direct method of getting anything.

"No, but we hinted. A lot better than a Chinaman would." Kennedy replied acerbically.

"Time for war by other means." Wu observed sympathetically while reflecting on Walter Aloisius Kennedy's personality evaluation that his contacts in the Chinese State Security Service slipped him two days earlier. The analysis was summarized: *Walter A. Kennedy has worked for the Central Intelligence Agency since his initial recruitment during the unprovoked Imperialist Aggression against the peace loving people of Korea in 1951. CIA leaders and compradors know that he is also on the payroll of the Corsican Mafia. He plays both ends to his own benefit and occasionally to the benefit of his American employers. He can be witty and charming or warm and concerned, but these qualities are always performances, produced as needed, and rarely prompted by genuine feeling.*

"You want to tap into their information network from the inside." Wu summed it up succinctly as he expertly skewered the last hunk of cake with his chopsticks. The Celestial's self- actualized sense of Oriental superiority kicked in and he obliquely quoted Sun Tzu. "Such information can't be divined from ghosts and spirits. It must come from people. And you think that we can help you? Maybe we can, but the CIA has been in the Corsican's orbit for many years." His tone turned wry, "I find it surprising that you'd need our help at this late date. After over thirty years of attempts at penetration you should be able to do whatever you want to with them. After all, the Corsicans like communists even less than you do. Then again, perhaps I am giving the CIA too much credit."

Ouch! Kennedy didn't like the way Wu put it. The little gook bastard wanted to play rough, personal and yes, Kennedy expected it from the Teochiu Brotherhood. Still, the insult could have been far more deftly delivered.

"Yeah. I think the Teochiu can help or I wouldn't be feeding you fucking cake." Kennedy now talked with flat, menacing tones. The love had gone. If anyone was keeping score and Wu certainly was, the first point went to the Teochiu Brotherhood.

"What makes you think we'll *want* to help even if we can?" Wu spoke fluent Fleet Street English, proof of having paid attention to the imported occidental instructors at the Glenealy School on Hornsey Road, the one that catered to select children of influential parents in Hong Kong. Since his father was incense master or Heung Chu of the Sun Yee On Triad, 'influential" wasn't the half of it.

"This war's heating up! That's why you'll help, goddamnit." Kennedy motioned to the waiter for a drink. The waiter, a Khmer Cambodian behaving like a wanna-be Chinese with a braided hair que running down the middle of his back, approached to take the order.

"Bushmills." The waiter stood ready to take Wu's order as well but Kennedy dismissed him with a wave of his hand and continued. "It's not like any other war before because *we* are running it. We've never had a theater of conflict all our own before. It's a CIA war in Laos, our turf. *My* goddamned turf, you wise ass commie."

Wu looked into Kennedy's cold, blue eyes. They reminded him of the eyes of a dead fish. To spite his familiarity with Westerners, they always appeared so alien to him. "The Russians and their Pathet Lao puppets have the clear advantage, publicly deferring to Souvanna Phouma on matters of government policy while secretly extending their influence at the grassroots level." Wu's eye's narrowed to mere slits. "It's a popular uprising. The peasants are susceptible to their control, making a Pathet Lao village a world unto itself. Their children act as couriers and lookouts, the young people join the village self-defense units, the lowest level of guerrilla organization. The men act as porters for the regular Pathet Lao and North Vietnamese Army units while the women make clothing, prepare food, and look after the wounded. I think you're out of your league Kennedy – you *and* the CIA."

Kennedy laughed. "How long do you think that's going to hold, Sherlock? A few months at most? When it pops into a million pieces, there'll be a lot of Virginia Farm Boys in Laos with fast moving jets overhead. When that happens, the way we feel about the Teochiu will have a lot to do with your level of support in this venture. In fact, it goes deeper than that when you analyze the bigger picture. Think of how you'll look when your New Righteousness and Peace associates find their narcotics supply interdicted completely. Maybe the 14K Triad can be the big dragon of white powder and you can serve them. It doesn't matter to

11

me who the comprador is that manages the supply side of the business, you greasy, slant eyed bastard."

Wu winced. That point went to Kennedy. New Righteousness and Peace was also known as the Sun Yee On Triad. They ran the Kowloon side of Hong Kong and prospered in a number of commercial ventures from prostitution to kidnapping for ransom. Of all that they did, the opium and heroin business was the most lucrative. It was also the most vulnerable because it required a steady stream of raw opium and the highest quality came from Laos and Burma.

Wu grunted, slyly glancing at Kennedy. "It seems that our interests do not diverge significantly." He drank warm tea to emphasize his request. A pregnant pause as he composed himself. "There is a matter of some delicacy that I should like some help on." The English accent was more pronounced now as he put some effort into it.

Kennedy turned from polite to profane. "My dick is high and hard if you help us with Unione Corse."

Wu didn't understand the colloquialism but continued, encouraged by Kennedy's attitude. "People in Yunnan Province, influential people, wish to expand their private interests in Laos the way they have in Burma and the Shan State but have no interest in developing a conflict with the Corsicans. Your tacit assistance and a pact not to interfere with our mutually harmonious venture would be gratefully accepted in a spirit of cooperation and friendship."

Kennedy smiled. It always came back to white powder.

FOUR

Sunday, 6 August 1961 – 1030 HRS
Military Region One - Near Ban Na Toum, Laos
Ten miles from the border of
the People's Republic of China

Burton's men followed the tributary, gurgling through the rocks, stammering through dark chambers as it followed the gorge. Rain fell, sometimes sheeting, occasionally slacking, then whipping into circles between the dark stone canyon walls. By that time the moisture had permeated every wrinkle of clothing and skin. Each man in file moved deliberately, carefully, each footfall planned, then executed.

Pools of water fed each other more hungrily as the canyon threw itself wide at an unanticipated lip, water cascading five hundred feet down into a deeper series of chasms. Jimmy Paint walked like a cat. His flat face with high cheekbones and alert, coal black eyes showed only steadied concentration. His uniform was French lizard pattern camouflage, nondescript, without insignia. He wore a faded green canvas Chinese magazine pack on his chest that stacked rifle magazines in pouches on his chest, providing easy access to more ammo to feed the AK-47 he carried. He'd pulled his slouch brim hat, dark now with rain running off in rivulets, low across his brow. Paint turned and looked behind. Three men stopped, freezing in position, stone statues on the trail behind him. None of them turned. He would alert them to danger. Jimmy Paint motioned slowly with his hand and slowly each turned to look behind them.

Thousands of feet up from the rocky crags, waterfalls cascaded. Waterfalls on waterfalls as if the windows of heaven burst out upon them to blast earthward for thousands of feet before erupting into mist. Some were narrow like great white cables. Others peeled off into streamers. Each of the men were caught up in their own thoughts briefly as the scene unfolded before them. The moment passed, there was work at hand and they turned again to descend the chasm.

Below them, each waterfall led to its own small gorge and from that gorge to another one. Canyons within canyons, a spider's web of stone, capped with thick foliage, interconnected, and sewn together by waterfalls. Deadfall trees provided mossy bridges across the creeks.

Burton, medium height, wearing the same green lizard pattern clothing and a sun-bleached green duckbill cap, also carried a Soviet style AK-47 rifle. He moved up next to Jimmy Paint, the point man, and looked over the rim of the canyon into open space. The steady flow of water hammered hard against the ledge below, pushed off again into space and tumbled into the rocks below. To his left was an echoing hole of canyons, obscured by mist.

They were referred to as the *Tartar Team* and they operated without indigenous scouts or support. Technically, they were an element of a White Star Mobile Training Team from the 7th Special Forces Group. Practically speaking, they were a force unto themselves.

Using his hand as a pointer, Staff Sergeant Jimmy Paint, US Army, offered his opinion to Captain Craig Burton, his commanding officer, "Take it to the right, down through that maze and I think we'll come out above their base."

Burton took off his hat for a moment. He was gaunt. They'd been out for a long time. Jimmy thought he looked dangerous. A battle scar that ran from his right cheek to the lobe of his ear made him look like a bad guy in a comic book. Two week's growth of stubble added to the effect. Burton un-tucked a gum rubber poncho from his pack and tossed it over his head, ducking under it. Sergeant Paint joined him underneath. It smelled like a combination of old socks, sweat and automobile tires. Burton scrabbled for the map. When he pulled it out, Paint knew that it had once been a map, but now it was more or less a folded pulp mass, having been worked hard by water and exertion in Burton's map case. It unfolded damp but legible if you used your imagination. They studied it together, unsure of where they were. It came down to guesswork and luck.

Rain not only played havoc with paper maps. It deprived the men of their ability to smell an enemy and the odors associated with that or hear movement. Most of the time they either heard or smelled the enemy before they saw them. It had the reverse benefit of obscuring their smell, the sounds they made, and most importantly, the tracks they left.

The other two men were up with them now as Burton slipped his head through the hole in the poncho, not wanting to hassle with repacking it. He replaced his hat with a slosh.

Sergeant First Class Paul Gorman and Sergeant Sam Willoughby looked at Paint questioningly.

"Don't look at me." Paint said. Then to Captain Burton, "They always look at me for directions because I'm an Indian, but it doesn't rain in Tucson, guys. This is Laos. And I'm just a reservation frybread Indian."

"Yeah, sure Jimmy." Captain Burton patronized. "Let's follow your best guess down the hill."

"Sir?" Willoughby asked, "Do you think it's a good idea to attack a headquarters given that there are only four of us?"

"How hungry are you, sergeant?"

"My belly's sticking to my backbone." Willoughby replied.

"That's why." Burton said, and turning to Paint, he motioned for them to move out.

Paint stayed in the lead, the file continued. Wider spacing. They all did it instinctively. They'd been together since Korea, all but Willoughby, and he'd been with them since they showed up in Laos.

The depot was the local headquarters of what Burton still thought of as the Viet Minh. Names changed as politics ebbed and flowed. Now it was the Soviet Republic of Vietnam's 148th Independent Infantry Regimental depot, and based on intelligence they developed themselves, it was also the repository of logistics and order of battle information for all North Vietnamese forces operating in Laos.

If past practice held sway, when the Monsoon hit, many from the North Vietnamese Army regiment would be furloughed home and the guard on the facility would be light. Burton decided on a snatch and run operation as the weather closed in and got so bad that tracking them on the way out would be impossible.

The cliff side they were descending was not guarded during monsoon according to one soldier that they had interrogated thoroughly. It was deemed impassable by the enemy.

Burton didn't think anything was impassable, or so it seemed to Jimmy Paint. Their climb down over slippery rocks and cliff faces was suicidal, but Paint trusted the boss's instincts.

Burton lifted his compass from his pocket, tugging on the parachute cord that connected the compass to a button loop on his shirt. He took a reading and instinctively looked up for the sun but all he could see was a leaden sky. The compass didn't do him much good without a grid reference since he wasn't sure where they were. There was only one way off the cliffs. Straight ahead and down.

Everything in nature is curved. Only man makes straight lines. Willoughby saw the building before any of the others did. Ninety-degree angles below them blended into the fog in a world of curves and shapes.

"Boots off." Burton whispered. Gorman was already exchanging his combat boots for sandals. It would not be the first headquarters they'd hit. The method was more or less the same. Always in the rain so the sound of rifle fire wouldn't carry, they'd recon the target thoroughly and once they decided on a plan of action they'd execute it. Willoughby usually provided covering fire while Paint and Gorman crept in and took out any sentries. It was rare that they found an alert sentry this close to China during heavy rain, hundreds of miles from the nearest hostile troops. More or less all of the sentries would be alert for hill tribes, intent on stealing supplies, but even the Hmong stayed in their villages during the height of monsoon.

A large building with a tall radio mast stretching skyward from the roof stood in the center of cleared ground, surrounded by half a dozen tumbledown wood frame shacks. Dirt surrounded the main buildings, making it a quagmire in the rain. Wood planks connected the main building to two of the small shacks.

Gorman pointed to the planks. "One of those has to be an outhouse. Maybe there are people in the other one."

Burton nodded. "I think you're right."

Trip wires connected to mines or booby traps concerned Burton as they approached the tree line that formed a perimeter to the camp. The rain made them nearly impossible to detect.

It took them the better part of an hour, circling the perimeter to find the principle pathway into the camp. It lay on the downhill slope and it was wide enough for a truck to drive it. Ruts in the mud, now running parallel streams indicated the presence of a truck or trucks in the past.

"Don't ask me to put my ear to the ground to find out how long ago the truck passed," Paint cautioned with a hit of a smile crossing his serious face.

"Huddle." Burton called quietly. The men ghosted into the heavy foliage and gathered briefly. "Recon the points of the compass by rank. I'll take west." The men knew they'd deploy in a clockwise direction from west, each sweeping his sector. "Meet back here at 0400. We'll take 'em before first light." He checked his watch. "It's 1400. Hooch up together. Paint, you're with me. We'll watch the main road." Turning to Gorman. "Stay up there in the rocks with Sam. You should have a pretty good view of the outhouse. That should get us a head count between now and dawn."

Looking closely at each man, Burton nodded. "Questions or problems? What have I missed?" They all seemed satisfied. "Paint. I'll see you back here at 2000 hours."

They all moved off mechanically, softly, without disturbing the world around them as they passed.

Burton didn't like to fight in good weather. More often than not you smelled your enemy before ever you saw him. And if you didn't smell him, you'd smell his shit. The food they ate was different. Even now, living on Vietnamese style rations, he could tell the difference between the Hmong, the North Vietnamese and his own men's scat. Rain cleansed that smell. It destroyed footprints and made tracking the team out of the killing zone almost impossible.

Left alone with his thoughts, Burton moved closer to the target, using the cover available, sampling the air with his tongue. They were cooking meat. His stomach growled. They hadn't had anything to eat for a day. The blend of garlic, spices and roasting water buffalo distracted him briefly bringing memory of home, another place and time.

He sniffed while closing his mouth, concentrating on his upper nose to try and identify something other than the meat and garlic, but the rain, still sheeting down, cleansed the place. He watched for unexplained shadows as the darkness grew deep and jumped slightly when a diesel generator kicked on. Dim bulbs flickered on inside the main building. Wooden window slats were down because of the rain, but they were not light proof. Neither were the walls. The light inside would destroy the night vision of anybody inside.

Voices, an intelligible laugh, scuffing wood on wood carried through the rush of rain. Light spilled from the front door of the large building and a man bounced along the planks urgently to one of the two outbuildings served by planking. His return was far more relaxed. Yep, it was the outhouse.

Something wasn't right. It didn't feel right. Burton wiggled closer to the building in the mud like a burrowing creature. The voices were still indistinct. It didn't feel like an ambush. There was no sense of a trap. He didn't know what it was, but it didn't feel the way it should. Backing carefully, using shadow and moving slowly, he disappeared into the darkness.

He found Jimmy Paint at the rendezvous.

"It doesn't feel right." Paint said.

"You think we're walking into a trap?" From Burton.

"Not a trap but it doesn't look right. This road for one thing, and the camp isn't the way it was described."

"Dinner smelled good."

"Like roasted dog, smelled a bit like home." Paint teased.

"You sleep first. I'll wake you in two hours."

Paint dropped off to sleep almost immediately and was breathing heavily within two minutes. You had to catch Z's where you could. The walk down from the cliffs had been arduous and even though they were accustomed to the privations of long-range operations, sleep was a treasured experience when you could take advantage of a moment.

They'd been out since the end of June. Typhoon #9 whipped its way through the eastern Pacific in mid-July. The steady weather fronts and moisture they dropped provided the means for them to remain undetected for three months. The pressure was telling on all of them. Burton scraped his face with a dull safety razor out of habit as he waited for dawn and one last hit. Then they could go back to civilization. They each knew that they had to re-supply and the only place to do that was in the enemy's parlor. They carried Soviet rifles, threw Soviet grenades and punched through bunkers with B-40 rockets because that's what was available. Food had been a problem since the beginning. The continual monsoon made matters worse in that regard. They'd been raiding the Pathet Lao earlier in the month and made a brief foray into Yunnan, China for food before dipping back across the border into Laos. Now they had done enough. They had photographic proof of Soviet artillery parks and vehicles in Laos and the identity papers of six now dead Russian military advisors. They also took thumbs from the Russians to vet the papers, but they rotted quickly in the monsoon heat and moisture. Willoughby tossed them in a swamp three days later. Burton reasoned that the papers would have to stand on their own.

The team was small and tight. Nobody outside Lieutenant Colonel Bull Simons, commanding the Military Assistance Advisory Group, knew generally where they were. If they hadn't come back in by September,

18

they would officially be listed as missing in action. They all understood the rules.

They were an odd group. Burton reflected that they learned so much early in their association together that went back to Korea.

Paul Gorman was the first and the only survivor of that original bunch of Rangers that worked with Burton behind the lines in Korea, all the way up into China. Gorman earned the unfortunate moniker, Goatman. Gorman unfortunately had pistol grip ears canted outward and wide set eyes that combined with a beard the color of flax, to make him look a lot like a goat. Booze and opium paralyzed him when he was in the rear areas but he was a different man when he was in the field. Steady, smart and a survivor.

Burton read something Napoleon wrote when he was in the Military Academy to the effect that the greatest danger on the battlefield was the moment immediately after victory. He experienced it with Gorman. Their newly minted squad pushed through horrible opposition in Korea and in that lull that came, they found themselves completely physically and emotionally exhausted. Napoleon understood momentum. He and Gorman understood it too because their squad was destroyed at that moment by a counterattack they were unable to blunt, though they should have. Only the two of them made it back, but it was only one in a series of hundreds of lessons learned.

They called Sam Willoughby 'Sparky' because he operated a radio. Everyone who touched a radio was known by a variation of that name. Willoughby started out in the merchant marine before he enlisted in the Army and was scooped off to the secret chambers of the Army Security Agency and training at Ft. Devens, Massachusetts. If Willoughby had been less enthusiastic and not prone to the blandishments of single malt whiskey, he might not have volunteered for jungle training. It's amazing what an evening of carousing can lead to.

The tall, skinny, Cajun hailed from the environs of New Orleans, transplanted in Laos, now seconded from ASA to the 7th Special Forces Group because he spoke French, the language of their allies. One of Burton's greatest joys came from reminding Willoughby that only an idiot would start his career in the signal corps and then volunteer for the infantry. Willoughby took the hazing with some grace.

Sam Willoughby had been reduced in the ranks from master sergeant to sergeant due to an unfortunate set of circumstances while misbehaving on leave, in front of the wrong witnesses. The Army Security Agency hid the hint of scandal in the jungle while Willoughby paid penance.

Jimmy Paint, a Mescalero Apache from New Mexico, found the Special Forces in a round about way. Burton didn't think he'd ever been to Yuma, but it was Paint's story and he stuck to it. The Army screened Jimmy and put him in with a group of Navajo Indians to be a code talker. It took the brass a year to figure out that Jimmy (a) was not Navajo and (b) didn't speak Navajo. He ran into Goatman and Burton in Pusan where they were running deep recon missions in Korea and stuck to them. After Korea he officially went through the Special Forces Q course at Ft. Bragg and did better than anybody thought he would. Jimmy never panicked. He was never flustered and you wanted him next to you in a firefight because he was as cold as ice.

Second Lieutenant Creed Taylor, the only one of their number who hadn't gone out on this mission, stayed behind, recovering from hepatitis. Creed spoke nearly every local dialect in Laos with varying degrees of fluency because he'd been raised in Laos and Burma by missionary parents. His father had juice enough with somebody to get his son sent to the Military Academy at West Point-on-the-Hudson. While Creed was superb on the ground, his military acumen hadn't developed to the extent it had with the rest of them. He graduated from West Point, completed training at Ft. Bragg and they shipped him back to Laos immediately. The brass calling the shots hadn't done Creed Taylor any favors. He should have been sent to a rifle platoon to figure out what the Army was all about, first.

If Burton's parents hadn't employed a Chinese nanny to rock his cradle, Burton would have his feet up on a desk somewhere. When he moved from West Point's long gray line to the green machine, his ability to read and write Chinese and speak the Mandarin and Teochieu dialects earmarked him for special duty. The Korean War was in full swing at the time.

Each of them had their weaknesses. Gorman chased the Dragon, Paint dabbled in Buddhism and considered himself a minor mystic, Willoughby loved Scotch Whiskey and pussy and Creed Taylor was greedy. To Creed money had a perfume that was irresistible. Burton wondered what his peculiar weakness was. Introspection didn't come easily when you were in charge. Maybe that was his Achilles' heel.

20

Burton forced his mind back to the subject of the attack. He mentally ticked through a checklist, a countdown to dawn, and thought they had the angles covered. It was never a good sign.

FIVE

Monday, 7 August 1961 -- 0400 HRS
Military Region One - Near Ban Na Toum, Laos
Ten miles from the border of
the People's Republic of China

Willoughby and Gorman arrived a few minutes early, and made a little noise on purpose to insure that the Captain and the crazy Indian knew they were coming in.

Burton and Paint squatted under a lean-to made from their connected ponchos, but water gently tumbled in through the holes the heads went through and the rain now came at them at an angle so all it accomplished was to keep the rain from their faces.

"One thing's for damned sure," Willoughby whispered, "we're having fun now."

"I wonder if we got the right place." Burton suggested when they settled in. "Maybe Jimmy got us lost?" Willoughby said dryly. The jab was meant in good humor and Jimmy responded with the finger.

Sam Willoughby was in an unusually good mood. Burton chalked it up to the imminent kills, the coming adrenalin rush and the unholy thrill that came from living on the razor's edge.

"How many, Sam?"

"Seven guys crossed the plank to take a crap, but I don't know if there were repeat customers. I couldn't tell from my vantage point. So plus or minus seven or eight assuming they're regular. Nobody came out of the shacks other than the outhouse. No light or movement at all. Nobody awake outside but I can't say what they're doing inside."

"Two of the guys who came out for a smoke were speaking Chinese, I think. Maybe Cantonese?" Gorman added. "It's hard for me to tell the difference."

"What do you think?" Burton asked.

"Maybe they're advisors. We've heard that the Chinks are down here training the North Vietnamese. We know the Russians are training the Pathet Lao, so it would figure wouldn't it? I mean, we're not more than ten miles from China."

22

"They'd be speaking Mandarin if that were the case." Burton said, thinking aloud. "Ok, we'll hit 'em as planned at 0500, it's 0424 on my hack, three-two-one, hack."

The men set their watches.

"Sam, you stay here. We'll hit them from the uphill side. If they bolt, they're likely to come down the road and you can polish 'em off." Willoughby nodded and removed his magazine, tapped it on the sole of his boot once and re-inserted it.

"We'll clear the building with frags. Use the *Degtyareva* stick grenades."

Paint raised his hand, then spoke, "I hate those damned Russian stick grenades. I'm always afraid they're going to go off in my hand."

"It's that or the F-1's. The F-1's have too much punch and the shrapnel is likely to come back at us through the walls of the house. We're gong to be close. Each of you arm up two."

Burton took two RGD-33 stick grenade components from his pack. Gorman and Paint followed suit. The grenades were twitchy and unreliable if handled without due caution. A shrapnel sleeve fit over the top of the explosive head. The handle housed the fuse. The three components were kept separately in their packs until immediately before use. You could never be completely sure of the fuse.

Sticking two stick grenades into the waistband of his trousers, Captain Burton moved off into the darkness followed by Gorman and then Paint.

In position, Burton moved the thumb safety to the left and held the head of the grenade while pulling back, twisting clockwise and then pushing in the fuse mechanism, cocking the grenade. He looked over his shoulder at Gorman and Paint who were completing the same process. Paint nodded and moved to the side of the building as rain padded against the roof. Gorman was about six feet further than Paint. Each positioned himself under a wood window cover.

The front door opened and a man trotted across the plank toward the outhouse running deliberately, urgently, directly at Burton. Burton lifted his AK-47 and fired once Crack – Thump. The round popped as it entered the man's chest cavity, directly through the heart. The man went down hard.

As Burton fired, Paint and Gorman lifted the window covers and threw their grenades. They counted to two and then ducked.

A crisp, rapid throwing motion was required to activate the fuse, timed for three seconds. As the grenades were thrown, the grenade heads shifted, freeing the firing pin clip, forcing the firing pin into the primer.

CRUNCH-CRUNCH-CRUNCH —CRUNCH. The grenades detonated. Shrapnel burst through the thin walls of the building over the heads of both Burton and Paint. The diesel generator that had been grinding stopped running and the lights went out.

A man staggered through the front door in the darkness and Burton put two rounds through him at point blank range. Dropping, Burton threw two grenades in rapid succession through the front doors of the outhouse and the other out-building with a plank leading to it. Then he ducked. CRUNCH-CRUNCH-zing as shrapnel passed overhead. Burton pushed onto his feet from the oozing mud, taking an angular path through the door of the main building, stepping clear of the dead men. Then in the doorway, a sharp move left and crouch on the inside of the building, well clear of the open door. A fire burned toward the back, illuminating the hut. There was nothing living in the building. The four Russian hand grenades did their grizzly work. The place was a slaughter-house.

He stood. "Clear!" And he took a few deep breaths. The fire grew brighter. One of the grenades had detonated over the top of several cases of canned Russian sardines, and the place smelled of cordite and fish oil with the metallic smell of blood and shit from the dead men mixed in. "Check the outbuildings then call Willoughby in."

"Problem, sir." Gorman said, pointing down at one of the dead men. "They're *Kuomintang* Chinese, not Vietnamese or Laotian. Nationalist Chinese uniforms."

What are they doing here? Burton asked himself, still taking in the carnage he wrought inside the building. The *Kuomintang* had been pushed out of Burma at the first of the year and were supposed to be over in Thailand.

"Whatever it is, I'm sure it has to do with opium." Burton guessed, looking closely at the dead men. He crouched and went through the pockets of a man at his feet, finding and taking papers and an envelope from the breast pocket of the uniform shirt the Kuomintang man been living in for a few weeks, by the look of it. "They were driven out of China by Mao and then driven out of Burma by the Burmese and Chinese. The only ones left in Burma are mercenaries working for the opium warlords in the Shan States." Burton was saying what they all knew and what they were all were thinking.

Reading the Chinese characters on the piece of paper, Burton confirmed, "We hit the wrong place." He pocketed the letter, concerned.

Outside, he checked the bodies of the two men he'd shot. He rolled the first body over. He'd given this one two rounds. Part of the man's cheek was gone along with his nose and left eye. His teeth were clenched. Burton checked his pockets and found an American made Zippo cigarette lighter. A Timex watch strapped to his wrist – was still ticking.

The second man was young, no more than a boy of sixteen or seventeen years of age at most. The heart shot stopped him. There was some soggy low denomination currency in one pocket and a piece of carved jade in another.

Sam Willoughby found a spot he considered to be as good as any other for a one-man ambush. Intersecting dead falls provided cover and concealment with a back door in the event that he had to shoot and scoot. He was thirty yards or so inside the tree line that bounded the compound. He checked his AK-47 once more, insured no mud or debris was in the barrel, checked his Makarov pistol and then checked the AK once more. Spare clips, knife, and just to make sure reached south and grabbed his balls. "Don't fail me now."

Rain pelted his face and Willoughby contemplated the new war in Laos. It was strange, even though it was his first war and he wasn't sure precisely how they were supposed to be. The primary thrust of American activity in the north, which is where they were now, had been directed toward having the Hmong and Montagnard defend their own land from the Communist Pathet Lao and Vietnamese. The Hmong in particular were willing to do this because by defending their territory, they were also defending their opium crops. Opium was the only currency in Laos that meant a damned thing, the only cash crop available. So in a perverse way, Sam knew that he worked damned hard and put his life on the line to preserve the Hmong way of life, the drug trade.

Opium in Laos and heroin in New Orleans were also two different things. At harvest time, Hmong subsistence farmers took their ball of opium resin, put it in their packs, and took the family donkey down to the nearest town. Every store in every village had a scale. The farmer set his ball of opium on one side and the shopkeeper put a little weight on the other. The farmer bought what he needed for the year with the ball of opium sap, loaded the goods on the donkey and went back to the farm for a year with his supplies. It was merely a medium of exchange. The farmer didn't care about communists or capitalists. He and his family simply existed and the opium helped them do that. The dynamic was far removed from drug addicts, social parasites, or liquor store robberies, to pay for the juice they pumped into their arms back in New Orleans.

Over the last two years the war took on a different character for him. He began his career dealing with radios and signals. It was technical work, associated with processes and machines: vacuum tubes, wires, circuits and solder. Now it was different. Real war, blood red war, cat and mouse where those roles could change instantly. The first few times he killed men he felt ill, remorse overwhelmed him. It wasn't so much the slaughter as it was remorse for the high, the euphoria of survival and the satisfaction that came with the experience. He didn't resort to cowardice, the dreaded *tiny heart syndrome*. He hit the target, saved a buddy, saved himself and it felt good. Feeling good at the sight of a dead man depressed him. Killing them all for the sake of opium seemed a trivial waste of life. He questioned himself for motives and couldn't find any that made sense. He also questioned his sanity because he knew of a certainty that he was addicted to the combat, not the purpose for the killing. None of it was about America, Louisiana or anybody back home. What started out as a job where he felt pride working on radios ended up as being pride in being a pretty good killer. What was sanity and what defined insanity?

A series of dull thumps in the distance, sound dampened by the rain, told him that the assault was underway. Burton loved to use hand grenades. More was better to Captain Burton. Then silence. Then a footfall through the darkness in the rain came slowly in his direction. Their shapes were ghostly and inhuman in the distance, framed by the edges of the road. No hurry, no concern, simply coming, walking, huge. His finger tightened on the trigger, sight blade on the shape. Then relief.

Elephants. Two big gray elephants lumbered down the path, apparently disturbed by Burton's grenades.

He caught his breath and smiled. Laos was called the Kingdom of the White Parasol and the Million Elephants. He almost wasted two of them. He laughed perversely to himself. They would have to change the name to land of 999,998 elephants.

The elephants passed down the path and out of sight before Jimmy Paint came for him.

SIX

Monday, 7 August 1961 -- 0520 HRS
Military Region One - Near Ban Na Toum, Laos
Ten miles from the border of
the People's Republic of China.

When Willoughby and Paint arrived, Gorman and Burton were standing in the non-privy shack that had a plank leading to it from the main house. A round three-foot hole in the dirt floor led to a dugout chamber below. Gorman dropped a lantern attached to a length of parachute cord hand-over-hand into the hole. A grimy white face looked up from the floor, another fifteen feet down.

He was obviously French, and happy to see them.

"Ask him who he is, Sam." Burton asked Willoughby to translate.

Willoughby asked and had to tell the man to slow down so his admittedly broken Louisiana French ear could make out the response.

"His name is Jean-Paul Cyr, he's a captured French soldier, and he wants us to get him up out of the hole. He seems genuinely happy to see us."

Gorman, unsympathetic and a Francophobe offered, "I can toss a grenade in on a short fuse and fix the problem. You missed with the first grenade – Captain."

"It went through the door and went off here on the floor. Bad billiards." Burton muttered by way of excuse.

Burton thought for ten seconds before speaking. While he thought, he gently kicked dirt down into the pit. "We can't leave the poor wretch down there to rot. But I don't want to bring anyone back with us. You know the bastard will talk about how we saved his ass, and it will get out that we were here. This whole *Koumintang* business doesn't need to be broadcast." He fingered a Russian F-1 grenade hanging from his belt absently.

"That's how they dry out addicts, Captain." Paint said, hoping the captain wouldn't toss the grenade down the hole. Burton usually questioned prisoners before killing them, but this man wasn't a prisoner and he wasn't an enemy.

28

"Ask him if he's an addict."

Willoughby asked. "He says he's had an addiction problem in the past but he's clean now. He offers a reward if we can get him out. I think he understood what Gorman was talking about when he suggested we frag him." Sam didn't add that the Frenchman's eyes were locked on the grenade Burton touched unconsciously.

"What kind of reward?" Gorman prodded, now interested and not nearly as Francophobic as he'd been moments before. "Ask him."

Willoughby asked. "He says gold. The people who had him captive were *Kuomintang* from the Shan State. They have a cache of gold taels."

"A tael is aboug 40 grams. 1.2 ounces." Gorman said, seriously, having a change of heart about the fate of the man in the hole. "$35 to the ounce. Round off to $40 per tael."

Burton said. "We can't get him to take us to the gold and then shoot him." West Point scruples were in play now and he hated having a conscience at the wrong time. "Where's the gold?" Burton asked and Willoughby relayed.

"He'll show us if we let him out. There's a rope ladder up here somewhere."

A wad of rags in a corner turned out to be a rag-rope ladder. Burton tied it off and Gorman tossed the ladder down into the pit. Willoughby invited him up. Paint covered the Frenchman with his AK, standing off to one side so that if he shot him, the bullets wouldn't go through-and-through hitting one of his own.

"Don't shoot him 'till we find out if he's bull-shitting about the gold." Gorman cautioned Jimmy Paint.

The Frenchman saluted and reported. Burton could make out that he was Adjutant-Chef Jean-Paul Cyr of the Groupe de Commandos Mixtes Aéroportés. He was a scrawny man no more than five and a half feet tall, with pale, leathery skin covered with a beard, bulging, clever eyes, and a bald scalp, that he covered with a filthy moth-eaten beret that might have been red once. He wore the traditional black pajama style uniform worn and favored by the Pathet Lao and North Vietnamese.

Jean-Paul smiled as Burton returned his salute. The Frenchman's teeth were heavily stained deep red with betel nut.

"He has to be a deserter." Paint said, now wishing the captain had dropped a grenade in the hole. The French soldier's face reminded him of a basilisk, or maybe the cross between a Pekinese dog and a snake, if you could cross the two. His eyes were intelligent, hooded and wary, but in no sense fearful.

"Sam," Burton said to Willoughby, "Ask Adjutant-Chef Cyr about the people we killed and find out where the gold is. When you're done with that, let me know what you found out and Jimmy will spell you while you're trying to dry out your radio. I'd rather not walk all the way back to Vientiane." Shifting focus to Paint and Gorman, "Let's round up whatever food and ammo we can scrounge and be ready to move. There's no telling when their friends might arrive and none of us have eaten for a day or two."

"What about the gold?" Gorman asked, clearly wanting to remain with the French sous-officer.

"Sam will handle the interrogation. I don't want to march without food and we're short of ammo. First things first." Burton took Gorman's bicep gently and pulled him out of the shack and across the planking to the main building.

"Yes sir." Willoughby replied, then he turned to the Frenchman, formulated his question in French and asked, "How much gold are we talking about?"

Jean-Paul straightened himself and said, " Trois Pikul."

Willoughby's eyes widened. "Trois—that's three. Hey Gorman."

Burton and Gorman returned.

"How much is a Pikul of gold?"

"A pikul is 133 avoirdupois pounds." Gorman said, knowledgeable on the subject.

"How much would three pikul of gold?"

Gorman ran the math in his head. "It'd be about $26,000 per pikul so figure $78,000."

"Taels shaped like boats." Jean-Paul said in very broken English.

"The food and ammo will wait." Burton said.

Six leather sacks of gold ingots sat between them as they divided the food and ammunition. The small ingots were each formed in the shape of a boat, each a tael in weight. Each of the sacks weighed roughly fifty pounds.

The eight dead Chinese were stacked in a corner, their pockets having been emptied for intelligence purposes.

Burton opened a can of French Boeuf Bouilli and sniffed it. An unpleasant rumor that circulated for years held that the tins often contained monkey meat, and were still referred to by the French forces as *singe*. Paint looked at the can skeptically, but when Burton dug in, eating with the aid of his knife, he opened a can too.

Gorman ate the Russian sardines that weren't punctured by the hand grenade shrapnel while he kept watch outside in the rain.

They stripped two cases of French T-Rations, throwing out the unnecessary items, keeping the Armee cigarettes, Royco Soup, tins of Morey beef, large chocolate bars, brandy, tins of pork sausage, a few extra P-51 can openers, coffee and sugar.

Willoughby played with the ChiCom radio that had been pierced by a few fragments from the Russian hand grenades. He started the generator and powered the radio but was having difficulty tuning it. They looked at the Army Security Agency man as a static-chatter of Morse code erupted from a speaker. He nibbled on a chocolate bar from one of the French rations.

"I think I've got it working." Willoughby said proudly, as Gorman came in, trading places with Paint who went outside as a sentry.

"There's something wrong with the oscillator. Hear that, the tone of the signal is bouncing up and down. BEEp, beEP, weePP, DIT dah, dit DAH. Chinese crap." Willoughby commented as he twisted a knob.

"It just has to get out to one of the ASA Listening posts. Can you do that?" Burton asked, now irritated.

"I don't think it's transmitting. Something broke inside. Maybe the shrapnel did it? The key's dead. I'll have to crack the case to see if I can fix it." Willoughby explained. He pawed through a flimsy cardboard box with Cyrillic writing on the side. "I'd have to test the vacuum tubes one at a time and they don't have any spare tubes I can find.

"Destroy the radio and let's get out of here. We can try to get your radio dried out enough to use it once we're well away from here." Burton said, gathering his gear together.

Burton did the math and didn't like what he was figuring. Nobody wanted to leave the gold behind, but each would be packing seventy pounds of gold, provided that they divided the load evenly. Willoughby's radio weighed an additional twenty-five pounds and he'd been playing with it to try and get it working. Water and radios didn't have an affinity for each other. Dropping the radio wasn't an option at this point and from the looks on the men's faces, neither was leaving the gold behind.

WHITE POWDER

Gold fever gripped them all. Even Burton felt it. In addition to the gold, they found bundles of colorful 100 Piaster banknotes from the *Institut D'Emission Des Etats Du Laos*, French Indochinese currency. Presuming they cut Jean-Paul Cyr in for part of the loot, which was the only way to hope he'd keep his mouth shut, each man would walk out with about $18,000. The sergeants, though at different grades and with different times in service, made about $550 a month with hazardous duty pay, jump pay and their off-base housing and food allowance. Burton made more, but not that much more. The haul would ease everyone's financial woes. It was never a question of whether they'd take the gold and currency. It was more an issue of how to manage the bulk and clank of the gold boats and the weight on the long hump out of there.

SEVEN

Monday, 7 August 1961 -- 0930 HRS
Military Region One - Near Ban Na Toum, Laos
Eleven miles from the border of
the People's Republic of China

The straps of the ruck bit deeply into Burton's shoulders and the slick mud made going very difficult while wearing sandals. About a mile and seven river crossings later, they shed their sandals and put on wet socks and sodden boots.

"Nobody's complaining about the weight." Burton said to them all. "Gold is heavy."

"Or ne sont pas trop lourds." Jean-Paul Cyr said, with a smile.

"He says it's not too heavy, sir." Willoughby translated with a knowing wink.

"Which brings me to my next question, Sam, we're going to have to climb one of these hills to get a radio signal out if we want a ride back, aren't we?"

"It'd work a lot better, Captain."

"We could leave the gold at the base of the hill, cache it, and then come back and get it later after we check in." Burton suggested. They all wore skeptical expressions on their tired faces. The gold bug still held its grip. They'd only gone a mile and it might take some time for it to wear off. "Suit yourselves, saddle up and let's get going. Paint, let's find a hill to spend the night, maybe four or five more miles from here."

It was very tough going with the rain, mud and additional weight. They were no more than four miles from the *Koumintang* stronghold, when they began to climb.

As they reached the summit of a ridge that ended where it drooped to intersect the base of a vast limestone pillar, called a karst, the rain slacked and the sun appeared as a dull orange orb on the western horizon. Jimmy Paint looked exhausted, but he ran the back-trail to make sure that their path was reasonably obscure, and laid a few booby traps constructed of hand grenades and tripwires against the possibility that a curious tracker would stumble onto their path.

Gorman and Jean-Paul Cyr made a shelter of the group's combined ponchos. Willoughby and Burton strung Sam Willoughby's radio antenna wire between two large trees. And then re-strung it twice until it suited Willoughby perfectly. Gorman scavenged food from their packs to make a stew.

The Top Secret AN/GRC-109 Transmitter/Receiver was the latest and greatest communicator available to Special Forces, even though it had been in use with the CIA for over a decade. The radio consisted of three black boxes with a hand-crank generator for power. Sam Willoughby didn't bring the battery because of the weight so they made each radio broadcast under cranking power. Rather than keying in Morse code directly, the AN/GRA-71 Coder/Burst Transmission Group module connected to the radio. Willoughby keyed in the transmission of dit and dahs onto a small tape cartridge, encoded from a one-time pad. He inserted the cartridge into the burst transmitter. The burst transmitter sent at about 300 words per minute and made it more difficult for a radio direction finder to fix their location. A length of wire that they usually strung out between two tree trunks served as the antenna.

Sometimes the radio needed to dry out before it would work. Burton plotted with Willoughby to compose a message to Military Assistance Advisory Group in Vientiane. It simply read. TO: UNICORN (which identified Burton's particular White Star Mobile Training Team as the one transmitting, allowing the Army Security Agency person at MAAG to select the correct one-time pad to decrypt the rest of the message).

REQUEST PICK UP GRID 192 ASAP 4+1<STOP>ADVISE WEATHER FORECAST<STOP>

The officer reading the request would consult a reference and would understand the first digit. In this case a 1 meant that it would have to be a helicopter pick-up. Landing Area 92 was a pre-selected location about two miles from their present position and it was presumed to be hot because of its close proximity to the border with Red China.

Fourteen additional H-34 Choctaw helicopters had been delivered to Air America in March, bringing the total operational to twenty, providing that none had been shot down or crashed in bad weather between then and the present. Weather was always an issue. Rain and fog grounded the helicopters far more often than they flew during monsoon. This particular trip required that helicopters at Ching Ri, Thailand fly about two hundred miles across mountainous terrain, find the landing zone and then fly back. Since the maximum range of the H-34 Choctaw was 180 miles, presuming no headwind, they'd have to refuel inbound and outbound. The easiest way was to fly three choppers, two full of fuel, land somewhere safe, and refuel the mission ship. One of the helicopters would wait on the ground until the mission ship came back with the payload, Burton's White Star Mobile Training Team. While they waited, they'd refuel the mission ship and then all of the helicopters would return to Ching Ri together.

It sounded easy enough, but making it happen and finding a truly "safe place" in war torn Laos required a rendezvous with a White Star team in the field to provide protection for the helicopter while it waited for Burton's taxi to return. If they had favorable weather and Special Forces people in the field in roughly the right spot, it could happen in a day or two. If not, there was no telling how long it might take to coordinate.

Clearly, waiting around was not an option, which meant that they'd have to cache the gold and come back later. It would be unpopular with the men, but necessary if they planned to get out of Northern Laos intact.

Willoughby's message went out, MAAG-Vientiane acknowledged, requesting contact the next day.

"We'll cache the gold here and recon the LZ in the morning. Two miles out and back without the additional weight. Down this mountain up another and return. We should be back by noon."

Jean-Paul spoke to Willoughby, clearly getting the gist of what Burton proposed.

"Sam?" Burton asked Willoughby.

"Jean-Paul volunteers to stay with the gold and protect it. He doesn't think we should leave it behind, unguarded." Sam Willoughby translated. Cyr nodded vigorously.

"Tell him he goes with us. If he makes noise or causes trouble, we'll kill him here and divide his gold four ways. Clear?"

Cyr made a bitter face and engaged in an animated discussion with Willoughby.

"The soup's cooking, Captain." Gorman said, throwing Burton a long chocolate bar from the stores. "But you might want to jump the gun a little. I'm making chocolate hardtack cake for desert."

Burton saluted with the chocolate bar, broke it in half, and handed one of the halves to Cyr. "A word, Sam?"

The Frenchman unwrapped it and took a large bite with his stained teeth, saluting Burton with the remainder.

Willoughby stood and walked with Burton out and away from the encampment. Burton broke the half chocolate bar in half again and handed a piece to Willoughby. They both ate, Willoughby wondering if there was a bee in Burton's jock.

"You held out on me." Burton said. "I'm the CO, I'm in charge of this mission and I'm accountable for everything, no matter how secret you think it might be."

"Did you see me take the codebook?" Sam said, reaching into his shirt, pulling out an oilcloth.

"No, I know you ASA types and how you treasure the enemy's codes. I didn't know you had a book until just now. I was bluffing."

"Fuck." Willoughby said, handing the oilcloth with its contents to Burton. "Its pages are rice paper so that you can eat them if you need to but it's sealed and packed in a blue waterproof cover."

"One-time pad?" Burton asked as he opened the oilcloth and saw the blue rubber cover. Then he handed it back to Sam Willoughby. "You keep it, Sparky."

"It's interesting," Willoughby explained, "When Morse code operators transmit Chinese characters they're faced with a problem. With 10,000 characters in existence, operators needed a means of converting the Chinese characters to Morse. It looks like they've assigned numbers from 000 to 9999. Each number corresponds to a character in the Chinese Telegraphic Code. That means the originator has to convert to numbers while the recipient has to convert them back to characters."

Burton smiled, "That's interesting, huh? I need to get you back to Madame Lulu's while there's still time for you to get a life.

EIGHT

Tuesday, 8 August 1961 -- 0500 HRS
*Laos, Military Region One – At Landing Zone 192, sixteen miles
southeast of the border of
the People's Republic of China.*

Burton couldn't stop thinking of Sergeant Sam Willoughby, the New Orleans code maven. The memory of their first meeting had burned into his memory. It was his second day in Laos.

It seemed so long ago, but it had only about eighteen months since he first set eyes on Sam. The circumstances of their first meeting certainly set the tone.

He recalled the morning shades of yellow-gold filtering through the loosely thatched wall of the hut. Birds wailed, monkeys chattered in the distance and he heard coughing from many voices. An occasional laugh, perhaps a private joke shared. A military encampment woke up.

He recalled the headache as well. His head swam but he couldn't tell if it was from an interrupted dream or if something was going on in the physical world. Burton drifted in that semi-intoxicated state that exists between slumber and consciousness. Slowly, and almost painfully, he drifted awake as the building he was in swayed rhythmically. French voices from beyond the wall strained with passion.

The three-stilted Laotian hut shook, suddenly twisting so violently that Burton flew, tossed from his hammock, encased in the white, gossamer mosquito net that smelled of creosote, fever sweats and vin-o-jel. He hit the dried reed floor hard, elbow punching through the now tilted floor so that he could see lush green vegetation below.

Panting and giggling: Two voices, male and female, from the other side of a thin wall of woven banana leaves that separated the rooms. Dislodged thatching from the ancient roof drifted to the floor like snowflakes around him.

Burton reached for a packet of vin-o-jel on the floor in his rucksack. Hanging onto the wall to keep his footing with one hand, he opened it with a pocketknife and squeezed the concentrated wine jell-o into his mouth and let it reconstitute. It was nasty, but the alcohol content provided the relief from a building headache, no doubt caused by vin-o-jel the night before. The giggling continued.

The Corporal Chef, opened the door, stuck his ugly face proceeded by a large veiny nose, into Burton's cubicle and gave him a terse but apologetic offering in German accented French. "Big Olaf was especially amorous." Olaf, a huge Viking of a man from somewhere in Scandinavia, came to Laos as one of the replacements for the killed or wounded. He'd just begun his second four-year enlistment in the French Foreign Legion.

The Corporal Chef, a friendly, squint-eyed, purple-nosed, jowly German named Kreutz, ran the Bordel Militaire de Campagne, or BMC that had been set up east of Vientiane, between the French Military Mission and Wattay Airbase. Corporal Chef Kreutz explained it all to Burton the day before. This particular BMC had been in Vietnam or Laos since 1953. It was originally placed on the hilltop fortress at Sapa, astride the peaks rising into the clouds that ran between Hanoi and Lai- Châu. The French army evacuated it to Hai Phong during the military disaster at Điên Biên Phú, and then relocated to Laos and handed the operation over to a platoon of legionnaires who were a bit long in the tooth to manage. They set it up north of the French Military Mission facility, which was located between the airport and Vientiane.

To spite competition from other establishments in Vientiane, the BMC did a brisk business. Corporal Chef Heinrich Kreutz oversaw the BMC and supervised the bar in the main hut.

As Burton was new to Laos and had been assigned to work with the French Forces in a liaison capacity of sorts, he had been quartered in the mobile military brothel upon his arrival. The French were a courteous people and knew that officers had particularly urgent needs because of the pressures of command.

He stepped out of the tilting hut through the back door and his unlaced boots sank three inches into red, sucking, mud. Behind him, Big Olaf sauntered away from the BMC with a spring in his step. Burton stepped out of his boots, pulled them out of the sucking red mud, shook his head and walked/slid around to planking that provided a walkway to the bar.

Corporal Chef Kreutz fell into step with him, speaking idiomatically correct English. "We'll fix that hut for you, sir. It's broken before." Burton picked up his step and the Corporal's shorter legs blurred as he kept up. His voice was apologetic and full of bon ami. "It's not bad here,

Captain, not by anyone's standards, though it's hot in the summer, hot enough to melt lead."

"I think I need to find a more restful place to sleep than in the bordello."

"This is the best place there is. That's why you're here. It's better than Maurice Cavalerie's Hotel Constellation in town and we don't charge you to stay because you are a guest. You have the bar close at hand, and if you wish to *tirez un coup*, uh, fire-a-shot, with the girls, you have only to ask. You're with the Legion now and we will take care of you as we do with our own." Kreutz paused briefly, gathering his thoughts, then continued. "There are three rules of the Legion. The first is a hot meal served wherever and whenever possible. The second is an ample supply of wine. The third is access to generally disease-free female companionship." He patted Burton's back and grinned. Two teeth were missing.

"I haven't seen a decent bottle of pénard yet. You promised wine." There seemed to be an endless supply of vin-o-jel, though. The French air dropped vin-o-jel to isolated garrisons as a substitute for bottled wine. For a taste of wine that surely wore a layer or two from your stomach, all you need do was pour in the water. Or you could eat it straight the way Burton just had. It's wasn't wine, but if you closed your eyes and thought of a good glass of wine, you might be able to fool yourself. Well, not really.

The bar hut, where the Corporal Chef slept, was larger than the four brothel huts lined up like dominoes beyond it. The windows had been shuttered closed and the exterior was draped with mosquito netting. Cotton field uniforms hung limply over a drying line. As they walked to the stairs, Legionnaire Smith, a prematurely balding Englishman, stepped out into the sun, his uniform sharply creased and spotless. He looked over at Burton with mirthful blue eyes and tapped out Camel cigarettes for the Corporal Chef and Burton. Kreutz tucked his cigarette behind his ear and continued up the steps. Burton stayed with Smith to pass the time.

Smith struck a match and offered Burton a light. "Do you like the *Carnet de Pouf*, Captain?" Burton didn't answer so he continued, lighting his cigarette as he spoke, "*Tire un coup en ville, chez les poffiance de ville.*"

"You're *controlle medicaile*, right?"

"Yep, I sit here at this desk outside the bar area. As soldiers pick up the ladies they come to me for a condom and registration in the Carnet de

WHITE POWDER

Pouf. I take the soldier's name, rank and compagnie he pulls out his knob, draws the foreskin back and squeezes to ensure there is no discharge typical of '*chaude-piss*' - gonorrhea which carries a mandatory seven day stint in the stockade for self inflicted injuries."

"Do you like the job?" Burton took a drag on the unfiltered Camel.

"Sometimes I'm teased by the other English speakers as being '*la Roi du Corvee Bit*'! Because I have to clean out the channel when it's been infected with gonorrhea but damn, they really could find me a more dignified job. I trained as a combat medic."

They smoked and watched a flock of white birds take to the air from the Mekong River, flowing to the south.

"I'm supposed to meet another American. His name is Sam Willoughby. Have you seen him?"

"He's in the bar. He's been here all night." Smith motioned to the bar with his thumb.

Burton climbed the stairs and opened the flimsy wood slat door.

Willoughby slung a long leg over a chair next to where he lounged in the dark bar, staring at the wall. A pretty, exceptionally petite Vietnamese woman sat on his lap.

"Is this breakfast?" Burton asked.

Sam Willoughby was drunk, rumpled and looked like he hadn't slept. He motioned to the chair offering Burton a seat.

"This is Lotus. We tried to do the Christian, Buddhist, Muslim trick last night. Lotus is a Buddhist." Lotus' eyes were sly as she slumped coyly against the man from the Army Security Agency. "Joy is from the North African Ouled Nail Tribe. She's fat, drinks mint tea and is Muslim, and Dao, that sacred, precious little thing shipped out of The Green Latrine to this God forsaken hole, is Catholic."

He waited for Burton's comment, but all Burton did was stand up walk behind the bar and pour a tall glass of pénard. Burton lifted the bottle as if he'd found a prize. Willoughby continued unbidden. "Corporal Chef brought Joy. Joy was a pain in the ass. No way was Lotus going to screw Joy, even to please me and it had nothing to do with racial politics. Dao took off with the Corporal Chef. So, Lotus and I just sat on the floor drinking Mekong. And here we are."

"I'm Craig Burton. You'll be working for me."

Willoughby replied with a wink. Then he squeezed the girl. "Lotus—My God, how I love you. I want to visit you on Sundays, when

40

we're both old." Willoughby looked up at Burton, "I told her, 'Lotus, you aren't a whore.'" He stroked her breast through fabric, tenderly. "She asked me where I met her. I said, 'Ok, in a whorehouse. But you're different than all those other girls.'"

Lotus smiled and some of her gold dental work gleamed in the light.

Burton probed. "Rumor has it that you closed one of those high class bars in Manila because the disquiet in your soul needed it."

"Now, who told you that?" Willoughby drew his oiled blue steel .45 Colt Model 1911 as he remembered. He brandished the handgun as he reminisced. "I brought along this secretary that I met there who worked for General Motors. She was a bottle blonde, the carpet definitely didn't match the drapes, but who cares, cause she was white.

"This is how it was. I've got a .45, but big fucking deal. So does everybody else in the joint except the Aussies and they're packing nine millimeter Brownings. This Mamasan legacy bitch struts up to me, arrogance personified. She starts in on me with a shrill voice. 'You got a problem? I don't know why you got a problem. I know who you are. I know you so goddamn important. Sam Willoughby, shit...you probably so *goddamn* important you came in here with your wife to get a girl. Is that your kink?"

"*Is* that your kink?"

"Sure, if I was married." Willoughby said sincerely. "I quickly and eloquently stuck the .45 in Mamasan's mouth and said, "*You've* got a .45 in your mouth."

"She blinked, 'Yes.'

"The music snapped off. Everybody with a mind left listened to the best of their ability because they were vicariously interested in *why* Mamasan wanted to have rough sex with me.

"I told her, 'I never said nothing about you. Why you say something about my friend, Mamasan?' I hit her upside the head with my left hand. 'I never called you bad names, but here you stand, with a singing ear and a fucking death wish, smart enough to stop sucking cock and stupid enough to start sucking guns.'

"She blinked a serious 'Yes' on that one. Who can blame her? Anybody would.

"I stood there with my .45 in her mouth and shouted so everyone could hear, 'Mamasan, your mouth is like a whore's pussy and I wanna cum. Know what I mean?'

41

"So the Army shipped you here to Laos so I could rehabilitate you." Burton summarized the outcome.

"And here I am in the French mobile military bordello in fucking Wattay Airbase, busted from master sergeant to sergeant, serving Uncle Sam." He lifted Lotus off his lap gently and whispered in her ear. She smiled at Burton and left through the front door.

"Sit down Captain and let me tell you something."

Burton sat.

Sam Willoughby continued, "I'm jealous of dead soldiers. Dead soldiers have friends to avenge them and family to mourn them. They lie peacefully in neat graves, their bravery and sacrifice noted; buried in smart uniform, medals in velvet boxes, citations to hang on the walls and a folded flag in a cupboard somewhere. They said what they had done and where they had been, and when they died, their friends told how they died, and, from time to time, why they died."

He motioned toward the glass of pénard Burton held. He handed it to Willoughby, who sloshed it in his mouth and then downed it with a toss.

"In the parlance of dead soldiers there is the front line. In the cant of my strange craft we call that place 'the end of line.' People in my business die alone. Our deaths are unsung, our motives unclear. So we die slowly. Every challenged moment of each belabored day is barbed and thorned with memory of the things we cannot tell. We die defenseless with naught to avenge us but the mute records of what we observed in the strange lands that swallowed us."

Then he drifted. Burton took a grey wool blanket from behind the bar and put it over him. "Nice to meet you, Sam."

Back in the present, his eyes open in the dim dawn light, Burton looked over at Sam Willoughby, standing the last watch of the night, nodding off. He'd taken to wearing a coned straw peasant hat he found in the house they had hit two days before. Or was it three?

Birds chirped, signaling the sun's arrival. He felt good for a change, and broken white clouds against a cerulean sky was a big part of it. The men were resting and... where was Jean-Paul Cyr?

"Sam," he whispered urgently. "Sam"

Willoughby turned to look at him, his eyes red, lids heavy. "Hey Captain." The cobwebs in his head translated to his slowly articulated speech.

"Where's the Frog?"

"Right over..." Willoughby pointed to a patch of compressed grass where Cyr had been sleeping.

"Everybody up." Burton's voice was not so quiet anymore but he didn't want it to carry. The urgency, not the volume, brought them all to life instantly.

They were on the trail in five minutes. Cyr, carrying his portion of their trove of gold, appeared to be attempting to cover his tracks, but Jimmy Paint had him almost immediately. They left everything behind but weapons, ammo, intelligence they'd been able to collect to date and Willoughby's radio.

They did a weapons count. Cyr hadn't taken one. Then again, since they all literally slept with their AK-47's, liberating one quietly would have presented problems for the French paratrooper.

The other side of the mountain had a broad base and then white limestone cliffs rose almost vertically up to where they stood. The entire western approach broke off into a sharp landslide. Cyr skirted the cliff. A few Hmong huts on stilts wound around through the bottom of the canyon like a ribbon, paralleling the river. There were plots, likely opium poppies, under cultivation.

"Are you sure you've got the trail, Jimmy?" Burton asked.

"Yeah, look here, boot sliding on the grass. He's got a heavy load, he's not striding out and we're not far behind at all. I wouldn't be surprised if we could hear him ahead of us soon. The ridge sloped down and as the grade became easier animal trails wound down through a double canopy forest.

Cyr took a game trail down the side of the mountain and then cut down over a rocky area. The moisture from his boots clearly marked his pattern over the rocks.

They all heard the noise ahead of them. It was a sharp snap and twang, not unlike the sound of a bowstring being released with a heavy thwack sound following. Not far away. Jimmy looked back at Burton, who shrugged, Willoughby mouthed, "what-the-hell?"

Burton slung his AK-47 and unlimbered a hatchet. It was polished sharp on the leading edge and the beard was honed like a razor. Jimmy paint took a similar hatchet from his pack. Burton made the hand signal for 'provide cover' to Gorman and Willoughby. They moved off down the trail.

Gorman whispered to Willoughby, "I've gotta get myself one of those Spitfire cockpit escape axes."

"Where'd they get 'em?" Willoughby whispered back.

"Fucking British Spitfires the French were using here. Jimmy and the Captain liberated them from the planes parked at Watay Airfield. I've been lookin' hard but I haven't found one yet." Gorman said a little sadly.

Burton motioned them forward and Willoughby followed Gorman, AK-47's ready.

Jean-Paul Cyr lay on a tree trunk that crossed the creek the led into the village, pinned to a booby trap constructed of sharp spikes affixed to a framework. The spikes took him in his midsection and he was still alive, groaning softly as blood poured out of a dozen wounds. Gold boats, one tael weight each, dropped from a hole in his faded green canvas backpack, plopping onto the log. Some of them remained, others bounced off the slimy edge of the old wood into the river.

Burton secured his hatchet and cut Cyr's throat with a knife, wiped it on Cyr and slipped the blade back into the scabbard.

He made a hand-signal to move the other way, back up the hillside.

"You want me to pull his meat tag, Captain? So his people will know what happened to him." Jimmy Paint asked Burton.

"No."

Gorman waited, looking anxiously at Cyr. "Aren't we going to get the gold, Captain?"

"Leave it," Burton said. "The trap was set by the villagers to protect their opium crop. They'll find him and the gold. People talk. It will get back that he stole at least part of the gold if not all of it. Maybe they'll think he buried some of it. No matter what, it will take the heat off us in the near term." Then he thought again. "Ok, Paul, take most of the gold from his pack but leave a quarter or something."

Gorman worked quickly, moving the load and hefted the gold in his own pack.

"Sam, take it easy going back up the hill. It's not raining now. We can't afford tracks. Not at this late date."

"Yes sir."

They took a break half way up the hillside while they waited for Jimmy Paint to work his magic on the back trail.

Sunlight broached the horizon and the beauty of the light on the verdant scenery belied the situation they just left.

"Sometimes this bullshit gets to me." Burton admitted to Gorman and Willoughby.

"It was kinder to cut the bastard's throat than to leave him there to bleed out slowly." Gorman said by way of consolation.

"The sad truth is that I would have let him bleed out naturally, but I didn't want anyone talking to him. He would have told them about us. I killed him for our benefit. Not for his." Burton spit into the grass. "I should have fragged the pit. Now we have the weight of the gold to consider and it might just get us killed."

"It's a lot of money, Captain." Gorman said, looking off at the village as cooking fires began to show their smoke smudges drifting languidly. "I have some debts that will be covered now."

"That gold belonged to somebody important. And we killed their friends. They won't know that we didn't know there was treasure there when we hit 'em. Since we have it, they'll presume that we murdered them for the money. It won't be about an act of war. I took a letter off one of those guys we hit. It's here." He patted his chest, the waterproof bag he kept under his clothes that contained the Russian identity papers and other scraps of paper that held potential intelligence value. The gold belonged to Chang Chi-fu who goes by the name U Kuhn Sa. It was a down payment from the government of Thailand, laundered no doubt, as their contribution toward a joint effort. The letter was no more specific than that."

"Fuck." Willoughby said. "So it's Thai gold?"

"It's tough to doubt the content of the letter when you consider how we came by it."

"What do you want to do?" Gorman asked, concern dripping from the words.

"I knew where the gold came from when we grabbed it. I read Chinese, remember? I'm as greedy as you all are."

Willoughby said, "You know the only thing Kuhn Sa wants to do is raise a bigger army so he can control the opium trade out of Burma."

Burton said, "No doubt. But it's still a payment from Thailand to him that we now have up there on the ridge in the form of little gold one-ounce boats."

Burton mopped his head with a damp green bandana. The continuous stress of the long duration patrols took a heavy toll. Seemingly endless surges of adrenaline and its chemical backlash were counterproductive because there, deep in enemy territory there was no place to run. Emotional and physical exhaustion compounded by the lack of sleep and food led to a state that was impossible to understand unless you experienced it. He wasn't at the end of his rope, but he could see the end. It was time to call for extraction and get out.

NINE

Thursday, 10 August 1961 -- 1100 HRS
Laos, Military Region One – At Landing Zone 188,
twenty-five miles south of the border of
the People's Republic of China

Two days later they popped purple smoke on a windswept ridge eight miles south at another pre-designated landing zone, 188. Jimmy Paint said that eighty-eight was a lucky number. Since the H-34 found them on the first pass, the rest of the men of the 7th Special Forces, White Star Mobile Training Team had to agree with Paint's assessment. They were superstitious during attacks and extractions.

Each of them had been played out. The combination of heat, mosquitoes, near constant partial immersion in water from the monsoon, lack of food and rest hit them once they were inside. The deafening roar of the helicopter masked the outside world and they simply lay there on the metal deck, limp, vibrating as the rotor churned the air overhead.

The helicopters refueled in a landing zone protected by Tony Poshepny's White Hmong who had been moving north in what he called 'a reconnaissance in force'. Bombastic, opportunistic and a vocally former Marine, Tony Poe was poaching over a hundred fifty kilometers northwest of his turf on the Plain of Jars. Tony served as the Central Intelligence Agency's paramilitary point man with the Hmong in Military Region Two.

Tony curiosity about what Burton had been up to proved boundless. As a result, Burton remained concerned the entire time that Tony would want to snoop in the helicopters for a hint of what they were bringing back. The curiosity factor peaked when Tony loaded fifty Czech Škoda automatic rifles in the cargo compartment of the helicopter that brought them out. The crates containing the rifles were stenciled, 'SEA Supply'.

"These rifles go to Walter Kennedy in the P. I." Poe told Burton sternly. He'll be expecting them at Watay Airport when you arrive. Burton hefted one of the Czech copies of the American made Thompson submachine gun, still covered in packing grease.

Keeping Poe on the subject of the rifles and off the subject of the exceptionally heavy battle packs, Burton asked, "Where did you get these, Tony?"

Poeshepny smiled and said, "Need to know, my son. Need to know. Just make sure they get to Kennedy."

"I heard the Agency cashiered Kennedy." Burton said inquisitively.

"Nah, the fucker is still around. He's like a cat. Nine lives at least. He's always in trouble."

"Maybe he's just a cat in a tree." Willoughby suggested, hanging on the conversation.

"No such thing," Tony replied, now facing Sam Willoughby, "I have yet to see a cat skeleton in a tree."

Burton stroked Poshepny's ego, praised his irregulars. Tony had them put a show on for the White Star Team, demonstrating the tactics Tony had been training.

"Ever thought of defecting to the CIA, Craig?" Tony Poe suggested blatantly to Burton.

"Maybe when I get some more experience, Tony. You've pissed more salt water than I've sailed over." Burton replied as he watched the White Hmong acting out a rolling fire advance along the ridge while the helicopter topped off with the last of the fuel. "I don't think I'm in your class."

Fueling complete, Poshepny lit a cigarette and handed one to Burton who put it in his mouth. Tony click-clacked open his Zippo and lit Burton's smoke. "Bullshit, I know what you and these guys do up there in fucking China. You're just the right sort." The helicopter's massive Wright R-1820-84 radial engine turned over behind them making it impossible for them to communicate further.

Burton took ten gold boats from his pocket and pressed them into both of Tony's hands, mouthing thanks as he backed toward the Choctaw, the rotor began to turn overhead. Tony waved and mouthed. "Think about it!"

TEN

Sunday, 12 August 1961 -- 0815 HRS
The Talat Sao Morning Market,
Vientiane, Laos

Burton's Jeep crooned down the crowded road and he turned to pull to a stop just as a black Citroen cut across in front of him and he slammed on the mushy military brakes to keep from plowing into the side of the luxury car.

Without a look over her shoulder, Charlotte Sabon slid a tapered leg from the car and walked into the morning market, oblivious of her transgression. A servant holding a wicker shopping basket looked back, glancing at him, embarrassed. The servant followed her into the rabbit warren of stalls and the shout of buyers and sellers that comprised the market.

Burton saw her before. She lived that way, without regard for anything but her next goal. Like a tornado ripping through a Midwest trailer park, she swept up what she wanted and never gave a second thought to the debris left behind.

He followed her inside with every intention of unleashing his pent up anxiety. "Hey!"

Charlotte ignored him, intent on other things. Trotting after her, he put a large hand on her shoulder and pulled her around to face him. She lowered her tortoise shell sunglasses and Burton knew he would never be the same. There was something about that moment. It was no *coup de foudre*, not love at first sight. The experience was neither sudden nor gradual; it was suspended. If he had to find a single word to define it, perhaps the best would be "coincidence." But something about the moment told him that from then on much of his life would be measured by the impact of that look.

"Captain Burton?" she said. Innocent of her effect yet carnal in her nature.

Burton stopped, lost for words, "Uh, Miss Sabon. I – well I thought you were someone else.

49

WHITE POWDER

***

Residual wastewater gurgled through a grill beneath Kennedy's feet wafting a complex odor of slaughtered chickens and rancid grease. Burton thought that perhaps lunch preparations were underway in the kitchen.

Walter Kennedy perched on a stool in a dark bar looking out onto the Talat Sao, marketplace in the center of Vientiane, he spoke to a person only he could see, presumably sitting on the empty barstool next to him.

His left hand scrabbled in a dish for hot pepper roasted peanuts. The cook fried them especially for Kennedy each morning with *prik ky nu*, rat-shit peppers, threw in some dried garlic and garnished with sea salt.

A hand gesture promptly brought two more drinks from the barman. One Mekong Whiskey, Thai style – with soda water, for Walter Kennedy and one for the invisible friend.

A week old edition of *Vientiane Wán Pha-hát* sat on the table next to him, unopened. He didn't want to deal with the problem that the weekly newspaper caused. There were other things on his mind.

"To my two favorite pastimes, killing and fucking." Raising his glass, he saluted his invisible friend.

Kennedy pontificated to thin air. "Killing produces the same satisfaction that accompanies masturbation. What did you say? Yeah, you're right, carrying a gun is something like having a permanent hard-on. Ok, I'll admit that it's a strange rite of manhood -- killing becomes like sex and sex becomes like killing."

Kennedy paused to sip his whiskey as he watched the people pass, seeming to listen to the person who wasn't there.

"Yeah, that's what I think too. I need to find a killer. A man who will do murder but who isn't a total sociopath. You know how hard that is to find? The Army ain't the best place to look. Plain truth is that most soldiers are motivated to fight by group pressures, not because they're murderers by nature. Some of them think they're bonafide killers because the business of life taking is laden with the baggage of false expectations and myth. It's just like sex in that respect. The problem is finding one who will deliver the goods without remorse or guilt *and* won't go off the reservation on me. Somebody who will attack problems like a terrier shaking a rat."

50

Kennedy finished his drink and shrugged toward the other. His invisible friend was devoid of thirst so Kennedy swapped glasses. He stared out of the bar window through wire frame glasses as sheets of shimmering heat hovered over the city, growing heavier with each passing moment. The merchants were aware of the approaching heat storm. On that day as on many others, the Talat Sao would end with the onset of mid-day. They scurried about like a thousand ants trying to empty their stalls before the heat dipped down and stole their breath away.

Burton stood in the door behind Walter Kennedy and could very nearly read his mind. He'd seen Kennedy muttering from a distance and decided to drop in and tell him about the shipment of machine guns they brought with them from the highlands.

Beyond Kennedy, into the mix of odors produced by blends of fish, fowl, oil, incense and spices and a raucous medley or voices shouting in lowland Leo, highland Hmong, Chinese and Burmese, walked Lieutenant Creed Taylor, US Army, a twenty-six year-old raised in Laos who could speak the local dialects without accent. Kennedy's attention shifted, immediately drawn to Taylor. He saw the man in action and knew that Taylor wouldn't falter when he needed to pull a trigger. Taylor had a reputation for competence in the private, intimate, destructive act that he, Kennedy held to be much like the procreative act. Might he be the one? Kennedy finished his drink and slipped off the stool to discretely follow Taylor.

Burton told the spy. "Last time anybody heard, you were in Manila."

Kennedy turned with a mystical dreamy look in his eyes, a dodge Burton saw before when he was playing the degenerate drunk. "Am I in Laos? I think the shell shock from Korea is catching up with me."

Burton motioned for Kennedy to sit back down. "The only shell shock you experienced was in the Pusan Pleasure Garden when mamasan took your wallet and vanished. I remember walking by on the street out front, watching you run out the door bare naked in hot pursuit."

The dreamy glaze vanished, replaced by his solid cold blue eyes. "So what am I going to have to give up to get Creed Taylor?"

"Taylor's daddy is a missionary somewhere up country in the Shan States and might raise a fuss if you drew him in. What do you want with an army officer with a sharp trigger finger who speaks Kachin?"

Kennedy moved to leave, "Been nice talking to you Craig, and I mean that sincerely. Fuck you very much for everything." He brushed past Burton, raising the middle finger of his left hand.

"Reverend Taylor is living up by Aungban."

Kennedy stopped and turned slowly, "Pindaya Caves?"

"Cave of Six Thousand Buddhas. Bringing Christ to the heathen nation, working to ease the white man's burden by making them one with Jesus."

"Ok, asshole, maybe we do have something to talk about."

"There's also a shipment of fifty Škoda automatic rifles that I socked away for you at Camp Chinaimo. Special delivery from Mr. Anthony Poshepny." Burton added.

"Shhh." Kennedy hissed, sitting back down. "Drink?"

"I'll pass."

"Suit yourself, but it won't dissuade me." Kennedy motioned for another two. "Which brings me to another question since you've been up in the border lands. Colonel Maurice LeBeau of the Service de Documentation Extérieure et de Contre-Espionnage bought me a drink the other day to see if I heard of anything from one of his men who did a special favor for his and our Thai allies. You ever heard of Jean-Paul Cyr?"

Burton kept a straight face and lied. "No, never crossed his path."

The drinks arrived. Kennedy downed one in a gulp. "Doesn't matter. Fucking Frogs need to keep better track of their own men."

Burton stood and walked out of the door. Kennedy, drinks in hand, trailed him like a recalcitrant hunting dog.

They both followed Creed Taylor, who stood about a foot taller than most of the people around him. A trained chimp could follow him with ease.

A submachine gun hung loosely across Taylor's chest distinguishing him most profoundly. The weapon, a well-oiled Swedish-made Carl Gustav M/45, marked him as an opium dealer or a bodyguard for someone rich and influential enough to pay dearly for a license to carry the gun. Burton knew he was neither.

Dressed casually, except for the weapon, Creed sauntered through the marketplace on sturdy sandals, his loose gait carrying him forward while his eyes darted in different directions.

"He's looking for the Corsican bitch," Kennedy said knowingly, finishing his first drink and setting the glass on a food stand as he passed.

Burton paused before a saffron-robed Buddhist priest and dropped a 1000 Kip note equal to two dollars American, into the priest's begging bowl. The more Burton gave, the more merit he supposedly earned.

"Don't bother with that," Kennedy counseled, eyes locked on Creed Taylor, browsing in a stand that sold cheap electronics.

A short, wiry Burmese man, his leathered face riddled with crow's feet, approached Burton and immediately demonstrated his manners by greeting him with his palms held together in front of his chest, a gesture called a wai.

Burton had been in Laos long enough to learn polite behavior and returned the wai without any conscious thought. Kennedy wai'd insultingly and then made the sign of the cross with his hand, holding the remaining glass of Mekong whiskey. The old man steered Burton toward a table littered with a combination of brass ornaments, carved teak animals and wooden prayer beads.

The old weathered merchant said a few words in his native dialect and Burton responded first in English and then in broken Chinese. The old man was confused, speaking neither language, but a Chinese woman, bent with age, who sold savory cockroaches fried in coconut oil in an adjoining stall translated in Mandarin overshadowed by the guttural dialect of Yunnan Province.

"He asks you, the great warrior, not to steal his goods as he is an old man and supports three wives and many children. If he does not make a sale, his children will starve."

"I have money if I see something I like." Burton responded in broken Chinese, with a hint of Michigan. "Tell the man I am a tame predator."

The translation and subsequent discussion between the old man and the Chinese woman turned into a brief argument that lasted a few minutes. Burton waited patiently. Finally, the old man compressed his toothless mouth into a flat line and then spoke in tones that sounded to Burton like an admonishment. "There are no tame predators, just well fed ones."

Kennedy snorted with a laugh, overhearing the conversation and finished his second drink.

The old man nodded and smiled, stubs of teeth, black from chewing betel nut.

As Kennedy and Burton continued, Creed Taylor looked over his shoulder at them. He'd been watching them through a mirror on the electronics stand.

Creed bought some fresh lotus fruits, breaking the thick woody pods and chewing on the marble-sized seeds, waiting for Burton and Kennedy to catch up. He offered the Lotus fruit to Burton. "It's an acquired taste, Captain." He told Burton.

"Lieutenant Taylor, this is Walter Kennedy, an admirer of yours. Mr. Kennedy is a cultural attaché at the Embassy in Manila, here for a visit."

"Lotus will give you the shits if your digestive system isn't acclimated." Kennedy said by way of acknowledgement. He didn't sound much like a diplomat.

"Lotus flowers?" A lilting voice asked from behind them. Creed made a slow turn.

Charlotte Sabon wore a pale blue pinafore and shopped with a servant who carried a large basket. "I've heard it said that once you've tasted the fruit of the Lotus that you can never go home." Her English was practiced and grammatically perfect but was spoken with a heavy French accent.

"Forbidden fruit?" Burton asked with a smile.

Charlotte smiled back and said to them all, "I fear that once tasted you can never go back to being the person you had once been." She tilted her head to one side and cocked a perfectly sculpted brow at Craig Burton.

"Will you take tobacco, gentlemen?"

Kennedy declined and produced a gold cigarette case from which he pulled his own smoke.

Charlotte took two from a bundle of freshly rolled cigars out of the servant's basket and handed them to Creed and Burton.

Creed twirled a butterfly knife open and cut the end of one of the cigars absently, handing it to Burton. Charlotte's servant slipped her a box of wooden Lucifer matches. She took one and she struck it on the box, and held it for Creed who puffed the acrid cigar into life. She struck a second one and held it. Burton looked over the flame into her mischievous face. Charlotte's eyes, large oval, green eyes and intelligent, sparkled with interest. Her skin held a delicate olive hue. Her hair tumbled down, curled, past her shoulders: Deep brown with a hint of auburn. She didn't have classic Corsican looks at all. Her bone structure hinted at Northern Europe, not the Mediterranean.

Puffing the cigar was very much like smoking dried cow pies but Burton knew from past experience that prolonged exposure brought a certain tolerance to the bitter taste.

"Gentlemen, if you'll excuse me?" Creed said as Charlotte took his arm, playfully.

Kennedy and Burton watched Creed and Charlotte stroll with the servant following down aisles of cheap electronics and kitchenware and past stall after stall of traditional Lao weavings. Gold-brocaded silks of indigo or royal blue from Luang Prabang, patterns of elephants pulling teak logs from Sam Neua in the distant north, and brass incense burners to carry prayers to heaven. Before they walked out of sight, Charlotte turned and held Burton's glance for a long minute.

"Does her husband know about Taylor?" Kennedy asked as they disappeared.

"What do you know about her husband?"

"Jacques Sabon is the front man for Unione Corse. But you know that don't you?"

Burton took a puff and blew the smoke at Kennedy. "I lead a sheltered life. I spend my life sleeping in the rain, spending night and day on merciless humps over tortuous terrain packing eighty pregnant pounds through brain-boiling heat, breathing red dust in the dry season and boot-sucking mud in the monsoon, leeches, malaria, dysentery, razor sharp elephant grass, bush sores, jungle rot, meals in green cans, fire ants, poisonous centipedes, mosquitoes, flies, bush snakes, vipers, scorpions, rats, and incoming fire." It was the canned response the Special Forces all gave with small variances to the specific rant.

"I drink rotgut whiskey, eat fine food and fuck to my heart's content." Kennedy said by way of repost.

Kennedy left Burton in the market and smoked another cigarette in the building summer heat outside the market while waiting for his car that should have been standing-by for him.

It was Sunday, so the usual Laotian driving pool that serviced the United States Embassy had been given the day off and stand-by drivers were used. That meant that while he scouted the market and drank, the driver was cruising Vientiane, handling his own business, carefully planning the time so as to return before Kennedy finished. The driver miscalculated.

When the black Buick arrived, Kennedy slid into the back seat and barked orders to the terrified Laotian driver in fluent Lao. "Take me to the *Vientiane Wán Pha-hát*!" He supplied an address. The driver tried to wai his respect but Kennedy ignored him.

The driver had difficulty locating the address as it was encased in a rabbit warren of tumbledown buildings in a bad part of town.

"Just park here. And wait or I'll skin your worthless hide and use it for a drumhead." Kennedy continued his rant in muttered Lao. The driver stepped out, opened Kennedy's door put his palms together tightly and bowed profoundly in a wai intended to show abject subjugation. Kennedy ignored him again.

"Asshole." Kennedy muttered as he entered the clutter of shacks and primitive shelters.

Under a full head of steam, he walked through the front door of the 'office' of the recently established *Vientiane Wán Pha-hát* (Vientiane Thursday) weekly newspaper. It had been established in a particularly dingy, decaying building in the center of the cluster of residential structures.

"It smells like a latrine in here."

Kennedy looked left to see an overflowing toilet. The lone one window, barred with steel and covered with nearly opaque canvas didn't offer ventilation. It made the filth of the shit-topped toilet and the heat inside the hut, enhanced by a corrugated steel roof, nearly intolerable.

A round-faced Laotian man sat at a desk in the corner reading a Thai newspaper, smoking a cigarette, holding it English fashion, with his thumb and forefinger. He seemed to be oblivious to the heat and smell.

With a glance both endearing and shy, the Laotian editor looked up at Kennedy and smiled nervously.

Kennedy put a hand into his suit coat's inside pocket. The man drew back in anticipation of a bullet. He relaxed considerably when the foreign devil pulled out a sheet of folded paper.

The pressman unfolded the document under Kennedy's merciless, ice blue eyes. His mouth dropped as he perused the crisp, white, page.

"Denounce that son-of-a bitch as a Communist."

The man pointed to the paper. "Him not Communist. Him read, him kill. Khun Sa hate communist. Khun Sa send men, shoot me in head, leave me on floor."

"Who you more afraid of?" Kennedy whipped out a snub-nose blue steel revolver, cocked the hammer and pointed it at the editor."

56

LARRY B. LAMBERT

"But him not Communist!"

"Everybody who reads the paper will think he is—so he is one now."

ELEVEN

Sunday, 12 August 1961 -- 1745 HRS
Mekong River, near Don Chan Island,
Vientiane, Laos

The languid heat of the August summer afternoon was cut in small part by the muddy-red water of the wide Mekong River. Two wooden canoes had been tied up under the shade of trees that spread their branches wide over the river. Each, anchored by rocks tied to parachute cord, contained two of the Tartar Team members. Jimmy Paint and Paul Gorman fished from one of the canoes. Craig Burton and Creed Taylor dozed in the other. Beer bottles, suspended from a net in the water provided a sea anchor and kept the bow into the current in addition to chilling the brew.

In Burton's canoe, the junior officer, snored lightly.

Burton thought ruefully that he must be exhausted from a rut with Charlotte Sabon. The notion that Creed and Charlotte formed some sort of connection bothered him. There was no rational reason for his irritation but it was there all the same. He kicked Taylor's leg with his toe.

Taylor's eyes popped open.

"I've got good news for you." Burton said.

After about five seconds of stretching Creed 'woke up'. "I'm all ears, Craig."

"Your cut of the last mission is about fifteen thousand dollars I haven't negotiated the exact price yet. We liberated some gold from some really nasty types by accident. We're a team, you share."

Taylor sat up, rocking the boat. More than a year's pay was no small thing. "Are you pulling my crank?"

"Nope, we all voted on it. You were sick so you couldn't go along on the trip, but you're one of us."

His eyes drifted for a moment, thoughts of uses he could put the money to, flashed in front of his eyes. "That means you snagged nearly eighty thousand dollars in gold?"

"More or less. I negotiated the price from Wu Ming. It's over three hundred pounds of gold. We left a little behind, cached, but this is most of it."

"Pathet Lao had that kind of money?" Taylor asked, still a bit stunned.

"They were *Kuomintang* from the Shan State with a trove of gold taels and Indochina Bank piasters we'll swap for Kip. And since you, and more importantly, your father live among the *Kuomintang*, I need you to keep your ear to the ground. If somebody asks questions, they're sure to include you on the list."

"So that's why you cut me in." It was a statement.

"That's not why." Burton asserted. "But since you're in, you need to know where the gold came from. They were shaped like little boats, one tael weight each, with characters in the bottom of the boat that said they were one tael."

"Odd." Taylor said, thoughtfully, "Mostly they trade in gold molded in bullion form or in thin sheets like thick foil."

"They're a special deal, a payment to Kuhn Sa from the Government of Thailand."

Creed explained, "They're trying to corner the white powder business and there are Red Chinese interests in the deal as well. The Nationalists and Reds hate each other, but I think they may be working toward a deal to divide up the opium crop and cut the Corsicans out of the business. That means everybody but the Corsicans get rich. Then again, there could be something else going on where they are keeping the Reds onboard until they have the deal sewed up and when that happens, the Reds will be cut out. The politics shift all the time."

Burton watched Taylor closely.

"I know Khun Sa", Taylor said. "He's my age--our age. I met him when I was with my dad before he sent me to the States. He came to our church a few times."

"What's he like?"

"Charismatic, wears Ray Ban glasses these days so you can't see his eyes. He likes gold. No question about it." Taylor said with a shiver. "He's young but he's like an old dragon guarding his treasure and he won't show mercy to those who failed to protect his gold."

"He's going to have a tough time with that." Burton said. "We killed them."

"Kuhn Sa will crucify their family members – as many as he can find. Children, women, men." As they're suffering he'll disembowel one

59

or two so the others can see it. The stated goal will be to find out who did it and who has the gold."

"They don't know. We ambushed 'em before dawn, grenades. They never knew who hit them."

"You think Kuhn Sa cares?" Creed Taylor asked carefully.

In the other boat, Jimmy asked, "How come Sam didn't come fishing with us?"

"The ASA is still debriefing him on the code stuff he found."

"Do you think he'll tell them about the gold?"

Paul "Goatman" Gorman stared into the water where his monofilament fishing line dipped into the murk. "Not Sam. He'll crow about the codes and all. Captain Burton is trying to get him his stripes back. The ones he lost in Manila—some time ago."

The conversation stalled for a few minutes.

"The river starts in Tibet," Jimmy said, "and there's gold that's washed down from the peaks. All you need to do is to get a pan and slosh some of that mud around in the water and it's said that you can be rich."

"Then why aren't you prospecting?" Goatman replied.

"Cause I like fishing better."

Goatman shifted in the boat as if he had something important to say, careful to keep one hand on his fishing pole.

Jimmy saw the book in his hand. "What's that?" Jimmy asked.

"A book."

"I didn't know you could read. I thought you just looked at the pictures." Jimmy said with a smile.

"It's a book by a guy named Nostradamus. He predicted a lot of things that came true." Goatman said defensively. "The day is coming my friend, and I can't say exactly when, but it *is* coming and blood will flow from stones."

"The next Pathet Lao patrol I run into will find that out the hard way." Jimmy said, patting his holstered Colt .45 handgun.

"No, this is like curses from the Bible. The dead will rise from their graves, the lame will walk, the blind will see and springs of magic water will burst from rocks." Goatman watched the tip of his rod for a moment. "It's big and this guy saw it all. A lot more than the Buddha I think."

"Where is this prophet?" Jimmy asked.

"He's dead," Goatman replied, "He lived five hundred years ago."

Goatman flipped to a dog-eared page and read for Jimmy's benefit. "Beasts ferocious from hunger will swim across rivers. The greater part of the region will be against the Hister. The great one will cause it to be dragged in an iron cage. The German child will observe nothing."

"That doesn't mean anything at all. You sound like a reservation missionary. I could write one of those. If I do, will you join my church and give me money?" Jimmy challenged.

Goatman changed the subject, finding that his pearls of wisdom from Nostradamus were dropping into the muddy Mekong. "You goin' to the movies at the assembly tent tonight?"

Jimmy shook his head.

"It's a John Wayne movie."

Jimmy said, "I hate John Wayne."

Goatman's mouth dropped open. "How could you hate John Wayne?"

"Cause he kills Indians, and in the movies they all just die easy." Jimmy pointed to himself casually. "Here's one Indian he'd have trouble shooting off a horse. If John Wayne missed and I scalped him and his buddy the Lone Ranger then the star of all them movies would be Tonto! Or maybe Jay Silverheels and me would both be stars."

Not wanting to argue, Goatman shifted the subject again. "I heard that Lieutenant Taylor's screwing some rich Frenchman's wife."

"Officers always get the pretty women." Jimmy said morosely. "Maybe it's the uniform."

"I heard you were tapping old Madame Lulu, herself, Jimmy." Goatman said with a knowing leer.

"That's just Commie propaganda," Jimmy's eyes grew guarded, "and everybody knows she has her girls do all the work."

"I heard she was taking care of you for free because you were a panther in the sack."

Jimmy grabbed his groin. "It's pure panther, all right."

Just then the tip of Goatman's fishing pole dipped once and then bowed as a large perch took the bait. All thoughts of Nostradamus, Madame Lulu, Creed Taylor's presumed affair and John Wayne's depredations against Native Americans were put in their proper place as both men focused on getting the fish into the boat.

When they all tired of fishing, drinking, telling white lies and

61

lounging, they pulled the boats to the shore where they'd found them in the first place and walked to their Jeep. The left rear tire was flat. Creed offered to change the tire while Paul Gorman helped and watched.

Burton and Paint took the fish back to the river to clean them for cooking.

Sweat rolled down Creed Taylor's face like tears, drenching his chest as he pumped the jack handle in the heat and humidity. The sweat glistened from the tips of his spiked crew cut like gems. Paul Gorman pulled the spare from the back of the Jeep and handed it to Creed. Creed stretched and twisted, limbering his muscles before he took it.

"Soft life in the rear area getting to you?" Goatman commented.

Creed smiled.

"Do you think there's a life beyond this one?" Goatman asked.

"Where the hell did that come from?" Creed asked.

"Jimmy's been talking about Buddhism. He says you get reborn again after you die."

"I think Jimmy's been on the spike."

Goatman said, "No sir, he's clean. He hardly even drinks these days." He winked. "Well, not unless you're buying and he's particularly thirsty."

Creed tightened the lug nuts.

"He says it's an endless cycle of life after miserable fucking life, each one a reaction against some imbalance from the one before." Goatman said with halting confidence.

"That doesn't sound much like heaven to me." Creed finished and jacked the jeep back down to the road.

"Me either." Goatman said.

Paint and Burton walked back to the jeep with the fish, now cleaned.

"I heard you, Lieutenant. It's not like the white man's heaven or the happy hunting ground. It's about perceptions. The world around you is a reflection of your reaction to the world around you. It's all an illusion."

"You mean this Jeep is a figment of my imagination? That would also mean by implication that you are a figment of my imagination." Creed sat behind the wheel, Burton rode shotgun. Jimmy and Goatman sat in the back.

"It's a persistent illusion. I admit it, sir." Jimmy said.

"Christ almighty." Creed said, "You need to get shot at again, Jimmy. Trigger time brings things into focus."

"Yeah, Jimmy," Goatman weighed in on the subject, "you need to lift a couple of scalps and you'll find Jesus again."

"We all like what we do, and when you consider what it is we do, you should be concerned. I thought about that the last time I called in an air strike on a PAVN base camp," Burton said referring to the People's Army of Viet Nam.

"Yeah," Creed said, "I remember. F-100's came in fast and low. Four of 'em—napalm. Incinerated every last one. And the secondary explosions were like the Fourth of July."

Burton nodded. "When that's a rush you want to repeat, there's something seriously wrong with you."

Jimmy reflected for a moment. "I'm a reincarnation of a white Indian Agent who sold guns and whiskey to the Apache from a reservation store. Subsequently I spent two, maybe three incarnations as Apache, none of them illustrious. Deep resentment toward the white man carried over from those lifetimes to this one and drove me to redirect my anger toward the yellow man. I won't find Jesus."

"Your mama and papa back on the reservation wouldn't like to hear that kind of heathen language. Where's the old Jimmy Paint they shipped off to war?" Goatman asked irreverently.

They rode the rest of the way to Camp Chinaimo in silence. Creed parked the Jeep and he and Burton took the fish to the commissary to have them cooked for dinner. Burton was strangely silent and though the men didn't know it, he had been thinking about Charlotte Sabon.

"Now see what you did?" Goatman scolded Jimmy. "The captain was enjoying his fishing trip until you started talking about being re-born."

"Sorry, Goatman."

"You should be sorry as hell." Goatman emphasized. "So who was I?"

"Who were you when?" Jimmy replied with a question.

"In my last life."

Jimmy asked, "You really want to know?"

"Sure."

"You were a teacher who molested a student and then you committed suicide and you're still trying to deal with it." Jimmy said gravely.

"A boy or a girl?"

63

WHITE POWDER

"Boy or girl what?"

Goatman became specific. "Did I molest a boy or a girl?"

"I think it was a girl." Jimmy said. "But don't hold me to it."

"Thank God I wasn't a homo." Goatman breathed a sigh of relief. "Sometimes you can know just too goddamned much about yourself."

TWELVE

Monday, 13 August 1961 -- 0900 HRS
Embassy of the United States of America, Annex,
20 Rue Barthlonie, That Dam Road,
Vientiane, Laos

Burton took a 1958 Vespa motor scooter, borrowed from the Australian Embassy, to the Green House for his scheduled debriefing by the CIA. Opposite the Embassy, he stopped at the massive stone Black Stupa, a monument built over the cave of a seven-headed dragon, which was said to have risen and rescued the population of Vientiane during the 1828 war with Thailand. He bought flowers and laid them near a gilded Buddha for luck.

His experience with the CIA had been memorable but not universally pleasant.

Adjacent to the US Embassy, the Green House housed the Central Intelligence Agency's presence in Laos. Burton wore civilian attire per standing orders. He presented his military identification to two uniformed Marines, who stood guard inside the foyer and they passed him through with a smart salute.

Inside a Spartan office on the second floor, Henry Dastrup waited for Burton to arrive. But when he did, Dastrup ignored him as he read from a sheaf of papers. Meanwhile, Burton took in his environment.

Henry Dastrup, an austere, balding, forty-something bureaucrat with a clean shaved hatchet jaw and tufts of hair growing from his ears, served as the Vientiane Station's section chief assigned to interface with White Star missions. He wore a bow tie, wrapped around the neck of a white shirt that had yellow sweat rings around the armpits. A diploma from Yale hung on the wall immediately behind Dastrup's desk. In a society where the criterion for acceptability was an Ivy League diploma, Dastrup was an up-and-comer with a bright future.

Dual photos of President John Fitzgerald Kennedy and CIA Director Allen W. Dulles looked down from their position on the wall. They reminded Burton of God the Father and his son, Jesus. Burton was not sure as he gazed which was God and which was the Son.

65

WHITE POWDER

Dastrup's desktop sported a framed photo of a plump middle-aged woman and two kids grinning at the camera, presumably Dastrup's family back home in the States. Burton wondered what the homely, wholesome Mrs. Dastrup would think of her husband if she could see his nightly forays into Vientiane's red light district.

A rusty air conditioner rattled in the window and a ceiling fan languidly rotated overhead. Burton focused on the rhythm of the fan while Dastrup read, not acknowledging his presence in the office until he'd read all of the daily message traffic.

After a lengthy silence, Henry Dastrup looked up. "Sorry to work you so soon after you came back in."

"It's not a problem, sir."

"How are your men?"

"Lieutenant Taylor seems to be doing better. We didn't take him the last time out– hepatitis. Paint, Willoughby and Gorman are taking a well deserved rest."

"Are we doing okay over here, Craig?" Dastrup asked, a hint of a New Hampshire accent crowding in.

Burton thought about the question for a moment and wondered if it was purely rhetorical. He wanted to tell Dastrup that the American efforts in Laos were clumsy and arrogant, but he decided on diplomacy once Dastrup's facial expression indicated that an answer was called for. "The Royal Laotian Army admires us and what we can do but instead of trying to emulate us, they sit back and let us do all their dirty work."

"That sounds a little harsh." Dastrup said, "Are you saying they're soft on Communism?"

"No, I'm saying that from what I've seen it doesn't have nearly as much to do with Communism as it does about just being Laotian."

"Maybe things have improved since you were actually training elements of the Royal Lao Army." Dastrup tightened his bow tie, absently.

"I stay in touch with the Laotians, sir. Some of the influential lower-ranking officers are very bright. They see what's going on. They're not at all happy with the way we encourage the corruption in the government."

Dastrup lifted a meerschaum pipe off a rack and he prepared to feed the bowl of the pipe. "We all know the metaphor of the farmer who was trained to use fertilizer to double his crop yield," he said imperiously. "After that the farmer only worked half as hard as before." Dastrup began to clean the pipe. "They need to be encouraged to join the Twentieth Century which means we have to give them a good Protestant work ethic."

Burton didn't respond. Maybe if he let Dastrup rant, they could get on with the debriefing and he could get out of here.

"What we're trying to do here, son, is an inexact art at best. Laotian politics being what they are, combined with the communist machinations, make it difficult for us to connect all the dots on our first pass. Look how long it took the French."

Burton wondered how many passes the Americans were going to make and how many Americans and Laotians would be lost. The French experience in Indochina after the Second World War had been an unmitigated disaster. They lost 23,000 men killed and wounded at the battle of Điên Biên Phú alone.

As Dastrup continued, he appeared to be trying to convince himself that mobilizing the Laotians en masse to defend their country from the Communists was a done deal. "Inside every Laotian," he mused, "is an American and our job is to pull that out of 'em. It wouldn't hurt if they'd drop the Buddhism and embrace Christ either."

Before Burton could disagree, Dastrup's boss Montgomery Keene, burst into the office. Also known as "The Monkey King," Keene gave a smug nod to Burton and got right to the point. "I hear you're on the team. That's great we'll read you into the program later and give you the down and dirty on everything – maybe tomorrow. But I have something for you to sink your teeth into right away. I want you to think up an angle. "We're looking to get a little closer to an influential Frog. Jacques Sabon has been a player here and in Nam for a while." He tossed a manila envelope to Burton. "Read it and leave it with Henry."

"Sir?"

"You must have met him," Keene said. "You and Lieutenant Taylor are invited to all of the French Embassy's power parties. You were their military liaison when you first came to Laos or did I read the file wrong?" He waited for an answer but when none was forthcoming, the Monkey King continued. "Jacques Sabon is a merchant, Craig. He imports and exports certain things. Runs with the Corsicans, but is joined at the hip with the French power structure here, or so it's rumored."

Burton could tell that Keene lied. For a CIA Chief of Station, the man was not an accomplished fibber. Best case, Burton knew Keene wasn't telling him the whole truth.

"I believe I've met him, sir," Burton said, visualizing the rich, sixty year old, cadaverously thin, mover and shaker married to Charlotte, who he suspected was having an affair with Lieutenant Taylor. The immediate, instinctive, mental image of the old bag of bones rutting with Charlotte turned his stomach.

The Monkey King clapped Burton on the shoulder and tossed a glance at Dastrup. "See, Henry! I told you he was a sharp kid. We need to see if we can keep him in the Outfit permanently. By the way, I got a cable from Tony Poe up in the PDJ and he said you're precisely who we need. He endorsed this deal one hundred percent, not that I need his chop. The point is, we're always looking for new talent."

Dastrup grunted his agreement.

Keene motioned Dastrup out of the office. "Read that for a minute, Burton. We need to talk shop."

Burton shook out three sheets of paper. The first sheet was captioned:

REDACTED TRANSCRIPION OF A CONVERSATION
PHOTOGRAPHED BY A MOTION PICTURE CAMERA–
DECIPHERED THROUGH LIP READING.

BRUNO JOSPIN, LEADER OF UNIONE CORSE AND
JACQUES SABON, OPERATIVE OF THE FRENCH
FOREIGN INTELLIGENCE SERVICE (SDCE)

10 FEB 61, NEW MANDARIN HOTEL, HONG KONG.
(TRANSLATED FROM CORSICAN TO ENGLISH)

JOSPIN: Time is important. The Teochiu Chinese are combining with the Thais and former Kuomintang Army to cut us out of the business.

SABON: What do you want me to do, Bruno?

JOSPIN: Conclude a deal with the Teochiu Chinese. Cut the Thais and the Kuomintang thugs out. None of us trusts the other and the Teochiu don't trust anyone. Maybe they're even more Corsican than I am. (laughter)

SABON: What of the Americans? Will they stay out

of our business?

JOSPIN: We have similar goals. Keeping the Communists out of Laos is in everyone's best interests.

SABON: (drinks from wine glass) I will see that it goes the way you want it to, Bruno.

JOSPIN: Remember that or I'll stuff your eggs (testicles) up your ass with a stick of dynamite.

The second page mounted a grainy photograph of Jacques Sabon shaking hands with a short, compact man who radiated energy like a coiled spring and wore a rumpled business suit. The third page showed a photograph of Jacques and Charlotte at what appeared to be a party.

Burton replaced the transcript and the photographs in the envelope and set them on Dastrup's desk. He didn't have to wait long before Keene and Dastrup returned.

"Did you read it?" Keene asked. "There is a picture of the old bastard and what is rumored to be a new wife from France. She's a looker and can't be over twenty. Dirty old man."

Burton thought, I can't tell them that I know her, that I saw her this morning with Creed Taylor. "He doesn't look Corsican, not like the other man, Jospin. The file says he's French Intelligence *and* an employee of the Corsican drug empire."

"What do you know about fruit, Craig?" Dastrup interrupted, in a hurry to get on with things.

"Fruit?" Burton asked.

"Come on, Henry," Keene interrupted, clapping Dastrup on the back. "Cheer up! It's time to head to the White Rose, for Christ's sake. It's a Monday, we need to start the week off right, and man doesn't live by fruit alone."

Dastrup's face lit up. He got to his feet and headed toward the door, having completely forgotten about both fruit and why he'd asked Craig Burton the question.

"We're on our way to the White Rose, Burton and there's room for one more. The White Rose is guaranteed to make you forget all about the Land of Flushing Toilets, mom and apple pie!" The Monkey King offered, making the sign of the cross with his hand in Burton's direction.

They piled into the black Buick sedan that served as an official Embassy vehicle.

WHITE POWDER

With Dastrup behind the wheel, the Buick roared off in a cloud of dust.

"Drink?" The Monkey King asked, offering a metal flask back to Burton.

"No thanks."

"You'll need to move out of Camp Chanaimo." The Monkey King said.

"I've got quarters in town," Burton replied, "I'm bunking with the Aussie military attaché. I've been there a little over a year now."

"Christ, now that should be a party." The Monkey King exclaimed. "The last time I ran with the Australians, I ended up with alcohol poisoning and was blind for three days." He reminisced for another moment. "The Company works in mysterious ways, Captain Burton. Congratulations and a drink are in order." At that moment, the Buick lurched to a stop in front of the White Rose. "And here we are."

After everyone had piled out of the car, the CIA Chief took Burton aside. "Next week you'll be in charge of the Consolidated Fruit Company's operation here in Laos. It's cover for status. My guys are looking for a good place for you to set up shop."

Burton observed, "The only fruit they grow in Laos ends up injected into a junkie's arm in the Bronx."

Ignoring him, Keen continued, "You'll like working with the CIA."

"Consolidated Fruit?"

The Monkey King put his arm around Burton's shoulder and spoke into his ear as if sharing a Masonic confidence, "Frankly, and this is secret, we've had a lot of luck in Guatemala with the United Fruit Company, and we want your cover to be a winner. I came up with this one myself. We don't want to tamper with success." He released his grip and changed he subject. "How's the up-country language coming along?"

"The word 'I' sounds just like their word for penis so I refer to myself as Craig and they try to imitate me. I can barely hold my own in Hmong. It's a very tonal language, sir."

"But you do speak Chinese?" The Monkey King asked.

"I speak Mandarin and the Teochiu dialect, and I write Chinese, sir." Burton replied.

It was pitch black inside the White Rose and the music blasted at maximum volume. Cigarette smoke floated in layers, thick and acrid. A mixture of foreign businessmen, diplomats and journalists were helping themselves to an early Sunday brunch as they clinched with the whores on a dance floor that was too small to accommodate the crowd. Their vibrations on the dance floor helped to circulate the cigarette smoke that passed for air. A plastic happy Buddha with a night light shoved where the light shouldn't shine, illuminated a corner of the bar irrespective of the karmic consequences.

Mamasan smiled so broadly that Burton feared the thick make-up would crack. Several girls emerged from behind a doorway covered by a blanket adorned with elaborate embroidery and looked at Dastrup and Keene expectantly.

Suddenly, the music stopped, deafening Burton with the silence.

"I have balls like an ox and a dick like a roasting ear!" The Monkey King roared like a lion.

Mamasan and the girls cheered as though they cared.

A man deep in the darkness toasted the Monkey King over the brash music streaming from the cheap metal speakers reverberating in their mountings on the wall. He spoke in a pronounced Irish accent, "Of all the tinkers, knackers and begrudgers in this God-forsaken land, 'tis yerself, Montgomery Keene!"

The man in the shadows with the brogue grabbed mamasan's arm, pulled her close and spoke a few words.

"'Tis myself," the man with the brogue announced generously, "and what are ye doin' here with the unwashed on the Saint's own day? You should be swinging the censer at Benediction in His holy house, praying to Saint Jude like all in your caste."

The music shrieked back to life, every bit as loud as it had been before.

"This is Walter Kennedy, and the less said of his profession the better," the Monkey King shouted over the wail of the music by way of introduction. "Walter, meet Captain Craig Burton from the Academy by way of Fort Bragg."

"We've done everything but fornicate with the same woman, Keene!" Kennedy said. "And maybe we've even done that unknowingly!"

The CIA Station Chief lost a bit of composure but snatched it back immediately.

Walter Kennedy's tousled, thinning wheat colored hair was only slightly askew. His prominent hooked nose split two eyes blue, cold and dead. Kennedy was cold sober. It was an act.

"What's a good, young, West Point man doing in this God forsaken backwater of sin and depravity?" Walter Kennedy's slurred, the shouted question was purely rhetorical, though it too was delivered in a pronounced high Irish brogue.

"I'm surprised the Controlled American Source allows one of its newest acolytes to be seen with me in public here in Vientiane." Kennedy paused with a loud, wet, belch. "But I heartily approve of the choice."

Kennedy gestured to a thin, dapper, pale man with a pencil mustache, a severe comb-over and bad dye job sitting next to him, "Allow me to introduce Colonel Maurice LeBeau, Captain Burton. I think the rest of you know each other." Everyone nodded, Burton shook LeBeau's hand, which turned into a brief squeezing contest. Burton immediately disliked the French spy.

Burton said to himself, so this is the big shot from the Service de Documentation Extérieure et de Contre-Espionnage, France's answer to the CIA.

Burton scrutinized Colonel LeBeau and decided that he reminded him very much of the late Jean-Paul Cyr. They looked nothing alike but both gave off the same shifty, flakey vibe.

The girl came for drink orders and Kennedy ordered for all of them. "A round of hot Powers." His Irish accent was so pronounced that it sounded like "hot Parrs".

The girls had anticipated Kennedy's order and mixed the drinks in front of them immediately. They all watched as scalding water was poured over a tall mound of sugar and cloves in a glass carafe, and then a few healthy slugs of John Power & Son Irish Whiskey were added. A portion was poured into each of five glasses. The carafe and bottle were both left on the table.

"So you are the famous Craig Burton." Maurice LeBeau said, his pomposity glaring like a flood lamp.

"Not so famous, only a simple soldier, Colonel."

"Don't be so modest," LeBeau pushed, "I've heard tales of your *hardiesse*." LeBeau grasped for the right word, "Of your audacity." When Burton didn't take the bait, "So tell me of your last foray into Region One, Captain."

"I'm not disposed to discuss anything I may or may not have done. I just returned from a flashlight repair course in Tokyo." Let's see if that shuts him up.

"Of course," LeBeau said, maximum solicitation and condescension.

Burton took a sip of the Powers and wanted to spit it back in the glass. But he didn't. And more than not drinking the Powers blended with sugar, he really didn't want to sit and drink with Kennedy, LeBeau, Dastrup and the Monkey King. He excused himself to the restroom.

"Take yer piss by all means," Walter Kennedy allowed.

Burton melted into the background while the Irish fraternity with a French guest toasted Irishmen worldwide. With as much grace as he could muster, he stepped out of the front door and into the light and heat.

As he left, two Russians in crudely cut civilian clothing, products of the Worker's Paradise, likely KGB, shoved past him into the White Rose looking as if they desperately needed a drink.

THIRTEEN

Monday, 13 August 1961 -- 1130 HRS
Setha Palace Hotel, 6 Pang Kham Street,
Vientiane, Laos

Burton's head spun. It had been one hell of a morning. The CIA was embracing him like an anaconda, the French version of the CIA thought he knew something of the fate of Jean-Paul Cyr, who turned out to be affiliated with them and nobody seemed to care about his mission report beyond the blithe acceptance of government paperwork.

The report carefully omitted anything to do with the attack he launched on the *Kuomintang* compound, the gold, or the situation involving what turned out to be a French DGSE spook, now dead of multiple puncture wounds and a ventilated throat. Likewise, he didn't share information about the Thai-*Kuomintang* alliance, and the potential complicity of the French and the opium trade.

Kennedy likely had some of the answers but Burton didn't trust him any more than he did the Frenchman spook, LeBeau.

"Ok, Craig," Burton told himself. "Let's focus on the gold, shall we?" The first order of business had to be a meeting with Wu Ming, a Teochiu Chinese gold merchant who dabbled in Lao politics. A number of gold merchants, mostly Indian and Chinese, conducted business in Vientiane. Of those who plied their trade, Wu Ming showed a greater tendency toward discretion and if a man, short on cash, wanted to impress an Annamite or Thai mistress with a bauble or trinket, Wu often provided it at a substantial discount. As a result, he was well received in the French Diplomatic Community as a friend and occasionally as a confidant.

Burton found Wu Ming sitting in the bar at the Settha Palace Hotel by himself. The staff hovered around him like attentive bees around their queen, concerned that the hive would be smashed very soon. Ming dipped a rice ball into papaya pok pok, a Thai sauce made up of a variety of ground up chili and papaya. Moving the rice ball expertly to his mouth with chopsticks, he chewed like a man eating a spam sandwich. There was no joy in the meal. A waiter delivered raw minced toad and spring onions as Burton gestured a greeting to the morose Mr. Wu Ming, and sat

74

across the table from him.

"Burton, I need a new girlfriend to take my mind off my wife." Ming lamented.

A waitress arrived over Burton's left shoulder to take his order but Ming beat him to it. "A Jamison's whiskey for my friend and a double for me."

The silence hung heavy in the humid monsoon air, no breeze, only a languid fan overhead, rotating slowly to dissipate the heat.

All discussions took time. Burton knew the Asiatic way. He was patient. "I'm sorry your home is not harmonious."

"Living with a woman from Chouzhou is like living with a dragon that requires tributes of gold to keep her satiated." Ming nipped at his drink, then finished it with a gulp and a flourish. Glancing furtively, he looked for one of the staff to bring the next one.

He ordered another with a flick of his wrist to the waitress then turned back to Burton. "Love and suicide are just different sides of the same gold coin, which makes me think of an old school Japanese woman. They're the most twisted creatures on the planet but one of those ladies would take my mind off my problems." He popped a few fried grasshoppers into his mouth from a bowl that sat on the table between them.

"Until Mrs. Ming found out." Burton offered.

"She'd slice my fragrant stem from my body while I slept. She's a Chouzhou woman and she has a reputation to maintain."

Burton said, "I'm in a bind at the moment and I hate to impose." Ming looked at Burton with pathetic blood shot eyes that gained some sense of purpose.

Ming smiled. "It would be no imposition to help. If I can."

"I've got about 300 pounds of gold in taels that I need to convert to US Dollars."

"Do you have a sample? The price is better if the hallmark on the taels is known and trusted."

Burton handed him one of the small gold boats with a closed fist. Ming swept his fist and the tael vanished. Then he looked into his lap and paled slightly. "Where did you find this? You say 300 pounds?"

"It's complicated. We need to keep the matter confidential."

"And in a sense it isn't. The world is a small place and karma holds sway upon the whole of it." Ming said sanguinely.

"So I have my hand upon an elephant's tail and think I am holding a snake." I said, reciting a proverb.

"Precisely." Ming said, happy that Burton, an American, could grasp the situation so completely.

"It's fortunate that you came to me because I'll pay well for the gold. Better for the gold and its source." Ming thought to himself: A masterpiece is rarely recognized in the day it is painted.

"So we're talking about the price of the gold with a commission for information?"

Ming grabbed more dried grasshoppers and chased them with the Jameson's. He nodded.

"How long have we known each other?" Burton asked.

"Two years I think. Maybe a bit more" Wu said in his studied Hong Kong British accent.

"What if I told you that I couldn't tell you where the gold came from?"

Ming sighed, "It is a statement on the condition of a man who is not free. Understanding your karma is a gift. And once understood, you can live harmoniously with it. Choice is an illusion in the ultimate sense. Nothing in the universe stands outside karma's domain. Even the concept of the independent, autonomous "I" we so dearly cherish is nothing but the product of karmic forces."

Burton translated it to US Military English. "So you're saying that my head is so far up my ass that I need a glass belly button to see out."

Ming thought about that for a moment and then winked a 'yes'.

It was Burton's turn to grab a few dried grasshoppers without the use of chopsticks and eat them followed by a deep sip of whiskey.

Ming said, "There are two types of karma. The first is the karma of effect. This addresses the age-old question of why our life is this way and not some other; it shows us that every aspect of our lives is the result of actions we have performed in past lives. It's," Ming struggled for the English word, "comprehensive. Think of your body, your parents and all other elements of your history, your relatives, your life situation and general state of mind. All of these come about because of specific actions that you have carried out in the past. They represent what is given in our lives and, as the fruition of past actions, stand beyond our ability to make them more or less than what they are.

"The second type is the karma of cause. This addresses the question of you or even whether you influence the future. It says that every action in the present is going to produce results of some kind further down the road.

"Everything you do affects the future in ever-widening ripples of cause and effect. If you are virtuous, then the karmic results will be positive, whereas if you are not virtuous, the results will be negative. Positive results include fortunate life circumstances, experiences and opportunities, while negative results include various forms of suffering, including poverty, sickness, oppressed circumstances, calamities and so forth."

"Ok, my team found them in the North." Burton relented without giving details.

"I'm not surprised," Ming admitted, "because they originated with me. When the Thais asked for £33,000 in gold for a very discrete payment, I provided the taels in boats so that it might be more easily traced. You see, I myself wanted to see where they went. That was two or three weeks ago. And here you are with what seems to be most of it. They took three pikul, 400 avoirdupois pounds."

"I have decided to move to Bhutan." Ming said abruptly, changing the subject as only a Chinese person could.

"I'm surprised. The trade is profitable, you're juiced in here." Burton replied, accustomed to the culture and the nature of oblique conversations.

"The King of Bhutan is my personal friend. In that country I will be treated like a living divinity and will want for nothing. When I go on a drunk, they will sit with ten scribes to take down every slurred word as if it were golden. When I get sick, they will send in doctors who don't need an x-ray to see inside, and give me medicines that won't make me sick. If my rivals or my wife's relatives come to visit the entire Bhutanese Secret Service Special Unit will swing into action: 12 black magicians and 1 skilled marksman who would rather throw their own children down deep wells than permit my tranquility to be disturbed, will deal with the source of my discontent."

"Did your wife's family come to visit again? The problem is not just with your wife?" Burton asked.

Ming frowned and said, "Yes and her shiftless Teochiu aunts as well. They eat as much as four water buffalo. The only thing they do all day is eat, dung, and complain about me. They are having a private party now."

Burton was relieved to have time to think about what Ming told him and suspected Ming needed to process it all as well. So he brimmed with sanguinity and offered advice while he was trying to make sense of what he just learned. "You should stay in Vientiane and throw your wife's family out into the river in weighted sacks."

Wu grunted, turning his thoughts back to Bhutan. "If I decide to embrace woodworking in Bhutan, a Royal Woodworking Shop will be established, and thereafter, as I walk through the town, dozens of men and women will shyly let it be known that they like woodworking too. If I later say, 'fuck woodworking,' there will be bonfires wherein tools are destroyed."

Burton thought it was a joke. "Really?"

Ming was serious. "In a previous incarnation, I am credited with single-handedly saving Bhutan as a nation. That act cursed me for centuries, and is why Tibetan Buddhists understand my strange ways and curious lifestyle. Of course, relocation to Bhutan does have a downside. If there is a big storm, I will be expected to subdue it, or if one is required, I will be expected to produce it and I can't do that in this incarnation."

They both drank and neither one spoke for long minutes.

"Important people risked a great deal to deliver that gold you found to a location far from here." Ming said. "We'll arrange for a place to make the swap." He picked up an abacus from the tabletop and flicked beads. "$80,000 for the gold and the information."

"Done." Burton said.

"If people found out what you've done, your life won't be worth all that much in Laos or anywhere else in Indochina." Ming cautioned as Burton stood.

"Don't worry." Burton said with a degree of confidence he didn't feel.

Burton walked out the door of the hotel, turned on Pang Kham street, walked to Tu Do Street and took an alley that cut between Tu Do Street and Hai Ba Trung Street, where there was a small US Army motor pool. It only took a moment to sign for one of the white Jeeps parked on the curb. He took the Jeep to the American Embassy where he parked it and swapped if for the Vespa he borrowed from the Aussies earlier in the day. He rode the Vespa out of town.

The Chinaimo military camp, a growing military sprawl six kilometers south of Vientiane, sat at the beginning of a big bend in the Mekong River. Chinaimo provided an entry point to the City of Vientiane proper. It also served as a choke point to block real and imagined coup instigators coming up from southern Laos. It was more than simply the Headquarters for the Royal Lao Army in Military Region 5. It provided security to the regime. In addition to the presence of the Royal Lao Army, a US Army detachment that provided administrative and logistics support to the White Star teams in the field.

Burton arrived, showed his military identification to the guard at the gate and was passed through with a crisp salute.

He parked the Vespa in front of the headquarters building and passed Ralph Syndergaard, an officer he knew slightly, a Wisconsin man who ran a White Star Mobile Training Team in Paksane. The officer wanted a word, but Burton brushed past him and into Major Owen Piper's office without knocking or announcing himself, slamming the door behind him.

"I just had a talk with the CIA, Owen." Burton said without benefit of preamble, "And they told me I've been reassigned. Either they're full of shit, which is probable, or you failed to mention that little detail during my debriefing yesterday."

Major Piper, Burton's boss, had been one year ahead of him at West Point. Burton's help with academics during a particularly rough year earned him the right to undue familiarity. Piper, a tall, phlegmatic Bostonian with a perpetual frown had been standing, punching pins in a map when Burton stormed in. He calmly set the box of pins on his desk and dropped into his chair, motioning Burton to do the same.

"I'll stand if it's all the same, *Major*."

Major Piper stood, walked to the door and shouted, "Corporal, bring us two hot coffees." On his way back to the desk, he put his hand gently on Craig Burton's shoulder. "Sit."

Burton sat.

"The cable came through this morning. I sent a runner to find you but he came back empty handed." Piper spun on his chair to a safe and dialed a combination. Once open, he thumbed through files and pulled one out for Burton. "Top secret, effective immediately, by order of General George H. Decker, Chief of Staff, United States Army."

Burton took the file. "Sounds like a two-dash-two." Burton

79

muttered, referring to a report issued at the United States Military Academy listing cadets who had been recently subject to punitive actions.

"Two-dash-two." Major Piper said nostalgically. "It reminds me of screwing up the days." Plebes were required to know the number of days until the next football game, the Army-Navy football game, Thanksgiving leave, Christmas leave, 500th Night for the junior class, Ring Weekend for the senior class, and so on. "When I first met you, I remember ordering you to 'Start the Days!' and you began the chant: 'Sir, the Days. There are 5 days until Army defeats Navy in football. There are 32 days until Thanksgiving Leave for the United States Corps of Cadets.' You were a salty bastard even as a Plebe, Craig."

Burton didn't look up and he didn't smile. He read, re-read and was reading once more when the Corporal came in with two china mugs filled with strong, steaming coffee and set them on Major Piper's desk. The Corporal left.

"How do I get out of this, Owen?" Burton asked plaintively.

"You'll note that you officially volunteered." Major Piper said, nodding toward the 201 personnel file.

"When chickens have teeth and pigs fly." Burton said. "I didn't know anything about it. Nothing."

"Oh, come on," Major Piper countered, "You've been operating up there in the hash and trash with that band of misfits, kicking ass, never getting caught, three month missions for Christ's sake. I don't know how you can look at me with a straight face and tell me you didn't see this coming."

"I wonder if it would be better to have the Pathet Lao torture me or to work for the damned Monkey King in the Green House?"

Piper laughed. "It won't be that bad, Craig."

"Fǎndòngpài zǒng yǐwéi zìjǐ liǎobuqǐ, qíshí bùguò shì zhǐlǎohǔ." Burton said in Chinese. Then he translated for Owen Piper, "The reactionaries always think they are terrific, but in fact they are just paper tigers."

"Right, I forgot about that. You speak read and write Chinese – more than one dialect as I recall. You're the man of their dreams." Piper prodded, good naturedly, handing a cup of coffee to Burton. "It's black, like your heart and your future job. In fact, I'm not even sure I know your name anymore. The memory faded when the orders arrived. Need to know and all that."

"So I'll be sheep dipped by the Agency no matter what?"

"You could resign your commission, I suppose. I've never seen them more adamant to lay claws on anyone as they were with you and your men. Lieutenant Creed Taylor, Sergeants Gorman and Paint are on the list too. It's not just about you." Piper tested the coffee, found it was scalding and set the cup down. "These things usually run their course. You'll spend a year seconded to them, and even if you screw the pooch, they'll make your record look like it's made of platinum because they want to look good."

Burton sighed.

"Colonel Simon endorsed your recommendation that Willoughby be awarded the Silver Star and have his rate reinstated to master sergeant. That was quite some write up. Sounds like he won the war all by himself."

Burton replied, "It's the least I can do. Not many Army Security Agency guys have a Silver Star. It'll put him their good graces, maybe even get him a commission in the Signal Corps. Sam Willoughby is a great soldier, good man in a fight and I'd like to see him pulled out of this meat grinder and sent somewhere stateside before he catches a bullet."

"The code book was quite a coup. The ASA is orgasmic over that one-time-pad." Piper added. "Sam Willoughby is on his way to stardom in the Black Chamber."

FOURTEEN

Monday, 13 August 1961 -- 2130 HRS
The White Rose Bar
The Strip (Red Light District),
Vientiane, Laos

At the White Rose, the afternoon stretched on for the American big men sitting at a corner table. "So how does he get away with it? The CIA Station Chief asked Walter Kennedy. "Craig Burton runs around this city like he owns it?"

"Captain Burton is a sharp operator." Kennedy said. "You have to be to survive up in the north surrounded by hostile Pathet Lao, North Vietnamese, Red Chinese, Shan State Thugs, and villagers that would turn you in for a wooden nickel."

"I heard he killed a civilian here in Vientiane?" The Monkey King wanted to know.

"So what? It was in a bar fight. A drunk German contractor working for who knows who drew down on him, just like the OK Corral. Burton whipped out his .45." Kennedy mimed the action. "Shot him once through the liver and once between the eyes. It sounds to me like a clear-cut case of self-defense. The Kraut didn't get a shot off. He just crumpled and croaked."

"What happened next?" The Monkey King seemed intensely interested.

"Oh, there was the usual investigation, and of course Burton was cleared. The local police said the shooting was self-defense. The Army didn't disagree. This is Laos and we're not exactly at a high school prom. Captain Burton is Special Forces and they are a high-spirited lot.

"Then there are the local cops. The Vientiane Prefecture cops like Burton. A month or so before the shooting, Burton saved a couple of Laotian policemen in a bar fight in the Green Latrine. That earned him a name with the local cops. In a further act of brotherhood and concern a few days after he saved their skin, Craig successfully liberated two dozen, Australian Owen MK-1 Submachine Guns on a midnight raid, from the Australian Embassy."

The Monkey King's eyebrows shot up so high that the sprayed-stiff pompadour actually moved on his scalp. "No shit?"

"It was a put up job," Kennedy calmly explained. "Pure theater. Burton and his buddy the Australian Military Attaché made the legal weapons transfer authorized by the Australian Government look illegal by taking the police commandant and a few of his most daring men on a raid at the Embassy. Mr. Burton's reputation grew when the Australians fired a few perfunctory parting shots at Craig and the local police as they slipped over the Embassy wall and he fired a few perfunctory shots back with a .45."

"Ballsy move," The CIA Chief muttered.

"The next day Burton's buddy from the Embassy of Oz formally reported to the Vientiane Prefect of Police that one of their men had been killed in the firefight and that the highly prized Owen MK-1 submachine guns had been stolen. Even though Burton fired high in the air and couldn't have hit anyone, his reputation became metaphorically chiseled into marble on the facade of the Prefect Police Headquarters Building. They'd eat the peanuts out of his shit if he asked 'em to." Kennedy took another drink and Mamasan, hovering nearby quickly recharged his glass.

"The fact that the reporting party was Burton's buddy was not considered significant?" The Monkey King asked.

"Hell no!" Kennedy slurred. "The Vientiane Prefecture Police had the machine guns and the fruits of theft had a far sweeter taste than if they'd been handed off legally through an act of Australian largess. So when he wasted the Kraut, the Police Prefecture left him alone not only out of respect and brotherly gratitude, but because they believed him to be a very dangerous man. They liked that and made him an honorary police *inspecteur divisionnaire*. Something like a major of police."

"To dangerous men," The Monkey King cheered, lifting his glass in a toast, then draining it dry.

Kennedy matched him and passed out, unresponsive as a sand bag.

The CIA's Spymaster handed Mamasan a wad of Laotian banknotes, stood up and looked down at Kenedy. "See to it that he's put to bed. He has a room at the Setha Palace."

With that, the Monkey King strolled out into the street armed with an understanding that Craig Burton was more complex and definitely more dangerous than he'd been led to believe.

The tea Mamasan poured for him for the past half hour while she

83

poured Kennedy whiskey went right through the Monkey King. He walked outside of the White Rose and released his stream against a small stand of bamboo. People passed on without giving him a second glance. It was Laos.

Burton scoured the city for Gorman and Paint and hit all of the potentially respectable places knowing that after the sun went down, the two of them would be living it up after their months in the north.

He wandered through the Dong Phalan Bar where the only source of illumination was gaslight and the women always looked better because of it. From there, he walked to the Vieng Ratry where the owner served Lucky Lager date-aged-beer, shipped directly from the General Brewing Company to the owner courtesy of the US Air Force. An officer married the bar owner's daughter and moved her to the States. The bar owner's rice bowl expanded. They didn't serve the beer cold but if you were doing a bar crawl and hit five other dives first, you wouldn't care. The generally accepted quality of the girls in the Vieng Ratry was on par with the beer: date-aged.

Sam Willoughby sat at a table with five other men in a corner of the Vieng Ratry. Burton knew two of them by sight but suspected they were all Army Security Agency. Sam stood and threw his arms around the Captain.

"That was one hell of a mission, Craig." Willoughby and the guys were drinking Mekong Whiskey and from the look of the empties on the table, they started early.

"Have you seen Gorman or Paint?"

Willoughby looked confused. "No. Not tonight. I did see Creed running around with the pretty Corsican chick, the married one. He's definitely throwing the meat to her."

Burton's face flushed, he balled a fist and then backed down without anyone noticing. He threw two-dozen folded Banque de L'Indochine 100 piaster banknotes from among those taken from the trove found up-country, onto the table. "Drinks are on me for the rest of the night, gentlemen."

Next on the list was Suzy Bar, in a house constructed by an American who had gone home. It looked as if it was plucked from the California suburbs and dropped onto the strip. The draw at the Suzy Bar was Burmese country girls from the Shan States. The bartender, a greasy

Khmer who served as an interpreter with the US Marines during the Second World War, said he'd seen Paint earlier. Burton had one beer and left.

Each of those and a dozen other watering holes comprised "The Strip", Vientiane's Red Light District. An exotic combination of stringers of colored Christmas lights illuminated the wide street. Some businesses used gas lamps with their white-hot mantles glowing to light the bars. The lowest class burned acrid pig fat in tiki torches. Each club or bar had a different singer or phonograph blaring, each clientele called the shots on what reminded them most of home or what they wanted to forget most about the life before Laos.

He walked down Rue Sampsenthai and stopped at the Constellation Hotel where he cruised the lobby bar and the lounge. There was the usual mix of journalists, expatriates representing a dozen companies on contract, do-gooders who had done good and lost focus of the 'why' and kept their attention on the 'how'. There were also the ubiquitous down-and-outs who had been in Asia too long. Though he doubted Sergeant First Class Paul "Goatman" Gorman would hang out at the nicer places, he drifted past The Spot, an elaborately decorated Corsican hangout where the women were double the price as were the drinks. The Coriscan mafia owners discouraged bar flies unless their pockets were bulging with money.

Burton's bar hopping was into its sixth door. He left the Riverside Tavern's earthy smell without taking a drink and headed for the Brass Monkey.

"Who are you looking for, Captain?" The question was asked in broken French from a Lao police officer standing in the shadows, carrying an Australian Owen submachine gun. Burton knew the police officer slightly. He'd been on the Australian Embassy raid and the entertainment at this end of the strip kicked down to the cop. The cop in turn kicked up to his boss and that's how the world turned.

"Raison pour laquelle?" Burton replied in broken French.

The police officer switched to broken English. "You stalking tiger walk."

"It sounds," Burton said, switching to English, "as though you have been keeping an eye on me."

"I keep zee eye on all thing." The police officer said proudly in French accented English.

WHITE POWDER

It was his beat, after all, Burton told himself. "You see the Goatman?"

"Goatman in Brass Monkey," the police officer replied, saluting casually almost as if he was wishing Burton luck.

Burton nodded to the police officer, smiled and turned toward the Brass Monkey.

Even Burton's most innocent smile sometimes twisted his face into a cruel leer. The scar tissue on the right side of his face crinkled and left the smile lopsided. The police officer appreciated the smile. It pleased him to know a strong man like Captain Burton who would shoot down an Australian to swipe badly needed machine guns for his friends without a backward glance. He'd also heard about Burton fearlessly shooting a legitimate German businessman over some slight or reproach. He respected that sort of ruthlessness. A man who had a plan to kill everyone he met was a man on his way up in society. Currying respect with such a man could carry you aloft in his wake. Men who didn't decide to be aggressive enough quickly were planted in the cemetery outside Vientiane.

Burton's nose led him to the Brass Monkey. The burnt cinnamon smell of opium grew stronger as he approached the bar. Two bouncers stood next to the entrance to the stairs that led to the Brass Monkey. They also stood next to the ground floor doors of a medical rehabilitation clinic catering to opium addicts. The Brass Monkey catered to the same clients, managing the supply side, upstairs.

Burton walked in. Even though it was dark outside, it took a moment for his eyes to adjust. A wasp-waisted Cambodian bar girl walked past him in absurdly high heels and bared her teeth toward him in what she hoped would pass for a smile. He didn't return her gaze.

Paul Gorman's eyes were locked on the tight skirt that stretched like a second skin over the Cambodian bar girl's well-muscled rear and thighs. Smoke from the opium pipes wafted between him and the object of his unwavering gaze.

Burton slid into a chair across the table from him but Goatman didn't notice. He was comfortably numb.

"I see you've been hitting the pipe again."

Goatman looked across the low table at him with a dull, uncomprehending gaze. He stuck the pipe stem in his mouth and puffed absently.

"Need a puff to calm my nerves. Just riding the Dragon, Captain. What a fucking relief from those endless humps, being chewed on by bugs—you know?"

"That opium skews your thinking."

Goatman's attention was drawn back to the bar girl who stood eyeing him with feigned longing. He picked up the pipe and silently toasted the girl with it.

"I can't believe Alvin Camacho is dead," he said morosely as he puffed on the opium pipe.

The comment came completely out of left field and Burton reflexively said, "I'm sorry." Then as an after thought he asked, "Who?"

"Remember, Korea. Big dumb beaner took a round for me."

Burton touched the scar his cheek absently, "Oh, yeah. That was while I was in the hospital." Burton paused and then spoke his mind, "You're a Ranger. Remember?" Burton tried to help Goatman to his feet but he sank back into his chair, limp as one hundred ninety-two pound lump of laundry.

"You've got to sober up, Gorman."

Goatman made an elaborate attempt at faux hubris, "I'm a civilian now, and I'm not in the real army. Major Piper told both Jimmy and me that we were going to be working with you on some sort of secret project. And -- I asked myself how best to celebrate. You know what I decided to do? Get so seriously fucked up on this shit that I don't come down for a week."

Burton threw Goatman's right arm around his neck and hoisted him aloft. They stepped out of the Brass Monkey and Goatman stumbled down the wooden steps on his rubber legs to the street. Burton kept him moving and erect.

A scrawny addict who ran the Brass Monkey followed them down the stairs, shrieking. "Goatman owe money."

Burton asked, "How much money he owe?"

The addict struggled for the amount.

"In dollars." Burton added.

The addict-manager paused and said, "One thousand dollar."

Burton knew that Goatman had a problem but didn't know he was in that deep. He handed the guy the rest of the Indochina Banknotes from his money clip and said, "That's all I have for now."

The addict took in the Colt .45 shaped bulge in Burton's waistband

and clucked with his tongue in acknowledgement. It was only then that he realized he was facing the bloodthirsty American gunslinger who was in tight with the police. A wad of piasters was a lot better than a double-tap from the Cowboy American's pistol. This was the man, he reasoned, who ruthlessly executed the German for reputedly slurring the reputation of the 7th Special Forces.

Burton hailed a three-wheeled, open-sided taxi called a tuk-tuk and the driver stopped. He paid double in Kip, reverting to the local currency.

"Take him to the Lido Hotel and make sure the desk clerk gets him to his room." He told the driver in French.

Goatman looked up at Burton, the pupils of his blue eyes constricted to a pinpoint even in darkness. "I'm fucked up." Goatman mumbled as he nodded off.

"Drive!" Burton told the driver and the tuk-tuk spewed thick blue smoke as it pulled laboriously into traffic, the loud engine blending with a dozen others passing in the night.

At the last minute, Burton sprinted and joined Goatman, fearing that the cab driver wouldn't be able to lift the now comatose Goatman and that he'd dump him in an alley.

Burton hoisted Goatman up two flights of stairs to his room slung over his shoulder in a fireman's carry. The Lido Hotel enjoyed the reputation of being one of the worst in town and he reasoned that was specifically why Sergeant First Class Paul Gorman stayed there. After he dropped him onto the bed and pulled the door shut, he walked out into the hall.

Jimmy Paint leaned on the hallway, smoking a cigarette. "Heard we're gonna be one big happy family: You, me, Lieutenant Taylor and Goatman. Major Piper didn't know about Sam. Goatman and I were there, checking in with personnel after you left and the major hauled us in the office. I don't think Lieutenant Taylor knows yet."

Burton thought that it wasn't Major Piper's place to tell his men. There was a chain of command last time he checked.

Burton sighed. "Yeah – well, then how's it swinging, Jimmy?"

"Swinging left and low at the moment." He paused. "Are you still a captain?"

"Maybe I'm a civilian now, Jimmy."

Paint fumbled for a pack of Camels, "Me too, huh? I wanted to get out of this chicken shit outfit and all of a sudden they let me out."

"Careful what you wish for, Jimmy." Burton advised as he started walking toward the stairs. Jimmy Paint fell into step next to him. "But you're not really out."

"I know."

They didn't speak again as they walked down the stairs to the street below.

"You been with me since the Brass Monkey, Jimmy?"

"Picked you up when you were talking to the cop. You're not watching your back like you used to, Craig."

"Captain."

"I thought you said you were a civilian." Jimmy replied quickly.

Burton laughed ruefully. "I'm not really sure who I am at the moment." They started down the street.

Burton asked, "Want to get a drink at the Continental?"

"Injun no drink firewater," Jimmy joked. "Not unless you buy."

"We'll drink to our new job."

Jimmy Paint slid under the table after three drinks and Burton helped him to the front desk of the Continental Hotel where he pre-paid for a room. Then he took him to the room and dropped him on the bed and pulled off his civilian shoes.

There were two choices. Go home or look for Sam Willoughby. He missed the Cajun and thought that the logical place to start was Vieng Ratry, the bar where he last saw Sam.

By the time he got to the bar, it was closed. It was just past 2 am. The Strip look like a ghost town. The only joint that was open was Mama Dai's. The red neon "Open" sign buzzed high over the entrance. Gaslight hissed and mantles burned white both inside and out. Two cops sat outside playing Thai checkers with bottle caps. Owen submachine guns leaned against the building. As he walked up they both stood and saluted him. Burton smiled and returned the salute. A third Prefecture policeman sat a short distance away. He was overweight, slovenly and had no machine gun.

Burton motioned to the other police officer and asked what his problem was in broken French. The senior of the standing officers explained, "His karma is such that he can't do sex because of some outrage in a previous lifetime. He is condemned to be poor, fat, flaccid and resentful."

89

WHITE POWDER

Burton smiled inappropriately, without a hint of due compassion and the officers returned his smile, equally devoid of compassion.

Inside Mama Dai's the girls were all there, eating and talking after a hard night's work. Some were playing cards. Others were in line to have their fortune told by an old crone who sat in the corner turning cards. A blind Vietnamese man chanted a dirge on stage as music twanged in the background.

Burton saw Lotus, the same girl he met sitting in Willoughby's lap his second day in Laos. She saw Burton at about the same time. She wore a tit hugging tank top, hot pants and high heels and sat in front of another fortune-teller. The Fortune-teller looked up at him and said, "Killer Buuton".

Lotus said, "Everybody know you."

Apparently she stayed behind when the French packed up their Bordel Militaire de Campagne and left town for Djibouti. Lotus was smart enough not to go to Africa.

"What card say?" Burton asked in pidgin.

"Same-same." A smile from Lotus carefully designed not to give offense. "Police say you major now."

"Honorary police major, former army captain." Burton tried to clarify the issue but Lotus was confused.

The fortune-teller offered a paper cone filled with fried grasshoppers by way of refreshment. Burton declined.

"Where Willoughby?" Burton asked.

Lotus said, "He go with Dao. Dao say you too big, Mister Sam pay extra, she go."

"You finished for night?"

The girl nodded her head vigorously.

"No pay bar fine, we go boom-boom, I go now."

"No. I not go you. I look for Willoughby."

"Creepy – he say job, you, him?"

"He job Creepy?" Burton asked, trying to decipher her English.

"Chiffrer de cryptogramme." Lotus clarified in French.

"Oh, a Crippy, a cryptographer?"

Lotus smiled, showing more gold dental work than before. "Oui, Creepy!"

"Why he here?"

"You get *secret jalousement garde from société secret Chinois*. He *traduire en Anglais.*" Lotus explained in her blend of fractured French and English.

The meaning was clear. Sam Willoughby, likely tight lipped under other circumstances bragged to a whore he was fond of that he was in town to manage decryption of something to do with the Chinese. She used the phrase "Chinese secret society" and that was telling.

Burton thanked her, gave her $5 dollars US and stood up.

Lotus said, *"Fais ce que tu dois fair."*

He took in a deep breath. She was right. We all have to do what we have to do.

From the street below, the lights in the second story of the Green House burned dimly, late into the night. From the street you couldn't see the copper screens affixed to the inside of the windows to block probing electronic eavesdroppers that may have been snooping.

In his office on the second floor of the Green House, Montgomery Keene handed his deputy two pages of carefully formatted text. "Read it and let me know how you think it'll play at headquarters."

Henry Dastrup took the document. His bloodshot eyes moved along the top. There was the operational title, routing, classification and usual security caveats. He scanned lower and the intensity of his review increased.

"Christ, Monty. You're changing the op again?"

"It was Kennedy's idea. He made a lot of sense."

Dastrup set down the message his boss planned to send to Washington D. C. "Kennedy's a maniac."

"Yes, but he made sense to me and *I'm* the Chief of Station."

"Why do you want me to read this, Monty?"

"I want your opinion. I'd like to have the cable on the boss' desk when he gets to work on Monday."

Dastrup counted to three in his head. "What a great idea!"

"So you like the plan?"

"Hell no. Why didn't Craig Burton tell us that his man was having sexual congress with the Sabon woman."

"You can say fuck." The Monkey King offered. "Nobody knows for sure, Lieutenant Taylor wasn't found *inflagrante delicto*, but he's been seen with her everywhere and who wouldn't tap that magnificent ass if it was offered?"

91

"There's no need to be crude. The issue is one of trust. You told Burton and Taylor that you wanted information on her husband and if I read this cable you propose to send out correctly, they have a little tryst going on. No doubt Burton knows."

"He didn't exactly lie. Give the kid some slack. He's protecting a junior officer. I don't think that he knows Charlotte Sabon is *Charlotte Jospin Sabon*, the daughter of Big Bruno himself."

"He withheld information that was critical and in my book that's worse."

"Ever been in love Henry?"

"Plenty of times. What's that got to do with it?"

"I don't mean with Madame Lulu's girls. Look, we didn't know that old man Sabon's child bride was Bruno Jospin's daughter either. I'm not sure that Lieutenant Taylor knows. I just thought she was a little gold digger. Until I find out otherwise, there's no reason to suspect that Craig Burton knows."

Henry Dastrup was caught short. "The cable doesn't explain that. You didn't mention Bruno Jospin by name."

"I didn't use his name because Old Bruno has a cryptonym. FRANGLE. He worked with us, well, with the OSS in the days of the Maqui and the French Resistance. Kennedy swears she's Bruno's kid. Think about it for a minute. They need to cut a deal with the Chinese but whether or not they're successful, we have a chance to get close to the man that's essentially running Marseille. Bruno Jospin is *the* shot caller, the man himself, *the* boss Frog. According to Kennedy, his favorite little girl is smitten by our man Taylor. Call it what you want. Kennedy says it's puppy love on steroids."

Dastrup complained. "Taylor won't go along with us manipulating him if he loves her. He's not a big-picture guy."

"Burton is though. Don't you see? All of those guys look up to Burton. He becomes our cat's paw with Taylor and Taylor in turn is Burton's cat's paw with the girl. If things go south, we blame whatever bad happens on Burton and ship him back to the army with our reputations intact." The Monkey King knew he had all angles covered. "Frankly, I don't see a down-side."

"So, we fly by the seat of our pants like always? Do we have to keep Kennedy in the loop? I don't trust him. I don't even like him a little. He's a drunkard, and he's been ducking his flutter for five months now."

Dastrup said, referring to Kennedy's reluctance to participate in a mandatory polygraph examination.

"Kennedy will do what he does best and we'll just have to keep an eye on him like always. Technically speaking he's not in our food chain, He works for Jack Beckman in Manila." The Monkey King decided on his course of action and would not be swayed.

The lights on the second floor of the Green House, dim from the street below, winked out.

FIFTEEN

Tuesday, 15 August 1961 -- 0930 HRS
Embassy of the United States of America, Annex,
20 Rue Barthlonie, That Dam Road,
Vientiane, Laos

Henry Dastrup sat in a slat back wood chair in the Station Chief's office and smoked his pipe. Montgomery Keene tilted back in his high-back executive chair. Both propped their wingtips on Keene's desk. Each read from a file in a manila folder with broad red stripes across the cover that indicated that some or all of the contents were classified. The Monkey King's personal safe stood open behind his desk with other similar files visible.

"Burton's appointment to West Point was nothing to speak of unless you consider the source." The Monkey King explained patiently.

"I thought you had to be appointed by a congressman." Dastrup flipped pages in the thick file looking for an answer and not finding one.

"He was appointed by Congressman Dan Woods, 5th Congressional District."

Dastrup looked up. "Ok, Monty, you have me on that one. So what?"

"If you read the whole goddamned file you'd have seen that his father, William Parker Burton died and his mother remarried, well as it turns out."

Dastrup wore a perplexed smile.

"Ellen Burton married Dan Woods. Our man was appointed by his step-father."

"It doesn't say that in the file in the West Point Section," Dastrup said, still flipping pages.

"It's in the personal history file, not in the military record," The CIA Station Chief clarified.

Dastrup continued to flip pages and read. "Class of '49—I didn't know Burton played football for Army. You know, I went to some of those games when I was posted at the UN in New York. Army almost went all the way in '48 and from what it says here Burton was on the team."

"Keep reading. He was a second stringer." The Monkey King said, looking up from the folder he had just been reading from. "Burton played half-back. Actually, he played most of his third and fourth year on the bench, watching Pete Jensen move on to the Hall of Fame. Pick any other four years and Burton might have made his mark. Tough break."

Dastrup returned to his reading. Then his eyes peered out over the top of the file folder at Keene. "How come Burton picked the infantry? He speaks Chinese. I think they would have put him on the fast track in intelligence."

"He wanted to be a grunt-warrior leading his platoon into glory or something like that. Isn't that what they teach? Maybe he wanted to bang and burn at Fort Bragg instead of troop with the paramilitary types at The Farm. Personally I always hated the Farm," The Monkey King said in annoyed tones. His own focus centered on file he was reading.

"I never went in the military. Yale, class of '40. Academic deferment during World War II."

"Congratulations, Henry." The Monkey King said, reminded now of how the Yale good-old-boy's-club ran the CIA, excluding him from higher offices that were populated with those who wore the school tie.

"There's nothing wrong with Southern Methodist University." Dastrup said generously.

"Nothing wrong with Yale either." Keene said from behind his file.

"This is in the language tab. Maybe it should be in the personal history section. Raised by his mother, who it would seem has family money. Father died when he was three—learned Chinese from his nanny. How improbable is that in Northeast Michigan? San Francisco's loaded with Chinese but finding one in sub-arctic Michigan doesn't make any sense to me." Dastrup continued speaking in tones just loud enough to cause his boss to raise his head again. "When he was at Fort Benning attending infantry training he was tested for language aptitude at School of the Americas by our people. Wow. He scored higher than I did. How'd Burton do that? That's a hard test to cheat your way through."

"Maybe he didn't cheat, Henry."

Dastrup continued to read. "He came out first in his class at Ranger School. Somebody must have noticed him."

"You and I noticed him too." The Monkey King said, setting his reading down in front of Dastrup.

Shifting files to one with higher classification, the Monkey King tapped it on his knee. "Burton is a star. He's a good leader, he is a natural for foreign languages but he's a bit rough around the edges. I'm not worried about him."

"What about Creed Taylor. He's not long in the Army, but he's the same age as Burton." Dastrup said. "Taylor's old man was one of us, OSS, before he took up the cloth."

"That's how the kid got into Officer Candidate School – favors for past deeds done quietly. And now he's back because he knows the people and speaks the language, but he's not cut from the same piece of cloth as Burton is."

The room beyond the mosquito net looked fogged-in.

Burton lay in the bed, his body covered by sweat. Light from the windows remained blocked by heavy black-out drapes, but the sun screamed through the gaps above and below and grew hot inside the room. His head pounded and it took a moment for him to focus on his wristwatch.

Cold chills began suddenly. The onset of Malarial sweats. It felt like the flu but the intensity would increase if he didn't have his quinine.

10:15 – What day was it? Saturday. No. Burton counted the days. Tuesday. Maybe it was a Tuesday?

Pressure on his bladder drove him to the toilet. Next to the porcelain throne, Soviet Premier Nikita Kruschev and his Defense Minister Rodion Malinovsky shared the cover of Life Magazine. May 30, 1960. He threw the magazine in the trash.

Opening bottles, he popped four aspirin, two metaquinine tablets and tipped the water bottle into a glass. A splash of Jack Daniels and he chased the pills. He washed his mouth out with a swig of Jack and then swallowed it and brushed his teeth.

Wearing nothing but white skivvies, he padded out to the hallway and then around and down winding stairs.

Chester Watson, a large, homely, pug nosed, jug-eared man with a perpetual squint, sat near the stairs wearing a Russian Army major's jacket that he acquired in a poker game two months before. Chester painstakingly and obsessively painted molded lead soldiers with a fine brush.

A pot-bellied, brass incense burner churned out spiced smoke in the corner behind him.

"G'day," Chester said in a distracted monotone without looking up or breaking his concentration. Major Chester Watson, Royal Australian Army, was the Aussie military attaché in Laos.

"Why are you wearing that commie's jacket like a cut lunch commando?" Burton asked.

"It makes you jealous because you can't play poker like the master, doesn't it?"

"Want a beer?"

"Scotch is better for breakfast but beer will do," Chester said, his concentration fixed on the soldier he was painting. "Bring in the tucker too, mystery bags on a plate in the icebox."

Burton walked into the kitchen, fetched two San Miguel beers from the refrigerator, scanned for the plate of sausages and then grabbed that too. On the way back Burton, opened the beers awkwardly as he walked back into the formal room where he set one next to Chester.

Chester sniffed the air, "beer." He took a long swig from the long neck bottle, draining it completely and then set it on the table where he was painting.

"Still working on Waterloo?"

Chester gnawed on a piece sausage. "Yer cunning as a dunny rat! Austerlitz, Imperial Guard." Chester directed his eyes to the painted lead soldier.

"I can't figure how Napoleon did so well with such small soldiers under his command," Burton commented wryly.

"All Yanks are bitzers," Chester said as he finished painting the boots of the Old Guard soldier. "Are you going to the party at the British Embassy next week?"

"Hadn't planned on it. The last one the Pommys threw was all men. A real sausage fest."

"Last one was dry as a nun's nasty but this one may be different. I heard a new crop of school teachers arrived three days ago to instruct the Limey ex-patriot offspring." Chester released the information gleefully. "I'm thinking of throwing a party with a theme for 'em right here at the house. How does this sound, 'Barbarians and Librarians'?"

"A come-as-you-are-party?"

Chester laughed. "Precisely."

"You weren't home when I came back from out there, the other day."

"Somebody around here has to work some of the time," Chester replied matter-of-factly. "I was off with a delegation of do-gooders from Sydney who flew in a few days ago. We were out in the buggery-back-of-Borque, flailing around. They needed protection while they figured out how much of other people's money they'd pitch at soap, rice and Bibles for the natives."

Chester shoved a whole sausage into his mouth and spoke as he chewed. "D'ya hear my mate Monty Banks is opening a place of his own?"

"That doesn't sound like a good idea, Chester. He'll drink all the profits and you'll help him."

"Monty says the girls will be clean as a whistle."

"Sure," Burton said smoothly, "clean as the last whistle they blew."

Chester moved on with only the twitch of a smile from the corner of his mouth. "He's calling the bar the Purple Porpoise. I think that's what he calls his dick."

"That's original." Burton quickly changed the subject. "Ever heard of a guy named Walter Kennedy?"

Chester sat up and put the lead soldier down to dry, squinting at Burton. "He's very shonky. Dobbs in for the CIA or so legend has it. I wouldn't trust the bastard. I met him once. Mean and flashy as a rat with a gold tooth."

Burton laughed.

"It's no joke, mate. He's a real bushranger. You know I'm not one to gossip."

"Not you, Chester, never."

"Right, but there's a rumor floating that the CIA put him on ice in the Philippines because he went rogue. There was a scandal about a year back where got himself caught by a Thai general, breaking into the general's house. Quite a rascal."

Burton smiled and stood, turning toward the stairs that led to his room.

"Who's the shiela that Lieutenant Taylor's running around with, mate?"

Burton turned. "Sheila?"

"Pretty as a button."

"I wouldn't know." Burton lied.

Chester turned his attention back to his lead soldiers and Burton walked up the stairs, past a servant and through the door into his room.

The Aussies ran their generator 24/7 on embassy fuel so there was always plenty of hot water and the electricity always worked. Hot water notwithstanding, Burton took a cold shower in an attempt to forestall the malarial symptoms. Sometimes it worked. This time it did.

He took an Australian staff car, a '52 Hudson, to the Continental Hotel and parked out front, throwing an Australian Embassy placard on the dash. A Vientiane Police officer hanging around the front of the hotel recognized him, smiled and saluted. Burton returned the salute and walked to the desk, put his hands together and greeted the desk clerk with a wai to be polite.

"Please call Room 32 and tell Mr. Paint that I will meet him in the bar."

On the other side of the bar, three pink knights were lined up wearing hot pants and halter-tops, pushing hard for a date with an Australian who looked like he might be one of Chester Watson's do gooders there for his church to bring Jesus to the heathen nation.

"You want love me long time?"

"You my first Australian!"

"I love you all day."

Burton ignored them. The headache got worse.

He wore plain, worn, khaki trousers, a pale blue button down collar shirt and polished loafers. The look, the deep sun tan, the scar on his face, the haircut marked him as a soldier.

"Can I buy you a drink, sir?" It was one of the Air America guys, new to Laos. Burton couldn't remember his name. Burton never gave the pilot his name. Customers such as Burton were more or less anonymous. Sometimes a code name was offered. The game was fun when it was new. It wasn't new for Burton anymore.

The Air America pilot ordered rye, neat, from the squat Chinese-Lao bartender who must have been tending the same bar for the last twenty years.

"Beer, with ice."

"Is that your drink?" The pilot asked.

"I've had hepatitis. And I *have* malaria."

"Oh."

WHITE POWDER

"Chances are good you'll come down with two or three of the nasty ones while you're here: Dengue Fever, hepatitis, Yellow Fever. Everybody has malaria. Beer with ice is a cure and I'm a mess today."

Jimmy Paint came into the bar and Burton made a brief introduction. The pilot shook his hand.

"He's another Air America customer and we need to talk." Burton hurt the pilot's feelings but his head throbbed and he needed to get the gold redemption underway before something popped up to interfere.

The pilot walked away and Burton told the bartender to keep the Air America guy's glass full, slapping down a few of the Indochina Bank piasters. He toasted the pilot with his beer and the pilot returned the toast. No hard feelings. The Air America pilots were never told anything about the cargo they carried or who "the customer" worked for. Air America types presumed most of them were CIA, also called the "Controlled American Source." It wouldn't have been true yesterday, because he was in the Army. Today, with the stroke of a pen in Washington, that all seemed to have changed.

"Jimmy," Burton lowered his voice. "Get the guys together with the 'stuff' and have everyone meet at Wu Ming's shop at two, this afternoon. Make sure Lieutenant Taylor is with you."

"Ok. What then?"

"You'll walk out with $16,000 and you can do with it as you please. I'm sure he's going to weigh it, so try not to let too many of the boats sail away before they make it."

Jimmy thought on that for a moment. "Have you thought about what you're going to do with your cut?"

"Bank it and worry about it later." Burton drained his glass and left, giving Jimmy Paint a good-natured pat on the shoulder.

Burton felt suddenly hungry, a steak sounded good. Once out the door of the Continental Hotel, he angled toward café Les Deux Magots. The Corsican mafia established the restaurant and they brought the principal staff and architectural design from the old country. The café's patio overlooked the slowly moving Mekong and he haunted the place on afternoons when he was in town and needed a meal.

Café Les Deux Magots catered to a wide variety of men, mostly European, who sat on the expansive patio with accommodating Lao or Annamite mistresses. If you didn't have a mistress at the moment, the local Lao geisha house next door would supply a young girl scented with sandalwood to meet your immediate needs.

The maitre d' seated Burton and he relaxed, taking in the scenery. Laos encouraged a languid lifestyle. A Theravada monk whirled his prayer wheel clockwise just outside the gate of the café. A fisherman cast his net into the Mekong River where the restaurant ended. Edith Piaf sang a sad song of lost love, broadcast over a phonograph speaker.

The Alsatian sommelier, tall, florid faced, waxed mustache, walked up to Burton and looked at him expectantly.

"Chateau Cheval Blanc '56," Burton ordered thoughtfully and then looked up at the Sommelier to see if he'd made a good selection. The Alsatian wine steward smiled, pursed his lips and then winked.

In his peripheral vision, Burton watched a skinny American wearing an expensive white silk suit weaving through tables generally in his direction. It was Walter Kennedy. He took a chair directly across the table from Burton.

How ya doin'?" Walter Kennedy spoke slowly, pleasantly, without his Irish accent. He offered his hand across the table. "Walter Kennedy, no relation to the Hyannis Port Kennedy Clan."

Burton reluctantly shook Kennedy's proffered mitt.

Kennedy sat down. "I looked for you at the Continental Hotel and when you weren't there, I asked myself where a young, strapping guy like yourself might want to go to cure a hang-over."

"Good guess."

"Yeah, it's bull shit. I had you followed. When you left the Australian manse, my man called me."

"Why have me followed?"

"We needed to talk and I didn't want to run around God's half acre looking for you."

"A friend told me you got into some trouble in Thailand and the Agency dumped you in Manila," Burton said, being deliberately provocative. "The word he used was, 'cashiered'."

"Cashiered? Hardly. A rose by any other name? We don't call it the Agency, the Company or the Outfit here in Laos. I guess the Controlled American Source is as good as any other name. Would you like me to tell you what tweaked the Agency's nose?"

"Why not?"

"The after action report didn't reflect the subtle nuances of the operation. It was last year about this time and involved me and my

Vietnamese wife, Ngoc. I never bothered to open Ngoc as an agent and the Outfit was upset about that. I was drunk all the time back then and they didn't like that either."

Kennedy waited for a comment from Burton and when none was forthcoming, he continued. "I black-bagged a Thai general's bedroom in daylight hours, mind you, and there was a commotion in the compound so I guessed I was in shit. Sure enough, I was in shit. There were a whole bunch of M-1 Carbines and Thompson guns pointed at us and I heard a bunch of cocking levers getting jacked. It looked grim. Ngoc just muscled her little self in front of me, protecting me like a mother tiger, and she said, 'you going to shoot a real Kennedy?'

"They all just looked at us, and then they hauled us into the living room. Cool room. The place was dominated by a large picture of the general getting sworn in by the king, sword on his shoulder and all that. Then they proceeded to ask me some pointed questions. The general asked the questions through his son-in-law, Thai Air Force Intelligence, US trained, very good command of the language. The general, Wattapongsiri Sithikit, spoke English well too, but then again, you know him, don't you?"

Burton said, "I met him at the French Embassy on Bastille Day, a year ago last July. I stood on one side of the Ambassador and he stood on the other side." Burton thought but didn't say, his clothes smelled like cheap bay rum and his breath smelled of spiced cabbage. "We sang the Marseilles together once but I don't usually move in those circles."

Kennedy grunted and then continued, "So you know the bastard. Anyway, the general asked, 'what are you doing in my house?' Ngoc said, 'We've been waiting for you.'

"The general's son-in-law asked, 'Why were you in the general's bedroom?' Ngoc said, 'We were looking for a place to go to the restroom.' The general's son-in-law said, 'shut up woman.'"

A smile crossed Kennedy's face as he reflected on the drama. "I told the general's son-in-law, 'you don't talk to a lady that way, you little cocksucker.' Ngoc said, 'Shut up Daddy, these clowns don't fool around.' Then we started to argue."

A laugh escaped Kennedy's thin lips. "I told her, 'I count five dead.'"

"Ngoc said, 'Daddy, please. I count three dead and you're one of them.'"

"I said, 'If you say so, but the general and the son-in-law are two of them for sure.'"

"Ngoc said, 'I have the son-in-law, you take the general and the daughter.'"

"I said, 'that's five dead, you're cracking under pressure and you can't count.'"

"The general is taking all this in and asked, 'is your name really Kennedy?'"

"I said, 'No, it isn't. It's Cassidy,' using my cover name."

"The general is thinking hard and you could hear the cogs turning in his head, 'I believe you are a Kennedy, using the name Cassidy falsely.'"

"Thinking fast, I told that prick, 'The Kennedy family could only wish they were Cassidys. My operational name is Walter Kennedy, but my true name is L. Robert Cassidy, and I am here to extend my government's request that you assist with an official investigation. Permit me to call the Embassy and we will have American Foreign Service Officers respond here at once to answer any further questions you may care to ask. In fact, some people in Washington are awake at this hour waiting to hear your response.'"

"The general asked, 'Are you CIA?' I told him, 'No, but my uncle is in the United States Senate. He controls the CIA's money.'"

"Ngoc got hostile, 'Did he just insult a Cassidy?'"

"The general asked me, 'Who is this woman?'"

"I introduced her, 'this is Madame Cassidy. She is Vietnamese. If you would be so kind as to politely offer her some refreshment, I believe she'll feel more at ease.'"

"The general began to relax and said, 'Aha! You are really a Kennedy!' They all shut up, Ngoc got tea, the situation calmed right down and we escaped with the information in the false bottom of a camera bag."

"Hmm," Burton uttered judgmentally, "that doesn't seem to be something they'd fire you for." He could tell from Kennedy's expression that his account was not exactly what happened.

"I wasn't fired, I was tactically reassigned for good cause." Kennedy reached into an inside pocket of his white silk suit, withdrawing a cigarette case. "I assure you that I'm not out of play. My mere presence here with the Monkey King and his deputy, that pervert Henry Dastrup, yesterday at lunch should convince you of that."

WHITE POWDER

"You're a pathalogical a liar." Burton said to Kennedy.

"When we hear lies, we immediately want to investigate the matter, in order to learn the truth. Thus, my only hope is that my lies will prompt your investigation. That, after all, is the reason I *may* have lied to you. Now, I will stop lying to myself. Do you speak Corsu, Captain? The Corsican dialect of lingua mizana in particular? Of course you don't. The English think everyone should speak English, the French firmly hold that the world should speak French and the Corsicans know each other by the dialect they speak which is culturally unique to the city they grew up in back on the island. That's why the Corsican mafia is effective. It's almost impossible to infiltrate. And infiltration is the name of the game."

Burton didn't understand where Kennedy was going with it, but before he could ask for clarification, the sommelier arrived with the wine, un-corked it and offered the cork to Burton. A waiter stood behind the sommelier waiting to take an order.

Burton deferred to Walter Kennedy. Kennedy sniffed the cork with his long snout and twisted his face into an accepting half-smile. The sommelier poured a splash of the Chateau Cheval Blanc into a glass and offered it to Kennedy who stuck his nose into the glass and swirled the wine to absorb the bouquet.

Kennedy took a sip and sloshed it in his mouth and took an educated guess. "It's a '51. Perfect."

The Alsatian sommelier smiled, his lower lip protruded with satisfaction and he poured a glass for Burton and then added wine to Kennedy's glass. The waiter scribed the order: dry sausages, cheese, bread, butter and fruit for Kennedy, who also wanted durian on the side on a separate plate. Burton ordered a beef steak, specifying that it not be water buffalo, t-bone, medium rare with rice and whatever vegetable they wanted to add.

When the waiter left, Burton asked, "Ok, what's this all about, Kennedy?"

"I'd like to have you and your men join me as my guests in Manila."

"When?"

"I can arrange an Air America flight out Wednesday morning. I'm leaving this afternoon."

Burton thought about banker's hours and the need to deposit the money he'd be collecting from Wu Ming shortly. "Make it noon. My guys like to sleep in when they're standing down."

Kennedy smiled but his eyes didn't. "Noon on Wednesday it is, at Watay Airport. I'll have my man meet you in Manila when you land."

"So what's going on? Why me? Why my men? You have to admit, Walter, that this is all very sudden."

"Opium and its derivatives." Kennedy shifted into high gear. "The French colonized Indochina for the purpose of creating their own opium trade. The British traded opium grown in India and Burma to the Chinese for silver in the 1800's and the French were jealous because the Brits made a fortune. The colonial government funded infrastructure development, irrigation and highways. Did you ever wonder why there were so many highways throughout Laos? They were expensive to build. Why build them? One word. Opium. The last country to abolish opium production officially was Laos—three years ago when the UN Single Convention on Narcotic Drugs forced the issue, yes?" Kennedy smiled like a Sphinx. "We can get into details when you're in the Philippines. There's a timetable but—." He stopped speaking when the waiter arrived with the steak and Kennedy's mixed plate.

They ate quietly. Kennedy waved at some patron he knew and they waved back.

Burton reflected on the Central Intelligence Agency while he carved the t-bone. He knew more about how things worked than he let on, but it didn't make much sense. Kennedy was a bit unusual. Clearly even the somewhat exotic members of the Outfit treated him like an outcast.

The ranks of the old Office of Strategic Services were being filled with frustrated, idealistic, naive students joining right after college. There were also former senior police officials with detective experience but they were in the minority. The Agency's recruiting tastes ran toward the Ivy League and keyed on inexperience. The $640.00 per month that they paid case officers was fine if you were single or a hustler like Kennedy with a lot of side action, but it wasn't enough to live well at all unless your cover required a stipend. The CIA tried to recruit him while he was in Korea and he turned them down flat. This time the orders came from the Chief-of-Staff of the Army and there wasn't any wiggle room. Orders are orders.

He compared CIA pay to his. The Army paid him $498.00 per month as a junior captain. Then there was $49.88 basic allowance for subsistence and another $98.20 basic allowance for quarters. If you included the $65.00 per month hostile fire pay and the $155.00 jump pay he was way ahead of case officer pay. A change of employer to the CIA wasn't one he'd welcome. The $16,000 he would put in the bank from the sale of Thai gold would offset any immediate need for money in Laos. At least something put his mind at ease.

The Fruit Company cover seemed stupid. He wasn't thrilled with the new boss. The Monkey King and his sidekick, Henry Dastrup, were both manipulative, small, unimaginative bureaucratic men who presented as very tarnished role models. Kennedy's persona was exponentially worse.

Burton took a gulp of wine, finishing the glass and tried to put the thought out of his mind. He thought instead of Charlotte Sabon.

It was a short walk for Burton from café Les Deux Magots to the Shanghai Spring Phoei Kwan shop, Wu Ming, proprietor. As he approached, he saw a Jeep with Jimmy Paint behind the wheel, looking around nervously, holding an M-3 Grease gun, Creed Taylor in the shotgun seat holding a 12 gauge pump action riot gun, appropriately, and Sam Willoughby and Paul Gorman in the back of the Jeep, each holding M-14 rifles with bandoliers of clips slung from their shoulders.

People passed by without a sideways glance. Nothing was out of the ordinary. Life rolled on as usual in Laos.

The Phoei Kwan (currency exchange) business existed inside a nearly square building. The blockhouse had been poured at the same time as the French poured concrete revetments for their Spitfires at Watay Air Base shortly after the conclusion of the Second World War when they reclaimed Laos and Indochina. Burton suspected that some of the concrete, paid for by the French taxpayers, had been diverted for this purpose by Wu Ming, himself.

Shanghai Spring Phoei Kwan Shop was built like a vault with two-foot-thick poured concrete walls reinforced with re-bar. There were no windows. Only one person at a time could enter, through a man-trap that insured very controlled entry.

"Where's your sack?" Sam Willoughby asked.

Burton grabbed his groin and feigned relief. "Still there, Sam." A roaring engine in the distance prompted him to look at his wristwatch.

Olive drab and dangerous, the Australian Embassy's Daimler Dingo armored scout car roared down the street. Chester Watson drove while another Australian officer sat topside with his hand on a .303 caliber Bren gun. Both smiled like Cheshire Cats.

"How low key can you get, Craig?" Creed Taylor observed dryly.

"Just a little insurance." Burton replied.

"What did you have to give 'em?" Taylor continued.

"Past favors repaid with gusto."

"G-Day mates!" Major Chester Watson called out, as he leapt awkwardly from the Dingo, wearing a bush hat with one brim turned up and pinned.

Gorman looked closely at the Dingo. "Diesel?"

"Nah," Chester Watson said, "A petrol engine that runs rough. It just sits out back of the Embassy and rusts. I think they brought it here in case of a riot or something but nothing ever materialized. It's been here on the order of fifteen years or so, waiting to be used."

Burton walked to the back and Chester handed down Burton's rucksack with the leather bag containing gold boats, one tael weight each, clinking in inside.

A wink and a nod from Burton and a hearty thumbs up from Chester in reply. The Dingo roared off and the men took the loot into Wu Ming's castle.

Wu Ming waited for them, and ushered them through another layer of security, into a room, thick concrete walls, steel security door. Inside the door was a table and on the table sat $80,000 in US currency, in hundred dollar bills.

"Is the money counterfeit?" Gorman asked suspiciously.

"You may examine it and count it." Wu Ming said magnanimously, pulling the steel security door closed behind him.

Creed Taylor and Paul Gorman appointed themselves as currency counters and examined every banknote as the rest stood near and watched, intent on taking in the entire process of examination.

"All there." Taylor pronounced.

"Divide it into five shares." Willoughby prodded.

"Wait." Burton said. Turning to Wu Ming, "The gold is here for you to weigh. I'm not sure what the weight will be. Some of the boats sailed here and there between the time we, uh, found it and now."

Gorman looked sheepish.

"I trust that the gold is all there as you said." Wu Ming said graciously.

"You should weigh it and pay us after you do that." Burton said.

"Leave a little money behind if you wish, but I am buying it as it is

107

for the amount we agreed on." Wu Ming insisted.

Creed Taylor, who was no novice to the Chinese having grown up in Laos said, "It's the first time I've ever seen a Chinaman give money without weighing and examining every tael."

"The door is closed, the world is out there," Wu Ming gestured vaguely with one hand, "and we are in here. Whatever shortfall and I'm certain there is some, is of little consequence. It's only important to me that you and each of you think well of me."

"What do you want, Wu?" Taylor said firmly. "What's going on behind those wicked slant eyes?"

"I know your father well, Lieutenant Taylor. We were acquainted before he took up the cross and Bible and we have had discussions at times since then. He and I have had our differences at times and in other situations and other times we were of one mind. I presume that you and I will find ourselves in similar positions in this incarnation. However, next time, in the next life, you may be me and I may be you. One needs to think ahead. Perhaps I will want help when that day comes and it will be important that you think of this moment when I was generous."

"Good enough for me." Gorman said, dividing the currency.

"I think we need to talk when the others have gone." Burton suggested.

Wu Ming put his hands together and offered a wai.

It didn't take the White Star Mobile Training Team long to scoop up the cash, once divided and stacked. Burton divided his between both front trouser pockets.

Willoughby was the last one out, "We'll wait for you outside, boss."

Burton nodded, closed the door and turned to Wu Ming, deciding to speak in Teochiu dialect instead of English.

"I was thinking of parables I could offer but the best one comes from the Trojan War, not from China."

Both sat across the table from each other.

Wu offered, "Beware of Greeks bearing gifts."

"Yes."

"The gold will be light." Wu arched a nearly non-existent eyebrow.

"I said it was."

"Of course."

Burton stopped himself. It was a Chinese thing. He had to start behaving and thinking in Chinese, not simply speaking Chinese. He pulled a pack of Camel cigarettes from his shirt pocket and pushed the pack across the table. Wu took the pack and tapped out two, offering them to Burton who pulled one. Wu took the other and pocketed the pack. Burton flipped open his zippo lighter and spun the wheel with his thumb, offering the flame to Wu Ming.

Three puffs later, Wu said, "Everyone tries to push down a falling wall."

Wu quoted an old Chinese saying that implied a show of weakness led inevitably to exploitation.

"Not if you have friends."

"No." Wu shifted to English, "Not if you have true friends. People willing to overlook a small thing like a few boats that might have sailed."

"Why us?"

"I like you, Burton." Wu exhaled smoke. "I know Taylor's father, therefore I know Taylor, the fruit that fell from the tree. Wu shifted back to Teochiu Chinese, "There is a proverb which Su Shi scribed. Once upon a time, there was a blind man who does not know what the Sun is. So he asks other people to explain."

"One man said, 'The Sun is shaped like a copper plate.' So the blind man banged on a copper plate, and listened to its clanging. Later when he heard the sound of a temple bell, he thought that must be the Sun."

"Another man said to him, 'The Sun gives out light just like a candle.' So the blind man held a candle to feel its shape. Later when he picked up a flute, he thought that this must be the Sun."

"Yet we know that the Sun is vastly different from a bell or a flute; but a blind man does not understand the differences, because he has never seen the Sun and only heard it described. Friendship and trust are the same. You can describe it to everyone but it can only be understood by those who somehow experience it."

Burton smoked slowly. Nodding his head.

"The people's popular uprising against the warlord, Generalissimo Chiang Kai-Shek resulted in the collapse of the Nationalist Chinese *Kuomintang*. They fled to Taiwan and to the Shan States in Burma. Once in exile, Chiang Kai-Shek lobbied and ultimately convinced the Truman administration that the best way to staunch the southward flow of communism into Southeast Asia was to use them, their army in Burma, where remnants of the *Kuomintang* 93rd Division could be reorganized if they had supplies and money. There were roughly twelve thousand

Kuomintang soldiers who fled into the Burmese jungle and they were battle hardened so they had potential. At the same time, Burma found itself invaded and sent an army against the *Kuomintang* who occupied a portion of their country. In 1950 your Defense Department extended military aid to the French in Indochina. In that same year, the CIA began regrouping those remnants of the defeated *Kuomintang* army in the Burmese Shan States for a projected invasion of southern China."

"And here we are, ten years later." Burton said, stubbing the cigarette out. "No invasion."

"No, the Kuomintang had no interest in invading Southern China. They had a pot of gold in their laps. Why look elsewhere?"

"Opium."

"Precisely. After the Japanese were defeated the production from Shan was less than forty tons a year, but the demand was much greater. Armed, strong and financed by America, the *Kuomintang* expanded Burmese opium production to around three hundred tons per year. America wasted money on thugs who are against communism, but have no interest in defeating the communists. You see the difference?"

Burton nodded.

"Now we come to the present. There is the *Kuomintang* Army and there are the warlords. The warlords have won and the army lost a battle for control of opium production. General Tuan has led his forces out of Burma and they are in the process of establishing themselves in Mae Salong, Thailand. In exchange for political asylum in Thailand, they have put themselves under the command of the Thai military with the goal of policing the area north of Cheng Mai against communist infiltration.

"Thailand seeks a better relationship with the warlords who won the battle for control of the opium."

"Therefore the gold." Burton interjected.

"A good faith offering."

"That never made it."

"And there are fingers being pointed in many directions." Wu said.

"At you?"

Wu blinked. "Yes at me as well."

"Maybe it's good that you have a grip on the gold again."

"Yes, Captain Burton." Wu offered his hand and they shook hands in the Western tradition.

As they walked to the door, Wu mentioned, "About a week ago,

Miss Sabon and Lieutenant Taylor came here to exchange Francs for local currency."

Burton looked at Wu from a corner of his eye.

"I took the liberty of checking their astrology as I have yours, Captain."

Burton turned to face Wu Ming.

"One can't do business without understanding the nature of one's—partners."

"Am I going to like what you tell me?" Burton asked.

"There is no like or dislike in astrology. It's all wrapped up with karma and the balance of past lives. Both you and Lieutenant Taylor were born in the year of the Earth Tiger. It explains why you are the way you are. Miss Charlotte Sabon was born in the year of the Iron Dragon both are dynamic in astrological terms."

"What does that mean?"

"I suggest that you advise Lieutenant Taylor—to be cautious in such a relationship as he has undertaken. It has nothing to do with her marital status or his status as an officer in the American Army, though both are clearly complicating factors.

"It's inevitable that the tiger would be attracted to the dragon and likewise the dragon to the tiger. You may have felt that yourself since you share the same sign with Taylor—and your karma is clearly linked to his. Karmic forces at work are not small things in matters such as the attraction of a magnet to iron, or to an Iron Dragon. Both signs possess magnetic personalities but attraction will give way to irritation. The Dragon likes to be in charge of everything and the Tiger insists on autonomy. It's like pouring kerosene from two cans into a jar and adding a match. The result is inevitable, its resulting karma unappealing."

Burton, now irritated, smiled nervously and left the building.

"Just like a Tiger," Wu said to himself.

Half an hour before sunset as the city came back to life following the heat of the day, Burton's White Star Team gathered at the behest of Sam Willoughby, who announced his intention to get everybody drunk before they boarded the airplane to Manila in preparation for an even bigger drunk weekend to come. The team called preparations of this sort, a LIV-EX, an acronym for *liver exercise*.

Creed Taylor was still on the OD roster for duty watch at Camp

Chinamo. Though he wiggled and begged, nobody wanted to take the duty for him since it was an open secret that he was about to be whisked away from the Army for indefinite special duty and would therefore be unable to repay the favor and take *their* OD duty at a later date.

Burton dragged Chester Watson along since his Australian liver was widely held to be superior to the American livers. Therefore if anybody passed out and needed to be cared for, the duty would fall to Major Watson. His payment for such services would be all he could drink and eat. The evening portended to be very expensive for Willoughby who insisted on picking up the check.

The place Sam Willoughby picked to start off the bar crawl was inauspicious at best, located at the dead end of Rue du Roi Anou where it joined Quai de Fangum, the street that paralleled the Mekong River. Since it was downstream from Perfume Creek, where much of the city sewage flowed into the Mekong, the place didn't smell exactly like perfume. The bar itself was little more than a long plywood sheet with a few tall bar stools with slightly uneven legs. Colored lights looking as if they had been torn down from a house in the US at Christmas time were strung over the plywood plank in a futile attempt at ambience. The bar's single grace was it's close proximity to the Mekong River, downstream from the sewage outfall.

An old Cambodian bartender with a pockmarked face served them. He had bad dentures that looked as if they had come from a 1920 Sears and Roebuck catalog. The false teeth were deeply stained reddish brown from the betel nut he chewed and they clacked when he talked because they didn't fit properly.

"Where did you find this class joint, Sam?"

"Been commin' here off and on for a while. I suggest you drink the bottled booze, though, because they wash the glasses in the river and we are only about a sixty meters down from the sewage outfall."

Immediately after the first round hit the plank/table, Jimmy Paint showed up with Paul Gorman. Both were dressed well, which provided something of a shock to the rest of the group who wore, "old G. I." clothing, which was to say, a blend of worn out tropical clothes that were clean, but about as stained as they could get.

"You two look like choirboys on the way to confession." Chester Watson offered with good cheer, taking in Jimmy's slicked down hair.

"Lieutenant Taylor invited the Corsican woman, Charlotte to join us since he can't make it." Jimmy Paint said. "Goatman and I wanted to look a little better than we usually do if we're watching out for her."

"I'm sure Charlotte Sabon will want to sit here at the bar down from the sewer and swill suds with us." Burton suggested sarcastically.

Chester replied, feigning hurt. "Why not? Is she that high and mighty that she wouldn't let my mate Sam pick up the docket for her beer?"

Paint looked around. "This place really is a dump," directing his comment to Sam Willoughby, "I like it. It reminds me of the Reservation, but classier."

"Ah, I see." Burton said, getting the picture, "I smell Goatman in this. You told her to meet us here so that you and Jimmy could ogle her while you sluice down drinks and tell lies about Taylor."

Jimmy's eyes twinkled with delight. "Taylor's been telling her how great he is and now we can hear the lies and set her straight."

Willoughby ordered bottled Korean Soju for the second round, and specified Chamisul, a more expensive brand.

"They have Chamisul here?" Goatman looked surprised.

"They stock it because of me." Willoughby replied, and motioned to the bartender. "Send a drink to the lady at the end of the bar."

Burton looked at the bar girl, sitting by herself on one of the remaining stools, looking forlorn. She didn't seem to possess the natural aggressiveness of most of the Asian bar girls he'd seen. She wasn't pretty. Nice figure, just enough silk to cover the budding nipples, somewhere between sixteen and twenty-five years of age. The girl spoke rapid fire Cambodian to the barman.

"I love Thai women." WoFat crooned lovingly to the bar girl.

"I from Cambodia."

"That goes double for Cambodian women. Your voice like golden bell my heart." The girl seemed to clearly understand Willoughby's pidgin English.

Chester butted in. "Hold on, we're not going to sit here all night while this bar girl plays you for drinks. I had my heart set on warm beer and a blowjob at Rendezvous Des Amis.

"That place is too far out of the way." Willoughby argued.

Chester puffed up. "No place is too far away for a blow job."

Sam Willoughby seemed to shake off his momentary lust. "You're right, damn it. The local moonshine must be getting to my head."

"A round for the house!" Willoughby shouted, looked over Creed's shoulder toward the river, and added. "Look at that fine piece of occidental talent. I'll bet she can suck-start a B-52."

Goatman tried to calm Sam down because he could see where his friend was looking but Sam was shifting into high gear. "Come over here baby. I've something for you that's screaming your name."

Burton turned around and saw Charlotte Sabon walking toward them, seemingly oblivious of Sam's boisterous entreaties. Paint and Gorman were off their stools walking toward her.

Sam looked at Burton. "Did I just insult the guest of honor?"

"I'm sure she didn't notice." Burton replied dryly, getting off his stool to shake Charlotte's offered hand.

"Nice to see you again Mrs. – uh – Charlotte. May I introduce our host for the evening, Master Sergeant Sam Willoughby, man about town, king of cool."

Willoughby kissed her hand. "Enchanted."

Charlotte smiled. She wore an outfit that was something out of a Marilyn Monroe movie. Blouse with a few buttons open, discrete skirt that accentuated her curves and tall spike heels.

"I'm sorry for what I said back there." Sam said.

Charlotte took Sam's hand and laughed. "It's so nice to be the object of a handsome man's attention."

"You met my buddy, Chester Watson?"

"We met at a party at the Embassy." Charlotte said with mirth and a twinkle in her eye. "It's a pleasure to see you again, major."

Chester beamed. Sam's dignity had been restored. Jimmy Paint and Paul Gorman looked on paternally.

"Would you walk with me by the river, Captain Burton?" Charlotte asked, then turned to Paint and Gorman. "I'll keep an eye on your boss. Nothing bad will happen to him."

Officially dismissed, both Paint and Gorman stood there with bottles of beer in their hands, not knowing quite what to do.

Craig Burton walked to the river with Charlotte, leaving the other two behind. She took his arm.

"Aren't you concerned about appearances?" Burton asked.

"No, not anymore. I'm the scandal of Vientiane, a fallen woman. Then again I'm French and at least to some extent it's expected. *Menage et trois* is a French phrase after all."

Burton found himself blushing and the mere thought that the girl could do it so easily to him made him uncomfortable. He didn't say anything, just walked with her, taking in the sights and sounds.

The sun dipped toward the horizon and the long orange light reflected off the river. They walked silently as the sampans, houseboats and junks in the main current drifted south on the Mekong toward Viet Nam, six hundred miles away as the river slinked its serpentine path to the ocean.

Closer to the bank a small, lean boatman poled his vessel north against the current while his wife operated the stern oar and children directed the rudder.

"Look! Fishing birds," Charlotte said.

Half a dozen black cormorants perched on the bow gunwales of a slowly moving sampan. Small brass rings were fastened at the base of their necks. Their eyes searched the water hungrily. Then, spotting fish, two of them dived into the river and disappeared beneath the surface with a plunk. They each returned to the sampan and flapped aboard, choking on their catch, complaining that they were unable to swallow because of the brass rings. Their master swept the birds up and turned them upside down over a basket to disgorge the live fish. The unhappy birds, still hungry, went back to their perches to repeat the process.

"The ring will be removed on the seventh fish," Charlotte said in a melancholy voice. "It's what we do now with our Hmong and Lao these days. We are made to turn to them for our livelihood while keeping them captive, in a sense. We permit them to keep and eat the seventh fish, the seventh part of the crop they harvest. It will not go on forever."

"What's going on, Charlotte?"

A woman in a bar a block over began a crooning rendition in Thai. The music was very loud and it caused both of them to pause. They walked further along the river in search of a place where they could talk. As they walked they traded the crooning Thai for the chatter of Lao children at play. Over a dozen impetuous nine-year olds streaked down the grassy riverbank on makeshift sleds fashioned from cardboard boxes. At the edges of the sandbars, thousands of tiny speckled frogs jittered like popcorn whenever they overshot their mark and sloshed into the shallows.

Charlotte sighed. "Bruno Jospin is my father. He is an important man in Marseille."

"I've heard his name before. People speak of him but they don't do so lightly."

"He's my father. Don't judge him or me harshly, Captain—may I call you Craig?"

"Yes, you can call me Craig." Oh, brother, where is this going?

"Craig. I know things are different in America. My father, Bruno, sent me to Massachusetts to a Catholic boarding school so I could learn about America. I lived there three years."

"Did you like it?"

"I hated every day of boarding school. But I didn't let anyone know it. Not until this moment."

"And Bruno Jospin is part of the mafia?"

"Unione Corse? Yes, he is a big man in the Unione Corse and has been since before I was born. Some would say it is a mafia and some would say it is a brotherhood for mutual protection. Who is to say what is right? Maybe each is true."

The cormorants dove for more fish and were not allowed to eat once again. The symbolism was not lost on Burton. "When I was a kid the circus came to town. Elephants, fire-eaters, the big top, clowns, and another tent not so big. The little tent had lots of mirrors in it. Some made you look fat. Others made you look thin. It was a small maze and no matter where you looked, nothing was as it should be. The reflections were all real but they were distorted. That's how it is here."

The Corsican side of her screamed that she must lie. The lover in her whispered that the truth might promote their budding relationship.

"Like the fisherman who owns the cormorant, we control much of the opium that comes out of Laos. We buy it, transport it, refine it and then we sell it on the market at a large profit."

Burton interrupted, trying to separate Charlotte from the drug trade. "You mean Unione Corse."

"I am Unione Corse," Charlotte said tenderly. "I am part of the whole process that begins here and ends somewhere else."

Charlotte seemed to accept it all as a matter of course.

"The cormorant will soon take control of all the fish it consumes and when that comes there will be no need for the fisherman. The Laotians see the profit in the opium trade and will force us out unless we are careful."

"Then let it go."

116

There was steel in Charlotte's words. "I have heard that you are now part of the CIA. No longer in the Army. Was it your choice?"

"That was supposed to be a closely held secret. I don't think there are all that many secrets around here though." *After all, you are Lieutenant Taylor's mistress.* He felt for his pack of cigarettes but realized that he gave them to Wu Ming earlier. "Your situation and mine are not quite the same thing."

"Maybe not in your orderly world of God Bless America, but in my world, number four heroin is no different than Southern Comfort or Marlboro. There are growers, refiners, packagers, middlemen, distributors, and customers. The demand sets the price."

She set her jaw just so, and in doing so, she reminded him how he felt in the market the day before. Everything about her was special and seemed wonderful. For some reason he consciously deflected what she told him of her involvement in the drug trade.

"We have a monopoly on refining the opium into heroin. It's done in Marseilles. It's been our family monopoly for a long time. Turning opium into number four heroin is not an easy thing to do. The Chinese would like to do it here in Asia and keep the profit for themselves. You asked. That's what's going on. There is a struggle for power, and there is a lot of money in the balance."

She touched his hand tenderly. "Leave the army or whoever you work for. Come with me and work with us. At least try to. We could use a man with your strength. Your exploits are well known. Did you know that the North Vietnamese have a price on your head? Do you know how rare it is to find someone who can do what you and your men have done again and again?"

"You sound like an Army recruiter."

"Unione Corse is an army. It has generals, and it has captains. It even has privates. But it has one thing that your army doesn't have."

Burton turned toward her and looked at her intently.

"It has me." She intertwined her fingers in his.

"So first it was Taylor and now it's me? Did he turn you down when you tried to recruit him? Is that why you're moving on to me?"

"No, he accepted the offer."

Burton felt as though he'd been hit between the eyes by a two-by-four.

"So did Sergeants Paint and Gorman, the one you call Goatman."

117

They were approached in a different way, but yes. And you are the last.

"Sam Willoughby?"

"No, we don't need him."

"I think I need a drink or seven." Burton confessed.

Standing under a ginko tree, looking at the peaceful river and stars blinking to light in the evening sky he wondered what he'd do. In another world, on the banks of the Hudson River at West Point things seemed so clearer, so much more sharply defined.

SIXTEEN

Wednesday, 16 August 1961 -- 0330 HRS
81 Boulevard Circulaire,
Vientiane, Laos

Charlotte walked through the hallway from the door of the ostentatious French Colonial house, holding her shoes in her hand and set them near the wall. Without consulting the label, she opened a bottle of red wine from a rack, poured a glass and then lounged quietly in a wicker chair as she recalled the events of the evening. It was unlike anything that happened before. She felt transcendent in the moment.

Craig Burton stood before her as the river flowed behind him. Lanterns appeared here and there on the river boats like stars set against the inky black sky above. Even though she attended school briefly in America, her French prejudice was intact and she tended to look down on Americans. She took in the simple clothing he wore, his youth and at the same time, his age. She saw the puckered, welted scars on his cheek, the width of his neck, the way muscles in his jaws stood out without being grotesque, his eyes sharp and intense as cobra's eyes. Suddenly she realized the effect he had on her. He frightened her. It was a shock. Men didn't frighten Charlotte Sabon. Men on the Marseille waterfront doffed their hats with sincere respect. Her father ruthlessly pursued the aims of Unione Corse, the waterfront, and politics from the highest level to the lowest. She was proud of her reputation for being cold, fearless and under control. Never before did Charlotte feel the sort of power that Craig Burton projected unconsciously.

She scripted the evening from that point.

They went to the house he shared with the tall, bombastic Australian Military Attaché. The place smelled of sandalwood and soaped leather furniture with an undercurrent of gun oil. A man's house without the slightest hint of feminine influence was a challenge to her. Could she add her distinctiveness to it? They climbed the stairs and then he swept her in his arms as if she was weightless and carried her the rest of the way to his room, draped with mosquito nets, austere, just a foot locker and a large bed surrounded by a teak frame.

119

WHITE POWDER

Charlotte stood quietly, watching, as Craig uncorked the wine, Chateau d'Yquem Sauternes. The sweet wine was a nice touch but it didn't matter. She would have followed him home if he'd asked her to have a glass of river water from the turbid, malarial, Mekong. The night was inevitable, the wine a polite excuse to hide behind. Polite behavior was only a mask to shade her intentions.

She liked the effortless way he slipped the cork from the neck of the bottle. It was a smooth, easy pull, belying the requirement of force, the certain ripple of muscle in his forearm that was hidden by his sleeve.

Thinking of the strength in those arms brought Charlotte a step closer, an unconscious response of longing and want but she did not acknowledge the emotion. He poured the wine expertly into a glass, tilting it and lifting it as the liquid spilled from bottle to bowl and then handed her the vessel. His hand cupped the bowl of crystal; her fingers encircled the slender stem. Slowly she slid the glass from his fingers, watching his eyes the whole time, wondering if he would, at the last instant, cinch his fingers again on the glass and lean in and kiss her. He didn't.

"Thank you," she murmured, their fingers tenuously united on the glass. His smile was quick and heart wrenching. The dimple in his left cheek winking as if communicating that she was welcome. Then his fingers slipped free.

When he turned to take another glass from the cupboard for himself, Charlotte seated herself in a teak chair a few feet away, slightly disappointed in the lost moment. She chastised herself for not taking matters into her own hands, so to speak, and leaning into him for a kiss. She knew he would not refuse her. The moment was lost now. With a small sigh, she sipped thoughtfully, pushing her regrets away and refocusing on the slow burn radiating through her.

Her eyes rose to study Burton, wondering how and when he would ask her to make love, no to have sex. That's what it would be with this man. Pure sex. And she would take him; it would not be the other way around. She knew he would offer no pretty words to woo her, no false promises uttered. And then, he was in front of her, his hand held out for hers.

Simple. No words. No phony pretense. The look in his eyes said only, "Now." She placed her hand in his. Strong, callused fingers wrapped around hers and lightly pulled her to her feet. Keeping her hand in his, he led her wordlessly up the winding staircase to his room.

A large bed, encircled by a froth of white mosquito netting, was the focal point of the room. With a small squeeze to her hand, he released her and moved to the side of the bed, parting the netting.

Craig looked up from the bedding and she heard the breath leave his lungs in a silent whoosh. Charlotte had moved to the opposite side of the bed. He had looked up just in time to see the silk fabric of her evening gown slide from her body, nude beneath the dress. With a shrug, Charlotte moved aside the netting and stood beside the bed opposite him.

The single muted lamp cast its light on her, blending with the shadow. Charlotte's breathing, the slight rise and fall of breasts and belly the only movement. The play of light and shadow mesmerized her as all of her senses were focused.

Her still form, her quiet waiting was for him. There was nothing evocative or seductive in the pose. Her eyes conveyed her unspoken words. "Look at my body; it is yours because I'm going to give it to you."

His fingers began working the buttons on his uniform, shedding the strictures of his rank, of his training, of civilization. His hands worked automatically, by rote, as his eyes took in the feast Charlotte offered.

Her body was long and slender. Her face beautifully shaped, in proportion from the line of her jaw and the angle of her neck to her full, wide mouth and graceful nose. Her eyes were bright sparks in the subdued light. His eyes passed downward, slowly, appreciating her high, pert breasts, nipples erect, a young woman's waist and then the gentle sweep outward of her hips.

Charlotte was aware of her body, but only dimly as she took in the young officer's response to her nudity. His hands were steady and sure as he removed his shirt. His breathe quickening. His eyes dark as their gaze traveled slowly over her. When the shirt and trousers had all fallen, one by one, into an untidy heap on the floor, Charlotte felt her own breath quicken, her heart race.

His body looked trim and dark in shadow, the light behind him. Then he placed one knee on the mattress and stretched the expanse, his arm reaching for her, his fingers splayed to take her hand.

She stood frozen a moment, too long, and he stretched across the bed. The hand sliding around her waist and caressing down her hip and thigh to the back of her knee, pressing gently into the soft flesh, urging her onto the bed. She felt the leap of desire at the contact, her body suddenly alive. Her hand trembled as she reached for the sheet, meaning to pull it back and slide beneath the covering.

"No," Craig told her softly, taking her hand now and guiding her onto the bed with him.

Charlotte reclaimed the moment she had lost earlier in the kitchen, pushing against Craig's chest and settling beside him on her knees. It was her turn to look, to explore his body with her eyes and her hands.

His close-clipped hair was spiked beneath her fingers, she smiled at the feel of the nearly shaven skin around his ears and then the slight bristle of beard that shadowed his jaw and chin. She watched the intensity in his eyes as she touched him, his eyes locked on hers. Long fingers slid over his mouth, probing gently at his lips. He kissed her fingertips and held her hand for a moment to pull one errant finger into his mouth, sucking and then nipping softly. With a gasp and then a smile she pulled her hand free. A sharp tap on his nose with the injured digit was his punishment. For now.

Her fingers skimmed lightly down his chest, his hip and down his leg. She ignored the pull of his fingers, scooting free of his hands. And then she bent her body, rubbing her cheek over his chest, taking a nipple in her teeth tugging until she heard the hiss of his breath, releasing him and smiling to herself. Her kisses grazed his skin as she moved her attention down over his stomach.

Then her fingers stroked down the length of him, curling loosely for a couple strokes and then back to the feather light teasing of her fingertips. She listened to him groan as her lips followed her fingers. One kiss, two and then she took him into her mouth. The suddenness of it forced the breath from his lungs in a whoosh, his entire body strained towards her, towards the moist warmth engulfing him.

Just as suddenly, cool air flowed over him again. Charlotte raised her head and slid up next to him, her mouth joining his, her fingernails gently raking from his temples to the nape of his neck, interlacing and locking behind his head. She looked into his eyes, looking for his reaction to her as she straddled him and then began to lower her body onto his. His eyes widened for an instant as moist heat started engulfing him again, different, richer, silkier. Barely joined, she stopped. Her gaze never shifted.

The first intimate contact was held for a long moment. Charlotte's fingers, which slipped to the base of his neck, and her knees against his thighs, were the only other places that her body met his. She kept him poised, just at the entrance to her core, the promise of fulfillment beckoning. He began to wriggle beneath her and then his fingers dug into her hips, threatening to disrupt her control by force.

"No," she whispered, resisting the urging of his hands, then lowering herself onto him at her pace, slowly, taking him into her, her heat claiming him, bit by bit, clamping tight. Her soft belly lay against his. Her breath left her in a rush of pleasure as he pulled her tighter, filling her completely. The dance began in earnest then, her breasts moving on his chest, tremors rippling through her body.

For a while Craig was passive, receptive. Then his arms went around Charlotte, one over her shoulder, holding her tight, the other lower to her undulating hips, resting lightly, shaping to the curve as he studied the rhythm for a moment. Then he twisted, holding her close as he pulled her underneath him.

It was a maneuver Charlotte had allowed, despite her resolve to take and keep control of the interlude. Instead Charlotte gave herself over to this rare indulgence, closing her eyes as her senses absorbed everything happening to her. She let herself go, gave herself over to Craig, completely. Later her mind would query "Why?" She would have no answer. Only that it was a selfish moment, one purely for her own pleasure. Who would hold her accountable? No one.

No longer leading, her control lost, Charlotte relaxed. His weight held her pinned. He was still, holding her still. She felt his mouth on her face, on her closed eyes and then her lips. Dimly she heard music, the violin strains of Bach? Maybe Brahms? When had he put music on? Or had it been there all along? The pondering evaporated as Craig began to move, the rocking of their bodies quickening. Their breathing drowning out the musical notes. His hands tightened on her flesh as their desire peaked.

Wanting their climax to be together, Charlotte thrust up to meet him. She felt the spasms in him, knowing she wasn't near enough to match him. Her body bowed, drawing him deep and she opened her eyes to watch him. Above her she saw the oiled blue metal of an American pistol suspended from the headboard by its sweat-soiled leather sling holster. And she came to the top suddenly, surprisingly, shuddering against him and sharing the moment together.

They lay for a long time, no words. Just feeling. Mostly his hands moved over her, stroking her skin, tangling into her hair and then sliding up her face to trace her features with his finger. Feeling, molding like a blind man, seeing only with fingertips. Occasionally he kissed her face, tracing its contours with his lips. Her fingers traveled his back, learning the pattern of his spine, muscles and ribs, curving over his ass and lingering on the lean, hard flanks. Her lips gently kissing his shoulder, wherever she could easily reach without disturbing the languid sprawl of their bodies.

Charlotte lay awake for a long while, long after Craig's body had sought a position of comfort separate from hers, listening to her lover's slowed breath, interspersed with a few soft snores, as he slept. She dozed here and there and then at first light, rose, careful not to disturb the slumber of the man next to her.

Slipping silently back into her blouse, Charlotte shivered slightly as the cool silk caressed her skin, chilling sensation after the delicious warmth of Craig's hands and mouth. Holding in a sigh of regret, she looked down on his sleeping face, the angular features softened by sleep and the faint gray light of dawn.

Quiet as a ghost, she left.

Now, as she opened her eyes, she realized that from this morning on, she'd think of nothing but Craig Burton.

SEVENTEEN

Wednesday, 16 August 1961 -- 0800 HRS
"Sidney House", 2 Thadeua Road,
Sisattanak District,
Vientiane, Laos

Chester sat painting lead soldiers on a table by the foot of the staircase, wearing an undershirt and boxers. A Browning semi-automatic pistol hung from the stairway banister in a shoulder holster, within easy reach. He'd seen her leave as he was coming home and he waited until she was gone before he went into the sitting room. Unable to sleep, he painted his small, molded lead soldiers.

"Boring yourself to death is just a form of slow suicide." Chester said to himself as he set one small soldier down and picked up a molded lead Napoleon gun attached to a caisson that had not yet been painted.

The BBC broadcast was on the radio.

Burton walked downstairs, holding a suit case, dressed in a blue blazer and gray trousers, white shirt and striped tie.

"So you're a civilian now?" Chester asked.

"I think that's a secret."

After dipping blue paint onto his brush he commented, raising an eyebrow to Burton, "Keeping secrets from me now?"

Taking his meaning, Burton shrugged toward the radio. "What's happening?"

"East German troops are stringing wire around Berlin. They're building a wall around the city. The Brandenburg Gate is closed and the Communists are on the move. Word is they plan to starve Berlin and when the allies leave, roll tanks through the free part of the city. The East German border guards have orders to shoot anyone crossing from the east into free Germany."

Burton commented, "The Russians don't find it strange that all the people in West Germany aren't racing to take advantage of the great jobs and living arrangements in the Worker's Paradise?"

"I'm just telling you what the announcer said ten minutes ago." Chester was not his normally cheerful self.

"I'm off for the Philippines with the boys. I should be back in three or four days."

"You have a key." Chester said, focused on his painting. "Cheerio."

He didn't approve of Charlotte. She was far more dangerous than Burton could be at his most vicious.

Major Owen Piper, in Class A uniform, stood near a silver, twin-engine Beechcraft C-45G Expeditor with Air America markings on the fuselage as its engines coughed to life. Burton and his men drove up onto the tarmac in two Jeeps driven by motor pool duty drivers.

The Air America Pilot commented to Piper, "The run of good weather may be past. I think we're okay for Manila but there is weather moving in."

"Your customers are here." Piper pointed to Burton and waved. Burton waved back.

"You're looking every bit like soldiers trying to be civilians." Major Piper noted with good humor to the group. He motioned Burton to one side as the other men dropped the luggage for the crew to pack and boarded the aircraft.

"Watch your back, Craig. For the record, I'm not comfortable with this whole sheep-dip thing."

"The Army Chief–of–Staff threw us to the wolves, Owen. I didn't have anything to say about it."

"I know. I have a bad feeling about all this. That's why I came out to see you off."

Burton shook Owen's hand and it ended in a hug.

"Did I tell you how much I appreciated you saving my ass at Hudson High?" Owen asked.

"Five dozen times, Owen." Burton said and then tapped him on the back. "See you when I get back – drinks on me."

"That would be a first," Piper said, "I'll hold you to it. We'll have all of the paperwork ready for you and your guys to separate from active service when you get back."

Slightly deflated, Burton boarded on the aircraft without further comment as the pilot shouted down to the co-pilot, "Kick the tires and light the fires!"

Burton found a seat. An In-Flight Ration rested on the thin web seat cushion. He picked it up, sat down and buckled up. As the engines spun to life, he opened the box lunch and took inventory. It contained a can of compressed, desiccated ham and lima beans from a C-Ration, a can of fruit cocktail from an Air Force In-Flight ration, canned crackers and a ration supplement sundries pack that included a plastic spoon, a pack of unfiltered Lucky Strike cigarettes with half of the smokes missing, matches, soluble coffee packet, chewing gum, a can opener, salt and pepper packets. It had been picked over. There was nothing worse on the planet than the ham and lima beans. Even gooks who would eat anything under normal circumstances rejected the ham and lima beans that the GI's dumped. He took the chewing gum and set the ration box on the deck of the aircraft as the twenty year-old Beechcraft began to taxi toward the runway.

"Welcome to Air America flight zero to Manila, My name is Skip Parnell and I'll be your pilot. My co-pilot is Fred Birch. We're flying tail number N7950C today because our sister ship and regular ride, N7951C, has clogged carburetors from bad gas. It remains to be seen whether or not this load of gas is bad too." Parnell shouted back to the passengers, not apparently paying any attention to the runway.

The flight crew was in good humor. Parnell and Birch wore white aircrew shirts. The co-pilot, Birch, wore a crushed pilot's hat. Parnell wore a red baseball cap with a US Marine Corps anchor, globe and eagle pinned to the face.

The Twin Beech roared and rattled over the South China Sea due east toward Manila and Burton had a moment to think about Charlotte, about what she told him of the decision his men made behind his back and of their night together. Was she part of the deal? The honey pot that attracted the bees? Is that how it worked with Creed Taylor?

Burton looked across the aisle to Lieutenant Taylor who smiled and handed a bottle of Old Harper to him. Burton toasted Taylor with the bottle, took a draw and handed it back, wiping the mouth of the bottle with his sleeve. "Thanks Creed."

He did not struggle through the rigors of the US Military Academy to be bootstrapped to the CIA. However he rationally thought through the problem, there wasn't much of an option. The invitation from the Unione Corse was another problem and he didn't know whether he'd be in more trouble if he reported the overture to the Monkey King or less. And what of his men? What if they really had turned as Charlotte said so confidently last night?

WHITE POWDER

Maybe Manila would give him time to think about it and an opportunity to speak with Jimmy Paint one-on-one. He felt closer to Jimmy than to any of the rest. Sam Willoughby wasn't part of it, so he needed to insulate Sam from any discussion.

Burton pulled a dog-eared copy of Robert W. Service poetry from the pouch in the seat back in front of him and tried to read through it over the loud drone of the engines. Before he read a page, Creed Taylor sidled across the aisle and spoke to him.

"How long has it been since you've been to Olangapo?"

Burton searched his mind. "Maybe two years, but we're going to Manila, Ermita District to be exact. If we don't like it there, we can always take a Jeepny to Olangapo for enhanced debauchery."

"When I was at headquarters this morning I heard Group Tactique Nord was hit by Pathet Lao up near Sam Thong about twenty-two klicks northwest of Pha Khao. Good weather is never good. It brings out the dinks."

"Did they get Rusty Kramer?" Burton asked.

"I don't know."

"Your girlfriend Charlotte showed up last night for Sam's Liv-Ex."

"She said she was going to drop by and say hello." Creed replied. "Did you guys talk about anything?"

"Just the weather." Burton lied.

Burton waited a moment and then went on, "She's married, right?"

Taylor gave him an evasive glance, shifted his gaze and said, "Yeah, but I don't think she and her husband do anything together."

"The CIA Station Chief said that her husband is in the white powder business, and I don't mean wheat flour."

Creed smiled, "I never heard that."

"Watch your ass." Burton admonished. Creed saluted him with the Old Harper and went back to his seat.

Fedor Ochoa, a short, pot bellied, lop-eyed, fifty-five year-old Filipino watched the passengers disembark at Naval Air Station Stanley Point from the Air America Beechcraft. The five soldiers in civilian clothing were an eclectic, fiercely individualistic group. Their look varied but their clothing was utilitarian, muted and, bulky enough to conceal weapons and ammunition from casual inspection. What they all had in common was the toughness, the wary eyes, leathery skin and the cool readiness of professional soldiers who had seen considerable combat.

Kennedy said that he planned to meet them at the airport but since he wasn't there and an hour had passed, Burton decided they'd head to the Ermita District and wait for Kennedy to find them. They didn't have hotel reservations but each of them had money to burn so there was no problem paying for the best Manila had to offer.

"We'll go to Ermita and look around. The better hotels are in Makati. We can always head that way if we want to." They all agreed with Burton.

Fedor made a call from a pay phone and then followed the soldiers in a brightly colored taxi, called a jeepny that he drove with reckless abandon.

Once the American soldiers paid off their hired jeepny and started off on foot, Fedor drove to the courthouse, transferred to a black staff car and picked up Kennedy, who wore aviator sunglasses and dressed in a white silk safari-style suit.

It didn't take Fedor long to find the soldiers again. He pointed to them and looked over his shoulder at Walter Kennedy, lounging in the back seat, smoking expensive British cigarettes. "Dangerous men, Fedor." Then he motioned Fedor to park the American-made car.

Fedor double-parked, got out and scuttled off through the crowd toward the soldiers who were walking toward Lim Boulevard. Walter Kennedy put a placard in on the dashboard of the car 'National Bureau of Investigation, Republic of the Philippines.'

When he positioned himself to his satisfaction, Fedor doffed a little cap from his head and approached them. The soldiers walked past him without giving him more than a glance. He turned and had to run to keep up with their stride. The soldiers spoke quietly among themselves and he thought he could overhear if he got close enough but that didn't work either.

"I speak English!" Fedor shouted from behind them in thickly accented English.

"Then you know what go to hell means." Creed Taylor hissed to him from a mouth that clenched a smoldering cigar.

"I'll be your guide for ten pesos. My little sister is beautiful and she has many friends."

Goatman spat tobacco at Fedor's sandaled feet but Ochoa moved quickly enough to avoid the jet of foul liquid that splattered on the uneven pavement. "Pimp."

"I know many things." Fedor said enthusiastically, "I can help you.'

The soldiers kept walking and Fedor stopped, looking at them with frustration as they disappeared into the mass of people. He darted through an alley to cut them off.

The tall Americans stood out over the short Filipinos, allowing Fedor the luxury of maneuvering once more to place himself in front of them.

Burton passed Fedor again, giving him a brotherly pat on the shoulder. "Do you know an American named Walter Kennedy who seems to know what's going on around here?"

Fedor was shocked he would be asked such a direct question about his esteemed and most secretive employer but he concealed his amazement. "Yes I do. He goes to a bar."

Burton took a deep breath. "This guy will take us to a great bar."

"About time," Paint said.

Fedor turned around and gave Walter Kennedy a not-so-covert wave. Burton took it in, glanced back through the crowd to a black Chrysler sedan, pulling slowly from the curb into traffic.

Fedor led them two blocks and then they turned took three steps down from the street into the Lotus Garden. A heavy, dirty, green velvet curtain was pulled aside by a fat, greasy Filipino soldier with a riot gun to reveal a stage behind the bar. Roughly thirty young Filipino women, ages fifteen to twenty danced with greater or lesser degrees of interest. They wore three-inch platform shoes; electric blue bikinis and each had a round plastic tag with a number printed on it. The music thundered with an ear splitting beat.

The soldiers found a seat and took in the action. Paint looked at Goatman with a measure of appreciation. This was more to his liking. Creed Taylor and Sam Willoughby were fixed on a tall girl wearing a red beret and nothing else. She had one foot on the stage and the other on the bar, engaging in intercourse with a San Miguel beer bottle held by an Australian patron. The boisterous crowd cheered her on without restraint.

Goatman leaned toward Willoughby and observed, "The patrons are all armed with handguns."

The master sergeant smiled and waved him off, "Of course they are. Welcome to the P. I., Goatman."

Taylor echoed Goatman's observation, "Hey, everyone's packing heat."

"No shit." Paint replied. His eyes were now also fixed on the tall girl wearing the beret.

Four paces behind the soldiers, Fedor Ochoa took a seat next to three Filipino gangsters, who watched the soldiers intently.

Walter Kennedy walked up to the gangsters, calmly smoking a cigarette, and said, "You wouldn't be planning on doing anything to those fine young men would you? Do you know how rare it is to find heterosexual men operating out of the American Embassy? It's almost an epiphany. You can appreciate that was something I had to see for myself to believe."

The oldest of the gangsters asked, "Who are you?"

Another gangster whispered something in the ear of the older thug. His demeanor turned from one of belligerent arrogance to humility in the blink of an eye, "We do not want trouble. We're minding our own business but I would be happy to buy the house a drink in the spirit of brotherhood."

He grabbed a wad of pesos from his pocket and handed them to the Mamasan who was standing near, hopefully.

Walter Kennedy snatched the money before Mamasan could take it and thrust the wad into his pocket. He smiled inwardly, walked up to the soldiers and sat at their table, "I am the Special Assistant to the President of the Philippines and you men are American soldiers from what I have been told." He winked at Burton.

"News travels fast." Burton observed phlegmatically, seeing Fedor bobbing and prairie dogging for a better look from where he stood behind Kennedy.

Two National Bureau of Investigation agents and half a dozen uniformed police officers from the Manila City Hall Detachment walked into the bar. Kennedy nodded to a Pinoy Gunman who took the stage. He wore dirty jeans, worn out tennis shoes, a t-shirt ten sizes too large, a small white towel over his left shoulder and he had a chrome Colt .45 Commander stuck in his waistband under the shirt.

The music stopped, the girls huddled back and the Pinoy Gunman made an announcement. "By order of His Excellency, the Governor of Luzon this establishment will close in five minutes and anyone remaining on the premises will be arrested."

The crowd voiced its displeasure but they began to leave all the

131

same.

Kennedy turned to the soldiers, "May I inquire what your plans might be for this evening?"

Goatman spoke for the group. "We planned to get drunk and laid, not necessarily in that order."

"Major Balagtas!" Kennedy went into action, "I want everybody out, I want the music turned on, I want the girls to dance, I want four cases of San Miguel for these visiting Congressmen here, I want the door locked and I want Remy and Baby on the front door until I come back tomorrow morning. Angelo can cover the back. Sigue! Sigue!"

Major Balagtas responded. "You have found no evidence of crime?"

"Yes," Walter Kennedy pronounced gravely. "Arrest Numbers 12, 71, and 108, charge them with whoring and hold them in my office at the courthouse."

"Yes sir."

Kennedy turned back to the soldiers and leaned on the table shared by Jimmy Paint and Goatman with both hands, "You can also appreciate that if they love me well enough, they are not whores but Madonnas in need of a manager." He paused pointedly. "This establishment is yours for the evening. Do as you wish but remember two things. Sometime next week I want 5,000 rounds of factory hardball in my office at the American Embassy in Vientiane and second, if you kill anything, let it be yourselves, understood?"

The soldiers all nodded. Kennedy nodded, winked again at Burton and then he left with his entourage. The music began and the girls started dancing again.

"Fuck!" Creed said with sincere appreciation.

Fedor edged closer to Burton. "My master would see you tonight?" It was phrased as a question and in light of the large number of available companions it was a question that Burton could have answered in either the affirmative or negative.

Burton made a move to follow Walter Kennedy and the dancers who had been taken into custody but Fedor shook his head and whispered. "Not now, later tonight." Fedor wetted the tip of a pencil with his tongue and wrote an address on a soiled scrap of paper. He handed the paper to Burton.

The brightly painted taxi stopped in front of a large colonial mansion

132

outside town. Burton paid the driver of the jeepney and stepped out. The taxi sped into the darkness. Burton melted into the jungle fringe at the same time, blending completely with the shadows within shadows in the oily blackness of the moonless night.

He did what he'd been trained to do, moving through the heavy undergrowth slowly and silently, spreading the foliage gently, bending it back, traversing the jungle as he did so.

A band of manicured grass stretched between the heavy jungle growth and the mansion. Lights illuminated the lawn providing a false sense of security. The house was magnificent, of Spanish design, two stories, large enough to house a battalion of soldiers.

Filipino sentries armed with American made M-2 carbines passed at intervals. Burton timed them and then moved across the open ground. Suddenly, he realized he'd been too careless. Somebody had him. He extended his middle digit toward a shadowed figure behind a window on the second story and noticed an open door on a tiled veranda on the ground floor.

The broad French door was open, spread wide and he simply walked into the mansion from the veranda.

The decor of the mansion screamed opulence gone berserk. King Louis IV meets Dorothy Gail as they both hold hands and walk through the Land of Oz. Burton walked quietly and carefully through the living area of the mansion, his clothing damp and limp from the humidity outside and the moisture that transferred from the leaves he passed through. He slid a Colt .45 semi-automatic pistol from his waistband and held it near his thigh.

Gilded frames held disintegrating oil portraits, the lives of the illustrious images cut short by the pervasive humidity. The furniture appeared to have been carved by a master. It was mahogany, upholstered by expensive European damasks and Jacquard brocades. A tarnished brass bust of an attractive Asian woman rested on one stand, a Tibetan rattle crafted of a human femur with a baby's skull attached by a lacquered leather harness perched for display on another.

The air was heavy with cloying incense.

Burton spotted a marble top table with a mahogany humidor centered on the marble. He walked to it shyly and lifted the lid of the humidor. The cigars were lined up neatly. He selected a likely candidate, withdrew the stogie, clipped the end and put a match to it. It had been soaked in tea and laced with vanilla. There was no doubting that Walter Kennedy knew Asian cigars.

Burton puffed the cigar to life, expelled vapor and through the blue-tinted smoke, he saw Walter Kennedy walk into the room nonchalantly.

"Nice work if you can get it." Burton commented with a confidence he did not feel.

"I see you found the cigars."

Kennedy headed for the bar and nodded toward the bottles standing like stalwart soldiers on shelves ready to sacrifice themselves to Kennedy's tastes. "Want one?"

"I don't drink on duty." Blowing a mouth full of blue smoke to the ceiling where it was picked up and dissipated by a slowly moving ceiling fan.

"I only drink on duty." The Kennedy replied with warmth in his voice. "But then again, I am always on duty."

"I'm not sure why I'm here."

"If I didn't want you here, I would have had the dogs patrolling the grounds the way they usually do. You're an invited guest and I wanted to make you comfortable. People like you never want to come through the front door. Hell, I never like to walk through the front door and I live here. So maybe we understand each other."

"I heard you made a connection with the girl." Kennedy appeared distracted. He was looking for a bottle. Then he found it and lifted it from the shelf. He opened it with a lack of ritual.

"What girl?"

"What girl? You're the soul of innocence. I'm going to promote you for the evening, Burton. *Now you're a General.*" Kennedy laughed as if at a private joke. "The fucking girl! The French-Corsican drop-dead beautiful daughter of Bruno-fucking-Jospin. And wife, God love you, Burton, the fucking wife of Jacques Sabon, that you bedded." He toasted Burton's success silently with the bottle.

Burton eyed Kennedy narrowly but remained silent.

Kennedy poured himself a stiff drink. "I haven't been sober for the last five or six years—at least that long. And to be honest with you, General, sobriety is not all that appealing."

He took a long sip and motioned to three comfortable leather chairs arranged around a zebra skin rug that centered a conversation area. Then he walked back into the bar, pried the cap off of a bottle of Coca-Cola and brought it for Burton along with half a bottle of Bushmills for himself.

Burton sat and so did Kennedy.

"I envy you a French woman. I really do. The Vietnamese speak their version of French but they can't curse effectively in French. I love to hear an honest-to-Christ Marseille woman curse at me in French in the throws of pleasure. Cursing in French has an elegance you can't capture in any other language. It's like wiping your ass with a silk scarf or the Russian flag, depending on the mood." Kennedy offered a silent salute with this bottle.

Burton took a drink of the cola. Walter Kennedy swallowed the Bushmills.

"It must have been a million years ago but somebody told me that watching politics in Laos is like watching chameleons making love. I told him I didn't understand and he told me I would one day. And he added that on that day I would have been in Asia too long."

"You've been here too long." Burton said. "We *know* that we're tilting with windmills."

Kennedy snorted. "You don't know what you're tilting with, General. That's why you're here with me tonight." He waved around the absurdly eclectic room with his glass. "Yep, I thought I'd strike it rich here and in Asia. Then I learned the hard way that the only way for a white man to become a millionaire in Asia is to start out a billionaire. I learned a lot about women too. My first wife was a poor woman, a Khmer. I thought she'd be grateful for what I could do for her and for her family financially. After three subsequent marriages, I realized that an Asian wife's loyalties belong to her parents, her brats from a previous marriage to a scoundrel who deserted her, any remaining blood relatives, the family goldfish and me—in that order."

Walter Kennedy lit a cigarette with a shaking hand. "I am a slow learner, General, but I ain't no liar, which, is why I frequently find myself having to think about Las Vegas. In Las Vegas they got this whole shit down so cold that they can call it shorthand and the one word they use to sum up the bullshit is 'rolling.' Every time in your life you find yourself in Las Vegas, and you hear some dealer say, 'rolling' then bet two dollars in memory of me and then press that motherfucker and I swear to you—."

He got up and walked, staggering slightly around the house while he spoke pouring another drink as he strided, downing it in one gulp. "I've been rolling, General. I have been rolling hard and I've got one big caper left in me. Maybe one or two. There are a hundred things you don't know about this shit going down in Laos and maybe two you do know about so ask me, General. And I'll tell you the truth."

He sat down hard across from Burton and thought about what he said. "Or maybe I'll lie to you. I'm not sure I can tell the difference."

"Why do you bother, Walter? You must have the cash to blow out of here to anywhere you want."

"I want you to remember me when this shit is over and I have been killed in your crusade because this is the bottom line. Life always comes down to this, either you want to believe in our essential spark of shared divinity, or you want to succumb to our human insecurity. And either way your conscience lets you slice it, the main thing is to earnestly do what is right at the time. So we'll stay here and we won't run to Rio and sit on the beach and watch the girls go by. We'll talk about this mess we're both in. That's what we'll do tonight."

Kennedy gestured expansively with his bottle and then charged a glass of Irish whiskey, sipped this time. Kennedy set the bottle next to the chair.

Burton looked at Kennedy without any hint of insolence as the CIA man began what he considered to be a teaching moment. "There was a tribe of monkeys living on an island ruled by a monkey king. One monkey discovered a treasure chest at the bottom of the sea surrounding the island. The treasure chest was too heavy for one monkey to recover, so he appealed to the monkey king for help. The monkey king thought for a moment. Probably he scratched his balls the way we see a monkey do, and then he came up with a plan. He decided he would grab the other monkey's tail, then that monkey would grab another monkey's tail, and they would get all the monkeys to form a chain so the monkey at the end could hoist the treasure. This is what he planned, but it didn't work out very well. When the last monkey grasped the treasure chest, the monkey chain could not bear the weight. They all tumbled head over heels into the sea and drowned."

Burton weighed the words, trying to figure out where Kennedy was going.

Kennedy continued. "The freedom of the Laotian people is like that treasure chest. A false guru is like that monkey king. False teaching is like that monkey king's plan. The sea is a sea of suffering. The island is

136

an island of mistaken belief. Unless you know how to escape the island, and unless you know how to swim across the sea, please learn to beware of monkey business."

"Hm." It was the only comment Burton could muster. Kennedy tried to tell him something but the prose was lost on him.

"What about the third option? Isn't that the policy in Laos now?" Burton finally spoke and Kennedy seemed pleased that it might turn into a debate.

"Sure, America doesn't want to use nuclear or conventional forces to defend its interests because that means American service men and God forbid American civilians, stand a chance of dying. For the record, that's bad during an election year. The third option requires that we rely on special, elite clandestine forces like yourself, General, to recruit, train and arm indigenous tribal forces to protect our interests and counter any annoying guerrilla movements. In short, we use mercenaries to fight our battles for us and let somebody die for our crusade." He lit a cigarette as an interlude. "How fucking vain-glorious can you possibly get?"

Kennedy took a sip. "I think your new boss, Keene is jerking us both off.

"Can you get to the point?" Burton asked.

"Ok! Let's start up country in Luzon. Manila, shall we? We've got to begin your briefing somewhere. Let's talk about this place."

Kennedy reached down, grabbed the Bushmills and topped his glass. Then he drank half the glass with one gulp. "This place is one big sewer. The American Foreign Service officers are partying at Spartacus, which is on Roxas Boulevard directly across the street from the Embassy. Spartacus has lady boys instead of girls. The Marine Guard is happy at the Firehouse and the spies are all up on Neptune Street. None of the white powder business is run out of the Australian Embassy, the Kingdom of Oz. They're into the flesh trade. And they don't mix with the Chinese who run the white powder game. Not at all."

Burton wondered whether or not playing both ends against the middle had begun to bother Kennedy's conscience.

"I always thought the flesh game was more interesting than the white power business but maybe that's because I'm a pervert. The better girls are sent to Makati, to a place called Nightwatch, which is secretly owned by the Chinese. The second stringers go to the Firehouse, which the Oz Embassy owns and the third stringers get exported. The really good ones are sold to the highest bidders—usually Binodo Chinamen who do white powder business at a very high level with the Frenchmen and Corsicans who are very busy in Laos, Burma, Thailand and Viet Nam.

Kennedy took a tablet and wrote on the paper for Burton. "My Manila girlfriend was Miss Cotobato City. I stole her from the Governor of Mindanao. She was a police captain's daughter. Then she was in the movies. Sometimes I miss her now that I am in Laos so much."

Walter Kennedy smiled in reminiscence and fondled the paper with a name and phone number on it. "But not too much. She tended to roll around in her sleep and it disturbed me. It got to be a chore tying her up and then untying her." He smiled broadly, sipping his whiskey. "She knows a lot about the white powder business and she'll tell you about any of that you may need to know." He began to offer the paper to Burton, had second thoughts, wadded it up and slipped it into his pocket. "There are things I can't part with."

Kennedy stood again and walked around the room with jerky movements like a pugilist sleepwalking. "Laos is a small country. The Philippines is even smaller in its fashion. Everybody knows everybody else. That's why you need women to help you if you want to understand the white powder game. A Chinese woman is ok. Or a Corsican, or a female Corsican if you could ever find one." Kennedy smiled knowingly and lighted yet another Dunhill cigarette with a gold tip with his twenty-four karat gold lighter.

"Charlotte?"

Kennedy snorted, walked behind the bar and pulled out a green canvas bag. From the bag he plucked a Sykes-Fairbairn knife in a leather sheath. He unsheathed the knife and began to play with it while he spoke.

"Does your mother know how to recruit an asset, General? Fuck no. There aren't very many groups that know the clandestine skills, and we'll call it tradecraft. Think about the essential skills it takes to mount an extra-legal operation, to have somebody killed, to motivate a crowd to righteous anger and do what it does when societies are in flux, when power is unclear and available to be grabbed and shaped and molded into a new state."

"I'm not a spy." Burton affirmed.

"Of course you aren't, you kill them off with the precision of a single thrust." Kennedy demonstrated with his knife. "I admire kinetic war! Ordnance on target and if we miss the target, oops."

138

Walter Kennedy reached into a bureau drawer in a mahogany credenza, dropped the knife into the drawer and pulled out a Browning High Power 9 millimeter semi-automatic pistol, dropped the magazine into his other hand and worked the slide absently. Then he set the pistol down, fiddled with his cigarette, ground it out, lit another and picked up the pistol again. "Say you want to overthrow a government like Diem's in Saigon and put a new one in because the bastard is out of control and he's screwing around with the Buddhists. A little bird told me that might happen next year. Providing that the bird is right, how would you do it? Who does this for you so your hand remains unseen? God forbid we can't take credit for cleaning up the mess we started."

"You need to find an agent provocateur, an operative you can send to incite a target group to action for purposes of entrapping or embarrassing them. Do you look for a person of that stripe among shoe salesmen and shopkeepers? They go to the store every day. Students go to classes. Maybe they're good for one riot or something, but they've got career dreams and are in a hurry to strike the establishment and then move on and become pediatricians or gynecologists or pediatric gynecologists. Where do you find people who have these skills?"

Kennedy got tired of fiddling with the handgun and he slid it back into the credenza and sat unsteadily in his chair. "If you're a foreigner, your capacity to make things happen in the streets is very limited. Maybe you turn to the underworld. That's why the CIA worked very effectively with Corsican syndicates in Europe and those bastards really have a horse in the race in Laos. They use the same tradecraft that we do. They employ the same techniques and share our values of mission before morality. Follow me?"

Burton had a sinking suspicion that Charlotte was going to be right in the middle of the whole mess that Kennedy was explaining. He nodded numbly.

Then he nodded off. Kennedy slumped in his chair.

Burton checked him. He had passed out. Burton picked up his silk bush jacket and draped it over Walter Kennedy's skinny frame.

After that, he stood uncomfortably in the living room decorated with Walter Kennedy's curiosities, not quite knowing what to do next.

Feeling eyes on the back of his neck, he turned. A pallid, willowy Vietnamese woman with long ebony hair and large black eyes stood in a hallway. The white silk dress she wore bore elegantly embroidered Mai

139

flowers. She was somewhere between eighteen and twenty-five years of age. Burton couldn't render a more accurate guess.

"Walter often sleeps in his chair. Sometimes I have a servant move him to his bed. Sometimes not." Her words were intoned musically in accented English. "I'm Mr. Kennedy's secretary, he calls me Mai and you can call me that too."

Burton nodded.

"There's a guest room made up for you on the upper floor."

EIGHTEEN

Thursday, 17 August 1961 -- 0710 HRS
"The Bluffs" 1 de Todos dos Santos Street
Paranaque City,
Republic of the Philippines

Burton slept soundly through the night and woke to an erotic dream. Charlotte lay between his legs, her velvet mouth taking him in deeply. It felt about as close to heaven as he thought he could get. Slowly he became aware that the dream wasn't a figment of his imagination. It had that quality that wasn't present in the ethereal musings of slumber. An expert worked his shaft and about the same time as he awoke completely, he finished.

Mai, Kennedy's secretary, rose from his bed, smiled beguilingly and trotted out of his bedroom, completely naked.

Burton felt guilt mixed with bewilderment and sat up in bed getting his head on straight when Walter Kennedy walked into the room.

"Good morning. There's nothing like a little release in the morning to start things out on the right foot." Kennedy held a drink in one hand, ice clinking against the crystal and a cigarette in the other.

"Haven't you ever heard of coffee?" Burton asked in a raspy morning voice, pulling the sheet to cover himself.

"Sure. I've heard of it." Kennedy sat on the foot of Burton's bed. "But why drink java when there's a nip of old Ireland available?" He stood, stubbed out his cigarette in an ashtray on a dresser and said, "We've got a long day, General. There are things we need to cover before you rejoin your men."

Without reply, Burton got out of bed and trotted to the water closet.

"Where are my manners? Shit, shower and shave and I'll have the staff whip up some breakfast. Steak ok? Say, medium-rare? Bar-b-qued steak and three or four eggs with buttered toast?" Kennedy said on his way out of the room.

After Burton pulled himself together, he walked downstairs, wandered a few hallways and located the kitchen.

Burton couldn't smell of steak cooking.

141

WHITE POWDER

Kennedy sat at a table with a drink in front of him. His cigarette smoldered in an ashtray as he read the newspaper. "Nothing above the fold worth reading. Khruschev's threatening to bury us—*again*. The Communist Krauts are walling up Berlin. Same old bullshit." Kennedy commented.

"You offered breakfast?"

"Sorry." Kennedy said though he didn't sound sorry to Burton. "We don't have steaks or eggs but the cook is whipping you up a bowl of soup."

A short Filipino woman who couldn't possibly have been a year shy of eighty shuffled into Kennedy's dining room as if on queue with a bowl of tepid noodle soup and a cup of coffee on a tray.

Burton was starved, his appetite whetted by the offer of steak and eggs. Even yesterday's warmed-up noodle soup sounded good. He sat down and decided to try the coffee. Burton slurped in some of the scalding hot coffee and spit it back into the cup. "This coffee tastes as if it was brewed from old socks and turpentine."

"The staff steels me blind." Kennedy said by way of excuse while reading the paper, absently turning a page. "I don't drink coffee so it might be ersatz. In fact, I'm almost sure it is. The booze is genuine though and the noodle soup might be ok."

Burton sampled the soup warily and found it to be good. He told himself that almost anything would taste good. He folded the soggy noodles into his mouth with chopsticks and then he drank the broth.

"You are here for an education and I'm no teacher." Walter Kennedy stood up and filled his glass with the remnants of a bottle of Bushmills and then he called for his cook. "Maria, more Bushmills, god-damn-it!"

He took a drink and then spoke, "Don't pussyfoot around with anybody in Asia. If people are going to help you in Laos, they have got to be getting wet titty. I mean big, juicy, long-nipple wet-titty. Even then, with a lot of cash, they will betray you unless you're careful. Giving money to the Royal Lao types is like pouring perfume on a pig."

From the tone of his voice, it seemed he had been having trouble with the Laotian government recently.

"Sly bastards." He muttered under his breath.

"Or pouring Bushmills down the throat of a drunk?" Burton added.

"Don't be bitter with me about the damned steak and eggs, for Christ's sake."

"You delivered dishwater soup and chamber pot coffee."

"I also told you that I am a liar but I'm not lying now. Prince Boun Oum runs the white powder business south and the Red Prince, his brother runs it north to China. The Red Prince cut a deal with an up-and-coming warlord in Burma named Kun Sa." Kennedy tried to get things back on track.

Burton said, "Creed Taylor, the guy you *wanted* to recruit out from under me grew up in Burma."

"You don't say? There was no *trying*. I recruited the lot of you. You read the orders from the Army Chief-of-Staff." Kennedy walked around to his chair, sat down and unfolded a map, sliding it over so Burton could look at it. It was a map of central Laos. "The Outfit is setting up landing strips all through Central Laos and they have the best of motives, but it won't keep the Communists from coming south in the end and it will facilitate the white powder business." His cigarette ash spilled onto the paper and he brushed it away. "Washington doesn't understand the dynamics and they won't listen so I don't really care. Fuck 'em."

"The Hmong in Sam Thong and Long Tieng? Yeah, I know about that. The money is about supplying the Hmong Army in the field." Burton replied.

"You know what I'm saying so don't be coy. This ain't a bingo game or taffy pull at St. Mary's Parish Church and we take our allies where we find 'em. Our allies against the commies grow the poppies and the Corsicans turn the opium into heroin for the European and American markets. I'm saying that your fuck-buddy—and a fine ass it is—has a father who runs the entire Laotian export market for the Corsican Mafia and God knows what else he has those wicked Marseilles rat claws into."

Kennedy took another sip from his crystal tumbler and howled for Maria again.

"None of those Lao politicians with property and servants is above corruption. Some of them are greedier than others and they want to keep what they've stolen. General Phoumi Nosavan is about the worst. Kun Sa is emerging as the dominant warlord up in the Shan States, very cunning, a survivor, and one of those people who make it his business to know what is going on around him, like me. However, that cocksucker wants to unbalance the whole damned arrangement we have with the Corsicans. I'm leaking word that he's a commie plant."

Morning rain began in earnest and the thundershower blasted down, rattling the inside of the mansion. The breeze kicked up and the windowpanes creaked. It roused Kennedy slightly and he looked through rheumy eyes toward Burton, "I've been to the Vietnamese central highlands where they refine some of the crude #3 powder. Not the Corsicans, the Khun Sa's Laotian-Burmese unholy pact. This time of year it looks like a sopping wet cross between Bayonne, New Jersey and a truck stop casino in the South Dakota boondocks. The Vietnamese can't compete yet, so it's a Corsican enterprise.

The Laotians want to cut the Corsicans out completely. The Chinese want the Corsicans in the game when it's convenient. Laotians won't do business with the Chinks because of America's pressure to keep communism out of Laos. It's all complicated and made worse because everybody in the CIA is a professional anti-Communist. I guess that includes me when it comes to Khun Sa, and he's not even a commie unless he reads my newspaper and decides to turn coat. It is confusing."

Burton scratched his brow unconsciously. Everything came back to the Corsicans, and by extension, to Charlotte.

A short, muscular Filipino man in chauffeur's livery appeared at the kitchen door. Kennedy set his glass on the table and snatched a silver hip flask from a cabinet, checking its contents with a studied eye.

"Get your gear, General, we're blowing out of this rat hole."

Burton looked at the bulge in the chauffeur's black jacket.

"What kind of heat is he packing."

"Czech Skorpion." Kennedy replied. The 9mm Kurtz, not the .32.

Burton followed Kennedy down wet flagstones to a black Chrysler sedan that had Philippines flags flying from standards on the bumper. The rain that had been torrential a few minutes before gave way to a drizzle and rain streaked skies in the distance. The air felt still, moist, musty, ripe and earthy all at the same time. A faint whiff of garbage drifted into his nostrils.

They both sat in the back seat, locked in their own thoughts. During the drive they swung through fields, dedicated to agriculture, near the ocean. Kennedy was remarkably silent.

"Pull over here," Kennedy instructed the driver. Gravel crunched under the tires as the car came to a stop.

A neighborhood of shanties and chicken coops bordered the road. The jungle seemed to be gaining on the ramshackle confusion. Kennedy

144

stepped out, unzipped and whipped it out. He pulled once or twice. Piss leaked out in a steady stream onto the ground, damp from earlier rain.

Back in the car, Burton closed his eyes and leaned his head back against the leather rest.

Sharp words. People were talking. He opened his eyes. Burton couldn't tell what they were saying because they were speaking one of the Philippines' languages. It didn't sound as though they were speaking Tagalog. He looked over at Kennedy, who worked to finish his stream.

"What's going on?" Burton asked.

"Welcoming committee I expect." Kennedy said, with a shudder as he completed and zipped up. Farmers approached the car and spoke loudly.

Kennedy shrugged and then translated for Burton's benefit. "They speak Maguindanao. I don't really but I can make out what they're after. It seems that there's a blood feud going on between this village and the one over across the jungle there. These folks are poor and the other village is rich because they work at a banana plantation."

The leader, with rodent cunning and beady unblinking eyes shouted a few incendiary words.

The voices of the crowd became louder and sharper. Kennedy turned to the car and translated. "They demand that the government do something about it. They want to work at the banana plantation and they want us to put the torch to the other village so they can get the jobs." Kennedy's reptilian heart did not swell in response to their plight.

Kennedy spoke in Tagalog. The villagers shouted back and as loud demands turned shrill, he pulled his Colt and fired two rounds in the air. The Chauffeur stepped from the driver's door, brandishing the Skorpion submachine gun. The villagers got the message, toned down and turned the other way, walking off, simmering in sullen anger.

Kennedy slid into the back seat next to Burton. "Let's get the hell out of here, Fidel!"

The driver dropped the car into gear. The engine roared and he scattered villagers into the weeds at the roadside as he passed.

"That's how you handle complaints in Asia. You don't put up with anything. I was taking a piss by the roadside and those rude cunt-lapping cocksuckers came up to me with their silly-ass problem. That's exactly what I'm talking about. That's not how you handle things back in the Land of the Big PX but it's what we do here."

"Actually," Burton said, "that is pretty much how the Rangers handle things in Texas."

Kennedy laughed and then Burton laughed.

"Get to the point." Burton asked five minutes later as they passed a Filipino police station surrounded by sand bags. "What do you want from me?"

"I thought we discussed all this last night and this morning." Kennedy replied.

"No, you beat around the bush for hours and I want you to tell me what you and the CIA want from me."

"You know--."

"I mean it, Kennedy."

Kennedy leaned forward and spoke softly to the driver. The driver pulled to the side of the road, ocean on one side, a small fishing town on the other. The boats were out in the small bay. Frangipani trees canopied over the slum. They both got out of the car again.

They walked. Locals looked at the tall broad shouldered soldier and skinny American in his white silk safari suit.

"It's the girl. We want you to get in with the girl. The world's first intelligence officer was in disguise as the serpent in the Garden of Eden. He recruited Eve to use feminine wiles to compromise Adam. There's nothing to say that you can't pull a reverse to the traditional mission of women."

"Charlotte?" Burton asked.

"Yep, she's the road to her old man and he's the king of the world." Kennedy assured. "And since you took her into your house at about 10:00 pm and she left on her own at 3:00 am yesterday if I have my days straight, you have your eye on the ball."

"She wants me to work for Unione Corse, and she said that Paint, Gorman and Taylor are already cooperating."

"The bitch has some moves, don't she?" Kennedy said with admiration. "We want you to take her up on it and this is the point. We want to know which politicians they pay off, where and how much. They've got big shots from New York to Moscow on the payroll. We want to know who they got to when so we can get to them too. That's the drill. That's the mission and that's what you need to do."

"I'm a soldier, not a spy."

"You were a soldier three days ago or so. Since then you've been a spy. A junior spy, I admit, but by definition, a spy."

"Am I getting a briefing on precisely what you want me to do? What about Jacques Sabon? Your boss, Mr. Keene wanted me to get to know him better. Is that what you want too?"

"Yeah, Jacques Sabon. Word is he made his bones killing Nazis during World War Two. He was in his prime then, running and gunning with the underground, doing the odd favor for the OSS and the Brits. Now, he's past his prime but he has your girl there to perk him up."

Kennedy never saw the fist. Pinwheels spun and stars spurted. The back of his head hit the paving stones that ramped up one side of a small bridge. He looked up and saw Burton standing over him with a .45 automatic in his hand, looking over his shoulder at Fidel, the driver, who dropped his Skorpion machine-pistol on the ground.

"You've got a mean right hook, General. I think I'm going to demote you back to captain." Kennedy massaged his tender jaw."

Burton scooped up the Skorpion. Fidel smiled putting his hands up with both thumbs extended.

Yeah, your boss is an asshole. You know it too, don't you Fidel?

Burton walked back reached down and helped Kennedy to his feet.

"You'd best leave Charlotte out of this." Burton cautioned.

Kennedy was all ears. "Sure. Sorry." He stood slowly and got a smoke out of his cigarette case and tapped the tobacco. His hands shook but he lighted the smoke with a gold Dunhill lighter.

Kennedy leaned over the railing of a stone bridge where a canal met the ocean, puffed on his cigarette and looked out as the car pulled up. He didn't say anything else. He just smoked and looked into the water. Boats glided beyond them. The water mirrored the bridge, hanging vines, trees and azure blue sky. It was a tranquil, picturesque setting on a calm, sultry morning. Kennedy massaged his jaw and wiggled a loose tooth.

"Did you box?" Kennedy asked.

"Golden Gloves, for Bay County, Michigan and won the state match against the tough gyms in Dee-troit in my weight."

Kennedy went back to the loose tooth.

"What city?"

"Auburn, home of the Auburn Warriors."

"Your dad's a big shot." It was a statement, not a question.

"Step-father, who married my mother. He didn't have any use for her kids."

"Got you into West Point, though. I read your file—twice."

Burton's fist unconsciously closed and Kennedy took a step back. "Hold on, slugger, I don't need another fucking lesson. I'm a fast learner."

"Hit him!" Fidel urged from where he stood by the car.

"Are you nuts?" Kennedy asked.

"I was talking to Captain Burton!" Fidel cheered.

Suddenly, Burton became aware of a commotion in the water among a group of sampans about fifty yards away. He heard a man shouting, then screaming in desperation, and spotted him thrashing helplessly in the filthy harbor water. Other boatmen within easy reach of him were aware of his perilous predicament and were looking right at him with some interest but none of them moved to help him.

"The guy is drowning!" Burton exclaimed to Kennedy. He yelled down to the boatmen, "Somebody help him!" Then he repeated his cry in Chinese.

None of the boatmen moved to help though only an oar's length separated them from the flailing man.

Still thrashing, the fisherman disappeared beneath the surface, struggled to the surface and then vanished again into the murky, opaque harbor.

Burton moved quickly, pulled off his shoes one at a time as he began to run.

"No! Don't interfere!" Kennedy warned sternly.

Burton ignored him.

"Let go, Burton." Kennedy grabbed Burton's arm. "They believe that if you save a man's life you are responsible for him for as long as you both live." Kennedy explained calmly. He gestured at the sampans moving away from the scene of the drowning as if it had not happened. "None of them wanted that burden."

"Forgive my lack of compassion." Kennedy said taking a careless drag on his cigarette. "The corpse will float to the surface somewhere in the tidal basin and will be taken away with all of the other detritus found along the shore. There is a lot of anonymous death here with no one to mourn."

"This whole place is completely twisted." Burton said, applying logic that worked in Saginaw Bay, Michigan.

"I've been trying to tell you last night and this morning that we're in a new paradigm here. That's why I wear white. In Asia, white is the color of death. Everybody around here knows that. When they see me dressed as I am they know what I represent and they leave me alone. Red is the color of luck and money. Being in the red here is a good thing." Then Kennedy smiled and said, "But bleeding isn't. Don't bleed for the Corsican girl, Burton. Use her for the sake of your country but whatever you do, don't fall in love."

Burton doubled his fist but kept it to his side. Kennedy noticed.

"This shit in Laos is the tip of what will be a very big ice burg. For the first time, the CIA has a war all-their-own and they're going to escalate with a vengeance. They want you to get in deep with the woman, and not just with your dick. You've bottomed out there now--up to your sack." Kennedy said, watching Burton tense. "And if you hit me again you may land it but I swear I'll shoot you in the kneecaps one night while you're sleeping."

Burton, disgusted from the sordid situation asked, "Is that what this American society has come to?"

"Society is produced by our wants, and government by our wickedness." Kennedy said. "It's not my quote. It's from Thomas Paine, philosopher of the revolution, author of *Common Sense*, Washington, Jefferson, Madison the patriarchs of American government relied on his acumen. 'Society unites our affections and government restrains our vices'. Or it tries to. You don't work for the American society, you work for the government."

"Fuck you, Kennedy."

"You ready to catch your plane back? Your men will be at the airport waiting for you." Kennedy said. "And I suspect they'll want to know your answer to the question Mrs. Sabon put to you. I want to know if she asked you before or after you did the dirty deed but if I ask, you'll hit me. Won't you?"

"Leave well enough alone, Kennedy." Burton menaced.

Now with his hands raised in mock surrender, having pushed Burton as far as he intended to, "Fidel, let's take this soldier back to Naval Air Station Stanley Point, then I need to see a dentist."

The flight back proved uneventful. Everybody slept. Kennedy ended up joining them on the Air America Beechcraft in lieu of seeing a dentist. He found a seat in the back of the aircraft and drank himself into a stupor, snoring during the balance of the flight.

Burton looked down at the endless ocean below and tried to organize his thoughts. First there was Charlotte Sabon. Why had he hit Kennedy? Why would he have hit the bastard a second time? Charlotte used her wiles with some confidence to pitch him on the idea of coming over to the dark side. After that, to seal the deal or perhaps to get something on him, she treated him to her rather exquisite charms. Charms she'd been using on god only knew how many men for how long. Paint and Gorman? Unlikely. The timing was off. Never the less either she or somebody else got to them, but who?

Taylor. He answered his own question. It was obvious. She seduced Taylor and Creed Taylor carried the message to Paint and Gorman.

Back to Kennedy. Why had he hit the man? Just because Kennedy suggested Charlotte Sabon was a whore or a slut?

Oh, God. No. He told himself that he had no feelings whatsoever for her. He used her as a self-propelled semen receptacle and nothing more. He used HER. Not the other way around. He flashed back to their meeting in the morning market after she cut him off in that big damned French limo.

He bounced to Wu Ming's pronouncement. *"The Dragon likes to be in charge of everything and the Tiger insists on autonomy. It's like pouring kerosene from two cans into a jar and adding a match. The result is inevitable, its resulting karma unappealing."*

Burton didn't believe in fate. He knew that he was in charge of his own destiny, was the master of his own life. Then again, a fisherman drowned in the presence of so many who could have saved him. How did that speak to destiny?

He started from his first day in Indochina and played it all back, thinking on small details. Some things were too small to be seen, other things were too big. It all seemed to be spinning out of control and he felt like a pawn.

NINETEEN

Friday, 19 August 1961 -- 1225 HRS
Headquarters, People's 14th Group Army
Chengdu Military Region
Kunming, Yunnan Province,
People's Republic of China

General Qui's office smelled of sour age masked by insecticide. Seated behind his worn wooden desk, he turned a page from the Hong Kong daily paper published in English the previous week but only just received. It appeared nothing newsworthy had occurred in the past week for the articles had little to report. Qui looked out from the top floor window of Army headquarters in Kunming through grime that had been collecting on the glass for years. The dismal, gray city he saw below the window, tinted ochre by the stain of accumulated filth had become a metaphor to him for the peasant's revolutionary paradise in which he lived.

As General Staff Advisor to the 14th Group Army, stationed along the Chinese border with Viet Nam, Laos and Burma, he had a small staff who did readiness studies and oversaw "warnings and intentions" on the other side of the Chinese border. In reality, his position was far more important because his duties were not confined to the military as a member of the Guojia Anquan Bu, or Ministry of State Security. In particular, he was Commander of Second Directorate Operations for Indochina. His area of command stretched over Viet Nam, Cambodia, Laos, Thailand and Burma. His headquarters provided direction, information collection priorities and served as liaison with worker's struggles and people's liberation movements in the lands under his oversight.

Under his scrutiny, clandestine agents moved abroad using covers such as cadres posted to foreign trade companies, insurance companies, banks, and other commercial ventures. Senior Bureau personnel working under diplomatic cover while performing intelligence functions staffed Chinese Embassies and consulates. *Renmin Ribao* and *Xinhua* provided cover for his operatives masquerading as journalists.

WHITE POWDER

Of all the operations underway, the most tenuous seemed to be that conducted in Laos under the aegis of Wu Ming, son of his wife's sister. The Americans arrived in Laos and Viet Nam in larger numbers. The British intelligence operatives were very active in Burma, all the operatives funded by the Americans with their never-ending supply of resources. When he commented to his superior, General Dirt Farmer Yee that the Americans never seemed to lack for logistics, the Colonel General screamed at him. The memory remained unpleasant.

In his mind he could still hear Dirt Farmer Yee's high, whining voice. There was the odor of breath that smelled like an old tent. "The Chinese Communist Party, its leadership, its cadres and its members fear no difficulties or hardships. Whoever questions our ability to lead the revolutionary war will fall into the morass of opportunism. The peasants' struggle has never ceased. Harassed by aggression from abroad, by difficulties at home and by natural disasters, the peasants have unleashed widespread struggles in the form of guerrilla warfare. This guerilla warfare is directed at the running dog lackeys of the intelligencia and will not stop!"

Qui firmly held that reason Dirt Farmer Yee was a general of higher rank than he was because Dirt Farmer could get all that out without taking a breath in between sentences. Dirt Farmer also foamed slightly at the mouth slightly while speaking and sprayed his audience. Dirt Farmer excelled at a show of Party zeal.

It was a verbal browbeating right out of the Little Red Book. Essentially it meant that results mattered. Qui had seen what happened to others who didn't produce. They were accused of being part of the enemy of the worker's struggle, put up against a wall and shot or shipped to a reeducation camp.

In order to insulate himself from failure, he hand selected Tieuchau men from the region surrounding his home in Shantow to support his operations and provide particularly attentive patronage. Of those, Wu Ming had never let him down.

General Qui looked at a portfolio on his desk, open to a grainy black and white photograph of Jacques Sabon, a French narcotics smuggler representing Bruno Jospin's Guerini Brotherhood, the dominant faction of the Corsican Mafia that oversaw the narcotics trade in Indochina since the end of the Second World War.

He tapped the photo. What to do about Sabon?

LARRY B. LAMBERT

Wu Ming traveled from Laos to Yunnan under short notice for the meeting. He used the pretext of compassionate need to comfort a relative at a time of death. They would meet, discuss the next step and foil both the American compradors *and* their allies. There was also the matter of white powder. Implicit in its growing and sale to the decadent West were profits that might ease the course of one's retirement.

Well after sunset, a new black Russian made Zhil limousine pulled to a slow stop in front of the Huashan Bao Mi, translated literally into English, 'Protected Secret Club'. A driver who wore the uniform of a lieutenant of the People's Liberation Army opened the passenger's door curbside. Wu Ming, who wore his baggy blue Mao jacket and trousers stepped onto the curb and then looked up and down the street out of habit. Nothing unusual. Knuckles scarred from youthful spirit knocked twice and a small window opened in the center of the door. Hushed password, the door opened discreetly and he walked in. The Zhil purred back onto the street and disappeared into the night.

"Hello Da ge." The girl behind the desk was breathtakingly beautiful; as were all the girls in the brothel but that night his business did not primarily involve women. Maybe later. Business first.

He nodded slightly and then turned left and walked up a gilded staircase to the private meeting room upstairs. He smiled to himself as he slowly ascended the staircase. At the head of the stairs, two more girls clothed in gossamer lingerie sipped coconut milk and munched cashews. They looked at him knowingly. He would pay later for both of them—after his meeting.

Contraband music played on the phonograph. "Earth Angel" by the crooning Penguins. Wu Ming didn't like the song, but understood the appeal of the forbidden, decadent West. The song finished and somewhere, girls flipped the record on the phonograph to "Hey Senorita". The Party permitted the record because Negroes who were engaged in class struggle against fat cat overlords made the recording. It became politically acceptable at the moment in a rare display of common cause between exploited workers' striving and yearning. Wu Ming didn't think that Earth Angel sounded like the groaning misery of struggling masses, but nobody else at the club spoke English.

Comrade Wu Ming walked along the empty corridor in step with the music. He had the kind of authority that didn't need to flaunt itself.

Brushing past the sentries, he walked in, finding a seat before he made eye contact.

General Qui remained seated when Colonel Wu Ming walked into the room.

Qui offered Wu a smile one size too small.

"I brought you here for one reason." General Qui said by way of preamble and greeting.

Wu couldn't have been more surprised if the esteemed general hit him across the mouth with a fresh fish. His face showed it. No solicitous comments about the health of his miserable snake of a wife, no concerns for his own personal wellbeing or of the family they shared in common? No concerns for the good of the Party, the continuing struggle of the workers.

"A revolution is not a dinner party, or writing an essay, or painting a picture, or doing embroidery."

First, a complete disregard for manners and civilized conduct and then General Qui quoted Chairman Mao. Things were going downhill fast. Wu decided to throw some Mao back at the General. At this point there didn't seem to be much to loose. "In time of difficulties, we must not lose sight of our achievements."

"I'm gratified that you haven't forgotten what the Revolution is all about. You said 'we' in quoting Chairman Mao. This is not about Wu Ming or his family. It is about all the workers advancing together in a common front. It's about taking the initiative when it is offered. Passivity is fatal to us. We must make our enemy passive."

Wu, eyes downcast, feeling as through a cattle prod was rammed up his ass, could only wonder whether he would be shot on the premises or driven somewhere for the bullet behind the ear. Things had been going so well. Penetration of the French Mission was complete, he made significant progress in his friendship toward Americans and a flea couldn't leap from a dog's back in Vientiane without him hearing of it.

"We think too small, like the frog at the bottom of the well. He thinks the sky is only as big as the top of the well. If he surfaced, he would have an entirely different view." Qui hammered with another quote from Chairman Mao.

Wu Ming, eyes lowered to reflect due humility. At the same time his mind was racing for a way out of whatever trouble he landed in. General Qui still hadn't told him what he had done wrong.

154

"We all grow older. And in the revolution you must take care that you are able to live to old age." Qui pronounced more softly, this time in the Teochiu dialect. "Comfort in age comes from one's family and they too must be alive to enjoy that comfort."

"The Proletarian Revolutionary Cause is progressing as we link arms and march forward." Wu Ming said, eyes no longer downcast, scrutinizing General Qui.

"Linking arms is what I had in mind. And helping the Corsicans keep their monopoly in refining for two years more must have value. And then there is the matter of Khun Sa. He remains valuable to us but he may be overstepping himself. I heard he's ordered a large dragon." General Qui spread his arms wide. "Very large—from the finest craftsman in Hong Kong, crafted in 24 karat gold. One may be taken to believe that he fancies himself a large dragon."

Wu Ming asked, "May I freshen your drink, General?"

TWENTY

Friday, 19 August 1961 -- 1400 HRS
Consolidated Fruit Company Office
23 Rue Nong Duoang
Vientiane, Laos

The Monkey King strolled through the front door of the newly minted Consolidated Fruit Company office in downtown Vientiane. He walked past empty desks, and joined Burton in a corner office.

They shook hands and Keene got down to business, opening his briefcase. He withdrew an envelope and slid it across the table to Burton.

"It's a sanitized copy for you to keep."

Burton opened it. Inside the envelope, a manila folder with information about Creed Taylor's father, he found four pages of typewritten copy, a grainy 8x10 photo and a large- scale map of the Shan State.

"Do I get to see the part you sanitized away?"

"It's classified."

"So I don't have a need to know?"

The Monkey King gestured in the direction of the file. "That's what you need to know. It's what we know that's germane to what we want you to do, which is a rescue effort."

"That sounds simple."

"Disarmingly simple. Easy enough for you and your team."

"What about the Corsicans?"

The Monkey King smiled, "That is the real mission, the end result. To get there, we want you to the first step, which is to rescue Creed Taylor's father. He's being held by Khun Sa. Read over what I gave you, think about it and we'll talk more later."

The Chief of Station stood and looked around the office. "Marvelous. This place is great."

Sam Willoughby passed the CIA Chief as he left the office. They exchanged polite greetings.

Willoughby locked the outer door behind him. Once the lock engaged, he walked to Burton's desk and slid a sheet of paper across the wooden, US Government issue, World War II vintage oak desk.

Burton scooped it up, squinting. The print was feint. "What's this, the twelfth carbon copy?"

"New orders," Willoughby said.

Burton scanned the orders from Headquarters, Army Security Agency, Pacific, 8621ST AAU, First Lieutenant Duncan H. Stern, Signal Corps, Master Sergeant Samuel K. Willoughby and five ASA men had been officially assigned to the 7th Special Forces Group.

It all looked kosher. He spoke to Taylor and the Monkey King. "There will be a radio watch section assigned to our operation. Lieutenant Stern is due in tomorrow or the next day and I figured you could brief him." Burton paused, to Willoughby. "Do you know Duncan Stern?"

"Yep. He looks just like Ichabod Crain, from the *Legend of Sleepy Hollow*. Pencil neck, huge Adam's apple, weak chin, long beaky nose and bulging eyes. Hell of a nice guy. He's married to a Thai girl named Beautiful Moon—that's her Thai name. Stern is a Mormon from Utah. Doesn't drink, smoke or fornicate excessively."

"What is excessive fornication?" Burton asked.

Willoughby shrugged. "I don't think I fornicate excessively."

"It sounds as if you have it all under control then." Burton summarized.

"I guess." Sam said.

Sam Willoughby announced he was going outside for a smoke. Burton took the hint and followed him. They walked fifty feet from the plywood building that housed Consolidated Fruit.

Sam lit up and said, "Look, Captain, something big is going on around here. I heard of a new communications net going up called BACKPORCH. It's still on the drawing board but they're looking for a contractor to build it. What it does is provide a strategic communications net all through Southeast Asia. They'll put up these huge billboard size antennas on mountaintops connecting five major cities in South Viet Nam with Thailand and Laos."

"So we'll be able to use it soon?" Burton asked.

"That's not the point. Something big is going on and they're throwing down big cash for infrastructure. The big show will be in Viet Nam if I'm any judge of things."

"How big?"

"If the communications infrastructure is any guide of what the Pentagon has in mind, I'm guessing a Corps level military commitment, maybe two. Fifty thousand men with Air Force and Navy support, as many as seventy thousand."

Burton whistled. "Really? In Viet Nam?"

"They have to put in the infrastructure first and communications is critical." Sam Willoughby stressed.

Willoughby then tapped the orders. "Look closer." Sam prodded.

Burton looked. "Sure. In this case I'm the installation commander so a certificate of non-available quarters is not a problem at all. You can keep your room at the Continental Hotel."

"It says Master Sergeant."

"That's you, Top-Sergeant." Burton smiled. "The orders must have passed the reinstatement of rank somewhere in the bureaucratic mess." He stood and took Sam Willoughby's hand and pumped it sincerely.

"I'm afraid that you're going to have to buy again, Sam. This time Creed Taylor won't have the duty. This heat brings out the thirst in a man."

Burton sat and handed the orders back. "There's also a rather impressive gong to go along with the stripes. Major Piper will present it to you for distinguished gallantry under fire while serving on assigned duty to the 7th Special Forces while engaged in classified military operations involving conflict with an opposing force with which the United States is not a belligerent party—yet. I'll let them read the citation and you can act surprised."

Sam's eyes were moist. "This calls for a drink."

"A Silver Star warrants several goddamned drinks, Willoughby." Burton sternly admonished. "You're not getting away with buying anyone 'a' drink."

A furtive glanced crossed Willoughby's features, "I've got a wad of piasters I found somewhere. We'll use those up first."

"Don't you have a radio to work on, master sergeant?"

Creed Taylor showed up half an hour after Sam Willoughby left. When he walked into Burton's office, Craig opened a desk drawer, pulled out a bottle of Jack Daniels and two smudged glasses. He dropped two fingers in each glass and shoved one glass across the table to Creed. Then Burton rested his feet on the open drawer and leaned back in his chair.

"Take a sip and come to Jesus." Burton admonished.

Creed tasted the Tennessee whiskey and said, "I'm not sure what you mean."

"Give me all of it. Every sordid fucking detail, it's a direct order and if you don't think we're still in the army to spite the Monkey King, the CIA and the orders from the Chief-of-Staff, just try me."

"Craig, I'm not—sure."

"Start from three months ago. We left on patrol. You were sick in the hospital. All was well with the world. I came back from patrol, the CIA is up my ass and the Unione Corse is up yours."

"I didn't want to involve you, Craig."

"Involve me in what? If there was a problem, why didn't you come to me? We've been to hell together, bled together, and maybe it didn't mean anything to you but it sure did to me."

Burton pulled the file that the CIA Station Chief gave him earlier and sat it on the table. Mr. Keene dropped this off for me. "The name on the tab is Halvard C. Taylor. Your father."

"They got my father. He's a hostage."

"Who got your father, the Corsicans?"

"No, it's a long story. Best start at the beginning. World War II ends and the Chinese Communists beat the Kuomintang. Most of the Kuomintang make it out to Taiwan but the 3rd and 5th Kuomintang Armies make it across the border into Burma. My father was with the Office of Strategic Services then, before it was wedded to the Central Intelligence Agency. We lived in Rangoon when I was a kid and dad worked up country. At some point my father resigned from the CIA and started up a ministry. It wasn't a front for anything. It was a real ministry. There were still a lot of British people around in Burma, most of them either worked for the Colonial government or they had plantations, import businesses and so forth."

"I'm with you so far."

Creed nodded, took a drink and continued. "Things were getting tense, the Red Chinese were threatening to invade Burma to root out the Kuomintang. The CIA took a real interest in rearming the Kuomintang in the hopes of sending them back into China to topple Mao. There was pressure on Dad to participate and he caved in. At this time I was living in Paris, Texas with family, going to High School, but I went back to Burma during summers. There were lots of flights in and out of Burma.

Some of the Kuomintang were ferried back to Taiwan, but a lot of arms and ammo poured in.

"The Kuomintang occupied the Shan state and because the chief cash crop is opium, they more or less enslaved the locals to produce more. Jungle slash and burn produced more land under cultivation and more opium poppies.

"At the same time the Burmese government is not at all happy with this occupying army and they make a deal with the Devil. The Burmese Army moves up from the south and Red Chinese come down from the north and root 'em out."

"And the last of the Kuomintang left Burma last January." Burton tried to be helpful.

"Yeah, sort of. The People's Liberation Army and the Burmese Army had them in a pincer and rather than fight to the death, the CIA their assets to Taiwan. The rest were pushed into Thailand. A few months ago the Thais said they could stay if they helped fight communists in Northern Thailand and protect the border."

"That was my understanding too." Burton said.

"Except that's not the end.

"U Khun Sa."

"Yeah, Khun Sa." Creed said, "Smart guy, good with people, knows how to make friends, lots of exposure to the CIA, British MI-6, French Service de Documentation Extérieure et de Contre-Espionnage, and a blend of spooks, mercenaries and drug runners including the Unione corse. He re-named himself U Khun Sa, which means prosperous prince. When I knew him, he was plain old Chang Chi-fu.

"So here's Khun Sa up in Burma, the Kuomintang is gone, the People's Liberation Army is leaving Burma, the Burmese Army is going back down to the lowlands and everybody wants a caretaker to manage the white powder business, which is exceptionally lucrative.

"The Kuomintang took over half of the opium harvest with them when they left so the upcoming harvest will be a big deal to my old buddy Chang Chi-fu, or Khun Sa. It will be his first big taste of power. Right now he's refining what opium he could pull together into morphine base. He wants to swap my father for the recipe for #4 Heroin so he can go into competition with the Corsicans. If they can figure out how to transform opium into #4 Heroin here rather than the expensive and risky trans-shipment to France they can keep the profit for themselves.

"Who besides the French have the recipe for #4 Heroin?" Burton asked.

"The CIA. And some of his buddies from the old days moved up in the Company so there's history there." Creed answered.

"And Khun Sa knows this."

"Absolutely." Creed confirmed.

Burton poured for himself and for Creed.

"So everybody is playing for high stakes." Burton summarized.

"Bruno Jospin is here from Corsica, though nobody is supposed to know that. The Front man is Jacques Sabon."

"How did they get to you, Creed?" Burton asked, knowing the answer.

"Bruno and Sabon visited me in the hospital. Sabon knows my father from back in the days when they were both in the intelligence game. Dad found Jesus and Jacques Sabon found heroin. Both are 'the opiate of the masses'." Creed ended with a quote from Vladimir Illyich Lenin by way of a joke. It elicited a forced laugh from Burton.

Burton picked it up. "So, Bruno Jospin is the shot caller in Marseilles, where the Corsicans refine the stuff." That would seem to confirm everything Charlotte told him.

Creed added. "Some of it's also refined in Sicily but the Corsicans and Jospin oversee it all."

"And he's here now. In Laos?"

"Actually he's staying across the Mekong in Thailand at a very well protected villa he owns. It's got a movie theater, swimming pool, indoor tennis court, runway, and one hell of a well stocked bar." Creed said, "It's a big deal for them. If they lose their supply of raw product, they lose their income. For Jospin to show his face is no small matter."

"Let me cut to the chase, Creed, and I'm going to be indelicate here to a brother officer. What will Jacques Sabon do when he finds out you've been having carnal knowledge of his wife?"

Creed paled slightly. "Who said I was doing that?"

"It's common knowledge. Kennedy for one told me so in no uncertain terms. Even Wu Ming talked about it."

Creed gave a nervous chuckle, "I only wish."

"What do you mean? I saw you two in the market the other day, before we went to Manila."

"Yeah, well that's part of the deal I have with Sabon and Jospin. I guard her when she goes out and about, or I did while you guys were gone. Now you're back they understand I have to be a soldier again at some point."

"So you never?" Burton didn't finish the sentence.

"—no, I never did. I can't say I wouldn't like to but she guards her virtue like it's locked in the gold depository at Fort Knox."

Burton poured more Jack Daniels and knocked it back in one throw.

Creed raised three fingers from his left hand. "Scouts honor. I was a First Class Boy Scout in Burma."

"Not once?"

"Nope." Creed leaned close to Burton, "and I'll tell you something that nobody knows. She's not married to Jacques Sabon. I'm not saying that old Jacques wouldn't like a rut with the randy little thing if given the opportunity. It was Bruno's idea to keep the Corsicans and French hound dogs from trying to hump her leg. Charlotte has a mind of her own. She's Bruno's only child, daddy's girl, the apple of his eye, and she's got a bit of the old gangster in her. The deal is if I play along with them, they'll help me get my Dad back."

"Do you trust the mafia?"

"Oddly enough, I do. And at some level the CIA does too, because their interests converge with the Corsicans at the moment."

"It would explain all this." Burton waved at the interior of the Consolidated Fruit Company office. "If Khun Sa is the hustler you say he is, making pure heroin would put him in a position where he wasn't dependent on the CIA or anyone else."

"The Red Chinese would protect him for a piece of the action." Creed speculated.

"What's Kennedy's angle?"

Creed thought for a moment. "I'm not sure. Maybe he's the go-between from the Agency?"

"And Charlotte isn't married." It was a statement.

"Frankly," Creed leaned close again, "I think that Bruno thinks she's a virgin, and for all I know she may be. What a waste."

Burton leaned further back in his chair and closed his eyes. "I've got a head ache."

Walter Kennedy knocked on the front door of the Consolidated Fruit Company office, let himself in, and walked back to where Creed Taylor and Craig Burton were sitting, speaking sotto voce.

"What's goin' on guys?" Kennedy asked as though butter wouldn't melt in his mouth.

Burton stood up, flexing his shoulders, rolling them slightly.

"Been meanin' to ask you Creed –the Corsican bitch ever let you take pictures of her naked?"

Burton hit the CIA man twice. A left broke his nose and the right uppercut took him under his chin, forward of his ear. Kennedy went down like a sack of potatoes.

TWENTY ONE

Friday, 19 August 1961 -- 2000 HRS
Seventh-Day Adventist Missionary Clinic
Vientiane, Laos

Burton sat next to Kennedy's hospital bed when his eyes opened.

"Where am I? Fuck! What am I?" He probed the bandages across his nose. His eyes shined black and blue, swollen and heavily bloodshot. "Mortar round?" He had some difficulty speaking.

Burton adjusted the ice pack suspended against his jaw by a bandage that wrapped from the top of his head to his chin.

The doctor, a Seventh Day Adventist, crusader and missionary, stepped through the door. "Hello, Walter."

"Hey there doc."

"The last time you crashed your car into a canal—drunk again. What happened this time?"

Kennedy, sifting through the fog of memory and looking at Burton accusingly said, "A bus hit me. Big goddamned bus."

The doctor consulted a metal chart with notes on it. "You're lucky Captain Burton found you and brought you in. We set your nose. It's broken but will mend. You took a tough knock there on the side of your jaw but the mandible isn't broken. We don't have an x-ray machine here but it looks as if it will heal normally without needing to wire it. I suspect you sustained a mild concussion."

Kennedy looked at both Burton and the Doctor with puffy, beady, angry, ferret eyes.

"Does it hurt?" The doctor solicited.

"A fucking bus hit me, twice, my nose is on fire, my sinuses feel as though somebody flushed them with burning kerosene, why would it hurt?"

The doctor tucked the chart under his arm. "Profanity is not tolerated here. Please gather your possessions and leave." He turned to the door, then looked over his shoulder. "Captain Burton, please make sure he doesn't steal anything. I missed a stethoscope after his last visit."

When the doctor stepped out, Burton raised an eyebrow at Kennedy.

164

"For listening at doors. Spy work. Something you wouldn't know anything about."

"I know a bit about boxing." Burton said flatly.

"You're a master of understatement, General" Kennedy replied without any malice as he sat up in bed, stuffing a pillow behind his back to support himself. "I've had my share of woman problems. After the last time you slugged me I should have known better than to make the naked picture remark."

"I'm sorry." Burton handed Kennedy a metal flask.

Kennedy unscrewed the lid and tried to sniff the contents but he winced in pain.

"Bushmills." Burton said. "Peace offering."

"It's not a problem. You just stay with her in spite of her family's proclivity toward homicide. Your country needs that love to blossom." Kennedy tried to sound convincing. "Marry the bitch with my blessing. Breed up a batch of little mobsters with wicked right hooks for all I fucking care." He paused, looking past Burton at the rotating ceiling fan overhead. "Marriage can be good within the Calinzana Guerini mafia family. It might even be good between you both. Might be good for me if you get that father of hers elevating you in the Corsican *Caïd*."

Kennedy stifled a sneeze. "If I sneeze it will blow my nose off my face." He said in abject terror.

"What happened to your wife?" Burton tried to get Kennedy's mind away from the impending sneeze.

Kennedy looked confused. "Which one?"

"The lady you told me about when you broke into the Thai general's house.

"Oh, her. Fourth wife. She went crazy." Kennedy said sadly. Then he tapped a cigarette out of his gold case.

Burton torched the tip and Kennedy inhaled painfully. "I think I have that effect on women."

Burton helped himself to a swig from the flask he'd given Kennedy and then set it on a side table.

"I've got a dirty mind, so I still think some details have been kept from me, to spare a blood bath. It was last year or maybe the year before in Saigon and she was with me. I think my cover was selling wheat or something when the Security Police made the big round up.

"She was in heavy custody, getting the shit slapped out of her

165

accused of being a communist, but it wasn't too serious by our standards. It was your typical heavy Vietnamese treatment with women—tie their ass up all elaborately for a few days, fuck up the shoulders and the arms, slap the face, talk smart, threaten rape but settle for denying shampoo and soap. It's strange about Oriental sensibilities when they set out to insult a lady as distinct from torturing a whore. I swear the fuckers are almost polite."

He fumbled for the flask and Burton handed it to him. "It must be respect. Anyway, in those days I had a hot asset working in the Defense Ministry. This guy had world-class stroke, but considering the time and circumstances, I had a communication problem that was beyond belief. Finally I tasked him with a vengeance and Ngoc was freed."

"So she takes about a month to calm down, and then she dolls herself all up and goes back to this Vietnamese Senior Colonel that had control of the situation. She tells him, 'I couldn't say anything because of what was happening. I didn't want to cause any problems in your job or your family, but I really admired the way you handled things and I'm sorry if I caused you any problems.' So naturally, this asshole is interested right away, but Ngoc excuses herself and dances away. Well, now he is really interested, and this thing goes back and forth for a while, with Ngoc all timidly concerned for the implications to his career like a fluttering dove."

"Anyway, this Senior Colonel is shortly found dead and the cause of death is found to be that he was buried alive in his dress uniform in a vacant lot in Thanh Binh district. I guess he thought he was going on an important date, eh?"

"And God forgive me but I smacked her upside the head, and I asked her, 'did you have to fuck that bastard to kill him?' She just smiled that Mona Lisa smile and said, 'don't judge me by what you will do, judge me by what I won't do.'"

"Did she do it by herself?" Burton asked casually, professional curiosity piqued.

"No, I don't think so." Kennedy replied. "My old driver was in on the scam and probably buried the asshole. He took me aside a few months later and told me, 'that woman has honor you still can't see.'"

"You love her?"

"Ngoc? Damned straight I love her."

"Is she here?"

166

Kennedy felt for the flask again and didn't find it. For a moment he looked helpless and panicked. Burton lifted it off the side table and handed it to him. Kennedy took a long pull from the flask. "As you might expect, she went through considerable stress being married to me."

Burton laughed heartily, from the bottom of his soul. Kennedy looked at him as if he was a lunatic. "That has to be the understatement of the year."

Then Kennedy laughed and a Laotian nurse passing the room stopped and watched through the open door at the display of emotion, amazed that Walter Kennedy had it in him to laugh.

"I took her back to the Land of the Big PX. This Agency psychiatrist was assigned her case because she was having problems because of everything she had been through with me."

Ngoc went everywhere with two stuffed rabbits back then. She named them Barbara and Elizabeth. She took them to the doctor's office down in Reston, not far from headquarters. Naturally, the doctor asked about them and she said, 'Why don't you ask them yourself, and I'll be your interpreter.' The Agency doctor asked why they couldn't speak for themselves, and she said, 'They can, but they only speak Vietnamese, and you don't, so I guess I will have to interpret, won't I?'"

"So the doctor agreed and he asked Barbara, 'How are you feeling today?' Barbara said, 'I don't feel well at all.' The doctor asked why, and Barbara said, 'Because that bitch Elizabeth is on my nerves and I want to kill her.' So the doctor asked Elizabeth, 'How do you feel about what Barbara said?' Elizabeth said, 'Let her try.'"

"So the Agency doctor said to Ngoc, 'You must be feeling some conflicts.'"

"Ngoc said, 'No, I'm sitting here interpreting for a doctor who can be persuaded that stuffed animals talk, so the only thing I'm feeling is disgusted.'"

"That's pretty funny." Burton was smiling broadly at the story.

"To tell you the truth, General, it's pretty fucked up. She's in a mental hospital even though she's just as sane as you and me. Ok, not me. Not me—as sane as you are. Maybe she's there because she knows I can't get to her there and persuade her to come back here running and gunning."

Then the sneeze came.

WHITE POWDER

***

A rainsquall swept the streets clean while he was in the clinic. It turned a hot evening into a hot and humid night. Outside the clinic a black Citroen sedan squatted low on the side of the road. A driver in black livery stood by the front fender, smoking. When he saw Burton he dropped the smoke and ground it out.

"Capitaine Burton?"

"Oui."

"Venez avec moi, faire plaisir."

Burton fingered the grip of his .45 absently. "Where do you want me to go?" He said the words slowly and deliberately.

"Le manoir Jospin."

"Charlotte ou Bruno?"

"Vous êtes invités pour le dîner."

Burton's stomach growled at the thought of a meal. "Ok, Je viendrai avec vous." And the driver opened the back door of the Citroen.

They passed the ride down Highway 2 past Camp Chinaimo to Tha Deua in silence driving on the right side of the road. From there they took a ferry across the Mekong River to Nong Khai. Both the driver and Burton presented their passports for a perfunctory inspection from a smiling Thai customs official, who clearly recognized the car. Once across the river, the driver began driving on the left side of the road because he was in Thailand. The road to Ban Dua and Villa Alaccio, home of Bruno Jospin and his daughter, Charlotte, was bumpy and very uneven. Burton looked for a metaphor.

168

TWENTY TWO

Friday, 19 August 1961 -- 2135 HRS
Villa Aljaccio,
Ban Dua, Thailand

Colonel Maurice LeBeau of the Service de Documentation Extérieure et de Contre-Espionnage, Jacques Sabon, Andre Zuccarelli all of whom worked for her father, and her father ranted and drank pernod in the library. Even though it was not adjacent to the expansive kitchen Charlotte could hear them. They were dangerous, secretive men, but men of great wit and humor. The belly laughs and bon ami were enhanced as the pernod flowed freely.

Charlotte began her preparations for dinner in much the same way as any Corsican woman would. She dismissed all the kitchen staff but Truc, a Vietnamese woman who served her family both in France and in Laos and traveled with her father. Truc, a short, sharp eye'd, petulant, demanding woman with a genius for cooking, handled much of the prep-work.

Truc complained about the lack of quality produce available in the Vientiane Morning Market compared with the Rue Mouffetard Market in Paris. "I don't know how you will make bouillabaisse for your father with no conger eel or red snapper." Truc barked as she added a pinch of salt to the soup. "You should let me cook. You're not making it right."

"We're having a guest for dinner, an American." Charlotte beamed.

"They're barbarians, those Americans." Truc countered. "I'm sure he'll want a fried minced beef on bread with fried potatoes."

"I'm sure he'll love my bouillabaisse. He's very tall, handsome, and he has a scar on his face." She sang the words.

"You always like men who look like—," Truc struggled for a word, "buccaneers."

"Oh, yes, he's my buccaneer." Charlotte agreed.

She heard the limousine's engine. "He's right on time." Turning to Truc, "If you burn the bread, I'll beat you with a switch."

Truc spit betel nut into the sink. "My bread is always perfect, which is more than I can say for that bouillabaisse."

169

WHITE POWDER

"Watch the soup, Truc, I'm going to look at him."

She ran down the hall lightly on the balls of her feet and peered discretely into the Library where the men were meeting. Craig Burton stood with his back to her. The other men stood and shook hands.

Colonel Maurice LeBeau, who was wearing his uniform, made the introductions. "Captain Craig Burton of the American 7th Special Forces, may I introduce my dearest friend, Bruno Jospin."

"I've heard a great deal about you Captain, and I'm pleased to say all of it good."

Charlotte tingled all over when her father said that. She wanted to burst into the room and hang on Burton's arm with proprietary pride but restrained herself.

Colonel LeBeau went on, "You've met Jacques Sabon?"

Jacques and Burton shook hands, "Yes," Jacques said, "at the Embassy. And speaking of the Embassy, the Ambassador, the French Ambassador, sends his regrets. He wanted to join us but the duties of high office prevented it."

Charlotte smiled outwardly. The Ambassador's new paramour occupied his evenings. Indiscretion fueled political gossip circles.

"Andre Zuccarelli, our one-eyed giant, and a colleague of ours." Andre Zuccarelli extended a scarred hand. He was over six and a half feet tall, salt and pepper hair with a mustache. The half of his face with the missing eye had deep, old, puckered scarring across it.

Zuccarelli pointed to his face and eye. "The Nazi Gestapo during the war. They wanted me to talk. I refused. People wonder so I tell them."

Charlotte loved the Cyclops, as she called him. Some thought of him as a warrior but Charlotte considered him a gentle bear who loved her as a doting uncle, having no children of his own.

As Jacques poured the pernod, Charlotte retreated to the kitchen to finish the preparations.

She served the bouillabaisse to the men with her own hand. Truc set two baskets of fresh hot, crusty bread on the table as Charlotte ladled the soup.

Before he dipped his round soupspoon, One-eyed Zuccarelli, her lovable bear and veteran of many tough fights, picked at the empty socket of his left eye absently. "Bouillabaisse must be made within fishnet-tossing distance of the Mediterranean and by a Marseillais."

170

It was a direct but friendly challenge to Charlotte because they were a long way from the Mediterranean. Zuccarelli slurped up a spoonful and his face reflected the bliss of a saint. "How do you make it so good?"

Craig dipped his spoon took a taste and a smile crossed his face, causing the scar to pucker. "This is really good. Did you make it Charlotte?"

Charlotte blushed slightly. "Of course."

"Charlotte is known for her bouillabaisse." Bruno confirmed. "Even though Truc is an excellent chef, occasionally the sous-chef makes an excellent bowl for us so we will remember that genius is hereditary."

Colonel LeBeau and Jacques ate without comment. They were noisy eaters, common men who were made uncommon by the Unione Corse. Zuccarelli tore the fragrant hot bread, slurped the bouillabaisse, burped slightly and ate and then ate more.

She beamed.

"I must have a recipe!" Zuccarelli barked.

"First the complex soup is made. I then ladle that over croutons dabbed with rouille and then sprinkle with gruyere; then I fillet fresh red mullet, monkfish, or sea robin, add conger eel, mussels, clams, sometimes crab. It all depends on what the fisherman drag from the sea. Since we are here, I make do with what I can buy fresh in the morning market in Vientiane."

As usual, Zuccarelli wanted to have the precise recipe and as usual, Charlotte left out one or two key ingredients.

It tickled Zuccarelli, who chuckled to himself before sucking down another spoon full of hot soup. Charlotte knew that to a Corsican woman, a secret is inviolate. To Zuccarelli, as to all of the men at the table, there was something intoxicating about a secret. Charlotte never divulged her secret ingredient. Everyone in the room including Charlotte knew that they would all suffer profound disappointment if the secret leaked. A secret was a holy thing to a Corsican.

She left them but she heard them talking through the wall between the kitchen and the dining room. She sat in a kitchen chair, leaned back and recalled Marseille. These men reminded her of home. Even Craig Burton reminded her of the man she always knew would sweep her off her feet. When she saw him, she remembered him from her musings as a girl. "He is the one," Charlotte whispered to nobody within earshot.

Charlotte walked back into the dining room and poured pernod for each of the men. She left the bottle on the table and walked back into the kitchen, listening from inside of the door.

"Burton, I asked Jacques to have you consider working with us because I knew that the Central Intelligence Agency's interests and ours coincided. I also knew that they would pluck you from the Army. We are not small men, we do not mince words and if you are opposed to serving your country's interests while serving ours, I will understand. I may not be happy about your decision, but I will ask mutual friends to release your from your CIA orders." Bruno said, plainly.

Charlotte's stomach twisted in a knot. Jacques confided in her that he was to approach Burton and she petitioned him to allow her to handle the business. Jacques would never betray the confidence, but Craig Burton, who had been her lover was quite a different matter.

"Nobody has told me what they want me to do. I know that Creed Taylor's father Reverend Halvard Taylor is under some sort of house arrest and I've heard that Khun Sa wants to cut you out of the opium trade."

Bruno clapped his hands and a small Lao butler walked into the room and gave a deep wai. "Get me the newspaper. It's on my desk."

The small butler returned quickly with a folded newspaper on a silver tray. Bruno removed it and tossed across the table to Craig Burton.

"It came out yesterday. *Vientiane Wán Pha-hát* is a weekly newspaper that comes out on Thursday in English, French and Lao. Each page has the same article in all three languages. It's an independent paper. Non-aligned with the Reds or with the Free World."

Burton read the headline, *U Khun Sa Now Folling Orders from Peking*. "Typo."

"Everybody reads the typo error." Zuccarelli said. "Read the article. It's well written. The bastard is not only betraying us, he's in league with the Communists."

Burton read the article. "Who publishes it?"

Bruno replied, "It's done locally, independent reporters. Of course they have their sources and their journalistic integrity to rely on. This is the same thing Colonel LeBeau and I have been trying to tell Mr. Keene, the Chief of Station. Now it's in the local press, common knowledge." Bruno said and then called for desert. "Charlotte, *café s'il vous plait et le dessert*."

Charlotte, who listened from behind the door, ran quickly to the coffee service Truc set out and whisked it into the dining room, where she poured for the men.

"Captain Burton," Charlotte explained as she poured his espresso, "this is a special blend ground in a shop on rue Stephanopoli, in Ajaccio. The best Corsican coffee."

Truc brought in a tray of small desserts and put them in the center of the table. "Charlotte made the Mendiant au Chocolat Blanc." Truc lied.

Charlotte, quick on the uptake said, "White chocolate with walnuts, dates, and orange peel mixed inside." She smiled at Craig Burton and couldn't take her eyes off him. "Please try one."

Burton popped on in his mouth and chewed. His face beamed appreciation. "That's excellent." He sipped his espresso. "Also very good. Maybe the best I've ever tasted."

Charlotte sat at the table and looked at Burton.

Bruno cleared his throat, "My dear, the men need to talk." To Truc, "teach her a new recipe or something while we discuss business." It wasn't a suggestion.

When Charlotte left, Bruno said to Burton, "My daughter is not often around young men. Body guards and old men such as we three. She is taken by you, but she is a good girl, a clean girl."

"Yes sir." Burton said, "Isn't she Mr. Sabon's wife?"

"Yes, she is." Jacques explained quickly. "Mr. Jospin, her father, is naturally protective of her as am I."

"As are we all," Zuccarelli said with slight menace. LeBeau nodded in agreement.

"May we move on?" Bruno said, changing the subject sternly.

"The dacoits in Burma have had their day but they are threatening our supply line of opium. He hit a caravan of ours last week, taking 700 joi," to Burton, "about one ton, of opium, seventy-one mules and killed forty two-men. Additionally, Khun Sa's revolutionary intentions have been made known as he has allied himself with the Communist Chinese."

"I heard the Thai's have paid him as well for the sake of brotherhood, cooperation and a piece of the action." Burton said.

Jospin's deep set eyes bored into Burton. "Where did you learn this."

The Corsicans were concerned, LeBeau looked at Burton speculatively.

"I can't say, except to tell you the information is reliable."

Bruno pushed, "Can't say or won't say."

173

"Won't say. I don't work for you, Mr. Jospin." Burton was wondering precisely who he worked for, but he tried to make his point.

"I would pay well for that piece of information."

"I'm not in need of money." Burton replied.

"Perhaps you came into money lately?" LeBeau speculated.

"Family money. My father is in the United States Congress." It was not a complete lie, and one that would sound accurate when the Corsican's checked.

"Most people don't tell me 'no'."

Burton shrugged and sipped his Corsican espresso. "At least you know the Thais want a horse in the race for horse." It was Burton's pun, *horse* being a slang term for heroin. Zuccarelli laughed.

Now Bruno shrugged, scooped a white chocolate dessert from the tray and ate it in one bite. "They are good."

"The CIA will soon be sending you north into the Shan State with your men to rescue Révérend Taylor very soon. We would like you to succeed. To that end, and for that reason we are meeting here. All my assets are at your disposal." Bruno said.

"It sounds as if you have the confidence of the CIA because that's news to me." Burton lied, but he found the lie to be foolish in light of the circumstances.

"People trust me because I am trustworthy, Captain."

Burton nodded. "I accept that in the spirit in which it is given, sir."

"However, if you should locate the l'expérimentation where Khun Sa is attempting to make #4 Heroin, that would be valuable to me."

"Can't you find it?" Burton challenged.

Jospin looked first at Sabon and then at Zuccarelli. "We've tried and failed. Time to ask the best to take a look for it."

"I may be in charge, but I also have men. I don't know how they're going to take any cooperation or any side deal I have with Unione Corse."

Sabon suggested, "As their leader, they will naturally follow you, no?"

Knowing that Charlotte wouldn't have divulged that his men were already bought and paid for to her father was an ace in the hole. However, since Kennedy said that his job was to become the confidant of Bruno Jospin and that was the reason for the CIA's cooperation, he decided to change tactics slightly.

"Yes, they will follow me."

Turning to LeBeau, "Colonel LeBeau, your man Cyr was a prisoner of Kuhn Sa up on the Chinese border when we found him. We also found fifty pounds of gold the villagers had hoarded and hauled it out. He fell into a booby trap on the way out and I cut his throat to speed him on his journey."

LeBeau's eyes narrowed but he didn't say anything.

Sabon said, "It seems only one more reason you don't need our money, Captain."

LeBeau added, "I presume you offer nothing for the maintenance of his family since he is now dead as you say."

"You presume correctly."

Jospin laughed, "Burton are you sure you're not part Corsican?"

"I'll work up a plan to recover Reverend Taylor but I don't need your money, Mr. Jospin. What I will need is full support from the French intelligence network. Specifically, Commandant Albert Grall's information. All of it—hold nothing back."

Jospin looked at Colonel LeBeau to answer the question.

"Yes," he said quickly, "Chef d'escadrons Grall will give you anything you want."

Burton said, "Grall is a good man, Colonel. He's not particularly a moral man but you can't be an intelligence chief in Indochina and keep any vestige of virtue can you? I'll be there tomorrow, Saturday morning. There has already been initial tasking from the Green House, they're going to be pushing me on timing and I want to be ready with some idea of how I need to go about this." To Bruno Jospin, "Are you in agreement sir?"

"And this laboratory or laboratories—this new refining location?"

"No promises that we can find or extract Reverend Taylor or that we can find out what Khun Sa is up to. There's no promise that I'll live long enough to snatch my next breath either. It's bad up there in the Shan State. Very bad."

Bruno sighed and ate a pastry.

"May I offer you advice, Mr. Jospin? I don't wish to be forward in doing so." Burton asked with dignity.

Bruno tipped his head toward Burton.

"The objective here is to make money, is it not?"

"Yes, we are engaged in a business."

"I don't know as much about the business as you all do, however I

175

have been in Laos and there are trends that don't favor your business in the long term. The war in Viet Nam will grow larger. That is a long-term inevitability. Would you agree?"

Jospin tipped his head toward Burton and he leaned forward.

"Invest all you can in companies that will be profiting from war manufacturing in the United States. Companies that make war materials including aircraft and munitions will increase in value in the coming years and one could be made rich from the increase in the value of their stock. It doesn't carry the social stigma of drugs and imparts stability and long term growth."

Colonel LeBeau's face grew red as a strawberry. "You impudent bastard, you sit here and eat Mr. Jospin's food and propose to tell *him* what to do?"

Bruno held up both hands. "Shhh. The captain is quite right. This one is smart, unlike you LeBeau. He thinks beyond the horizon. Maybe we will speak of this further but not now. Agreed?"

Burton nodded. "I meant no disrespect."

"I didn't take it that way. You are a smart boy and I like you. But now it is time to say good night. It was a pleasure to meet you, Captain Burton." Bruno stood. Dinner had ended.

On the way out the door, both Truc and Charlotte stood to wish Burton a safe return home. When Burton took Charlotte's hand, she palmed him a note, which he deftly slid into a pocket of his trousers. Once home, he opened the note, which read: *Meet me where the birds catch fish. Tomorrow at noon.*

LARRY B. LAMBERT

TWENTY THREE

Saturday, 20 August 1961 -- 0900 HRS
Boulangerie Moulin Rouge
Samsenthai Road,
Vientiane, Laos

A high white façade and a large glass window marked the bakery on Samsenthai Road. One-way traffic headed toward the French Military Mission Compound and the Airport beyond. Traffic returning to Vientiane took another one-way road on the river-side called River Road. Closer to town, the east and west bound traffic merged into one road called Airport Road. Things were simply not that complicated in Laos.

The bakery opened late on the weekends because the Westerners who frequented it didn't get up early. A florid faced, pot bellied ex-French Army Mess Sergeant ran the bakery the same way he ran the mess back in the old days and the bread was crusty, hot and delicious. Burton pulled the Australian Vespa to the curb, slid off and walked inside. His senses were assailed by smells of home. Because the Mess Sergeant, known only as Marcel, made his own butter, it was as fresh, sweet and delicious as the bread. Good quality butter and cheese, a rare thing in Asia, could be bought at the Moulin Rouge Bakery.

Burton broke out his 100 piaster banknotes and bought éclairs, canelés, bichon au citron, and four baguettes. Marcel packed the pastries in boxes and the baguettes in paper. He added a pound of fresh butter in a tin and sealed it.

Another hundred meters and Burton swung the Vespa right, onto the road that led to the French Military Mission. The guard recognized him, lifted a barrier gate and waved him past, but Burton stopped and offered the sentry one of the éclairs. "Pâtisserie à la Boulangerie Moulin Rouge de Chef Marcel." Burton said in his fractured French, with a heavy American accent.

The sentry lifted it from the box as if it was made of gold and helped Burton repack the box on the back of the Vespa. Once packed and secure he said, "Merci!" He saluted, and Burton drove up the road onto the compound. One additional sentry was stationed there, and he opted for a bichon au citron.

Grall stood on the stoop of the white wood frame headquarters building in civilian clothing that sagged limply from the humidity yet at the same time looked as if he'd slept in them. He had the look. Thinning dark hair with a cheap dye job, the belly, and the face, that one associates with late nights and long hours in bars. A pencil thin mustache, flecks of white that the dye brush missed. His shoes glowed; spit shined leather. Nobody would mistake him for a civilian if they but glanced in his direction.

Grall waved limply. Burton worked with him when he first arrived in Laos and liked him very much. Burton waved back, more enthusiastically and collected his boxes of pastries and bread from the back of the Vespa.

Grall motioned Burton to follow and walked back into the building. Burton walked in behind Grall and set everything down on the adjutant's desk. "I brought peace offerings."

"I always thought you were trouble from the first moment I set eyes on you, Craig." Grall said with a growl. His voice was at least one octave below normal and he had a whiskey and tobacco rasp, accented by a coughing fit that subsided eventually. Once the coughing was over, Grall led the way up the stairs, wordlessly.

They turned left into Commandant Grall's office. Grall had a cup of coffee, half empty sitting on his desk. He refreshed it and poured one for Burton in a green china mug with a French parachutists emblem blazed on the porcelain.

"LeBeau woke me up somewhere around midnight." It was an accusation. "Some high priority cable from Paris." He lit a cigarette and offered one to Burton, who declined. "So I woke up Captain Jean-Marc Barguille, who was in bed with the Malaysian Ambassador's secretary at the time. He thanks you too."

"If she put him to sleep before midnight, he should be thanking me. I've seen her, she's a beast."

"Don't be brutal so early, Craig." Grall cautioned, smiling. "Americans always need to go on the offensive. They wake up early on a Saturday, which is a sin according to holy French tradition."

Burton slurped his coffee. It was scalding hot. He took a seat on Grall's couch and closed his eyes.

"If you go to sleep on me after have me work all night to get things together for you, I swear I'll shit in your pocket while you slumber." Grall said, attempting humor.

"Did Colonel LeBeau tell you what I needed?"

"He said you could have anything you wanted, authorized by General Headquarters. I doubt that it's authorized. It never is. He lies. He lies even when telling the truth would serve him better. He's been here too long, like me. It's a bad habit. The dangers inherent in clandestine military operations such as those we undertake here and in Algeria are self-evident. By allowing us carte blanche to violate any or all military regulations and moral laws they create brutal monsters. Calculated acts of sabotage and terrorism, systematic duplicity in international dealings as an integral part of national defense policy has allowed us to become involved in the Indochina narcotics traffic. It is just another consequence of allowing men to do whatever seems expedient. But there are prices to pay and those prices are exacted as a toll on our eternal souls."

Grall flicked ash from his cigarette, took a drag and then continued. "As evidenced by our change in leadership in Laos. Our masters are not the People of the Republic anymore, but the drug mafia."

Burton looked down.

"And now you are in their orbit as well, like the Russian Sputnik spinning around Earth, eh? You know the Russians put a dog in orbit a few years ago too. It didn't survive—came back down to Earth dead. Somehow I find it incredible that your army would involve itself with Unione Corse."

"I don't work for the army anymore."

Grall's eyebrows arched. "The Monkey King is your master now?" A piece of the puzzle clicked into place for Grall. "You know I saw Walter Kennedy at the White Rose last night. Somebody broke his nose. I asked him if he'd been looking through one-too-many keyholes. You know what he told me?" Grall waited for Burton's response.

"No, I have no idea."

"Walter told me that a bus hit him in the face. Interesting. You used to box – amateur boxing, yes? If you are the bus, I envy you. Have you any idea how many times I wanted to break that bastard's nose?"

"What's your point, Albert?" Burton asked Grall.

"Everybody wants money. And most people don't care how they get it. The Chinese did well in the opium trade but as is usually the case with Chinese, they tended to loose everything they earned in drugs at the

179

gaming tables. Those who ran the gambling halls made the real money from opium. France has profited from opium. That's why the army is still here. We still have a Corsican horse in the race. Where will it lead us, Craig? To grief. That's where."

"Let's get started." Burton said finally.

Commandant Albert Grall shrugged, took another drag on his cigarette and stubbed it out on the ashtray on his desk. "The invasion of the Shan State by the fleeing 3rd and 5th brigades of the 93rd division of the Kuomintang army after the communists took over in China led to collaboration of those forces with your American intelligence. Your people worked with the exiled government in Taiwan. Your people facilitated their involvement in the opium and heroin trade as a way of sustaining themselves economically. All approved by the Truman Administration."

"Are you with me?"

"Lock step."

"Good. Then comes the subsequent military coup in Rangoon and the invasion of the Shan State by the Burmese army using the excuse that they were trying to drive out the Kuomintang. The Burmese and Red Chinese franchised the white powder trade to keep their hands clean as far as the public was concerned. It was transferred under force of arms to Khun Sa, who is an enterprising little shit. He's not at all a fool."

"Khun Sa sees far more profit to refining opium into Number Four Heroin than simply transporting raw opium out of the country to the Corsicans. So the Corsicans are worried. Everybody is squeezing the Guerini Family, run by Bruno these days, from every direction. Bruno Jospin is here with precious little Charlotte because sitting in Marseilles does not solve his dilemma.

"The Red Chinese made a move to take over the Corsican drug base on Coco Island in the Burmese Andamans in concert with Khun Sa's efforts to find the recipe for Number Four Heroin and to make it work. The Corsicans handed them their ass but they'll be back and Jospin knows it.

"Khun Sa holds venerable Reverend Halvard Taylor, father of your officer Lieutenant Creed Taylor as ransom for the recipe, which your CIA definitely has, along with the expertise to train the tribesmen and to supply them with the chemicals they need. The Corsicans know this. They were the French underground during the war with the Nazis and have old friendships with the OSS and its successor, the CIA. Bruno Jospin approaches your spies in person or perhaps by though old man Sabon who has been *our* man for thirty years, and a plan is hatched. Khun Sa is no longer taking orders from the CIA and he needs to be brought to heel. The best way to do this would be to humiliate Khun Sa in his own house and steal back his hostage while at the same time destroying his efforts to produce China White." Grall paused.

"Enter the deep penetration team." Burton said.

Grall made a grand sweeping gesture with his arms. "The Seventh Special Forces has a team that has been running around Northern Laos, into China, into the Shan State, collecting this, killing that, sabotaging this, photographing that and they're good. They're very good. They've never been caught. They have Red Indians, back woodsmen and people like Creed Taylor who grew up there. They spend months at a time under the enemy's nose. Who better to fix the problem? One day you will have to tell me how you keep coming back but—nobody can be lucky forever. No matter what they say about you, Burton, you have been lucky. And you only have to be unlucky *once*."

"Do they want Khun Sa dead?"

"God no," Grall exclaimed! "He's a good minder. He can baby sit the opium farmers. Under normal circumstances he collaborates with everyone. That's his genius. To remove him would be to create chaos and a disruption in the flow of opium. Everybody needs him. He simply needs to be reminded that he's not nearly as big of a player as he's pretending to be at the moment."

"I don't see as we have much of a choice but to go along unless we pack our bags and desert the Army or the CIA or whoever it is that we work for now."

"The Pathet Lao have a price on your heads."

"Yeah," Burton said. "I know. So do the Vietnamese."

"Same thing." Grall said with studied cynicism.

"Let's break out the maps and tell me what and where."

"I don't know all that much," Grall confessed. "Most of it is guess work on my part, reports from unreliable agents, most of whom ride the dragon regularly. That's all I can give you, Craig, but I'll give you what I have."

Grall pushed a file across the desk. "And so you know, so you have a warning, you will be asked to take some *ensanglanté boucaniers* who are former Foreign Legionnaires with you. They work for Jacques Sabon now, which means they have divided loyalties as he does. None of that loyalty, however, would extend to you."

"They won't be going with me." Burton said flatly, without a hint of emotion.

"Maybe they will go separately? I can't say. It's not for me to decide. But the Corsicans will take out an insurance policy and you should take care." Grall shrugged.

TWENTY FOUR

Saturday, 20 August 1961 -- 1130 HRS
The Mekong River,
Vientiane, Laos

Burton walked from the Wat Chanthabouli with its smiling, gilded Buddha, down to the river. He arrived early because he needed time to think and was trying to figure out precisely what was going on. The Wat was full of people, many from the West, who needed a place to sleep. The monks let them bunk at the Buddha's feet because they couldn't even afford a roach-infested windowless room. He looked around at them: English, Aussie, Americans, Germans, who thought they had been called by the Great Zamboni to walk around the world, or ordered by the Mad Hatter to go into the jungle and find enlightenment. They slept at the Lord Buddha's stone feet, spending what money they could scam from parents back home or from their respective embassies, on opium. Burton shrugged and walked out of the temple.

The Lord Buddha must have forgiven them, one and all, for Burton had never heard of the stone statue rising and stepping on any of the human lice.

There weren't many people outside because it was very hot and humid. The place was lethargic, as if somebody overdosed the city on opium. The water drains on the side of the street contained a pungent soup of smells, none of the fragrant.

Potholes in the road were never filled or if they were, the road crew didn't do a good job and they managed to wash out at the next heavy rain. Burton stepped over a large one and as he did so, he saw Charlotte walking near the Mekong River alone.

"Hello." Meeting Charlotte mid-day brought with it a sense of awkwardness. The city slept in the humid summer day but there would be prying eyes even though the place seemed asleep.

She wore a pale yellow sundress and a wide straw hat with a blue band.

"Oh, Craig, I'm early. I went to Habeeb's General Merchandise store and looked for something to bring you, but I couldn't find anything I liked. This is not Paris."

"Where's your bodyguard?"

"Lieutenant Taylor dropped me off at your house. The house boy let me in and I simply walked out the back door."

"He's here for your protection."

Charlotte shot back, "I don't need to be protected."

"Your father obviously thinks you do."

"Then you can protect me." She linked her arm within his and strided out, goading him to walk with her.

"Charlotte, I don't quite know what to say."

"Tell me you love me, then."

"My heart says yes, my head says, no."

She swung his arm, intertwining his fingers with hers. "Follow your heart. I loved you from the first moment I saw you."

"You have no idea who I am." Burton said in an advising tone.

"Then tell me all about you."

"There's not much to tell. I grew up in Michigan. When I was a kid I spent every possible minute out in the woods, up in the wilderness near Lake Huron. I tracked game, especially wolverines, because they were dangerous. My mother worried about me when I didn't come home at night."

"What about your father?"

"He died when I was four years old. I hardly remember him. He worked too hard, died young, Mom moved home to be close to her parents and brought us with her."

"You have brothers and sisters?"

"A brother, in college. He wants to be a doctor. And now you?"

"Bruno isn't my real father. I'm a bastard. My mother was a mistress to a German officer during the war. He was a rich Schutzstaffel officer from Hesse, the Höherer over Marseilles and Southern France. Of course, he was married with a family back home. I was a Nazi's love child. He died in bombing when the Americans invaded southern France.

"My mother was beautiful. Bruno took up with her and she became his mistress. He has another family in Corsica, many children. My mother died when I was young, he sent me to America to school to be out from under foot. When I came back to Marseilles after school, he watched out for me. Bruno Jospin is the only father I've ever known."

184

She stopped and released his hand. "Oh, my God!"

Burton stopped and looked at her, completely confused.

"You're married aren't you? You have children?"

Burton shook his head. "No wife, no girlfriend, no mistress in Laos. With what I do, there is no telling how long I'll live. If you ask Commandant Grall, my life expectancy is not very long."

"Why is this?"

"I work behind the lines, far behind the lines. If things go wrong, there's nobody to save us. And things can go wrong in a New York minute."

"What is a New York minute?"

Burton snapped his fingers. "That quickly."

"Then you won't go on any more of these assignments. You work for Walter Kennedy now?"

"After a fashion, I do."

"I will tell Walter Kennedy that you will remain behind to stay with me."

Burton was not used to dealing with women in general and certainly not with a woman like Charlotte.

She took his hand again and they walked.

"Walter Kennedy told Bruno that your father is in the American Congress."

"Step-father. He doesn't like me very much. I like him even less."

"My step father adores me." Charlotte said matter-of-fact.

Burton suspected that the last statement was simple truth, beyond dispute.

Charlotte turned and pulled Burton behind her up to a large mansion.

Burton observed. "This is the Ambassador's residence."

"He is at some stuffy meeting with Bruno and Colonel LeBeau."

A young Lao servant girl opened the door. "Lizette, this is my fiancé, Captain Burton of the American *Groupe de Commandos Mixtes Aéroportés*. I don't know what it is in English."

The girl curtsied formally and led them to a room, closing the door behind them.

"I'm not used to this." Burton said, embarrassed.

"You can learn—now make love to me."

TWENTY FIVE

Saturday, 20 August 1961 -- 1730 HRS
Setha Palace Hotel
6 Pang Kham Street,
Vientiane, Laos

Wu Ming sat at his table, surrounded by attentive staff and waved cordially to Burton when he walked into the restaurant dining area.

He'd been pondering on the Ministry of State Security's dossier on Craig Burton It couldn't be more different than Walter Kennedy's. The analysis was summarized: *Craig Burton is the step-son of the Capitalist leader Congressman Dan Woods, Democrat from Michigan. Mother Ellen Burton Woods, is the widow of William Parker Burton, Senior Vice President, General Motors Company, known to be a bitter enemy of progressive people's movements and worker's rights. An exploiter of the poor underclass and abused, oppressed workers, William Parker Burton died when his son, Craig was four or five years of age.*

Craig Burton entered the American Running Dog Academy for the subjugation of peace loving people, Military School, West Point and graduated 15th in his class. Since graduation, he specialized in operations against the Peace Loving People's Republic of China and has worked diligently to replace legitimate leaders and cadre with warlords and wicked commissars.

-Served with Ranger units during the unprovoked Imperialist Aggression against the peace loving people of Korea in 1951-53 during which time he was wounded at least once, and was awarded the Silver Star medal for valor.

-Suspected to have been a junior officer assigned with others in an advisory roll, promoting the agenda of reactionary forces in Indonesia to tread on the rights of legitimate workers struggling for freedom. Particularly supporting the Javanese General Suharto.

-Instructor, Special Forces Qualification Course, specializing in jungle warfare.

-Liaison Officer, Tentera Darat Malaysia (Malaysian Army) Rejimen Renjer DiRaja (Royal Malaysian Ranger Regiment) and Kor

186

Risik DiRaja (Royal Intelligence Corps). Graduated from Malaysian tracking and infiltration course.

-Assigned to Program Evaluation Office, Vientiane Laos as French Military Liaison in 1959, transitioned to training team oppressing the legitimate rights of the Laotian people.

-Suspected infiltration of the homeland of the People's Republic of China on many occasions. Speaks fluent Teochiu and Mandarin dialects, reads and writes Chinese. Is known to be an effective murderer with little regard or remorse for his victims, which include a German worker who accidentally bumped into him in a bar, and who he subsequently shot to death without provocation.

"Please join me," Wu said graciously.

Burton sat across the table from Wu. A circular "lazy susan" held a wide variety of dishes.

Pointing with his chopsticks, Wu recited the menu. "Sea slugs, boiled horse tendons, fried eels, birds eggs—not like your runny American eggs, these have chicks inside and best of all, a *pla buk* catfish, hauled from the Mekong this morning. The cat fish was huge, had been cooked whole and rested on a platter where Wu had picked a few morsels of flesh from the carcass."

Burton sat and chopsticked fried eels into a bowl.

A pretty waitress poured tea, followed by another pretty waitress who brought a drink.

"Jameson's neat." Wu pronounced. "I'm glad you came, Craig. I have a favor to ask."

"I came to ask you a favor as well." Burton admitted.

"Before we ask favors and before we eat, I must confess that I saw Walter Kennedy this morning and it seemed as though he had an accident."

Burton said, "I wouldn't know about that."

"You are not inscrutable. That is our way as Chinese. He told me you hit him and that I should beware."

"He said that?" Burton asked.

Wu chomped on horse tendons and spoke as he chewed, "I have known Walter for a long time. I don't like him one bit. He's abrupt and bombastic. My heart swelled with joy to see his broken nose."

Burton sipped the tea.

WHITE POWDER

"You are like Sun Tzu, Burton. You move in and out of the People's Republic of China like a ghost. Your reputation with the *Guoanbu* is impressive. Do you read Sun Tzu?"

"In Chinese," Burton replied in Teochiu, then quoted Sun Tzu, "*Be so subtle that you are invisible. Be so mysterious that you are intangible. Then you will control your rivals' fate.*"

"Of course. You would know that. It's how you out fox everyone."

"Sometimes the wisest fox falls into the snare." Burton said.

"Confucius?" Wu asked.

"Burton." Burton replied.

Wu spun the lazy susan so that Burton would have access to the horse tendons.

"You learned to speak Teochiu from a nanny?"

Burton nodded as he chewed the rubbery tendons. "She was *Chao-yang Hsien*."

Wu looked closely at Burton. "As am I."

"I never knew her Chinese name. She went by Sue."

After another drink, Wu said, "Let me tell you about the Teochiu people. They came south from Northern Coastal China originally to escape one invasion or another. Once they were firmly established in South China, the northern families set about taking over the livelihoods of all the weaker people around them. This was not easy because there were many warlords who held power, had armies, and had *guanxi* with other important warlords.

"Powerful clans, and mafias became involved in predatory commerce, not just deciding who could raise the largest hog or the most delicious dog. They went to war to decide who would prevail. This made them more aggressive, more imaginative and far more avaricious. They invested sums to expand their networks but there was never enough and among these northerners greed remained insatiate.

"The wars continued until they began to destroy each other. Absolute loyalty bound the ruthless clans of moneylenders, rice brokers, gold traders, silk merchants and banking clans. The code of loyalty and the tyranny of trust held each clan together. No matter how far you traveled from home or how much time passed, you belonged to a secret clan.

"The Three-Generation Curse took hold of the most prosperous. The first generation sacrificed everything to get rich, the second lost momentum and the third wasted it on gambling, drugs, whores and expensive things that brought no wealth. After several cycles the clans began to learn their lesson. The only way to dodge the Three-Generation Curse was never to admit that an objective was achieved, to train each new generation as if prosperity were forever distant. Thereafter wealth vanished. Rich men dressed in threadbare gowns, everyone worked in shabby storefronts, feigning poverty. No matter how much money these families accumulated, they practiced extreme frugality.

"As with your army, risk taking is avoided. 'Go along to get along.' Confucius himself condemned risk taking, but as born gamblers, these Chinese believed that fortune rewards only those who dare. They made every effort to be calculating, hence their endless fascination with Sun Tzu's *The Art of War*. They adopted the God of War, Kwan Ti, as the God of Wealth. They taught themselves to stay invisible. Only those who remained invisible could expect to hold on to their wealth in the face of continual extortion by imperial eunuchs and bureaucrats."

Burton said, "And the clans remain as they were. A secret society curled within an enigma."

Wu nodded. It amazed him that Burton grasped these concepts so readily. He must have been taught well as a child.

"What does this have to do with a favor?" Burton asked.

Wu reached in his jacket and pulled out a small, elegantly carved 24 karat gold dragon, not more than three inches long. He put it on the lazy susan and twirled the carrier so that the dragon ended up in front of Burton.

"Pick it up, Craig."

Burton turned it over in his hands. "It's beautiful."

"Give it to Khun Sa when you see him. It will mean more coming from you than it would from me."

A question crossed Burton's features, unasked.

"You see, Khun Sa commissioned the greatest craftsman in Hong Kong to carve a solid gold dragon." Wu spread his arms wide. "His pretense is unconscionable."

"And this is what is delivered?"

Wu nodded.

"A message that he is not as big of a dragon as he presumes himself to be?"

Wu nodded again.

189

"What makes you think I'll meet Khun Sa?"

Wu lifted his glass of whiskey. "I'm simply following what Sun Tzu set down. I'm trying to be so subtle that I am invisible and so mysterious that I am intangible."

"Now, I see the bird's eggs do not entice you?"

Burton smiled and shook his head.

"They're cold anyway and there's nothing worse than a flaccid bird embryo."

Burton pocketed the gold dragon.

"You have a favor to ask of me?" Wu Ming asked.

Smiling, Burton said, "I came here to ask how I'd go about finding Khun Sa."

"The opium trail winds down from the Shan State in Burma through Laos and into Thailand. Khun Sa's particular route crosses from Burma into Laos north of Muong Mounge. From there it winds down to the Mekong River, crossing into Thailand at Chiang Saen. Sometimes they unload the opium onto boats and float it down the river. Usually that is only done if bandits are operating in the district. Boats can be easier to protect depending on the circumstances.

"It sounds too easy. Go to the head of the trail." Burton suggested.

"It is no more complicated than that." Wu Ming affirmed. "It's a very open secret."

"Why don't they fly it out?" Burton suggested.

"Too high profile. Three hundred tons is a lot of opium. It means over a hundred flights in a C-47. People would get suspicious. Even if you broke it down to #2 Heroin, you would still be making thirty or more flights to get the shipment out. Range is also an issue with the aircraft fully loaded, depending on where you are flying. Aircraft runways can be disabled by the competition, it marks a location to attack. There are many problems associated with airplanes unless the CIA does the flying for you and those days have passed now that the *Kuomintang* have been pushed out of Burma. Mules are safer, more reliable, and they don't crash in bad weather the way airplanes are prone to do. Airplanes are expensive and they need parts. Mules breed and only eat grass and drink water. When the airplanes no longer fly they are hulks. When the mules no longer work, they are killed and used to feed the mule drivers. The Corsicans have small air charter operations but they buy the opium from Khun Sa that comes out on mules mainly. Airplanes are a status symbol."

190

"So we follow the yellow brick road."

"The road is paved with skulls, not with yellow bricks." Wu Ming said seriously, not understanding the colloquial expression associated with the *Wizard of Oz*.

Burton left Wu Ming and met Chester Watson at the Australian Embassy. They had dinner at the small canteen and bar to the rear of the building on the ground floor.

Chester wore his uniform and looked fit and polished.

"You clean up well." Burton observed.

"I've been in air conditioning all day. You on the other hand look like somebody dumped a bucket of water on you."

"Cuppa tea and some ANZAC biscuits while we wait for supper?" Chester offered.

Burton nodded, "Sounds great."

Chester nodded to a tiny Laotian lady who went for tea.

"I saw that dag, Kennedy. Definitely a few Kangaroos loose in the top paddock there. Somebody must have knocked him arse over tit and broke his nose. I asked him what happened. He said it was a bus that hit him. I told the bastard, 'cods wallop'. Figured you were the bus."

"What did he do? Insult the Shiela?"

Burton's face told the story.

"The married one?"

"She's single, not married. I found that out."

Chester cautioned, "Don't forget to use a franger."

"What's that?"

"A rubber, mate. A condom."

Chester offered a pouch of chewing tobacco. Burton declined with a shake of his head.

"Ever try betel nut?"

"That shit's for gooks and only gooks. Don't tell me you tried it?" Chester said, incredulous.

Burton nodded. "I thought I could get a buzz from it when I first got here."

"How'd it taste?"

"Terrible, bitter and weird—almost like acid. I was in the South training the Royal Lao Army and I was bored so I went into a hamlet and bought some. My lips and tongue were numb for two days after I tried it.

191

I would have puked it up but there were Royal Lao types there watching my reaction and it would have been a loss of face. So I sucked it up."

"It smells a bit like lime," Chester observed, "not bitter." He hinted at an interest in trying the local peasant narcotic in the past. "I always figured you could get away with chewing it in the out-back on patrol since the locals chew it. They wouldn't think twice about betel nut odor. Tobacco's another matter. It's a certain give-away."

"It smells one way when people are spitting it but it tastes differently." Burton affirmed.

Thai vegetables with a mutton chop arrived on platters. The Australians tried to blend home and Laos and always got it wrong. Burton's conversation with Chester revolved around Burma and Chester made few suggestions. He'd been there and like Burton, understood that Burma was hostile ground, a long way from help. After dinner they went home sober and made an early night of it.

TWENTY SIX

Sunday, 21 August 1961 -- 0700 HRS
Chinaimo Military Camp,
Vientiane, Laos

Burton drove out of Vientiane on the Australian Vespa, following the Mekong River, south to the Chinaimo Military Camp, a few miles from the center of the nation's capital. The Monkey King planned to meet them at a satellite facility to the Consolidated Fruit Company office that had been designated within the camp. Paint, Gorman and Taylor worked on it while Willoughby oversaw the installation of a powerful radio transceiver.

At the gate, and checkpoint to the camp, Burton saw that the Royal Laotian army Light Infantry, or *Batallion Léger Laotien* had been replaced by the more reliable and seasoned *Battalion Parachutistes Laotians*. Laotian politics was tenuous at best with the different factions within the Royal Family swinging toward the US, Russia and neutrality, respectively. The presence of the parachute battalion could mean anything but likely presaged some sort of expected trouble. Internal political instability was nothing new in Laos.

He presented credentials to the sentry who called a non-commissioned officer to approve Burton. The NCO knew Burton on sight, saluted and passed him.

Burton parked the Vespa in the nearly deserted parking area of the military headquarters, an old French provincial plantation house. The building projected a sense of dilapidated grandeur. Two other Jeeps were parked there as well, painted white in honor of the neutrality of Laos.

The French whitewashed plantation house had been ringed with defensive sandbagged gun emplacements and barbed wire. Laotian paratroopers lounged near two vintage Bofors 40mm anti aircraft guns that provided the centerpiece of the defensive preparations.

The Monkey King arranged for a thirty-foot-long wooden ISO hooch, a combination building and tent. There was no pretense of security for the building. Each end of the pre-fab structure had been covered by screen. Rolled up canvas was placed so that it could be dropped in the event of severe rain. A moat-like trench had been excavated around the outside of the building as a catch basin for the monsoon. A slab of plywood bridged the moat. In the center of the hooch, a seventy-foot antenna mast was in the process of assembly. Sam Willoughby directed four other soldiers in civilian clothing as they strung guy wires to support the antenna.

"Hey Sam, are these the new ASA guys?"

"No sir," Willoughby responded. "They're marines from the Embassy guard who offered to give me a hand in exchange for beer and steaks."

"So we're still having a Sunday Bar-B-Que?"

"It begins my three-rocker reinstatement."

"I thought the Bar-B-Que was our official celebration of the opening of the US Agriculture Mission to Laos."

"That too. I've invited some of the Air America guys. They're smuggling the steaks that I have it on good authority were stolen by my Army Security Agency buddies from some Navy Officer's Mess in Japan. The Australians are coming and bringing the beer. They'll also be roasting a whole mutton. Major Piper and the officers are tending to the bar, and the Laotians are coming too."

"How many Laotians?"

"The officers from the parachute battalion and they're bringing their families. This is their camp."

"Who else?"

"Some of the Company spooks invited themselves, Tony Poe is coming down from Long Cheng and he'll be coming with the Marine Aviators."

"So what's the head count?" Burton asked, amazed.

"No more than a hundred and fifty. The Laotians have cooks making traditional food. Tony Poe is bringing General Vang Pao and a couple of the Hmong leaders. Habbib is bringing kabob from town."

"Vang Pao doesn't see eye to eye with the Royal Laotian Army."

"He promised no politics."

Burton nodded, dubious.

"No Chinese or Russians?"

"I figured they were all spies." Sam Willoughby said firmly.

"Carry on, master sergeant and make sure that you get a guest list to the Parachute Battalion so they can be passed through."

LARRY B. LAMBERT

***

Theoretically, the Consolidated Fruit Company officially assisted the Laotian government under a US Department of Agriculture grant.

Creed Taylor, Jimmy Paint and Paul Gorman had been officially stripped of US Army identity and were accredited agricultural advisors to the Royal Laotian Interior Ministry. Burton was accredited as their manager. Sam Willoughby and the ASA communications team who were due in the following week were horticultural specialists whose work was largely administrative under the terms of the hastily assembled grant. A powerful radio transmitter and receiver was deemed necessary for the field representatives of the Consolidated Fruit Company to communicate with a distant and unspecified headquarters regarding immediate needs of Laotian horticulture. When the ASA Team arrived, they were expected to improve the security arrangements at the ISO hooch.

The inside of the Consolidated Fruit Company hooch was anything but an agricultural support mission for the needy Laotian people. Four sets of bunks occupied one end of the hooch. Five very old US Government desks edged against the walls in the other half. A worn and torn North Vietnamese trophy flag hung from nails in the thin plywood wall. Under it were media photos of Steve McQueen, James Dean and The Lone Ranger and Tonto. The Lone ranger had a large X drawn over both him and his horse. Tonto looked fierce and defiant. An arsenal of captured arms and ammunition and a small quantity of American munitions were scattered in crates and on pallets under drop cloths between the bunks and the desks. Cosmaline and grease scented the air.

A dilapidated wood desk had the words C.O. written on a piece of paper and taped to front of it. An in-box brimmed with typed copy, routine unclassified telexes, black and white high-resolution photographs of hills, roads and vegetation and a well read copy of *Playboy* with 'property of Goatman' written neatly on the cover in black magic marker. There were also half a dozen guard mail envelopes.

"Are we making the world safe for hypocrisy as usual?" Creed asked sarcastically, looking up at Burton from where he was banging the keys of an Underwood typewriter.

Jimmy Paint read a *Superman* comic book, Goatman slept soundly.

"Jimmy."

Paint set the comic down, dog-earing a page as he did so to mark his

195

place. "Sir?"

"Get some coolies to work filling sand bags. Doesn't matter if it's Sunday. I want them six feet high and at least three bags deep all the way around the perimeter of the hooch before the job is done."

"Yes sir."

"Jimmy."

"Yes sir?"

"I want them sturdy just in case we take mortars or rockets— and you're a fruit horticulturist now. You don't need to sir me."

"Can I swap out the trigger assembly of this Chinese AK-47 for the same assembly on this B-40 rocket launcher, first?"

"Better that than a *Superman* comic—and wake up Goatman, have him help you police up this place. We're expecting company."

"Yes—Craig."

Burton thought that it sounded wrong but smiled and walked on to Taylor.

"I'm surveying out all this equipment as shipped to the Royal Laotians and lost in combat." Creed Taylor said.

"The army marches on a sea of paper."

"It would be nice to get a clerk typist here to handle this." Creed said dryly.

Burton reminded him, "The Security Agency will have a team here Monday or Tuesday and they can pick up the slack. They'll have a lieutenant with them as well. If things get out of hand, I'll have the Monkey King send one of his tame spooks from the typing pool to help out."

"There are a lot of people coming to Sam's party."

"Seems as if the war took a holiday." Burton replied. "I didn't complain because we're going to be mounting a mission to recover your dad, Creed. Soon. And it has all the makings of a real nasty one."

Creed's eyes were locked on his fingers as he banged on the typewriter.

"Before the Monkey King gets here with his entourage, you need to seriously consider staying behind on this one. I can't have you getting twitchy on me out there."

"I'm going, sir."

"Give me one good reason?" Burton demanded.

"He's *my* dad."

196

A knock at the door announced the Monkey King and a short, trim man, whose eyes were obscured by aviator sunglasses. He wore impeccably clean creased khaki civilian clothing and a Chicago Cubs baseball cap. The Monkey King wore a white shirt, tie and corduroy trousers.

"Craig Burton, this is Lieutenant Colonel Howard Sevigny, US Air Force. Call sign Skids."

"Colonel Skids Sevigny?" Burton shook Sevigny's hand and then the CIA Station Chief's.

"Belly landing during training – Skids." Howard (Skids) Sevigny explained, as if he'd been explaining it for a long time.

Burton nodded and introduced Taylor. "This is Creed Taylor, my executive officer." Creed stood and walked to them, shaking hands in turn.

"I brought Skids along because we need to talk about the up-country mission your team will undertake." The Monkey King was expansive in his arm movements.

"What mission would that be, sir?" Burton played dumb, but the Monkey King plowed ahead.

"I call it Operation KNUCKLEBALL and we're going to use your people here, the Air Force who are operating under Operation MILL POND and whatever indigenous people you think you might need for support.

"Mr. Keene," Lt. Col. Sevigny said, referring to the Monkey King, "told me about what you might need in the way of resources and I'm here to see that you get whatever it takes."

"I have no idea what the operation might be sir." Burton looked at Taylor who also shrugged. "We're simply setting up the communications and logistics office for agricultural support here."

The Monkey King took a deep breath. "This building's not secure, we can't talk here." Keene pronounced.

"It's where you wanted to meet, sir." Burton commented.

"Let's go back to the Green House."

Taylor, Burton, Lt. Col. Sevigny and The Monkey King piled into the black Embassy Buick and headed into Vientiane.

"So what's your story, Skids?" Creed asked once they were on the road.

"We have sixteen B-26B Invaders at Takhli Royal Thai Air Force

Base. They're wicked on strafing runs. Six fifty-caliber machine guns in the nose and another eight on under-wing pods if you want us to tear up the jungle. For longer-range missions we can put fuel bladders in the bomb bay and get 1,800 nautical miles out of the ships if we have to. Full bomb load, figure 1,100 nautical miles."

"Markings?" Burton asked.

"They're clean, no national markings or tail numbers." Skids Sevigny replied.

"I'm thinking a special mix on the fifty-cal ammo. Alternate armor piercing incendiary and tracer on all aircraft, all guns."

"You don't even know exactly what the mission is yet, Burton." The Monkey King interrupted.

"If I'm wrong you can countermand the suggestion, Mr. Keene."

The CIA man looked at Burton seated next to him, in the passenger seat, but didn't say anything else.

"What sort of comms?" Burton asked.

"Long range to call up the mission and then you can guide us in with handi-talkies when we're close. Better if you pop smoke on the target—if it's possible. We'll be White King One through however many are in the flight. We can talk about the targets and bomb load outs when Mr. Keene tells us what we'll be hitting but I favor Mk81 snakeye and Mk47 napalm combos for most applications in Laos. We get a better disbursal from more, lighter bombs than we do with one or two heavy bombs, we can drop them from lower altitude and even put parachutes or retarding fins on them if we need to come in on the deck. We're limited in how many bombs we can carry based on the range. Most of the targets in Laos are soft skin buildings, troops and such. As far as aircraft, we can bring them all if you want to obliterate something. This mission has priority, right?"

Mongomery Keene nodded. "Cleared by the Chief of Far East Ops himself."

"Weather?" Skids asked the CIA Chief.

"We'll be doing this soon, so plan on monsoon sloppy."

"If you guys can carry a man-portable TACAN radio transmitter in with you. It has enough power to get out of whatever valley you drop it in. The CIA has them. It might help us find you. Laos is hell during the monsoon. Lots of weather, bad ground fog. Impossible at night."

"It might take a couple of days to get them here." Keene said. "I'm not so sure how much it weighs, but it's designed to be run out under low visibility conditions. We have them stored in Japan. I'll send a cable out on that." He pulled out a fountain pen and scribbled in a small notebook as he drove.

"We're limited on the weight we can carry." Burton suggested and Creed Taylor nodded. "Batteries are heavy."

"You'd only be carrying it on the way in." Keene added.

Sevigny voiced concern. "The down side of a TACAN is that once you turn it on, anybody with a radio direction finder will know where it is. The enemy can use the range and bearing to attack the TACAN. They're accurate. The new ones use a two frequency principle that will bring us in right on top of them."

"Maybe we could load up Sam with all the Comm gear?" Creed suggested. "We could pack his stuff until he dropped the TACAN. We can load out light with ammo and replenish it from the Pathet Lao, wherever we're going." Creed looked at the CIA Chief. "Mr. Keene, I expect that we'll be going where the enemy is."

The big black Buick pulled into the parking area next to the Green House and they all got out.

"You know, Creed, you are a fucking smart ass." The Monkey King said after thinking over his sarcastic tone.

Once cloistered in the secure briefing room, Keene opened his briefcase and pulled out four thick folders. The covers had a broad red stripe diagonally across the face and the words Top Secret – KNUCKLEBALL, were stamped onto the covers.

"The mission is two-fold. To recover Halvard C. Taylor from whatever location he's being held and to repatriate him to friendly forces. Secondly, your team needs to find and destroy opium refining and processing factories that have been set up by Khun Sa in the Shan State. We don't know precisely where they are."

"It's a big area. Like the size of Massachusetts or something." Creed interrupted.

Keene continued as if Creed Taylor hadn't said a thing. "First, Burton's Tartar Team will handle the recon. They'll insert into the area by any means they choose, scout and report. Once they know where Halvard Taylor is, they can come up with an operational plan to spring him and then extract him. Because we think he's in Burma we can't use our Hmong allies or the Royal Laotian Army. That shouldn't be a problem for your men, Burton, because you work alone, don't you?"

"Yes, almost all the time, sir."

"Colonel Sevigny will have aircraft on call and you will have first priority. Once you develop an operational plan I'll need to approve it. It shouldn't be a problem, Burton, because you and Creed, here have forgotten more than I know about this sort of thing. I suggest that once you have approval, you transmit your coordinates and time-on-target. The B-26's will be in the air. Switch on the TACAN and it will bring the aircraft right down the chute to you. Mark targets and then get out of the way and let the White Kings do what they do.

"I need you two," The Monkey King pointed vaguely at Taylor and Burton, "to come up with an operational plan, logistics requirements, and everything we will need by Tuesday. That only gives you the rest of today. I want it on my desk Tuesday by noon. I'll QC the plan and forward it to Desmond in Japan for his reaction."

"What sort of intelligence support do we have in this?"

"If you're asking me where Reverend Taylor is, I don't have anything on that. Same goes for the drug labs."

"So we have until Tuesday to come up with a detailed Op plan." Creed said.

"Why so much time, I thought you were in a hurry." Burton added, straight faced. Keene didn't pick up on any of it and plowed ahead. "We have some scouts we'd like to send along with you so plan for another four men. They'll be first rate."

Burton stood, surprising the spymaster. "No, it will be the five of us. Five fingers on a hand. Five fingers on the team. That's it."

"You work for me, Burton."

"I'm not in the army. I'm a civilian. I can quit."

Keene stood, his eyes roughly even with Burton's chin. "You can *try* to quit."

"What's the *real* objective here? Why do you want *me* involved in KUNCKLEBALL?"

Keene sat down, remembering that the mission was designed to ingratiate Burton with the Corsicans so that they'd include him in their ranks, embedding him. He licked his lips. "All right, Burton. Just the five of you, but keep the goal in mind."

"Walter Kennedy and I have an understanding."

Three deep breaths later and Keene said, "You're all dismissed. Get that plan to me and we'll go from there."

They left Keene's office.

"You want to come to a party, Skids?" Burton asked.

"Only if there's beer."

"Australian beer." Creed assured him.

Skids Sevigny, Creed Taylor and Craig Burton walked out of the Green House, past the Marine guard and took Keene's Buick back to Chinaimo.

By the time they arrived back at Camp Chinaimo, trucks were unloading. The coals were hot and uninvited guests joined the throng.

The Air America crews flew in an unbelievably large number of stolen t-bone steaks, full racks of pork ribs, Idaho potatoes and corn-on-the-cob that had all been earmarked for officer's clubs throughout Japan. It was all either on the bar-b-que or staged for when space became available over the coals.

A few of the Laotian officers lit off ant-aircraft artillery simulators to signal the official beginning of the celebration. Burton opined that once they were liquored up, the twin Bofors mounts would be pumping 40mm tracers across the sky.

Winthrop G. Brown, ambassador extraordinary and plenipotentiary of the United States of America introduced Craig Burton as the contract representative from Consolidated Fruit Company, working on behalf of the US Department of Agriculture to bring better crop diversity to Laos. Burton mumbled a few words of thanks and told everyone to have a good time.

The party took on a dimension out of all proportion to the original intent. The guest list blossomed as the Laotians invited friends and friends of friends. After all, it was their base.

"It's like Jesus feeding the five-thousand," Burton commented to Willoughby, who was drunk but still standing on wobbly legs when the party began in earnest. Willoughby replied but Burton couldn't understand a word he said.

Burton led Sam Willoughby to the ISO hooch and put him on a bunk. Goatman snored in a bunk, cradling a nearly empty bottle of Crown Royal.

When Burton got back, Chester Watson, Albert Grall and Creed Taylor were deep in discussion.

Grall defended the French. "Laos is too mountainous for plantations, there's no mineral wealth so no mining, the Mekong has cataracts and is not navigable from the ocean. Farmers tried to cultivate coffee and rubber but the only thing that grows here with any value is opium."

Chester weighed in, "The French became addicted to the opium and the Laotian women and left the administration to Vietnamese civil servants."

"Let's face it," Creed said with a smile, "there's nothing here worth dying for but opium. It's the only reason the communists want to be on top—so they can control the trade."

The discussion depressed Burton, who pointed out the Monkey King who was fetching drinks. "Would it be possible for Mr. Keene to get his snout any farther up Ambassador Brown's ass?"

The conversation shifted to a game of whose-boss-is-the-biggest-asshole. Each had contributions with the exception Creed Taylor, who wasn't drunk enough to lay into Burton.

Chester Watson hoisted an impossibly large mug brimming with frothy beer and offered a toast, "To the finest Jungle Warriors in the world!"

Albert Grall lifted a glass of red wine and said fervently, "To the Centre d'Entrainment a la Foret Equatoriale and all who are trained there!"

"I beg to differ, my son." Chester said, "The best are trained in Queensland at the Jungle Training Center at Kokoda Barracks in Canungra. All the rest are cheap imposters. And the best instructor, I'm forced to admit, is none other than yours truly, Chester Watson."

Grall replied with Gallic sarcasm, "Those who can not survive the training in the jungles of Guiana might find the Australian course a welcome vacation."

Burton hefted a bottle of Australian lager, "To Australian beer, French women and Kem Sungai Udang where they've forgotten more than the Aussies, French and Americans know combined about jungle warfare."

Grall squinted at Burton. Chester, whose eyes were in perpetual squint mode anyway, squinted at Burton even harder. Slowly majors Watson and Grall lifted their beverages in a toast to the Malaysian jungle warriors and trackers.

"That's why you lace your boots that way. You were there." Grall pronounced.

"Two years."

"But," Watson countered, "the Maylay aside, the best is still Ganungra."

As Grall and Watson had at it over whose training was more difficult, Burton looked across the grinder at Jimmy Paint.

Paint sipped rice whiskey with some of the Lao officers as the sun dropped. When he had enough of that, he handed out candy to the children who came with their parents. The kids circled like chummed fish.

At one booth, manned by a senior Laotian non-commissioned officer, a dozen twelve-year-olds crowded around a table, placing 10-kip bets onto a grid featuring cartoon fish, crabs and shrimp.

He saw Jimmy passing and asked, "Luck, soldier?"

Jimmy squatted in the midst of the children and won six consecutive pots by betting on the crab, the children stared at him in reverent amazement. He handed his winnings to a younger child. That child was immediately pressed by the others to bet his windfall.

Two Thai generals and their staffs came from bases over the border and Madame Lulu brought her girls, admonished to remain on their best behavior. Chester Watson and the Australians brought two full muttons and a lorry full of cases of iced beer. The British diplomatic corps remained aloof, concerned lest they be seen to be enjoying the party. The French Mission brought wine, cheese and hobnobbed only with those of higher social standing. The entire diplomatic community attended unbidden with the exception of the Russian and Chinese contingents. A party in Vientiane tended to bring out everyone.

Walter Kennedy never showed up to the party, which wound its way long into the evening.

TWENTY SEVEN

Sunday, 21 August 1961 -- 1900 HRS
Villa Aljaccio,
Ban Dua, Thailand

Petru Batisti cracked his knuckles and looked hard at Walter Kennedy. Petru had been a professional boxer. Unlike Burton who seemed to have achieved a measure of fame without having his head pounded soft, Petru had a flattened boxer's nose, two cauliflower ears and a hulking physique. Bruno Jospin plucked him out of a le Jardin d'Eden where he was a doorman and bouncer. Petru killed a customer in a routine eviction because he didn't know his own strength. Indochina was the alternative to twenty years confinement in the *Marseilles Baumettes Geôle*.

He had long arms like an ape, with heavy muscles and a neck too thick for any but custom shirts. Petru wasn't tall, he was menacing. Through eyes under heavy Neanderthal brow ridges, he took the measure of Walter Kennedy and found him wanting.

Kennedy decided to ooze charm. "Petru, it's been nice spending the afternoon here in the air conditioning but I really must go."

"You will stay until Signore Jospin is ready to receive you."

"Can I have another drink?"

Petru snapped his fingers and the butler moved forward from his position near the door. "Get him what he wants."

"Grappa."

"Bassano del Grappa." Petru commanded.

It took some time for the crystal water glass, half filled with clear liquid to arrive.

"Thank you," Kennedy said, and raised his glass, *"Di tutti scunsulati, Di tutti tribulati."*

The toast to the disconsolate and unfortunate moved Petru. It was a Corsican toast and he smiled slightly at Kennedy to convey his appreciation.

The smile had a chilling effect on Kennedy's mood because Petru's love of brutality spilled as if from the center of his soul.

Bruno Jospin swept into the room with two accountants and a lawyer on his heels.

"Bruno!" Kennedy said, brimming with good will.

"I've made a decision where Captain Burton is concerned. He will remain in Vientiane." His words were flat, his mood somewhat stressed by the staff who followed him. "The French High Command will cable the American Army at Supreme Headquarters Allied Forces Europe and will issue an urgent request from Général de Gaulle himself, requesting that Captain Craig Burton be transferred as senior liaison officer to the Second French Foreign Legion parachute battalion at Calvi, Corisca. If there is any problem, le Grand Charles will call President Kennedy on a private line and make the request personally. I spoke to Prime Minister Debré personally this morning, which is last night in Paris. He sees no problem."

"Hold on!" Kennedy stood suddenly, causing Petru to draw a heavy revolver and point it in Kennedy's direction. "Just one goddamned minute. I don't know who the fuck you think you are—." Then it struck Walter Kennedy that Bruno Jospin knew precisely who he was. He instinctively touched his bruised and broken nose and turned to look down the barrel of Petru's handgun. Kennedy raised both hands slowly. "There's a lot riding on this, Bruno."

"What sort of betrayal do you plan against me, Walter?"

"Nothing. Nothing at all, but the CIA is involved and they won't like this."

"Have Allen Dulles call President Kennedy then and your president can talk about it with my president." Bruno wasn't bluffing. Bruno didn't bluff. He simply didn't need to.

"The whole thing will fall apart without Burton."

"What whole thing? Not my business. Charlotte says he intends to propose marriage and I will recognize the matter."

Kennedy took a moment to gather his wits. "Isn't she married to Jacques Sabon?"

"No, she will be married in the Holy Roman Church to Captain Burton."

"Does Burton know this?" Kennedy asked, now calm.

"They are in love. Their union must be pure. She is a virgin. There will be no long courtship. No mistakes. This is a matter of my family, and it is also a concern of State, which means of le Grand Charles, Eighteenth

President of the French Republic and Co-Prince of Andorra, who will be godfather to their first child."

Walter Kennedy was speechless. Burton did it. The son-of-a-bitch did it. But he didn't do it the right way because the problem of Burmese and Laotian opium had not been settled and the CIA's position, which is to say, Kennedy's position remained unresolved.

"At the moment, I am trying to decide whether to hold the wedding at the Vatican and asking the Pontiff, Blessed John the twenty-third, Vicar of Christ, to join them or whether it will be at the Paris Archdiocese, where they could be wedded by Maurice Cardinal Feltin. Charlotte will have the wedding she always wanted to the man of her dreams. I so swear it by the blood of *your* head, Walter!"

Bruno's staff, cowed by the magnitude of what they just heard, looked on in wonderment. The attorney crossed himself solemnly.

Kennedy picked up the glass of grappa and said with utmost sincerity, "To the happy couple."

TWENTY EIGHT

Monday, 22 August 1961 -- 0620 HRS
"Sidney House", 2 Thadeua Road,
Sisattanak District,
Vientiane, Laos

Charlotte woke him with a kiss that he returned passionately until it dawned on Burton that he recalled going to bed by himself. He opened his eyes and she was there, bright, cheerful and looking more beautiful than he had ever seen her.

"You are looking at me like a confused dog." Charlotte pronounced.

"Did we sleep together?" Burton asked, not quite getting it.

Charlotte feigned hurt. "Oh, I am that memorable?"

When he didn't respond she said, "Get out of bed, we're going flying."

"Huh?"

"I'll be outside waiting for you. There is breakfast in the car."

Ten minutes later, Burton emerged from the house to find a hulking chauffeur standing next to the black Citroen. He smoked a cigarette with a sense of bitter resentment directed toward Burton. Charlotte stood by the chauffer, buoyant.

"My love, this is Petru, my chauffeur and new bodyguard."

"Mr. Petru." Burton said, extending a hand.

Petru studied Burton and the proffered hand, dropped his cigarette, crushed it with a size 15 oxford and opened the back door of the car.

Charlotte cast a sideways glance at Petru as she entered the car. "Petru takes time to get to know you but he's my big champion."

She opened a wicker basket filled with croissants, a jar of strawberry jelly and showed him a thermos. "Coffee."

The coffee turned out to be half a gallon of powerful Corsican espresso, the croissants were crusty, warm and delicious.

"So where are we going?" Burton asked.

"It's a surprise." Charlotte said, smugly, enjoying her secret.

"I have a meeting at the Embassy."

"They'll wait. This is Laos. Everything is slow here."

207

Burton resigned himself to the breakfast and Charlotte's delightful company. The ride to the airport passed very quickly between Charlotte's comments on the scenery they passed as they drove through Vientiane to the airport and the food.

At Wattay Airfield, Petru drove onto the runway near where an Air America C-46 Commando was taxiing for a take-off.

"Are we going in that?" Burton asked, innocently curious.

Charlotte punched his arm playfully, "I can't fly that airplane."

Petru continued to a Cessna L-19 Bird Dog. Burton recognized the aircraft. The Bird Dog served as a taxi for the big brass in Korea and also filled the reconnaissance and artillery observation role. The L-19 had a haze gray paint scheme with French Air Force markings: Red-white-blue roundels with the legend, *Groupe marchant de l'extrême-orient*, blazed on the side in black lettering.

"I wanted to fly the *Criquet*, but it was in use." She pouted. "It's more intimate. It was built by Morane-Saulnier under the Vichy government. It's the same thing as a Fieseler-156 Storch."

"You are a women of many surprises, but I can't fly an airplane, Charlotte."

"Silly, not you, I will fly the airplane."

"You can fly?" Burton asked dubiously.

"Of course I fly. Come, get in the airplane and I will do the walk around."

Burton complied, taking the rear co-pilot's seat, while Charlotte walked around the aircraft. He looked at Petru, standing by the car, smoking nervously, looking at Charlotte inspecting the aircraft.

"Dual controls?" He asked Charlotte, wiggling an aileron.

"It's a training aircraft so there are controls for both the pilot and the passenger." She spoke, examining every detail of the aircraft, never taking her eyes off the aircraft. Then she looked up at Burton and smiled. "The weather is clear and it's a beautiful day for a flight. Put the radio headphones on and I'll be in soon."

Burton looked at the controls until Charlotte entered the cockpit. She flipped switches.

"Clear!" Charlotte yelled through the open window of the L-19.

The propeller spun once and the engine caught and roared. The entire airframe vibrated.

Charlotte spoke to Burton through the intercom in the aircraft. Her voice came through the headphones. "We get permission to fly and then we fly."

"Wattay Tower, Armée de l'Air 447 Able on one-two-two-point-two, over." Charlotte spoke into the microphone ad if she'd been doing it all her life.

"Armée de l'Air 447 Able Wattay Tower, over." The voice was American, Southern drawl.

"Wattay Tower, Armée de l'Air 447 Able, request VFR Traffic Advisories for Vientiane and permission to taxi."

"Armée de l'Air 447 Able, Wattay Tower, the pattern is clear, you are clear to taxi, hold at the threshold, runway one-nine Left."

Charlotte motioned to Petru, who stood by chocks that held the wheels in place. His face wore a concerned grimace. He pulled the chock free and the aircraft began to move.

She steered the little Cessna to the beginning of the runway.

"Wattay Tower, Armée de l'Air 447 Able, request permission to take off."

"Armée de l'Air 447 Able, you are clear to take off, have a nice day, Wattay Tower."

Impressed, surprised and curious, Craig Burton watched the landscape speed by and Charlotte eased the aircraft off the runway, executing a gentle bank to the left, over Highway 13 and then over the Mekong River.

Burton picked up the microphone, made sure the switch in front of him was pushed to the intercom setting and keyed the hand set. "I'm impressed, Charlotte. How long have you been flying?"

"You are my first passenger. I flew solo last week for the first time."

A shot of bile came up Burton's throat as he thought, 'she's not lying'.

"You're doing very well."

"Merci beaucoup!"

"Where are we going?"

"To the Snow Leopard Inn."

Burton knew of the Snow Leopard Inn by reputation. It was a hunting lodge in the village of Ban Phong Savang in the Southern Laotian Panhandle roughly equidistant between Viet Nam and Thailand. Based only on gossip, it was the location where most of the opium business was conducted. He'd never been there, but he'd been close. It was in Military

WHITE POWDER

Region Three on the Nakay Plateau, east of Highway 8, not far from bases named 'The Dropzone' and 'Yankee Pad', both of which were staffed by White Star Mobile Training Teams.

They flew in silence except for a few times when Charlotte commented on items of interest below. Burton grunted responses, calming from his original concern.

"Nakhon Phanom Radio, Armée de l'Air 447 Able requesting VFR traffic advisories."

Burton listened as Charlotte interacted with the Royal Thai Air Force Base at Nakhon Phanom, located on the Thai-Laotian border, not far from their destination. A flight of Laotian T-28 aircraft engaged with a ground target some distance to the northeast and a passenger flight from Hue, Viet Nam to Cheng Mai, Thailand flew not far to their southeast. Otherwise, the air was theirs.

About the time Burton became comfortable with the flight, Charlotte called to him on the intercom. "My love, we will land now."

They had been moving lower for some time and after they crossed over a hamlet with a broad dirt runway, Charlotte banked hard until she was roughly lined up with the runway.

Her landing proved to be rougher than the take-off had been. All in all, Burton felt lucky to be alive, true to the axiom, there was no such thing as a bad landing. If you could walk away from it, the landing was good. She taxied to a small shack and killed the engine. Two men stood by to secure the aircraft in what passed as a tie-down facility.

"Get car—me go." Charlotte said in Pidgin English to one of the ground crew. "Get petrol, put in airplane." The man smiled with betel nut stained teeth.

They got out and an ancient moped putted up, driven by a local taxi operator. Burton and Charlotte sat down behind the driver, who putted off the runway toward the Snow Leopard Inn.

A platoon of Royal Laotian paratroopers lounged outside of the inn.

Two men lounged in the lobby, near clones of each other: Black hair –slicked back, white shirts, chamois colored cotton trousers and sandals – aviator sunglasses worn indoors. Charlotte introduced both to Burton as Prince des Ténèbres (Satan), with buckteeth, and le Couteau (the Knife) with obviously false teeth. They were both employees of Bruno Jospin and were very solicitous of Charlotte. She introduced Burton as her fiancé, which came as news to Burton. The men looked at Burton speculatively as if perhaps he was a new American drug connection.

Two Laotian paratroopers stood at attention, holding American-made M-3 Grease Guns that looked a size-and-a-half too big for the soldiers.

"This must mean that General Ouane Rattikone is here. Uncle Ouane is an important general of the *Force Armée Republic*." Charlotte said conversationally. "He is also chairman of the Laotian Opium Administration."

"I know who General Ouane is." Burton said in hushed tones.

"He's my honorary uncle." To the clerk, Charlotte said, "Please inform General Ouane that Charlotte is here with her fiancé."

She waited while the clerk wai'd the telephone before picking it up and calling the suite occupied by the commander-in-chief of the Royal Laotian Army.

"Everyone thinks they can make heroin," Charlotte said. "Khun Sa wants to try now. They've been trying for a long time. There is too much acid in their #3 Heroin and it destroys the brain of anyone who uses it. None of them have successfully made #4 Heroin. It is only made in Marseilles successfully, and only by us." She had a definite sense of pride in their product. Burton wasn't quite able to make the connection between drug fiends, who he formed a stereotypical image of in his mind and Charlotte, Bruno Jospin and the others he'd been introduced to. To them it was only a business like making shoes.

"What if, and I'm only saying if, somebody was able to make #4 Heroin here in Laos?" Burton postulated.

"It has never happened." Charlotte said confidently.

Burton pushed gently, "But if it happened?"

"Assassiné." She looked at him. "There is no place for competition in this business. The raw opium purchased from the farmer is not expensive. We pay $1,000 for two kilos, about five pounds of raw opium from the farmer. In Marseilles the same quantity is worth $8,000 if it's in the form of morphine base, #2 Heroin. It's not usable and must be refined. #4 Heroin, the best grade of China White has a value to us of $50,000 wholesale on the street of New York. By the time it is sold on the street the actual price is nearly $650,000 for that five-pound quantity of refined opium. It no longer weighs five pounds. Refining reduces the weight considerably. We don't realize that profit, of course. There are costs associated with shipping, refining, protecting shipments,

211

commissions and so forth as you would expect. The opium we buy for $1,000 has a profit to us of about $40,000."

The numbers staggered Burton. "How many pounds of raw opium do you collect in a growing season?"

Charlotte did some mental arithmetic. "Last year was a dry year, bad harvest. The competition makes lower grades of heroin and a considerable quantity of opium harvested is smoked in Asia. In a bad year, we manage about one hundred tons. In a good year, nearly double that. The rain came last month but it's been another dryer-than-usual August. Planting began for the early harvest but will begin in earnest in a month for the Spring crop of 1962. When they are not growing opium, they grow rice. If insects come or there is bad weather they starve or get nothing."

"How much does the average farmer make in a year?"

"In a good year a farmer can earn 100,000 Kip - about $200. In a bad year they will earn nothing. I'm not saying that it's fair. It is what it is."

General Ouane Rattikone strutted into the lobby, flanked by staff officers and bodyguards, smiling broadly. "My dear sweet Charlotte," the General said in French, "and this must be Mr. Burton from the American Consolidated Fruit Company."

Charlotte kissed is cheek reverently, as if she was kissing the Pope's ring. "*Oncle*."

Switching to Chinese the General continued, "Mr. Burton, it's an abundant pleasure to see you here and I want to assure you that every effort will be made to make your fiancé and yourself comfortable."

'He knows I speak Chinese.' Burton said to himself. 'And he referred to Charlotte as my fiancé.'

Burton gave the Royal Laotian General a deep wai.

The general replied with a bob of his head.

"You will join us for our mid-day meal?" Though phrased as a question, it was a decree.

Charlotte accepted graciously on behalf of herself and Burton and they were swept away with the General's entourage.

Seating became an issue, and in the end, the General, himself, placed people at the table based on his inclination to speak to them. Burton and Charlotte sat directly across the table. The General didn't order food, that task had been subordinated to a staff officer, who ordered for them all.

Burton decided that General Ouane Rattikone looked corrupt, if 'corrupt' was a look you could cultivate. He had beady eyes behind horn rim glasses and when he looked at Burton, it was as if he was measuring him for a coffin.

"You have been in Laos for a long time, Mr. Burton? Not just this last month." It was a statement.

"First with the Army, now as a civilian. I came here for the first time about two years ago." Burton explained.

"I am a leader of my people. A father figure to them." The General said with considerable pride. "Some say I will one day rule, but I am content to be a humble servant of the King."

"Everybody works for somebody." Burton said in an attempt to be affable.

The General didn't seem to like what he said. "Lao leaders have knack for acting on impulse. In 1550, for instance, King Potisararat was crushed to death while attempting to impress a group of visiting ambassadors with his elephant-roping skills. In 1817, a pagan priest named Ai-Sa briefly seized the southern royal palace at Champassak through his fearsome power to create fire. Later people found that he had merely been using a magnifying glass, he was trampled to death by elephants."

"You strike me as being far smarter than that." Burton tried to regain lost ground.

"Our legacy for impulsive behavior was first documented in 1478. The governor of Kenetha captured a rare white elephant and gave it to King Chaiya. The emperor of Vietnam dispatched a delegation to ask for a few tail hairs from the sacred beast. The Lao king's son, who thought the Vietnamese were no better than rabid dogs sent the delegates home with a box full of the elephant's feces. War ensued. Luang Prabang was sacked.

"The Americans would have us be impulsive where their interests are concerned. The Corsicans have a more harmonious approach. Where do you fit in the picture, Burton?"

"I'm not quite sure. Perhaps I will work as a lowly clerk in one of Mr. Jospin's businesses, when Charlotte and I are wed." Burton patted Charlotte's hand. "Perhaps Entretenir des Relations Commerciales du Laotian would need somebody to balance the books?"

"You have not given her a ring, yet you both say you are to be married." General Ouane said, looking into Burton's eyes carefully.

"We're more engaged to be engaged at the moment, but it doesn't diminish our love for each other, does it sweetheart?" Burton moved to kiss Charlotte's cheek and she turned to offer him her lips.

"Or, perhaps the day will come when all Corsicans will be asked to leave Laos forever." It was a statement Ouane delivered flatly.

"Impulsive—," Burton said, "but I wouldn't give Bruno Jospin a box with the shit from a white elephant in it unless you want to see Luang Prabang sacked again."

Charlotte put a cautionary hand on his.

"When foreigners come there is war. When you go, there is peace."

"I read it on a Communist PAVN leaflet." Burton replied, sharply.

"Does that make it less true?"

"Whose side are you on?" Burton demanded.

"I'm on my own side." Ouane pronounced, then stood. The entourage followed suit even though the mid-day meal had not yet been served. They trooped off.

"Perhaps lunch could have gone better?" Burton said.

"His greed and his ego are boundless. He will be trouble for us." Charlotte replied. "For the moment, he uses our airplanes to fly his opium. He has it refined into #3 quality, which kills the users very quickly. The only market is local. Hong Kong does have chemists who can refine opium into #4 Heroin of comparable quality to ours but the British keep it under control so there is a market for Marseilles heroin there as well. There are about two hundred thousand heroin addicts in Hong Kong. They pay the Teochiu for the drugs – Sun Yee On Triad. That translates to about fifty tons of raw opium a year to satisfy just the Hong Kong market and Chinese refiners. We wholesale #4 Heroin to the Chinese in Hong Kong and maintain a cooperative working relationship with the Triads. General Ouane aspires to control the whole of it."

"How does Khun Sa fit in to the picture?" Burton asked Charlotte.

"He is the comprador for the Chinese, the Laotians and us in Burma. He controls the growers, arranges for stable, harmonious relationships between buyer and seller and keeps interlopers at bay."

"Have you met him?"

"No. What I know of him comes from what I have heard from Andre Zuccarelli and Jacques, my false husband. Andre represents the Guerini Family and Bruno. Jacques represents the French Intelligence Service and

214

Bruno. General Ouane Rattikone doesn't sit at the table but he would like to."

"Why would he want to refine opium into heroin if he has all these relationships?" Burton said, expressing his thoughts out loud.

"I'm not sure he would. Maybe to transfer opium to #2 Heroin, morphine base because it is easier to transport. If he went into the refining business he would no longer be a comprador and he would have no value."

"What about kidnapping Halvard Taylor, Creed Taylor's father? How would he gain from that?" Burton asked.

Charlotte shrugged. "I don't know. He is a warlord, maybe he does it for ransom?"

"Since the discussion with General Ouane is over, are we going home?" Burton asked.

"I didn't know he would be here." Charlotte said. "I brought you here to the Snow Leopard Inn to make love with you all afternoon."

TWENTY NINE

Monday, 22 August 1961 -- 0930 HRS
Embassy of the United States of America, Annex,
20 Rue Barthlonie, That Dam Road,
Vientiane, Laos

"Where is he Henry? Burton was supposed to be here an hour ago."
The Monkey King looked at his watch yet again as he paced.

"I don't know." Dastrup admitted, "Not my day to watch him. You should ask Walter Kennedy, he's Walter's problem."

"And mine."

"And yours." Dastrup parroted.

"And your problem too, Henry, since you work for me."

Dastrup picked up a desk telephone and turned the rotary dial. "Have the runners come back on the Burton matter?" He listened for a moment.

He hung up the phone. "Burton isn't home. They spoke to the Australian Military Attaché, Major Watson. Watson doesn't know where he is. Says he left early."

"I'm not a man given to fits of rage." Keene said, looking at Dastrup for affirmation.

"Yes sir, but you have your limits." Dastrup placated him.

"That's right, I do. Where in God's green acre is Kennedy?"

"Right here." Kennedy said softly and smoothly, with serpentine guile.

They both turned to see Walter Kennedy standing in the doorway, his nose taped, his eyes black and blue.

"Where's Burton?" The Monkey King demanded.

"I don't know."

"Why not?"

"Because he's not here and he's not at home, so I don't know where the love bird flew off to but I know who he's with."

Keene was out of patience. "Who would that be?"

"Charlotte Jospin, his fiancé."

"Fiancé?" Keene and Dastrup spoke at the same time.

"I thought Creed Taylor was throwing the meat to her last week.

216

Now Craig Burton is and they're engaged? That's a bit far fetched even for Laos." Dastrup said.

"They are to be married by Pope John in St. Peter's Basilica. Their first child will be baptized and President Charles and Mrs. Yvonne DeGaulle will stand in as the baby's god parents."

"She's pregnant?" Keene asked. "Who's the father?"

"She's a virgin." Kennedy said.

"You've been drinking or injecting, Kennedy, get the fuck out of my office!" The Monkey King said. Dastrup pushed Kennedy out the door and closed it behind him.

"Order a psych evaluation on Walter Kennedy." The Monkey King said imperiously.

"He's assigned to Manila." Dastrup said.

"Then get Jack Beckman on the line and tell him that Walter Kennedy needs to be committed."

Kennedy opened the door, bandaged nose leading the way. "Before you do something you'll regret—if I'm right, aren't we on track with KNUCKLEBALL?"

"What about Khun Sa?" Dastrup said. "Infiltration is a benefit to us, but we want that son-of-a-bitch humbled and the only one of our people who has a chance of making it in is Burton. If he's successful the Corsicans will be happy and he'll have his chance to get in good with them."

"Yeah. I know what the Op is." Kennedy said, lighting a cigarette. "Remember who thought it up so Mr. Keene could take credit for it?" Kennedy winked at Dastrup. "But what if Burton was already on the inside with the Corsicans. What if he moved a whole lot quicker than anyone gave him credit for? What if—?"

"What if he's off the reservation and running his own game?" Dastrup worried.

"Are you saying that he's engaged to Charlotte Jospin Sabon, Jacques Sabon's old lady? She of the fine ass?" The Monkey King intoned.

"Sabon's out, Burton's in." Kennedy said flatly. "Bruno told me the Pope would marry them and if he couldn't get the Pope, he'd have the Archbishop of Paris handle the honors. Frankly, with his pull, my bet is on the Pope. Oh, and he's asked Charles de Gaulle to get Burton reassigned as a military advisor to the Foreign Legion's Parachute

Regiment. They're stationed on Corsica."

"DeGaulle. Really?" The Monkey King asked.

"And the Kuhn Sa problem?" Dastrup asked.

"We have our cake and eat it too." Kennedy suggested.

THIRTY

Tuesday, 22 August 1961 -- 0415 HRS
23 Singha Road
Ban Phonxay,
Vientiane, Laos

Montgomery Keene dreamed the bizarre and slept fitfully. The ticking clock on his nightstand read 4:15 am. He didn't hurt anywhere but it felt as if a rat had been gnawing at his ankle. Maybe just a dream? He looked around the room and pulled the mosquito drape aside.

"Who's there?"

"Nevermore."

He reached for the Walther semi-automatic pistol but it wasn't where it was supposed to be.

Adrenalin surged. "You'd better get out if you know what's good for you."

"Nevermore."

He stopped for a moment, thinking that it must be a dream. "Burton?"

Burton sat in a comfortable chair in the corner of Keene's beautiful European bedroom looking out over the carpet. The place had been elegantly furnished, although the house itself was old and decaying.

He stood. "You wanted the Op Plan turned into you this morning. You were adamant."

"Huh, the—Oh, yeah, KNUCKLEBALL. Right."

"I'll leave it here for you. Burton dropped a sheaf of papers on the chair behind him."

Old photographs of Colonial Laos hung, framed on the wall. "Did these come with the house?" In one photo, people stood around a car in front of a rubber plantation. In another colonists stood arm in arm, hopeful, optimistic, with their children standing in front of them, unposed.

"Why would you care, Burton?"

"I've been sitting here, watching you sleep. Wondering what kind of heart beats in your chest."

219

"What do you want—Craig?"

"If I wanted you dead, you be long gone by now. You're a sound sleeper."

"I have a clear conscience." The Monkey King said.

"Is that the same thing as having no conscience at all?" Burton smiled and the scar puckered, making it three quarters of a smile, one quarter leering grimace. The bed frame was teak, the spread elegant, the washbasin, porcelain. Burton looked at his face in a mirror over the dresser briefly. His brother wouldn't recognize him. He barely recognized himself. "Good bye."

From Montgomery Keene's perspective, Burton vanished into the darkness. Maybe he simply walked behind furniture? He slipped out of bed and padded to the place he last saw Burton. No sign of him. Except for the paperwork he left behind and Keene's Walther with the clip out of it and the ammunition spilled on the carpet.

Keene switched on an electric light and examined the document. It was all very well conceived, worthy of a West Point graduate. The only question in his mind was whether or not Burton planned to execute the operation the he told Burton to manage it.

He called Kennedy's Room at the Setha Palace and advised the hotel staff to let the phone ring until somebody picked it up. Keene counted the rings. On the eighteenth ring, Kennedy picked up.

"Whoever you are, you better have a good reason for calling me." Kennedy's voice sounded very nasal over the phone, and then Keene recalled why that would be.

"A friend of yours came calling this morning. He left something for me."

Kennedy allowed it to sink in. "Did he break your nose?"

"No."

"I take it you didn't mention the bitch."

"No."

"That was wise."

"Meet me at the office in—," Keene looked at the alarm clock on the nightstand. "Make it seven o'clock."

Keene arrived early for the meeting. So did Kennedy.

"Walter, you look like fifty miles of bad road." Keene observed as Kennedy drank coffee.

"A nip of old Ireland would go well with the coffee." Kennedy's tone resentful, "How can we hold a respectful conversation completely sober?"

"I'm sure you still have plenty of alcohol in your system from last night."

"That's not the point." Kennedy groused.

"I've had time to think about KNUCKLEBALL."

"Me too," Kennedy said, recalling Bruno Jospin's stern warning. "We need to shut this whole thing down before it gets out of control. I'm not saying that my idea wasn't brilliant, because it was—is. Sending Burton and friends north will only lead to trouble at this point. He's in with the Corsicans, we can find somebody else to fuck with Khun Sa."

Keene thought hard. "I agree. We need to nip this thing in the bud." He shivered at the thought of Burton being able to come and go from his bedroom at will. There were options and then again there were options.

THIRTY ONE

Tuesday, 22 August 1961 -- 0820 HRS
Shanghai Spring Phoei Kwan Shop
Sisattanak District,
Vientiane, Laos

Wu Ming sat in his cramped office in the Shanghai Spring Phoei Kwan shop when Burton came to call.

He stood and ushered him into the office as he would have a dear friend. Tea service arrived automatically, ritualized and the beverage had a particularly sweet taste accompanied by an aroma reminiscent of Magnolia blossoms.

"The good stuff?" Burton asked.

"Huang Shan Mao Feng is as you say." Wu Ming replied. "I had it brewed for this occasion since we are saying farewell."

"In America we simply say, 'until we meet again'."

"Karma, Taoism, teachings of Buddha and Confucianism is something now lost in Mao's China. A communist believes only in the revolutionary struggle. However, they look at it, karma is karma and it remains to be seen whether or not we will meet in this life or not. I expect that we will be friends in ensuing lives as w were in past lives."

"I'm leaving soon."

"I know. Soon you will be transferred from this land. Or maybe you will die here."

"What would make you say that?" Burton asked.

"The Pathet Lao have put price on your head, which means Ho Chi Minh is paying for it with Russian money. They know who you are. There are *dac biet cong* squads looking for you in the North. Do you know what they are?"

"Elite Vietnamese commandos. Sometimes just called scorpions."

"I think the translation works. They are very good, Burton. They will be patient, and once you have been seen, they will converge to pick up your trail and kill you." Wu Ming said with slight emotion. "You won't be killed for the reward. They will do it out of a sense of honor. They respect you and your men but you are no longer anonymous."

222

"People have been trying to do that for quite a while now." Burton said with a touch of ego.

"Not like this," Wu Ming cautioned. "Not this time."

Burton sipped the delicately delicious tea and as he felt the surprising yet subtle burst of flavor, a beautiful Chinese woman delivered morsels on a silver tray.

"She is beautiful?" Wu Ming asked.

"She's stunning." Burton said without exaggeration.

"You can have her for the evening if you desire since you are going away." Wu Ming offered. "She is as skilled at rain and clouds as any in China," Wu promised sincerely.

"I will have to take a pass."

"So perhaps your French woman, the one from Corsica will be your companion. It's said that you love her." Wu observed.

"Who said?"

"You did when you told me you were not inclined to have Jade for the evening."

"I'm a fool." Burton said.

Wu Ming pulled a bottle and two shot glasses from under the table. "Today is a day for cognac, not for tea. Not even for Huang Shan Mao Feng, the finest tea on Earth."

Wu poured two drinks and offered one to Burton.

"Many years ago there was a Chinese general of some renown. His name was Ts'ao Ts'ao. He is perhaps the most popular hero in Chinese folklore, whose genius as a general saved North China from chaos when the Han dynasty crumbled at the end of the 2nd century A.D. Tung Cho captured the Emperor and burned the capital. He threatened to obliterate the Han Empire completely. Ts'ao fled to the provinces, where he raised his own troops who then marched to the rescue.

"They were besieging a town controlled by Tung Cho when his supply officer came to him and told him, 'we are running short of food'. General Ts'ao Ts'ao ordered him to put the troops on half rations. The supply officer said, 'the men won't like that'.

Ts'ao tells the supply officer, 'follow my orders and I'll manage the rest'. As expected, the soldiers complained bitterly since an army moves on its stomach. General Ts'ao called in the supply officer and told him, 'I need to borrow something of yours to placate the men because they are restless now they're on half rations'. The supply officer supplicated and asked what that might be. General Ts'ao said, 'Your head'. Executioners beheaded the supply officer in front of the troops and the general had his head impaled on a pike for all to see. Under his head was a sign that read, *'Supply Officer Wang Hou Sheng, punished for stealing from the storehouse and giving the troops short rations.'"*

"So you think I might be the supply officer?" Burton asked directly.

"It's difficult to know for sure. Much depends on what happens. If a goat needs to be sacrificed, you will be the goat—for the greater good and glory of your superiors at the Central Intelligence Agency. You're not one of their own, you know precious few secrets with which to bargain your way out of trouble, and you are known as a young man who is not beloved of his step-father."

"So if the *dac biet cong* don't get me, my own people will?"

Wu Ming poured more cognac and picked up a morsel delicately with chopsticks, dropping it into his mouth. He chewed as he spoke, "No one knows the future. You are lucky Burton and you have audacity. They can only carry you so far when so many would profit from your disgrace or death."

"My options?"

"I would simply be circumspect." Wu said honestly. "You have been fair to me and I have been fair to you. Maybe in the next life you will be me and I will be you? Who can say? I am thinking of undertaking the eight-fold path to nirvana and ending this endless cycle of rebirth. My karma from this life will be horrible and I may spend the next one as a louse living near the anus of pig. However if I change and commit myself, I might be able to improve things. So it's important for me to be faithful to you."

Wu Ming pushed a manila envelope across the table. "Open it."

Burton tore the end. Inside was an eight inch blue steel tube and what appeared to be a specially machined barrel for a Colt 1911A1 handgun. "What's this for?"

"For the day you'll need it. Replace your barrel with this new one. It's threaded for the silencer."

"Do you still want me to give the present of a small gold dragon to Khun Sa?"

"It might save your life. He will think you are acting under the direction of the People's Ministry of State Security and won't want the certain retribution that will come from your death."

"So that's who you work for? The Guoanbu?"

"I'm Teochiu. It means I'm self-employed no matter who I work for. However, if the question should come up in polite conversation, my superior is General Qui."

Burton nodded and rather than finishing his cognac, drank the tea. "This tea is remarkably good."

Wu Ming smiled.

The houseboy led Charlotte into the kitchen where Chester Watson had just finished his breakfast.

"Please sit and have something to eat. The cook will make whatever you want." Chester said, standing to take her hand.

"Thank you but I'm looking for Craig." Charlotte explained.

"You missed him but he left a letter for you." Chester pulled a chair back for her and Charlotte dropped into it. She reached for Chester's coffee and drank down the scalding coffee. It tasted weak an ineffective. So unlike Corsican espresso.

Chester handed Charlotte the letter and she tore the envelope open as he sat down.

"Oh, no. I must find him." She said, stood, thanked Chester for his help and left the house.

Chester picked up the note and read it. *Gone up country to meet the man you've never met. Be back soon. Don't worry. I love you! Craig.*

THIRTY TWO

Saturday, 26 August 1961 -- 1045 HRS
Takhli Royal Thai Air Force Base
Takhli District,
Nakhon Sawan Province, Thailand

The B-26 Invader pilots and flight crews mixed with the pilots and ground crews of the 524th Tactical Fighter Squadron of the 27th Tactical Fighter Wing, who were on loan to the Thirteenth Air Force, headquartered at Clark Air Base in the Philippines. The 524th flew the F-100D Super Saber and they were nominally assigned to Cannon Air Force Base in Clovis, New Mexico. Though a collegial atmosphere existed between the two groups, nobody spoke about what it was they did. The 524th dropped napalm on Pathet Lao troop concentrations in northwestern Laos. The mission of the White King Squadron of unmarked B-26B's remained unspoken, though it was rumored that they had all been seconded to the Central Intelligence Agency.

The same Air America H-34 Choctaw helicopters flown by former Marine Corps pilots out of Ching Ri that extracted Burton's Tartar Team previously, provided Combat Search and Rescue for the 524th. Nobody was precisely who they were supposed to be, nor if they doing what they were supposed to be doing. All of three groups were there never the less, on the taxpayer's dime.

Nobody asked any questions about the four men from the 7th Special Forces and the Army Security Agency man who joined them the previous week. They were more or less invisible at Takhli Royal Thai Air Force Base.

Lt. Col. Skids Sevigny sat down next to Burton, who perused charts with one of the F-100 fighter jocks in building that served as the air intelligence office for both the White King Squadron and the 524th.

The only reliable intelligence on current Pathet Lao formations that Burton tapped into came from the pilots who interacted with the White Star Mobile Training Teams on the ground who called in the air strikes.

Sevigny wasn't uncomfortable helping Burton's team. Burton's orders came from CIA Far East Division Headquarters in Tokyo. Still, it

226

seemed unusual that Burton wasn't able to interact with the rest of the network.

"Craig? A word if you will?" Sevigny asked.

"Sure." Burton said. "Hold that thought."

Sevigny motioned him outside and offered him a cigarette. Burton declined. "Interest in your whereabouts has become fucking strident," Sevigny advised. "The Laotian Army, the Controlled American Source, Air America at Udorn, Bird and Sons—who run an Air Force contract operation out of Cambodia, E-Flight at Naha, the US Embassy at Bangkok, the Army Security Agency, Aviation Royal Khmer and every other spook and near spook outfit in Southeast Asia wants to know where you are."

"What's Aviation Royale Khmer?"

Sevigny said, "That's the Cambodian Air Force. I know you probably didn't think they have one but they do."

"What did you tell them?"

"I told everyone the truth – never heard of you." Skids Sevigny said with a wink. "Want to grab lunch in town?"

"Thai food?"

Sevigny laughed. "Yeah, Thai food."

On the road, Burton said, "I need to draw some heat in Laos up near the Burmese border. I want to see a certain class of people flock to an area like fruit bats on a mango tree."

"What do you have in mind?"

"I was thinking a demonstration of air power. Maybe a joint strike by the White Knights and the combined efforts of the 524th. Is it doable?"

"The man said *you* had priority. The order still stands as far as I'm concerned" Sevigny confirmed. "I'll tell Colonel Purdue to release the 524th for a few sorties based on priority needs and he'll rubber stamp it. When do you want to plow up the jungle?"

If weather permits, let's do it Monday.

Skids pulled a letter envelope from inside the bellows pocket of his GI issue trousers. "Maybe this will help. I purloined from the Air Intel weenie."

Burton looked at the cover. It was classified Top Secret with caveats for no dissemination to foreign nationals, sensitive intelligence methods and sources used, limited distribution with control maintained by the report's originator. Past the cover, the Assistant Chief of Staff for Intelligence of the US Military Assistance Advisory Group, Laos summarized the enemy order of battle in Houa Khong Province, Military Region One.

Burton read the document and asked, "How did you know what I was interested in?"

"I know you think all the zoomies are cretans, but I simply watched you looking at charts for the past three days and figured you had an interest in Houa Khong Province." Sevign tapped his head while he drove. "I know! You don't have to say it! I'm a genius."

"How many sorties can you fly on Monday?"

"It depends on how many aircraft are mechanically able and the weather here and at the target. Best case I can put fifteen B-26's and I'm guessing about the same number of F-100's. We can fly, rearm and hit them again, so figure sixty sorties."

Burton smiled and it was a wicked smile. "Make it happen colonel, have them arm with napalm. More is better. I'm also going to need a C-47."

After lunch, while Skids Sevigny greased the mission with the commanding officer of the 524th Tactical Fighter Squadron, Sam Willoughby met Burton near a green C-47 Dakota on the ramp.

"You wanted me to meet you, sir?"

"How tough would it be to rig a streaming antenna behind the C-47 for your GRC 109 radio?"

"Can do. We can run it out the door after we're in the air. No sweat."

Burton looked at the aircraft speculatively.

"What's going on, sir?"

"You're going to send a distress message, requesting immediate air strike MAYDAY-BUSTER. You're going to call in Napalm, safety released, on our position because we'll be over-run."

Willoughby said, "That'll suck."

"You have the TACAN?"

"I got one from the ASA. The CIA didn't get it to Vientiane fast enough."

"Set it for Channel 43 at 268.7."

Willoughby pulled paper and a pencil from his pocket and scribbled down the information. "I don't understand?"

228

"We'll go in first with the C-47 and drop the portable TACAN in with a parachute. It will broadcast a signal that the ASA will pick up at Camp Chinaimo won't it?"

Willoughby nodded, "And in Thailand, Cambodia, Vietnam. Not just us, the NVA, Chinese, everybody will get the signal."

"Great. Don't tell anybody what we're doing. Now, round up Taylor, Gorman and Paint and tell them we're meeting at the intel shop at 1500 for a briefing and everyone will have liberty tonight."

Paint wore a gold chain with a large jade pendant around his neck. Gorman looked hung over and Taylor was obviously pissed off. Willoughby had a pencil out to take notes. All of them sat around a table. Burton had a map sitting on the tabletop.

"We're parachuting into Burma on Monday, August 28." Burton turned the map around so everyone could see what he referred to. "We're going in near Wan Pai. Equipment check 0200 Monday, Prep and on the runway by 0500."

"What's going on, Skipper?" Taylor asked.

"We're going to repatriate Reverend Halvard Taylor."

Taylor looked annoyed but he feigned enthusiasm. "That's great. I can't wait to see my dad again. That is if we can get to him."

THIRTY THREE

Saturday, 26 August 1961 – 1200 HRS (noon)
Douang Deaun Hotel
192 Loykroh Road, Chang-Klan,
Muang, Chiang Mai, Thailand

Jacques Sabon called a meeting at dawn in the hulk of the burnt out Douang Deaun Hotel, in Chiang Mai, a little over three hours by car from Vientiane, Laos if the roads were dry, were in good repair and you drove like a bat out of hell. The hotel was in the process reconstruction having been gutted by fire but the construction moved very slowly. Everything in Laos and Thailand moved slowly.

Walter Kennedy never stayed there before the fire but he knew where it was and he arrived ten minutes early in a black Embassy Buick with a bodyguard driver named Danny DeMill. DeMill was one of those uni-brow gofer types that weren't good at much, but they were endearing and were kept around just because. At least that's how Kennedy viewed him. Kennedy called him Fred. Danny corrected him four or five times on the trip south from Vientiane but eventually gave up. He didn't know that Kennedy called everyone Fred that he didn't like. It was Kennedy's own personal acronym for, *Fucking Retard—Extra Dumb*.

As soon as Kennedy walked into the abandoned hotel, he could see why it had even been rejected as temporary lodging by displaced war refugees. The former roach motel smelled of damp extinguished fire and it was as dark and as forlorn as a crypt. The fire had licked its way across the polyester carpeting, destroying the lobby, noodle shop restaurant and rooms above. The blaze spooled soot up the walls and ceiling, leaving patterns of permanent shadow. It was a place of putrefying shoddy construction, now made bare from the fire. He walked through the rotting lobby that would require more will to rebuild than could be found in all of Thailand. Even seemingly useless items had been looted from the inside, leaving it barren, raped and dead. Most of the tiles in the terrazzo floor had been pried from their base in an effort to salvage everything of value from the corpse-like building. It was like walking through a morgue. The only item of elegance was the caged skylight above the lobby where

230

morning light filtered in through glassless window frames.

Jacques Sabon, Charlotte and three Corsican thugs arrived before Kennedy in the French Ambassador's Citroen driven by a bodyguard who remained with the car. The heavies carried American M-1 Thompson submachine guns.

They met Kennedy in the lobby and he put on his I-don't-give-a-shit mask immediately

"Good morning," Kennedy said buoyantly, radiating sanguinity.

Jacques turned to Danny DeMill and said, "You can go. We'll give Mr. Kennedy a ride back."

Kennedy lighted a cigarette and nodded to Danny with a confidence he didn't feel.

Two of the Corsican thugs followed Danny back to the car.

You could cut the silence with a knife but Kennedy just puffed on his cigarette, flicking ash periodically, playing chicken with the coming verbal exchange.

Jacques spoke as soon as he heard the Buick start. "Time is precious. What information do you have for us?"

Usually they beat around the bush for hours while everybody snacked on smoked liver sausage called igatelli, ate pasta stuffed with brocciu cheese and drank grappa before getting to the point. Kennedy thought that something was happening and he was uncomfortable to be so out of the loop as to not know precisely what that might be.

Kennedy tried to ingratiate himself. "Miss Sabon, your perfume is exquisite. Boucheron perhaps?" She did smell good and he opined that one wouldn't necessarily scent up if things were going to get rough.

Charlotte looked at him with ice daggers.

"There's nothing going on folks." Kennedy said with a relaxed menace that he studied and cultivated. He did not take Charlotte lightly. She was snobbish, willful, and cunning. In truth, he envied Burton a woman like that.

Charlotte spoke quietly. "On s'aperáoit toujours d'un mensonge."

Jacques nodded and Petru Battesti, the huge, sullen thug with his nasal cartilage crushed and twisted from years of bare knuckle fighting, appeared from a room behind him breathing evenly from his mouth. Petru hulked like a big, broad granite cliff.

She translated for Kennedy's benefit. "It's a Corsican proverb that says you can tell when somebody lying."

231

Kennedy looked around furtively contemplating a run.

Petru spoke in a voice that sounded like gears grinding, "Celui qui vit mal, meurt ègalement mal."

"Petru said, 'he who leads an immoral life dies an immoral death.'" Charlotte translated again for Kennedy's benefit.

Petru took Kennedy's .45 automatic from its shoulder holster in one hand and then dragged him through a charred door into a filthy room with the other meaty fist.

There was nothing in the room but a chair and two car batteries. Kennedy's blood froze.

Kennedy tried to charm Petru as the big man tied his hands, wrists and arms to the chair but it didn't mean anything to Petru. It was a job to him. He moved quickly and expertly as if he had done the same job many times before.

"You've done this before?" Kennedy said. He told himself that it was a stupid question right after he asked it.

Petru smiled. Then he shrugged. Just business, but he liked his work.

The rain began pouring down outside. Kennedy could hear it from inside the room within the burnt out hotel. He wondered if it would drown out his screams.

Jacques hooked up an alligator clamp to the tip of his penis.

Kennedy groaned as Petru handed Jacques the other clamp, which he clipped to Kennedy's ear lobe. Charlotte looked on, almost bored.

"Details." Jacques said as if he didn't expect a response from Walter Kennedy. It was a pro-forma statement that Kennedy recognized for what it was.

"Details? What do you want to know? Look, I may know people but I am not a decision maker." Kennedy knew they'd zap him to get his attention no matter what he said. He would have done the same thing if he stood in their shoes. He played for time out of habit.

This time Jacques offered yet another proverb before he hit the switch. "La compagnie entra ne l'homme l'èchafaud."

Kennedy didn't need a translation. *Company drags a man to the scaffold.*

The juice flowed. Kennedy bucked, clenched, bit his tongue and cracked his partial plate. He spit the worthless dental appliance out as soon as they turned off the electricity.

"Sweet Jesus," Kennedy gasped in his Irish accent.

Charlotte sighed. If you wanted something done right, you had to do it yourself. She bent down over Kennedy and ripped the bandage from his nose.

Kennedy strained against the cords that bound him. They were tight, professionally tight.

Charlotte changed the clamp on Kennedy's ear to his nose, closing the alligator clip onto the septum separating his nostrils. This time she flipped the switch herself and then walked out of the room with Jacques, allowing Kennedy to think about the question. Petru remained behind keeping an eye on Kennedy.

Walter Kennedy didn't think about anything except that his balls and dick were on fire and his sinuses were bursting as the electric current coursed through them. He bucked, he tried to kick, the chair jumped as he convulsed but it didn't break.

Charlotte walked back in and flipped the switch. The pain stopped but Kennedy still thought the juice was flowing. Hot heavy corruption flowed warm from his bowels outward and down the legs of his trousers.

Even though he didn't think he'd talk, the words came unwillingly through Kennedy's bleeding mouth, "General Ouane. An ultimatum for our cooperation."

Charlotte leaned in close, wrinkled her nose at the smell of his bowel movement and spoke softly to Kennedy. "Vendetta is a Corsican word and we take treachery very seriously, Mr. Kennedy. We paid you fairly and you played us falsely." She repeated it for effect in the Corsican: Lingua Mizana.

The Corsican thugs brought Danny DeMill, who Kennedy hoped had made it clean away. Kennedy didn't know him well. He was just another *Fred*.

"This guy doesn't know shit." Kennedy said through swollen lips, his speech slurred with the loss of his denture.

Charlotte picked up Kennedy's .45, thrust the muzzle of the pistol into Danny the driver's mouth

Kennedy heard the barrel click against his teeth.

Charlotte shoved it in deeper, gagging Danny and he and closed his mouth around it like a child sucking on a licorice stick, closing his eyes.

"We are Corsicans, Walter, and I want you to remember that. I also want you to remember that you are about to do murder. Or your pistol is. The police can trace the bullet to the gun that fired it."

WHITE POWDER

The flesh and bone of the driver's skull muffled the pistol's report. Danny's head altered shape. It swelled like a balloon filled with high-pressure gas. His eyelids flew wide open and for an instant his eyeballs bulged from their sockets before rolling upward into his skull.

Kennedy closed his eyes and heard the contents of Danny's head spit out through the back of his skull against the wall beyond.

Dead silence.

Like an old crypt.

Like the guts of a deep cave.

Charlotte fired another round into Danny the driver's chest. He was dead. This one was for evidentiary value. She handed the automatic to Petru.

Kennedy sweated like a pig, his nose ran—snot and thick black blood, "I don't know where Burton is. Honest."

Charlotte's lips pursed, she attempted to brush bits of skull shards and blood from where they landed in her hair. "You sent Burton into Burma to be killed?"

Kennedy looked Charlotte in the eye reluctantly, his eyes shifted warily to Jacques Sabon and back at Charlotte who had a murderous gleam in her eye.

"Bruno told you he wasn't to go north and you were in charge of the operation called KNUCKLEBALL."

"It's called knuckleball because when a pitcher throws a knuckleball nobody know where it's going to end up."

"So you planned to sacrifice Craig Burton to see what reaction there would be in Burma?"

Charlotte's eyes turned from murder to worry and Kennedy filed it away. The Corsican princess-viper was in love with Craig Burton. As impossible as it sounded, the evidence laid before Kennedy was absolutely convincing.

Kennedy couldn't tell them that Burton's primary mission was to infiltrate the Guerini Family of Unione Corse. They'd chop him into pieces and feed him to pigs if he said that, even if it was true.

"I have an idea. I can get him back." Kennedy said.

The Corsicans listened intently to Kennedy's plan.

Charlotte looked at Jacques Sabon. There were hushed words with the thugs and they turned and walked from the room. Through the door, Kennedy could see the Citroen they got into, idling in front of the hotel.

Petru, the knuckle breaker remained behind and disconnected the electrodes.

Walter Kennedy thought that was the end but he was wrong. Petru hit him in the nose. Pinwheels of light, eyes teared, blood spurted, and the bone broke a second time in a week with a squeezing snap. He found himself hands-and-knees on the filthy floor, alone and bleeding, thrilled to still be sucking oxygen.

Danny (*Fred*) the driver hadn't been so lucky.

Picking himself up from the floor and looking through rapidly swelling eyes, he stumbled through the door. He bumped into walls, he tripped and fell and got up again. He bumped again and fell, not knowing on which planet he was on or where on that planet he happened to be. Eyes focused slightly to light filtering down the throat of the building, through a caged skylight at the top of the open elevator shaft. Then he lost his balance and slid to the floor.

"Merde!" The word through his cracked, parched lips was an inaudible croak.

Kennedy's view of the world was sandals and dirty feet. He followed the sandals up to the blurred face of Wu Ming, inscrutable as ever.

"Walter." His name spoken with a blend of compassion and stern feeling, "Your imprudence seems to be catching up with you."

Kennedy felt as though it was precisely the right thing to say under the circumstances.

THIRTY FOUR

Monday, 28 August 1961 – 0330 HRS
Takhli Royal Thai Air Force Base
Takhli District,
Nakhon Sawan Province, Thailand

Lt. Col. Skids Sevigny drank a beer in the briefing room when Burton walked in wearing full battle gear, carrying an AK-47 rifle.

"Hell of a breakfast, Skids."

"Weather's in up in Burma. High clouds, low clouds, ground fog. Want a beer?"

"Well don't that beat all?" Goatman said, trailing behind Burton.

Paint added. "Maybe it's karma."

Goatman looked at Paint, perplexed, "Karma controls the weather?"

Paint nodded seriously. "Can't fuck with karma or karma fucks with you."

Creed Taylor and Sam Willoughby came in.

"What's going on?" Taylor asked.

"The mission is scrubbed." Skids said. "Bad weather. Have a beer, with ice."

Willoughby seemed happy at the news. "That means I can go back to my rack and sleep late when I'm done drinking this morning."

"What's the forecast?" Burton asked Skids.

"I can't even guess. I tasked the Air America guys at Ching Ri to make a midnight flight up there in a Helio Courier and give us a weather report. It's standard operating procedure if we're going to make an early strike anywhere in northern Laos. Bad weather means bad weather. Sorry."

Tuesday was a repeat of Monday. The weather at Takhli reported clear with high clouds but two hundred miles away it was socked in. Burton's plan, inspired by his reading of Sun Tzu, required the cooperation of the weather gods.

On Wednesday, the news changed.

Lt. Col. Skids Sevigny stood in the briefing room. Thirty-one pilots and sixteen co-pilots for the B-26B's sat in the room along with Burton's

236

7th Special Forces Team wearing full gear including parachutes. Paint, Gorman and Willoughby looked fresh and hungry. They were going back to war. Taylor looked worn, the dark circles that ringed his eyes were obscured by black face paint.

Sevigny pulled down a chart of northern Laos. "This briefing is classified Top Secret; No dissemination to foreign nationals is authorized, sensitive intelligence methods and sources have been used in the collection of information that will be imparted."

He tapped the chart. "At about 0545 Hours, local time, a C-47 carrying a portable TACAN will drop the beacon near the city of Muang Sing in Houa Khong Province, Laos. The beacon will be dropped near a heavy concentration of five regiments of Pathet Lao soldiers and their North Vietnamese Army advisors. The target will initially be marked with yellow smoke. The smoke will dissipate well before you all hit the target because we're using napalm, so each ship should plan to drop just short of the previous impact point.

"We're going to be dropping about six nautical miles outside the People's Republic of China so we will anticipate a response from them. Four F-100's will fly cap, designated Blackjack One through Blackjack Four. That will be Captain Slim Barry's flight. Eleven F-100's armed with napalm will be the strike element, designated Clubs One through Clubs Eleven. Colonel Jackknife Perdue will be Clubs One. When the Clubs aircraft have completed their run, the sixteen White King aircraft will make their run. I will be White King One.

"The strike elements will ingress from roughly 180 degrees and will egress at roughly 300 degrees. Any bombing corrections will be made by White King One or by Captain Burton who will be designated Roughrider One.

"Captain Burton?"

Burton stood and walked to the front of the room. Sevigny pulled out a reconnaissance photograph, blown up. Major Sevigny handed him the pointer.

"I'm Captain Craig Burton. The target is this area, designated strike zone on your individual briefing sheets. It's the home of the 17th, 23rd and 24th Infantry, 37th Engineer and 605th Artillery Battalions of the Pathet Lao. North Vietnamese advisors will be present. The 605th has four, Norinco Type 55 single barreled 37 mm anti-aircraft rifles mounted on four-wheel gun carriages, much like the Soviet Zu-7. Practical air range is

10,000 feet or two and a half miles. Each battery is served by a crew of eight men and the weapons will fire up to eighty rounds per minute. They are equipped with Soviet OR-167 point fused frag ammunition dated, 1940. That means that there's no proximity fusing."

"How do you know, Captain?" One of the F-100 fighter jocks asked sarcastically.

Goatman answered out of turn. "Because we infiltrated the 605th and grabbed some of their ammo without them knowing about it. It's unlikely they've been re-supplied in the last three weeks."

The pilot looked sheepish.

"Thank you Sergeant Gorman." Burton said. "That's how I know, gentlemen. The anti-aircraft artillery crews look very rusty. It doesn't mean they won't shoot. It simply means they're not front line troops."

"Thank you. Colonel Sevigny will provide the Mission Execution Forecast."

The weather briefing called for scattered clouds, a very small chance of rain in the afternoon and the wind over the target was likely less than five miles per hour out of the south, which would be good for the planned napalm runs.

Colonel Purdue presented flight information with details including alternate landing fields. When he was finished, he turned the briefing back to Lt. Col. Sevigny. There were no questions.

"This briefing is classified Top Secret; No dissemination to foreign nationals is authorized, sensitive intelligence methods and sources have been used in the collection of information that was imparted." Skids Sevigny looked at Burton as if to ask if everything was presented to his satisfaction. Burton gave him thumbs-up.

Sam Willoughby's radio antenna streamed back from the fuselage of the C-47 Dakota as it rumbled through the sky over northern Laos on the Burma border.

"What's he doing?" Creed Taylor asked Burton.

"He'll be sending out a Mayday requesting an air strike to support us at Muang Sing. We're on the ground, under attack."

"He can't do that!" Taylor protested.

"Why not?"

"It's not right, what if people think we're really under attack?"

"People should think we're under attack. That's the purpose for the message. Thirty minutes later there will be twenty-seven aircraft dropping napalm on the site, doing some serious damage to a reinforced Pathet Lao regiment and supply dump. We should see some impressive secondary explosions when their magazine heats up and the ammo starts to cook-off.

"I just think it's not right because—our guys back in Vientiane might send in reinforcements."

"The Air Force will fly another mission in the afternoon, same location, to polish off the area. I don't think there will be a cockroach left to crawl up the side of a ration can."

Burton shouted to Willoughby, "When you're done sending the message twice, let's get the TACAN ready to shove out the door."

"You can't put the TACAN out here." Taylor said.

"It will give our location to everybody in Southeast Asia in case there are any doubts."

Taylor said, "Oh."

Since the bombing would progress south from the initial impact, Willoughby and Gorman shoved the TACAN out the side door of the C-47 when it was roughly above the mountain located north-north-east from the village of Muang Sing. The green silk parachute canopy deployed and the radio beacon, broadcasting on its band, settled down into the verdant landscape.

Banking in the early dawn, with the light dancing on the wings, the aircraft made a low pass over a group of buildings on the road leading south out of Muang Sing toward Luang Nam Tha, thirty-five miles distant. Paint threw the smoke grenades out the door of the aircraft on Burton's command. A static line attached to the pin rings armed the grenades and released the smoke grenade spoons. The aircraft banked and Burton could see the yellow smoke drifting bright and heavy in the center of the military compound. There was activity around an anti-aircraft gun as foliage was removed to bring it into action.

Burton and his men were transfixed as the F-100's began their run on the military camp. Just under over twice a minute for six minutes, all eleven jet fighter-bombers released napalm tanks, blowing hot jellied flames across the compound.

Putting his hand to his throat and depressing the switch, Burton communicated with the inbound B-26 Invaders, armed with a combination of heavy machine guns and napalm. "Roughrider to White

King Flight, be careful of possible secondary explosions."

No sooner had he spoken but a huge detonation rent the jungle. The concussion wave spread below the C-47 through the lush green landscape. A large mushroom cloud formed. The flight of B-26 bombers orbited and watched as white phosphorous, large explosions and other detonations shook the area.

Within ten minutes the secondary explosions diminished even though the flames from the original napalm strike still consumed the jungle. Sixteen B-26 Invaders finished whatever there was to finish.

"Roughrider, White King One."

"White King One, Over."

"Bomb damage assessment is one hundred percent destruction of target. Additional sorties are not required. Over."

"Copy your request, Roughrider."

The aircraft containing Burton and his men climbed and as they did, they could clearly see the smoke from the explosions passed eight thousand feet as it towered into the air.

Burton turned to Creed Taylor. "Somebody will pay attention to that!"

Taylor just looked at the destruction below as they flew north into Burma. He started getting ready for the jump, securing and checking his gear.

"Relax, Creed, we've got a long way to go."

"I thought we were jumping at Wan Pai?"

"Change of plans."

A shadow crossed Creed Taylor's face and then he smiled and shouted over the roar of the engines. "Ok, you're the boss!"

"We're not jumping. We'll be landing at a jungle strip near Pindaya. Everybody's used to see American planes flying in and out of Burma. The Corsicans fly some of the C-47's and the CIA flies others. We'll be long gone into the jungle before anyone knows we're there. I hate the idea of parachuting into a jungle, myself." Burton smiled.

LARRY B. LAMBERT

THIRTY FIVE

Wednesday, 30 August 1961 – 1230 HRS
Eight miles northwest of Pindaya,
Southern Shan State, Burma

The water sang its way through the narrow blood red slot canyon and they used it to mask their tracks. Paint's fist went up. The rest slowly lowered themselves to the ground, weapons off safe.

Burton went forward slowly.

"I smell *Ba Mu'o'i Ba*." Paint whispered.

"Vietnamese beer?"

"Yep."

"Sure you're just not missing the White Rose?" Burton asked soto voce.

Burton inhaled deeply, smelling with his nose and with through the back of his throat with his mouth slightly open. He smelled it too. "And nuoc-mam." The fermented fish sauce used by the Vietnamese as a condiment.

"You all smell nuoc-mam?" Gorman said when he moved in close.

Taylor and Willoughby closed the gap.

"I can't wait to get out of the water. These Ho Chi Minh slippers don't do anything to keep my feet warm." Taylor carped about the sandals made from tire tread he wore.

"I can only hope you have those weapons properly zeroed in because it might get hot. We have to move down, out of this gorge. I'm guessing the locals have some sort of sentry post at the mouth of the canyon. If they knew we were here, they would have hit us from above before now, but stay frosty."

Floods burst down the slot canyon in times past. The soldiers crept past mute testaments of wilder days: torn pieces of re-bar and concrete, a third of a water wheel, a child's toy. Today there were flowers growing in silted loam and nothing but the sweet, adorned sounds of water weaving between the rocks and of small air bubbles murmuring whenever they were caught. Burton stepped carefully over a small waterfall tipping over the edge of a moss pillow. He kept his head on a swivel, moving, high,

241

low, turning and he felt for footholds, dropping his feet blindly for a crack without dislodging rocks or gravel. It was slow work, intensified by the rancid, fishy odor of nuoc-mam that was subtly present on the breeze.

It wasn't a sentry post, more of a garrisoned cantonment of the local warlord's mercenaries. The fortification sat high on the side of a rolling hill where the gorge met a valley, now open to cultivation of rice in terraces as the hill descended. Once the rice was harvested, the opium poppies would be planted for springtime harvest. Guarding rice did not require the same degree of vigilance that guarding opium demanded. As a result, the soldiers were all resting from the building heat, smoking opium and eating a morning meal.

One sentry, posted on a low tower constructed of wood dozed, snored contentedly, with his Simonov SKS semi-automatic carbine lying across his legs. The Americans passed them like a passing cloud.

Burton reflected on the words of Sun Tzu. "Be so subtle that you are invisible. Be so mysterious that you are intangible. Then you will control your rivals' fate.

Once through the village, they stopped while Jimmy Paint rigged two Russian hand grenades on a tripwires about a hundred feet apart. They'd know if anyone spotted them and followed their path.

As with everywhere else in Southeast Asia, agricultural techniques were still rooted firmly in medieval times. Oxen pulled plows and worked the rich Burmese soil.

When Jimmy Paint called a halt to clean up their back trail, Creed Taylor moved forward and spoke to Burton. "These are the Palaung people. They live here in the highlands because the problem with Malaria isn't as great. Most of 'em aren't too bright, but they're very friendly to everyone."

"How far are we from Kalaw?"

"Is that where we're going?" Taylor asked.

Burton nodded.

"A day's walk from here if we move carefully." Taylor replied. "I like Kalaw. It's a quiet, peaceful place. We lived there during the British days." He thought for a moment. "So that's where Khun Sa is. That would make sense."

Paint returned and moved them forward, silently.

Thirty minutes later there was a distant crump. Nine minutes later, as second.

Goatman set a false trail through a stand of heavy, deep, elephant grass while the others curled up onto a promontory knoll that provided a textbook location for an ambush and waited.

"They'll move slower now—more carefully." Creed Taylor said quietly.

"Who will?" Burton questioned.

"Whoever set off the grenades," Taylor replied. "I hope it wasn't some farmer."

"Farmers?"

"Maybe."

"They set off those grenades in quick succession. I don't think whoever is behind us are farmers." Burton said, looking closely at Taylor.

Taylor shrugged.

Burton seemed to be off in a world of his own. "Chester Watson wants to retire and open a bar in Chiang Mai. I could never figure out why."

"Chiang Mai is Thailand's G-spot," Creed explained, "and I never met an Australian who didn't want to open a bar and whorehouse there. It's the marrow in the bone, the center of all gratification in jems, guns, drugs, girls, jade, teak, whatever. I've thought about Chiang Mai myself. It's not a bad place to plant roots."

"Maybe the Thais would have a different opinion of your intentions?"

Creed smiled a winning smile. "It doesn't matter to me who holds the cow so long as I can milk it."

Burton ordered Jimmy, "Go down the reverse slope of this hill and see if you can't find some good killing ground. Take Sam with you. We'll be along shortly."

Jimmy gave Sam Willoughby an odd look and went down the hill with Sam close behind.

"What gives?" Taylor asked.

"We have time before they get here. They won't want to trip another trap and they'll be moving slow."

"They'll move up the back of this hill and try and take us from behind."

Taylor sounded skeptical. "How do you know that?"

Burton said, "I don't know. If they're good that's what they'll do and I suspect they're plenty good. If they follow Goatman through the elephant grass, they'll learn that he's circling so they'll back out of that most riki-tick. Maybe they'll have one guy in front of us, but they'll be certain that we set up an ambush for them on this knoll."

"Ok, makes sense."

"Once Goatman circles with his false trail, he'll come back and he won't do anything until we open up. If the odds are too long, or if we're killed, he'll E & E the heck out of here. With the money from the gold and what the Corsican's paid him, he could do ok if he left Laos today and was presumed lost by the CIA."

Taylor nodded weakly. "I wondered when you'd get around to the Corsicans."

"You pitched the team without talking to me."

"It's about my father."

"It's about your greed. Your father's fine."

"How do you know that?" Creed demanded warily.

"When you put the pieces of the puzzle together, they don't fit any other way."

Creed became a bit more confrontational, "You got Charlotte. She always had the hots for you, asked about you non-stop. She's rich as a Bey's daughter. Maybe richer? If you have her, you have the key to her family's money."

"Then it's all about money?"

"And power. If you hadn't been around, I would have had her. Luck of the draw?"

"What did you tell the guys?"

"The same thing the fool Monkey King told you. That my dad had been kidnapped and that the only way to get him back was to play ball with the Corsicans."

"With a sweetener?"

"Ten thousand US, each. Paid in advance with another ten when we got my father back."

"You planned to kill them and me. Didn't you? You'd go back and console Charlotte."

Burton didn't have much time to consider his next statement because Creed's right hand moved fast as he un-holstered and drew.

Creed Taylor never heard the bullet that took his life.

Neither did anyone else.

Burton unscrewed the silencer from the muzzle of his Model 1911

A1 Colt handgun with its modified barrel. When Creed made his move, Craig Burton's pistol had been in his hand, behind his right leg, not in a holster.

He rolled Taylor's lifeless clay over and took the pistol that had been pointing in his direction, from the lieutenant's hand without emotion. Burton removed the clip, stripped the ammunition from Taylor's magazine pouches. Then he rifled Taylor's first aid kit and took a gauze compress and the morphine syrettes: collapsible tubes of morphine attached to a hypodermic needle. The contents of the tube were injected by squeezing it like a toothpaste tube. They deadened pain. Burton thought it ironic that they brought morphine from the US to Burma, the likely birthplace of that very morphine. That accomplished, Burton left him where he lay.

Burton met Willoughby, coming up toward him.

"There's a very small village at the base of the hill and the fields are cleared. They'll have to cross them if they want to come this way."

"Anybody see you?"

Willoughby shook his head. "Jimmy's in a good spot. Where's Creed?"

"He took off, looking for his dad. I didn't have the heart to stop him?"

"What?" Willoughby hissed urgently. "We have to go after him."

"Now is not the time, Sam."

"Are you sure they'll be coming?"

"Somebody dropped a dime on us or there wouldn't be anybody behind us."

"I've been thinking that," Willoughby confessed. "Is that why you changed the drop zone to the landing strip."

"Yeah."

"So you think the pilot told somebody where we landed?"

"Yeah. If somebody good is onto us this quick, it had to be the pilot or co-pilot. Nobody else knew about the change in plans. They must have radioed right after they took off."

"Who's paying them?"

"I think we'll find out."

THIRTY SIX

Wednesday, 30 August 1961 – 1230 HRS
Six miles west of Pindaya,
Southern Shan State, Burma

The movement surprised Burton. He saw the first one of the soldiers moving. The man was far more than good. He was world class. The tradecraft was only familiar to him because he'd been there himself. *Grup Gerak Khas*, Malaysian Special Forces. If the man moving so subtly wasn't Malaysian, he had trained with them at Kem Sungai Udang. Grup Gerak Khas taught the best in the world about jungle warfare and tracking. The man crossed fifty meters of open ground without being spotted by either Paint or Willoughby. *That* impressed Burton. It was impossible.

Too bad. Burton put the blade of his front sight on the man's waist and squeezed the trigger slowly. Bang – pop. A hit! No return fire. Well there wouldn't be, would there? Not from these guys. They wouldn't give up their position until they had you firmly in *their* sights.

"Christ, where did he come from?" Paint exclaimed when he saw the man Burton shot.

"We need to back out of here. They'll be flanking us."

"Who?" Paint asked.

"I'm not sure who, but they trained with the Malaysian Special Forces."

Burton led Paint and Willoughby back the way they had come, now, cutting through the hamlet.

"STOP!" Burton shouted, carefully unslung his AK-47, set it on the ground and then raised his hands in the air. "Drop your weapons."

"What?" Willoughby asked.

"Aasalaamu Aleikum." Burton said in Arabic

"Wa-Aleikum Aassalaam, Brooton." Came a voice from the jungle immediately in front of them.

Willoughby and Paint dropped their rifles.

"What's going on?" Paint asked in a hiss.

"They've got us."

"Who has us?"

"Kayf Halak?" The calm voice from the jungle asked.

"Qwayyis." Burton replied, calm.

"What are they talking about?" Willoughby asked Paint, sotto voce.

Willoughby replied, "He either said hello or he told the captain that he liked his pizza without anchovies."

A soldier in impeccable camouflage stepped from the jungle, now visible. "IL-Hamdu-Allah. You cost me three good men, Brooton."

"As you say, Sergeant Yahya bin Haji Morhd Siraj. But I do not grieve for them, for today they will be eating dates in paradise and I remain here, in the company of whores' sons."

Three more men appeared from the jungle. The Malaysian sergeant introduced them as Lance Corporal Yahya bin Aziz, Lance Corporal Hassan bin Mohamad and Sergeant Ibrahim bin Darus.

Burton introduced Willoughby and Paint and once manners were made said, "I have another man laying a trail on the other side of the hill."

Chester Watson walked through the Jungle, followed by another Malay soldier and Goatman.

"I got the drop on 'em and recognized Major Watson." Goatman explained.

"Yep, he's a royal prick." Chester said in good humor. "I worked for a banana bender that reminds me a lot of him once. Bloody bad luck though. A krait found its way into his kit. He should have been more careful since those snakes are deadly. Now he's in the national cemetery and they mourn him officially on Remembrance Day." Serious now, he added, "We lost two men to your booby traps, Craig."

"And a third to his bullet," Sergeant Yahya added. "We should bury them promptly."

"What are you doing here Chester?"

"Parachuted in yesterday looking for you."

"But the weather?"

"We jumped blind in the soup. Somebody was worried you'd need our help."

Burton looked completely confused.

"Your girlfriend. Kennedy suggested that she have me speak to the Grup Gerak Khas contingent training the South Vietnamese in Saigon. She and I flew there and she hired them with a suitcase full of British

Pounds. Then they dropped us in here, thinking you'd be making for Khun Sa. This morning we heard on the wireless that you were bounced down in Muang Sing, calling in air strikes on your own position and decided it was time for us to get out of the bloody back of borque since you were likely fertilizer. We used the slot canyon and picked up your trail there. Pure luck. Sergeant Yahya said you'd grown soft since you left a trail. The size twelve sandals gave away that you were farangs."

Burton nodded.

"Sorry about Lieutenant Taylor."

Goatman said, "We found his body."

Paint and Willoughby looked up sharply.

"I shot him." Burton said simply. "Long story. He's on top of the hill. We'll bury him with the others." To Watson, "How many of you are there?"

"We started with nine, down to six now including me. What's the deal with Taylor?"

"Later." Burton said softly.

They moved into a village about five miles north of Kalaw at dusk.

Goatman walked point into an obviously friendly crowd that formed from the village and walked out to the soldiers out of curiosity, led by a herd of happy children.

The Malaysian Special Forces soldiers leapfrogged forward through the village.

Jimmy Paint instinctively broke out hard candy and passed it out to the obvious delight of the kids.

A boy not older than ten chattered to Jimmy amiably. Jimmy looked plaintively at Goatman for a translation. "I don't speak their language. Taylor was the only one who did." He wanted to ask about Taylor but didn't. As the captain said, there would be time for that later.

An ancient, stooped, one-armed villager standing well under five feet in height wearing an old French uniform shirt and fatigue cap walked up to them confidently. His voice was soft like seeds rustling inside a gourd, but it was distinct. "I am called Caron for Auto Dèfense de Choc, et associèe des hommes dangereux." He smiled showing three teeth, each of them rimmed in gold.

Chester whispered to Burton, "Looks like those French dentists had at him."

248

Willoughby whispered, "That's the militia the French set up ten years ago when they were here. The Self-Defense Shock Force hasn't been in play for a long time and never in Burma."

"Parlay vous Anglais?" Gorman asked in chopped up French.

"Oui," Caron replied in English. "We welcomes you from far away."

"Communists?" Burton asked. "Are there communists or warlord army here?"

"No. Qui sait?" Caron said and then added, "Un coup de feuî and pointed to his heart. "Assassinat?"

"In English?" Burton asked Willoughby.

"He wants to know if you want them to go and find one so you can kill him. They're trying to be polite." Willoughby offered an opinion.

Caron nodded, validating Sam Willoughby's translation.

The Malaysian troops and Jimmy took up defensive positions. The children followed Jimmy, pleading for more candy. The children were clearly delighted to have them there.

It didn't feel like a trap. The villagers seemed to be precisely what they appeared to be.

"What do you think? Is it a trap?" Burton asked Sergeant Yahya in Malay.

Sergeant Yahya said that he didn't think so, but deployed his men to search the village and then form a perimeter anyway. Chester Watson went with them, sharp eye'd.

Dinner boiled, cooked in the shanty houses and old men and women squatted, sipping rice whiskey or smoking opium.

Jimmy Paint started handing out candy again and the kids circled. Chester took some of Paint's candy and handed out the sweets too.

Caron motioned them to follow and took the lead. Sergeant Yahya and his men followed.

"Where are we going Craig?" Chester asked.

"To the head man's house to be introduced." Burton replied. "He lives over there." Caron gestured vaguely in the direction of a hill on the other side of the village.

Gorman walked rearguard, scanning the crowd and the village behind them.

Caron led them past small homes set just off the main trail. A few children trailed them at a discrete distance.

The homes were constructed of hand-sawed lengths of wood placed vertically. The roofs were thatched. More children peered out through windows and doors at the tall, strange men who passed. Women sat in the doorways as they embroidered. They didn't seem surprised by the appearance of the American and Malay soldiers in combat gear.

The village chief, Sawng, met them on the trail and bowed deferentially toward Burton in a respectful wai. His skull was wrapped in a gray turban. Bright, bird-like eyes sparkled from within folds of wrinkled, dried skin, which formed a topographical map of a hard life. A wispy white mustache hung from the corners of his mouth limply. His voice was sharp, spoken through a toothless mouth that collapsed in on itself like a bellows.

Caron and Sawng shared a few words quietly and then Sawng led Caron and the Americans down a side path to his house, a building over thirty feet long, fifteen feet wide, with a plank and thatch roof. The house followed the terrain and was at least a foot lower on one side than it was on the other. There were two low doorways, one to the living area and an even lower one to the kitchen. He beckoned for the guests to enter through the main doorway. Burton turned to Chester, Goatman, Willoughby and Sergeant Yahya. They'd go with him. Caron could translate. The rest would form a perimeter.

Burton stooped to get through the front door, passing under two sharpened bamboo spikes suspended from ropes. Access to the house was made even more difficult for Burton and his men because they had to un-sling their heavy rucksacks and push them through ahead of them while balancing the weapons they carried.

"Why is there sharpened bamboo over the door?" Burton asked Caron.

"Not sharp bamboo. Swords! Keep demons out." Caron explained succinctly in broken French, that Willoughby translated.

Burton's nostrils filled immediately with the sooty, foul aromas that wafted around the interior of the house. The floor was beaten earth. There were plank partitions separating the main room, sleeping area and the kitchen. In the room where they stood there was an open fireplace with a blaze going; there was another fireplace in the kitchen. Cast iron lamps were burning wicks that were set in rendered pig fat but there were no flues, no window through which soot and smoke might escape. There was a layer of greasy soot and dirt over the disarray of crude furniture, implements, possessions and people in the interior. Only toilet smells were absent.

Burton spent enough time with the people of all the hill tribes to know that they relieved themselves merely by wandering out into the brush and he would be expected to do the same when the urge took him.

Caron made an obeisance at the simple family alter that was propped against the wall opposite the entrance. A bamboo cup, gray with age, rested on a shelf holding sticks of incense with their bases resting in grains of rice, and Caron lit one of the sticks of incense and placed it in a holder. On the wall above the table colorful strips of paper and some cock's plumes were affixed as decorations.

"They're offerings to the spirits of his ancestors." Chester said.

Caron turned from the altar and with Sawng's approval, seated his guests on bamboo stools around a low table. Sawng moved them slightly. When he was satisfied, he brought out an earthenware jar, inserted bamboo straws and offered them the drink with ceremonial gestures and words. Burton tasted the strong liquor made from corn mash and fermented rice previously, so he barely wet his lips, then smiled diplomatically at Sawng and Caron. Gorman, a self-described alcoholic, drank deeply and approved of the blend. Chester drank a little less than Gorman. Willoughby took a sip and left it at that.

Two village women scuttled into the house to prepare a meal. They wore blouses, skirts, aprons, turbans and leggings, but their clothing was more stylish than the other women's that Burton saw as they walked through the village. The dresses were more colorfully and more carefully embroidered.

The women served rice, corn, vegetables and chicken. They ate with chopsticks and wooden spoons and drank water and more rice liquor. The serving of poultry was in itself an honor.

After dinner, Sawng took down a porcelain jar.

"Opium," Chester said in a guarded tone.

"Fuck yes!" Goatman said with enthusiasm. "You must have read my mind." He looked longingly at the jar of opium.

I'm afraid we'll have to decline," Burton said to Caron. Willoughby translated.

"Please inform our host that we do not mean to be impolite but our army has regulations and we are obliged to observe them." Burton said it first in English and then in English accented Mandarin.

"For these people, it is the only joy and abandonment they'll ever know." Goatman explained to justify his participation. "It's wonderful stuff for people who have nothing else. The best opium in the world is grown near here on top of the holy mountain. It's famous for it's quality."

While they ate, Caron and Sawng spoke with Caron taking a moment to explain to Willoughby before continuing.

Willoughby summarized, "Our host advised me that a young man has decided to take his daughter to wife tonight. He does not wish you to think his people are barbarous, however in this culture, when a man chooses a bride, he will forcefully abduct her from the home of her parents with the help of his friends. Then he takes the girl to a home he has made for their honeymoon. He wants you to know that he has given consent and he likes the boy. This is their way. I think it's going to happen some time tonight and he doesn't want you to shoot his future son-in-law. Better that we find a camp farther away from this house and allow the abduction to take place as planned."

"They view our arrival as a good omen for the wedding," Willoughby explained further. "This is good luck for us because they could have just as easily found a reason not to like you, which would have meant they'd have sent a runner to the warlord's house in the city of Kalaw.

Sawng passed a brass opium pipe back to Caron, who applied a flaming stick to the bowl and took another puff.

Caron commented and Willoughby translated. "This is very good opium, you really should give it a try."

"How many men does Khun Sa have at Kalaw?" Burton went through the translation chain.

"He says about a thousand." Willoughby said.

"Crew served weapons, vehicles or are they armed the way we are?" Burton asked.

"Trucks, some with what sound like recoilless rifles, mostly infantry with shoulder weapons." Willoughby said. "He doesn't seem certain about the number but many times our strength. The chief is worried for us if we are not in Khun Sa's favor.

"What about foreign soldiers, Chinese, Burmese, British, Russian. Even if he can't tell the difference, let's see how he answers it."

"He doesn't know. The villagers avoid Kalaw even though they live in its shadow. He recommends that we move on for our own sakes."

Burton summarized his position in Chinese, "bù rù hǔ xué yān dé hǔ zǐ". "How can you catch the tiger cubs without entering the tiger's lair?" The cultural translation to English was simple. "Nothing ventured, nothing gained."

They all passed on the opium and having served the obligations of good manners, set off after dinner with Sergeant Yahya in the lead and the Malaysian Special Forces soldiers cleaning up the trail behind them.

For Burton, the late afternoon was an exercise in will power to keep his composure and energy under control. They moved under the stained glass light of a double canopy jungle and then down through a creek that ran steadily, then drained into a downwelling zone only to appear later, farther down the rock bedding, or around the next serpentine turn. Dangling throngs of vines draped over them, snaring their ankles, and occasionally forming a hedge-like barrier that they had to push through. The air inside the streambed was a potent marinade of humidity and heat that caused him to sweat profusely.

Burton pulled his canteen from its canvas case, popped salt pills and washed them down with a few swallows. His exposed skin had become a magnet for blood sucking insects and in the gathering gloom of sunset. Back home, in the world, he'd have slapped at them. The discipline of silence and slow movement in the hostile world of the Shan State forbade it.

The silent flow of water changed to a clattering sound like dishes being put away, as a small waterfall tumbled into a pool. Sergeant Yahya waded through the water ahead of Burton, his rifle high but ready. Fish, some a foot long, swam away from the sergeant with purposeful but smooth deliberation. A brilliant blue-green dragonfly dodged up and down the stream corridor, it's vellum wings broadcasting the dry, rasping buzz like rustling leaves.

Burton stepped carefully into the water, following the track the Malaysian sergeant blazed. A spring came in from a rock wall to his left, draining down a shear wall of white limestone. Shrouds of fern and vines blanketed the rocks, their roots having found a purchase in the cracks.

He followed Sergeant Yahya out of the water and felt something wiggling in his groin. Leaches. Discipline would call for allowing them to gorge themselves and drop off, but at least one was on his scrotum and Burton's resolve wavered. He unbuttoned his fly and saw the four-inch sightless slimy black parasite attached to him with its sucking mouth. He slid his fingernail to break the seal of the oral sucker. As his fingernail pushed along his skin against the leech, the suction of sucker's seal was broken and the leech detached its jaws. It dropped onto the muddy earth with a plop, leaving a read circle and mucus slime where it had been. Burton shuddered, knowing there were more leaches on his legs but he needed to move on, to keep focused. There would be time later to remove them properly if they didn't drop off first. Burton applied sticky antibacterial salve to the wound to prevent infection

They climbed up the side of a hill covered in thick pines and formed a perimeter along the ridgeline. No sound, no cooking, no talking.

Sergeant Yahya moved up next to him and spoke in a whisper. "We're about two miles from Kalaw, Brooton. We can be there at sunrise."

"Or I can be there at sunrise."

"You go in alone, Brooton, you die there alone." Sergeant Yahya said.

"What if I sleep on it? It's been one hell of a long day and I'm played out." Burton rolled up in his poncho and went to sleep, forgetting about any other leaches. The rain came, but he didn't feel it or hear it. Sergeant Yahya squatted in a vigil next to Burton in the darkness. Paint and Gorman dropped to sleep immediately as well.

Only Willoughby stayed awake and that was because he needed to string the radio antenna between trees in case Burton wanted to use it in the morning.

LARRY B. LAMBERT

THIRTY SEVEN

Thursday, 31 August 1961 – 0430 HRS
Near Kalaw Hill Station
Southern Shan State, Burma

The Americans and Chester ate Meal, Combat, Individual rations in the dark. They huddled together as they ate. Burton had Turkey Loaf and followed it up with a can of Beans w/Frankfurter Chunks in Tomato Sauce. It actually tasted good, mute testament to his hunger. The Malaysians ate dry rice rations that Burton had eaten years before when he trained with them. Somehow a hand full of dry rice simply wasn't enough of a payback for the tortuous previous day.

Fog replaced the rain, and it hugged the earth like a blanket.

"You want me to put a message out?" Willoughby asked.

"I harbored notions of air support today but I don't think the weather will cooperate, Sam."

Burton handed the last of his rations to Sergeant Yahya. A can of pound cake and a can of fruit cocktail. "Sometimes rice isn't enough."

Chester said, "There aren't enough of us to get Halvard Taylor out of there. Even if there are half a thousand and we have the best trackers in the world, it's not going to be enough."

"I know," Burton said. "I think I've pieced the whole puzzle together. Creed Taylor, his father, Khun Sa, the CIA, Unione Corse, the Laotians and the Chinese. It took some time."

"Maybe they think we're dead back in Muang Sing? There have to be hundreds of charred skeletons there after the jets and B-26's got done working the place over." Goatman suggested.

"That's what I thought too when I planned it, but I planned wrong. We wasted the Pathet Lao but the Air America pilot that flew us into the L-Z didn't hold his mud. People know we landed and people know we're here in the area. They're not certain where we are but they know we're here."

Jimmy Paint said, "They don't know about our Malaysian Army buddies in the Gerak Khas or our eminent Australian jungle fighter." He thought for a moment, "Unless the Corsican's blabbed."

"No." Burton said. "Corsicans are many things but they don't talk. Vendetta is a Corsican word. They live by their word and die by it as well." Turning to Jimmy and taking his hand, "Which is why I need to go in there alone."

"The Lone Ranger always had his faithful Indian sidekick when he went after the bandits." Paint muttered.

"Sergeant Yahya bin Haji Morhd Siraj, my old and dear friend, it was a distinct pleasure to meet you here again. My life is in the hands of God and I hope we will meet again, inshallah."

"Inshallah." The sergeant said, his eyes curious and fixed firmly on Burton.

"I'm very sorry about your men." Burton added.

"They are in paradise. We shall not mourn today."

"I have one last order to give you. Don't follow, don't be dead heroes. If I live out the day, I'll meet you at Pindaya by the Golden Pagoda on the south end of the mountain. If I don't show up, God speed and maybe we will meet somewhere else."

Sergeant Yahya quoted, "'And angels shall enter unto them from every gate saying peace be upon you for you persevered in patience! Excellent indeed is the final home!'"

If they all went in, there would be a fight. One man might have a slim chance because the threat wouldn't seem the same. Burton would have preferred to take all of them but it would have been a selfish act that would have surely resulted in their deaths. Now, if one of their number should die, it would be Burton. However he didn't plan on a suicide mission.

Craig Burton stood, stretched slightly and slung his AK-47. Then he turned and walked into the mist.

The path through the fog was not difficult for all he had to do is walk downhill to reach Kalaw. He hadn't walked half a mile when he found a wide dirt track and followed it downhill. A donkey cart rattled ahead of him, ladened with vegetables. It must be market day. He strided past the donkey cart to the surprise of its owner, and kept walking, leaving the donkey, cart and owner in the mist behind him.

Even though the pine forest surrounded him, he couldn't see the trees, he could only smell the sweet, fresh aroma of pine, of blooming wild ginger and the subtle aroma of wild flowers. The scents and subtle perfumes were all contained in the thick morning mist, now lighter with the coming of dawn.

Where the dirt track crossed train tracks, he followed the tracks for about a mile until he came to a locomotive steaming up for the day. Train men congregated in front of a wooden clap board train station lodge with its individual rooms each emptying to the outside. A woman prepared rice flour and butterbean pancakes in front of the old brick train station for the train crew and passengers. Burton walked up boldly and pointed to the cooking pancake topped with red peppers, butterbeans and scallions. He handed a damp 100 piastre note. The heavily armed and dangerous looking Burton surprised the lady when he did nothing more than take the food without asking for anything else.

Burton ate as he walked past men repairing a bicycle and nodded. They nodded back.

The trail led through stands of red Poinsettia. A hidden Buddhist shrine called a stupa rested patiently in the mist, off the path but not so far off that its influence couldn't be felt. He looked up and to his right. The pagoda overlooking the town could be seen faintly as the morning sun struck the gilded temple towers.

He walked as if he hadn't a care in the world and in truth, he didn't. There was no hurry. Khun Sa would be waiting.

Finding the warlord's headquarters proved to be more difficult than he thought it would be. People left him alone, ignoring the tall Caucasian soldier, so very much like others who had been in Kalaw for generations.

Burton's green clothing looked nearly black because it was soaking wet. The duck bill cap pulled low across his eyes, and the presence of his AK-47 and Chinese Communist chest pack of ammunition stacked in clips did not mark him as one thing or another. The warlord had many mercenaries and all white men looked alike. A sentry challenged him briefly and Burton chopped back in rapid fire broken Arabic. Satisfied, the sentry let him pass even if the sentry didn't understand a word of Arabic.

The garden spoke to Chinese architecture. A stone zigzag footbridge crossed a pond full of golden koi flashing under the surface. An ancient willow arched over the water, draping languidly toward the surface. Burton understood the significance. Evil spirits travel in a straight line. The bridge symbolized a refuge from bad spirits within the house beyond.

Across the bridge, Burton heard a phonograph needle scratch and then catch. Edith Piaf sang La Vie En Rose. The surrealistic situation overwhelmed Burton so he followed the music through the door of a large two-story brick building. Two guards at the entrance stopped him. He gave them two rounds each from the silenced .45 pistol. Cough-Cough—Cough-Cough. Both men dropped. The bullets took each in the throat and forehead at close range. Their rifles clattered on the highly polished, lacquered wood floor. Burton looked at them briefly. He didn't feel anything at their deaths except a smug acceptance that he hadn't lost his touch. He released the clip in the .45 and slid in a fresh one with another 7 rounds, pocketing the partially expended clip.

He kept walking and found a handsome, Burmese-Chinese man in his late twenties, presumably Khun Sa, sitting comfortably in a parlor with Jacques Sabon, One-eye Zucharelli and two officers wearing the uniform of the People's Republic of China.

"Chang Chi-fu?" Burton asked.

"Yes?" Khun Sa said, taking a sip of tea.

"You are my prisoner."

"Craig." Burton turned to see Charlotte walking toward him.

"What are you doing here, Charlotte?"

"She is my prisoner." Khun Sa said.

Burton did the math. And since you are my prisoner that means she's my prisoner too.

"If you accept the situation the way you paint it, that's true." Khun Sa said with a measure of humor. "However you may find it more difficult leaving than you did entering."

"I don't plan to leave. Do you have any idea how much trouble I took to get here?" Burton said, laughing nervously.

Khun Sa laughed with Burton, but nobody else did.

Khun Sa turned to Jacques Sabon, "So this is the famous ghost soldier from the Americans—Burton." Turning back to Burton, "Your reputation precedes you."

The Chinese officers apparently did not speak English and didn't have the benefit of Khun Sa's education at the hands of the British at the Kalaw Hill Station.

Burton spoke to them in fluent Teochiu, Chinese—Chao-yang Hsien dialect. "You lice don't belong here. You disgrace us all with your lack of skill in dealing with this problem."

The senior of the two, a full colonel, looked at Burton as if

258

somebody hit him between the eyes with a bamboo rod. "You sit there like a fat beached carp, report, Colonel!"

Burton had Khun Sa's and the Frenchmen's full attention. Things became very serious.

"Who do you think I am?" Burton demanded in English, looking at Sabon.

"You're the CIA's cat's paw. You are expendable, as is young Charlotte, I'm afraid.

There were armed men behind Burton now, but he kept his silenced .45 at his side and Khun Sa made no move, fascinated by the turn of events.

With his left hand, Burton reached into his shirt pocket and flashed an object that landed on the table in front of Khun Sa.

Now it was Khun Sa's turn to be flabbergasted. "Burton, what—where did you—my dragon—."

"You ordered it, I'm merely delivering it."

Burton switched back to Teochiu, playing his bluff to full effect. "General Qui has arranged your retirements." Burton shot the junior officer through the forehead, splattering brains on the back of the teak chair where he sat and onto the wall beyond. He returned the .45 to his side immediately.

"Wait," the colonel from the People's Liberation Army said in Teochiu. "I'm General Qui's nephew but I don't know you!"

"Behind an able man there are always other able men." Burton quoted a proverb. "You are Guoanbu, and yet you don't understand the nature of the Chairman's influence?"

"And you?"

"Flies never visit an egg that has no crack. Your aid was a spy for the Imperialists and he has died for his falsehood to the workers and the glorious revolution. The question is not him anymore, but you, colonel."

"But you are American." The PRC Colonel said in Teochiu, not fathoming how the secret dialect of the Chao-yang Hsien could be spoken so perfectly by a barbarian.

"Judge not the horse by his saddle and you may live to prosper." Burton said with finality.

Charlotte held onto Burton now. She whispered up at him. "When they kill you, they will have to kill me as well."

"Kill them both," Sabon said without emotion to Khun Sa.

WHITE POWDER

Khun Sa examined the tiny dragon, crafted with meticulous attention to detail. He turned to the Colonel and spoke in crude Mandarin, "Who is this man?"

The colonel's mind flashed to the proverb that it is better not to lift a stone larger than you are for it will only drop on your own feet. "He is my superior officer."

Khun Sa's eyebrows shot up. "Truly?"

The colonel averted his eyes.

Khun Sa hefted the dragon. "Where did you get this?"

"From the Vientiane Rezident, Wu Ming."

"As grand as your reputation seems to be, Burton," Khun Su said with meaning, "it would seem that it's underestimated by all." He looked at the Chinese officer with the partially excavated cranium, lying on his side, bleeding on the floor. "Why don't we move into the other room so we can drink tea and discuss this further?"

With a dismissing wave of Khun Sa's hand, the men standing behind Burton pointed the muzzles of their rifles at the ceiling. The young warlord led the way into another room and everyone followed.

"What are you doing here, Charlotte?" Burton asked.

"I came to rescue you. After Chester and the Malaysians parachuted in, I didn't hear from them and I worried. So I took the airplane, the same one we flew to the Snow Leopard Inn, Armée de l'Air 447 Able."

"The Cessna?"

Charlotte nodded. "Jacques and Andrei were here. They said you had been killed with your men in Laos but I didn't believe them. Then they said you didn't die, you survived and were here. They planned to use me as a hostage, as bait to kill you."

As everyone situated themselves in the new sitting room, Khun Sa asked Burton, "What do you want?"

"These men betrayed Bruno Jospin, their boss."

"Jospin is finished!" Sabon said and One-eye Zucharelli agreed. "We will divide the profits from this new operation here between ourselves and we will all be fabulously rich. Khun Sa is the big dragon now!"

"Maybe not so big as I had hoped." Khun Sa said thoughtfully. "Did Creed Taylor come with you?"

"No, he had an accident on the way here. He won't be joining us. He cut a deal with Sabon and Zucharelli." Burton said.

"Deal?" Charlotte asked.

"You," Sabon said. "I promised him he could have you once Bruno was dead, and a piece of the business proportionate to his contribution."

"You sold me?" Charlotte sneered. "Bruno will feed your testicles to the pigs."

"I'm afraid your days of threatening are over, young Charlotte." Zucarelli said. "Bruno has become a slave to your whims. Allowing a woman to do anything but cook, clean and breed diminishes a man. He was blinded in the way he cherished you, perhaps because he loved your mother so much and it will be his epitaph."

Charlotte struck Zucarelli's cheek and the big man didn't see it coming because her hand came from his blind side. All he did in response was laugh. Charlotte walked to Burton and stood close to him, whispering the word, "vendetta."

Khun Sa took a native spear from the wall where it served as a decoration and struck the butt of the spear onto the wood floor. "Now everyone will listen to me because all of you are in my house."

He spoke to the People's Liberation Army Colonel in Chinese. "Zhang, what do you have to say?"

The colonel replied in rapid-fire Chinese. "I defer my interests to those of the American *dai lo*."

"I presume you speak for the People's Guoanbu—thus for both the intelligence service and the Peoples Liberation Army?" Khun Sa replied in Chinese.

The colonel nodded.

Khun Sa continued in Chinese. "Your position, Captain Burton, would seem to be unique because the Frenchmen here say that you speak for the Central Intelligence Agency."

Burton lied, "I do," in Chinese. "And for interests in Hong Kong where you recently commissioned a rather large gold dragon."

Khun Sa nodded with sobriety. "Yes, there is that matter as well."

In English, Khun Sa said, "Mr. Burton seems also to speak for Charlotte Jospin, though a girl, the daughter of a venerated business partner."

Charlotte nodded.

"Before I ask Burton what he wants to do, who do you speak for Jacques and what is your present position."

Sabon spoke in French. "For too long all of the profit from Opium

261

has been shared to the detriment of the Shan people. I will manufacture #4 Heroin in this place and the profit will remain here, shared among the people." Zucarelli shook his head in ascent.

"Burton?"

Craig Burton stepped forward and said, "Chang Chi-Fu became Khun Sa because he was wise enough to remain a middle man, insuring the farmers were paid for their crops and that the refiners of opium received their deliveries. It's important that everyone understands their position in the world and what serves their best interests."

"Creed Taylor made his move and tried to kill me and ended up like that lump of flesh in the other room. It was a small thing for me to kill him. It would be a small thing for you to kill me in your house, on your land. It would be a small thing for the Americans to bomb the Shan State to a pulp or for the People's Liberation Army to send a million soldiers across your border. There were five battalions of Pathet Lao in Muang Sing last Wednesday morning before the sun hit the peaks around valley. There were large piles of smoldering bones and nobody left alive when the light touched the rice fields. Fortune is a fickle mistress."

"Kill him!" Sabon demanded.

"Continue Burton. This is my house. Show some respect, Frenchman." Khun Sa replied with ice in his voice.

"Bind these curs and deliver them to Bruno Jospin for his justice. Do business as you have been doing it because it's what keeps you and your people safe. It's a lucrative trade and one where you are neither too big nor too small." Burton sat on a wide wicker lounge and Charlotte sat next to him.

She reached out for his hand. It tingled at his touch.

Khun Sa beckoned to two soldiers, who approached. His pointed to Zucarelli and Sabon. "Crucify them. When they're dead, cut off their heads and send them to Bruno Jospin with my regards."

He asked Charlotte, "Will you forgive me for holding you as a prisoner?"

"You were a perfect gentleman." Charlotte said by way of reply as Sabon and Zucarelli were dragged from the room. "And I believe the punishment is just."

To Burton, Khun Sa said, "What now?"

"Where's Halvard Taylor?"

"Creed's father. He was the man who arranged the meeting with

262

Sabon and Zucrelli." Khun Sa replied.

"He still works for the CIA." Burton said.

"I know."

EPILOGUE

Three Weeks Later

WALTER KENNEDY sat comfortably in his mansion in the Philippines, surrounded by books, drinking with Harold Dastrup, now Deputy Chief of Station, Manila. The tape on his nose was down to two strips. Both were well into their cups. Kennedy waxed philosophical. "When the colonialists were running things they wanted others to think they were intelligent and well read, even if they couldn't read their own names." He gestured expansively at the expansive collection of literature.

Dastrup's vision was blurred and he saw twice as many books around him as were actually there. He mumbled something in a language that may have been English.

Kennedy continued, undeterred. "So they bought lots of books. I've liberated them. These are some of the most valuable books in the French language here. Pages not cut, unread. Silly bastards."

In an unusual moment of clarity given the level of alcohol in his bloodstream, Harold Dastrup admitted to himself; 'Kennedy you're nothing but a wasted intellectual with the heart of a Frog.'

Kennedy sloshed whisky in his tumbler and sipped. "Everybody wants to recognize unrecognized genius these days. It pushes the culturally astute to accumulate worthless works of art. The trashed life of Vincent Van Gogh is their mantra. How many pictures did he sell? One or two? Maybe three? He couldn't give them away. Even I buy into the concept of not wanting to ignore another Van Gogh."

He stood and walked, supporting himself on the back of a chair and flung aside a canvas that covered hideous paintings. "See what I mean? They'll be worth a fortune one day"

"What about Burton?" Dastrup managed to ask in understandable, if slurred English.

"Oh, yeah, he's on his way to France with his fiancé. It will give me an excuse to look for masterpieces in Paris when I go there to manage his career in the Unione Corse."

MASTER SERGEANT SAM (SPARKS) WILLOUGHBY, US ARMY, fed the birds in the Cheng Mai Zoo.

Harold Young ran the zoo but he wasn't famous for running the zoo. He trained Merrill's Marauders to maraud against the Japanese. His was the legend of the soft-spoken jungle master who was dangerous as a spitting cobra. William Young, his eldest son ran the CIA's show in Tham Na Province on the Laos-Burma border where the Shan States butted against China and the Teochiu Chinese were bidding top dollar for the spring poppy harvest.

Harold Young found Willoughby sitting on a bench in the zoo, throwing birdseed and said, "What's going on Sam? How did you find Laos?"

"Everything's the same."

Young thought for a moment and asked, "Is Theo Meier still living in that cheap hotel near the river painting his masterpieces by throwing paint at the canvas during his drunken binges?" He paused. What's the name of that hotel?"

"Vieng Veli." Willoughby threw the last of his birdseed. "Walter Kennedy's sure the hideous paintings will be worth a fortune one day. He's buying 'em all."

WU MING watched his relatives board the Soviet Illushin passenger aircraft with undisguised joy. His wife's aunts who had been devouring food like mongrel dogs waddled up to the metal stairs that led to the open hatch where the pilot stood, his face a mask of worry. Wu chuckled. Placing them inside the airframe to keep the aircraft in balance would be a fine trick.

CRAIG and **CHARLOTTE** sat in the terminal, three time zones to the east as the Lockheed Starliner's engines spun up. It was a long trip from Indochina to France and they spent two days in New Delhi while morning sickness laid her low. Curry made Charlotte nauseous and everything in New Delhi smelled of curry. By the time the next scheduled Pan American Airlines flight arrived, Charlotte was excited to leave no matter how airsick she got.

"Have you given thought to a name for our baby," Charlotte asked casually?

Burton smiled boyishly. "How about BIP?"

"BIP? What kind of name is BIP?"

"Baby-In-Progress. Maybe it's an army thing but I thought it would be fun?"

"My baby isn't in the American Army." Charlotte was serious as a heart attack. "Neither are you anymore Craig. And I will never call my child BIP."

"It was a joke." Burton maneuvered in an attempt to find redemption from his unintended gaffe.

"I do not find my pregnancy to be a joke." She sobbed softly, implying that he was less than serious in his love for her and by extension for the baby.

Craig Burton groaned inwardly. "Seriously, I thought that Bruno would be a great name if it's a boy."

Charlotte's sullen mood swung instantly. "Really?

Craig nodded, taking her hand, kissing it tenderly.

"Oh, my father would love that very much!"

Even though the name Bruno Burton didn't strike him as particularly poetic, it would do for the moment. They had eight months ahead of them. As he navigated the perilous waters of life with a pregnant woman, he was learning that there were very few safe topics of discussion and little room for humor.

THE MONKEY KING strolled down a disserted quay at the United States Naval Base, Yokosuka, Japan, speaking with Gerald Miller, the Chief of Far East Operations for the Central Intelligence Agency. The sun was a blood-red orb, suspended in Tokyo air pollution as it dropped toward the skyline.

"Thanks for coming to Japan, Monty," Miller said seriously. "We needed to talk about Operation KNUCKLEBALL and I thought we could walk and talk. They serve a great prime rib at the Officer's Club."

"It's my pleasure." The Vientiane Station Chief said.

"I don't know when I've seen an operation come off closer to plan. Minimal collateral damage—acceptable casualties, the Laotian Chief-of-Staff loves you, and our guy is embedded in the Unione Corse. You hit one out of the ballpark this time, Monty and I think it's time we start thinking about moving you upstairs with a rotation through headquarters. That new headquarters building is going to be quite something. It's

266

scheduled to be completed in 1963, and I think you need a corner office in that very structure

Montgomery Keene blushed under the lavish praise.

"Walter Kennedy has had a spotty career, but he's done well on this one. I have to admit it. I cabled my praise to his boss in Manila," Miller said with pride.

"We all try to do our part." Keene said sincerely with deep humility.

"I'm serious," Gerald Miller continued, "knocking up Bruno Jospin's daughter binds our man with blood to the Corsicans. It couldn't have been better. We need to do something special for Craig Burton too. I was thinking that a Distinguished Service Cross with ambiguous language about valor in the face of overwhelming odds in a classified operation might be just the ticket."

"It would be no less than he deserves." The Monkey King said, excited at the prospect of a promotion.

WHITE POWDER

HISTORICAL CONTEXT AND PRECEDENCE

In 1945, the United States transported the French Army to Indochina to reclaim the colonial possessions they lost to the rampaging Japanese Imperial Army during the Second World War. Ho Chí Minh's dreams of an Indochina free from foreign domination were dashed and his Viet Minh began a guerilla war with the French forces, which continued to receive support from the United States.

On May 7, 1954 the French suffered what was to be their last major loss in Indochina at Dien Bien Phu. Following their defeat, they slowly withdrew from Viet Nam, Laos and Cambodia. Nature abhors a vacuum. In December 1955 the US Department of Defense established a disguised military mission in Laos called the Programs Evaluation Office (PEO) to get around the prohibition against foreign military personnel imposed by the 1954 Geneva agreement, which the United States had pledged to honor. The PEO worked under the cover of the civilian aid mission and was staffed by military personnel and headed by a general officer.

Between 1955 and 1961, the PEO gradually supplanted the French military mission in providing equipment and training to the Royal Lao Army. With increasing numbers of Laotian officers receiving training in Thailand and at staff schools in the United States, there was a perception that the French military mission in Laos was a relic of colonialism. In 1959, 107 United States Army Special Forces soldiers of the 77th Special Forces Group (SFG) entered Laos in civilian attire and Operation Hotfoot began with the aim of providing ongoing training to the Royal Laotian Army in the field. In April 1961, the PEO was upgraded to a Military Assistance Advisory Group (MAAG), its members were allowed to wear uniforms, and the operational name was changed from Hotfoot to White Star.

By the summer of 1960, Civil war had broken out between paratroop commander Kong Le and General Phoumi Nosavan. The Communist Pathet Lao supported Kong Le, while the US military and Central Intelligence Agency lined up behind Phoumi. Admiral Harry D. Felt, Commander in Chief of the Pacific Fleet, put it this way: "Phoumi is no

George Washington. However, he is anti-Communist, which is what counts most in the sad Laos situation."[1]

At a meeting in Vienna in June 1961, President John F. Kennedy and Soviet Premier Nikita Khrushchev issued a joint statement of support for a neutral and independent Laos. At the same time, negotiators met in Geneva to try to work out the details. It seemed evident to the US Delegation that only United States personnel in Laos could ensure that the Royal Lao Army was capable of meeting the threat posed by the Pathet Lao backed by North Vietnam and the Soviet Union.

In 1961 the Viet Nam War wasn't the lead story on the evening news and wouldn't be for three more years. The developing war in neighboring Laos was never to make a headline. It was a secret war, managed under the auspices of the Central Intelligence Agency. In Laos the only cash crop was opium. Opium grown in Laos was purchased and refined by the Corsican Organized Crime Group known as the Unione Corse in clandestine laboratories in France and later also in Viet Nam. The distribution network it spawned was later coined *The French Connection* in popular print and film in the United States.

---

[1] Admiral Felt is quoted in Edward J. Marolda and Oscar P. Fitzgerald, *The United States Navy and the Vietnam Conflict: From Military Assistance to Combat* (Washington, DC: Government Printing Office, 1986), pp. 24-25.

GLOSSARY OF TERMS, THINGS AND HISTORICAL PEOPLE

7ᵗʰ Special Forces–In 1960, the 77ᵗʰ Special Forces Group was reorganized and re-designated as the 7th Special Forces Group. The 7th Group was active early in Southeast Asia, first operating in Laos and later in Viet Nam.

AK-47—Perhaps the most widely used infantry rifle in history. Inspired by the German Sturmgewher 44, Mikhail Kalashnikov, developed a rifle for the Soviet Army that was cheap to produce, easy to maintain in a combat environment and fired an effective 7.62x39mm cartridge. They were manufactured in most Warsaw Pact countries under the rubric "AK-47" and in China and Viet Nam as "Type 56" rifle.

Annamite & Tonkinese—A person from Annam or Tonkin. Viet Nam was a country amalgamated from three countries: Cochin China, Annam and Tonkin. In the novel, Tonkinese refers to one who identifies themselves as a descendant of people of Tonkin (Northern Viet Nam) and Annamite as a descendent of people of Annam (Southern Viet Nam). The countries were unified under French occupation in the late 1800's as Viet Nam.

Army Security Agency (**ASA**)—From 1945 through 1976, the United States Army Security Agency served as the Army's electronic intelligence branch. In some cases, ASA personnel were assigned to operate in the field with US Special Forces.

BACKPORCH—In the novel, *White Powder*, there is a discussion between Captain Craig Burton, USA and Master Sergeant Sam Willoughby of a new system of communications in Southeast Asia that was on the drawing board but not yet deployed. In January 1962, Secretary of Defense Robert S. McNamara approved the installation of troposcatter communications equipment within South Vietnam to provide the backbone of a strategic network known as BACKPORCH, which would connect five major cities in South Vietnam with Thailand and Laos. Because the Army had little experience with tropospheric equipment, Page Communications Engineering installed BACKPORCH at a cost of $12 million, and the company agreed to operate and maintain the system for a year. Huge "billboard" relay antennas began to appear on mountaintops.

Ban Na Toum, Laos—A small town in Northern Laos located near the border with the People's Republic of China.

Banque de L'Indochin—A bank established in Paris, France on January 21, 1875 for the territories of France in Asia. It currently operates as the Banque de Suez.

Burma—Known in the present day as Myanmar, it is referred to as Burma in the novel because that was the country's name in the referenced time period.

Central Intelligence Agency—A civilian agency of the United States government. Prior to 2004, it was the central intelligence organization for the United States.

Currency—The novel refers to piaster as the denomination of currency issued by that Institut d'Emission des Etats du Cambodge, du Laos et du Vietnam. Originally the piaster was equivalent to one silver dollar. The piaster was still accepted as currency in 1961 even though the official currency of Laos was the kip. In 1952 *Institut d'Emission des Etat du Laos* issued banknotes with dual denomination as piasters and kip. By 1957 government banknotes were denominated only as kip.

Dacoit–A member of a class of bandits in Burma and India who specialized in robbery and kidnap for ransom.

Dae Biet Cong—People's Army of Viet Nam (PAVN) special purpose /elite troops who were the counterparts of the Russian voyska spetsialnovo naznacheniya (SPETSNAZ) or special purpose soldiers. They were also referred to as scorpion teams.

Điên Biên Phú—A climactic battle between the French army in Indochina and Viet Minh communist revolutionaries that took place in the Northwest highlands of Vietnam between March 13 and May 7, 1954. It ended as a military disaster for France. 11,721 French soldiers were taken as prisoners and subjected to a "death march" to prison camps 250 miles away. Four months later, only 3290 prisoners survived to be repatriated. Of those who died, some succumbed to wounds sustained in combat. The majority were either executed or died of starvation and/or disease. The conduct of the victors was one of the more shameful in the annals of military history.

GRC-109 Transciever (radio)—This radio, designed for clandestine operations, originally went into service with the Central Intelligence

Agency as the Model RS-1 in 1950. They saw extensive use in Southeast Asia with Army Special Forces beginning in 1961. Functionally the RS-1 and GRC-109 are identical in appearance, operation and nomenclature. Many of the first radios of this type used by the Army were on loan from the CIA. The early RS-1 transmitter components (T-784) were modified to accept the GRA-71 burst coder.

Groupe de Commandos Mixtes Aéroportés—The French military operational branch of the *Service de Documentation Extérieure et de Contre-Espionnage* (see this glossary for further information). The CIA paramilitary personnel were the general counterpart to the GCMA, but operationally they functioned in a very differently from one another.

Guoanbu—The intelligence agency for the People's Republic of China (sometimes referred to in this novel as "Red China").

Hand Grenades, Russian —The novel makes mention of the use of two distinctively different types of Soviet Russian hand grenades. The Degtyareva (RGD-33) stick grenade and the F-1 hand grenade. They differed in function design and operation intent. The RGD-33 could be used without a shrapnel sleeve as a concussion grenade for close use when you didn't want your own shrapnel coming back at you. It was discussed in the novel used with the shrapnel sleeve. The F-1 hand grenade was a 'baseball style' explosive grenade.

Heroin—An opium derivative (see appendix 1). There are many slang names for heroin which include but are certainly not limited to: smack, horse, China white, blue velvet, antifreeze, hero, red chicken, scag, the beast, white nurse, etc.

Hmong—An Asian ethnic group living in China and Southeast Asia.

Hồ Chí Minh—(also known as: Nguyễn Tất Thành)(May 19, 1890-September 2, 1969) Vietnamese communist revolutionary leader who served terms as prime minister and president of the Democratic Republic of Vietnam (North Vietnam).

Indochina—(Indochine-fr) Viet Nam, Cambodia, Laos, Thailand-Siam, Burma-Myanmar, Singapore, all of which were colonized by France. The name is derived from the cultural confluence of both India and China on the area.

Khmer—The Khmer people are the predominant ethnic group in Cambodia.

Khun Sa—Real name Chang Chi-fu (February 17, 1934-October 26, 2007) was a very well known warlord and opium kingpin in the Golden

Triangle, operating primarily in Burma. He led the Shan United Army in an attempt to wrest control of the Shan State from Burma/Myanmar. He was ultimately unsuccessful. In 1989, a US District Court in New York indicted him for smuggling 1,000 tons of heroin. Though the US Government attempted to extradite him, the government of Burma refused to cooperate.

Kuomintang—The Chinese Nationalist Party, currently the ruling party of the Republic of China (Taiwan). It ruled much of China from 1928 through 1949 when it was defeated by the Communist party of China. The Kuomintang relocated to the Island of Taiwan.

Montangnard—A French term used to denominate the "hill people/tribes" of Indochina.

MI-6 —The British Secret Intelligence Service Agency focused on collection of information outside of the Commonwealth.

One-Time Pad—A method of encryption where the key material is distributed as a pad of paper, so the top sheet could be easily torn off and destroyed after use. Since the key is used only once (and usually only for short messages), the code/encryption system is considered unbreakable.

Owen submachine gun—An Australian made version of the British Sten submachine gun.

Pathet-Lao—A communist political movement in Laos, which was equivalent to the Việt Minh and Việt cộng. They were successful in assuming political control of Laos after a civil war lasting from 1950 to 1975.

Phnom Penh—(nom-pen) The Capitol city of Cambodia.

Phoei Kwan—(fooey-kwan) Phoei Kwan shops such as the Shanghai Spring Phoei Kwan shop mentioned in Chapter Thirteen of this novel handle currency exchange, currency remittance outside established banking channels. As such they are often utilized for both legal and illegal purposes. Legal of transfer of funds between countries, inevitably involving currency exchange, are used widely worldwide. Illegal money laundering is also conducted through the Phoei Kwan system. Other names for this method of currency remittance are hawala, hundi, fei chien, and underground banks. Locations to manage these transfers are currently (as of this publication date) available in all larger cities in North America, South America, Europe, Asia, Australia, the Asian Subcontinent and Africa. You need often look no further than ads in a local newspaper to find them.

WHITE POWDER

Poeshepny, Anthony—(Tony Poe) A legendary CIA paramilitary officer who served in Laos principally with the White Hmong in Miltary Region Two (1960-70). The author was invited to attend his funeral in 2003 but was unable to do so due to personal illness.

Rezident—Soviet Russian term of art denoting a member of the State Security Agency who directs a group of agents or co-opters. The term used in the novel defined the position of Wu Ming within the Communist Chinese intelligence structure in Laos. Rezidents are tested, disciplined intelligence officers, many of who are operating outside diplomatic cover within target countries.

Ride the Dragon—Use opium or heroin (smoked or injected).

Sahmanakkhaogrong-hangshaat—Secret Intelligence Service of the Kingom of Thailand.

Service de Documentation Extérieure et de Contre-Espionnage — The External Documentation and Counter Espionage Service was the French foreign security and intelligence service until April 2, 1982. During the time period of this novel it was subordinate to the Prime Minister. It was responsible for military intelligence as well as for strategic information, electronic intelligence, and it is also responsible for the counterespionage outside the borders of the national territory.

Shan State—An administrative region of Burma, named for the Shan people which borders China to the north, Laos to the east and Thailand to the south. Much of the opium grown in Southeast Asia was produced in this region. Though titular authority resides with the constituted government, operationally it's run by warlords with private armies who profit from the narcotics trade to the present day.

Škoda Automatic Rifles—A Czech-made version of the British (BSA-1926) version of the American M-1A1 Thompson submachine gun in 7.63 mm Mauser.

Sun Yee On Triad—(also known as: New Righteousness and Peace) An organized crime group composed primarily of Teochiu Chinese, it continues to operate primarily in Hong Kong and it's territorial strength is traditionally in the Kowloon District. Their traditional sources of income include extortion, prostitution, entertainment and narcotics trafficking.

Teochiu Brotherhood—An extremely powerful, very successful organized crime federation comprised entirely of ethnic Chinese, many of whom continue to live outside China. The group's origins began in and around Swatow, China. There are several Hsiens or "families" within the umbrella of the Teochiu Brotherhood.

Unione Corse—An organized crime network that dominated the Southeast Asian heroin market through control of French Indochina's opium production from the 1930's through the 1970's. Reputed to be far more secretive and violent than their Sicilian counterparts, the organized crime network continues to operate through political and criminal connections worldwide to distribute narcotics. It currently controls much of Southern France including the city of Marseille and runs a thriving black market. There are several families within Unione Corse whose individual fortunes have ebbed and flowed over time.

Việt Minh—The League for the Independence of Vietnam. It technically ceased to exist on October 11, 1954 when Hồ Chí Minh was appointed Prime Minister of the Democratic Republic of Vietnam (North Vietnam). The word carried on as a term of art for the next decade and is included at places in this novel for that reason.

Vientiane—(viang-chan) The Capitol city of Laos.

Weights and Measures—1 joi = 1.6 kilograms = 3.52 pounds. The joi is a standard measure of the weight of opium used in Burma and more particularly the Shan State.

White Star, Project—The code name for the US military advisory mission to Laos in the time period in which the novel is set.

Yord Serk—A protégé of Khun Sa, currently commands the Shan United Revolutionary Army in Burma/Myanmar. When Khun Sa became too physically ill to carry on his operations, the mantle fell to Yord Serk.

APPENDIX

Manufacturing Heroin

Heroin is derived from the fruit/flower of the opium poppy. In Southeast Asia, the growing season begins in autumn and about 120 days later harvesting can begin (in the spring). *Papaver somniferum* is one of the few species of poppy that produces opium. The flowers are colorful and vary in hue. Once they fall away, a green pod remains, which continues to grow. Opium alkaloid is only produced during the terminal ripening process, which lasts about two weeks.

While the fruit is still on the stem, incisions are made in the sides of the pod. Common practice requires the sap to seep out of the pod overnight for collection each morning for (roughly) the ensuing week.

Raw opium is converted to morphine base through boiling. The raw sap that was collected from the plant pod dissolves in boiling water and any obvious impurities such as plant fibers are scooped from the liquid opium. Quicklime is mixed with water and is then added to the boiling liquid opium. The morphine alkaloid reacts with the lime and impurities precipitate to the bottom of the pot. The liquid is poured through a filter into another container and ammonia is added and the mixture is heated. As it heats, the morphine solidifies and precipitates to the bottom of the pot. The liquid is separated off from the solid and what remains is *#1 Heroin or morphine base*. Within the time period of this novel the process up to this point was usually managed within Indochina.

The next step in the purification process necessary to create a usable narcotic requires acetic acid to combine with the morphine base. The mixture is heated to 85 degrees centigrade for two hours. This process chemically binds the morphine to the acid and creates *chemical heroin*.

Water is added to the chemical heroin and since heroin is water-soluble it becomes a solution. Common sodium carbonate is added to the heroin solution and the precipitate is taken from the bottom of the pot. That is *#2 Heroin or heroin base*.

From heroin base the manufacturer can make **#3 Heroin** (20 to 30 percent pure), often called brown heroin or smoking heroin. It has the general granular consistency and color of (unrefined) brown sugar. To make #3 Heroin, hydrochloric acid and caffeine are mixed with the heroin base and stirred until it dries.[2]

In order to make **#4 Heroin** from heroin base, hydrochloric acid and ether are added. The process is complex, toxic and hazardous because of explosive fumes. Once the heroin base passes through this process, it's usually around 90 per cent pure and is referred to as **China White**. China White (or #4) Heroin is a fine white odorless and colorless powder.

---

[2] Mexican Heroin, also referred to as "black tar heroin" is essentially crude #3 Heroin with more impurities in it than is typically found in #3 Heroin. The impurities make the drug more toxic but occasionally add a more potent effect (depending on who made it).

About the Author

Having spent his entire adult life in the service of government, the author has had the opportunity to travel and to operate in places and in situations denied to many people.

Larry B. Lambert served in various capacities in the intelligence community, as a commissioned officer in the United States Navy, serving with the SEAL Teams in large and small wars and in law enforcement, managing very complex cases.

Made in the USA
Lexington, KY
19 March 2010